Creatures of the Continent

Book II of the Shapewalker's Song

JH Tomen

ISBN: 978-0-578-78323-9
ISBN-13:

<u>Dedication</u>

To you, Dear Reader, for joining me again! I can't tell you how honored and moved I've been that so many incredible people decided to take a chance on Sumi and her story. This book has brought me so much joy, but what really matters is you and your commitment to reading. Even when the world becomes a very hard place, I'm so grateful that we still have this. Stories have been with us since the beginning — one of the most human acts of all. I believe that books are like liquid empathy, and by choosing to open ourselves to the worlds of others, I hope that we can take that empathy and make the world just a little brighter. So, thank you, for everything you are.

For Karl. I can't thank you enough for being so fully in this with me. You say you read slowly, but you also notice every single detail. It feels like you've traveled to Anushai with me, and your presence on this journey has given me so much courage. For Joe, for always asking about Sumi, even when your world is exploding with important and vital work. For Austin, for being my champion, you told SO MANY people about these books. For Analise, Chelsea, Jenn, Mike, Buddy, Augie, Meech, Liana, Dom, Torie, Javi (on the audiobook, of course), and Liz. For Devin, Angelina, and Esi, I'm so humbled and honored. For all my friends; to have you be the first, that you took the time to read the ramblings of a friend for no other reason than that friendship. You all mean the world to me.

Life without friendship has no shape.

Cover by Karl Nilsson (@sigvardnilsson)
Map of Wellonai & The Three Sisters by Jeremy DeBor (@jeremydeerboar)
Creatures of the Continent drawings by Shawn Russell (@shawnerussell)
Editing by A. K. Edits (@AdotKEdits)

Content Warning: This book contains flashbacks to the deaths of loved ones, as well as scenes of civil unrest and capital punishment.

Maps

WELLONAI
ISLES OF DAWN
GOLDEN COAST
ITORUNAI'S GAP
ANUSHAI
THE VOID
ERRIL SEA
EAST LINE
THREE SISTERS
BERRIL
EKOSINAR
AMORIAI
RELIMORA
ALARA
SOUTH LINE
MESOP
MESOPYN
VILODAI'S HEART

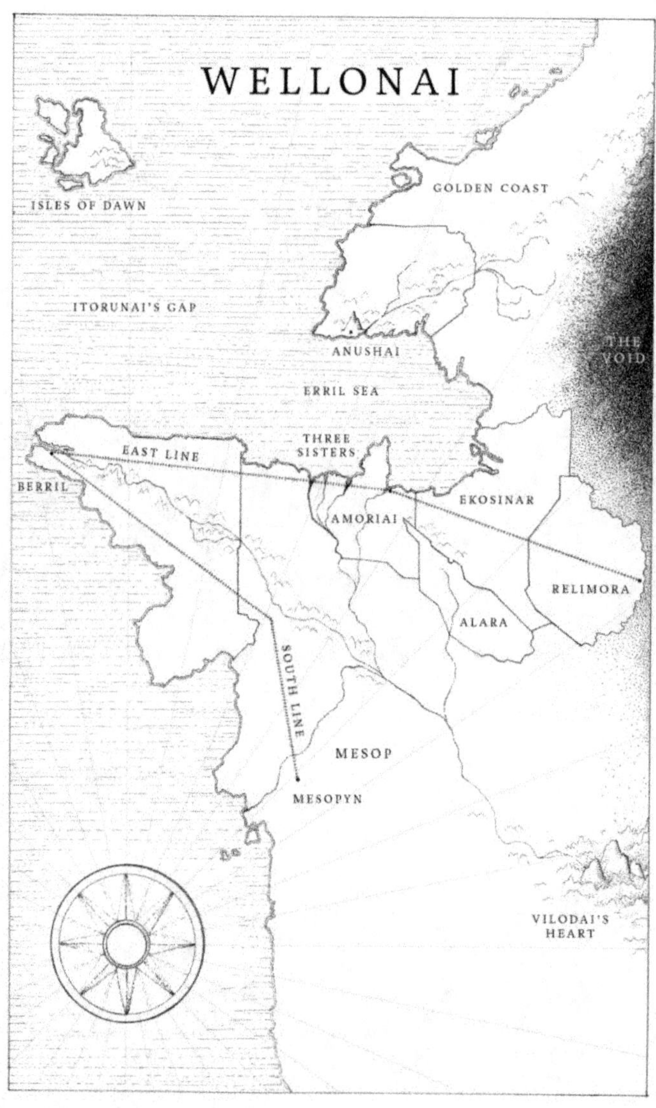

THE THREE SISTERS
VOLNEERAN PENINSULA
CÖTTHURN
HAFANELLE
STRUSSFARAN
CAPE OF V'INIEL
BERRIL
LUTERRIN
KASELDA
ENOZEIRA
KOLBENZ
AMORIAI
KO'LESTA
EL'TIMEIR
MESOP
MALDEGURN
MIEDARAL

Salnyeom
Common Name: Grass Cat
Location: Anushai

Arnisole
Sketch captured on the western coast of Ageleat

Mulakerri
Sketch captured in the eastern forests of Amoriai

Hagelnyeong
Common Name: Granite Bear
Location: Far west of Berill & mountains north of Seongbelm

PART ONE

1

Wellonai both was and was not. In the Void, there was nothing, and there was everything. Wellonai desired to become, and so became the land. The land was blank, but in it was her blood, her breath, and her voice. Partaking of the land and its awesome power, these pieces of Wellonai became her Daughters. Her blood became Essomuai, her breath, Itorunai, and her voice, Vilodai.

-Verses 1-5 of the Anushgiar Leyosil

—:—

Empress Mother Hiyelleom, one hundred thirteenth regent of Anushai and keeper of Stone House, was tired. She entered her study, placing her diadem on a stand and easing into the chair by her desk. She pulled the long braid out of her snow-white hair and breathed out a long, steady breath, closing her eyes. Her lady's maid would be chiding her for taking the braid out on her own, but she just didn't have the energy tonight.

She was feeling tired more often now, though she would have her rest soon enough; it was beginning to look like her reign may be coming to an end. She had just left a meeting with the other houses, and their rumblings were growing worse by the day. Yet, after thirty-five years on the throne, she couldn't seem to find the energy to mourn this ending; it would simply be the way of things.

When she was younger, of course, she had often wondered how it would all end. There was no shame in your regency ending before your death, obviously. It had happened under nearly half of all Anushai monarchs. Her favorite had been Emperor Piloriae some seven hundred years earlier. From her own house, he had called his own meeting of deposition. It had been time for a change, and he had personally nominated Empress Mother Culyugang from Grass House to take over in his stead. She prayed she would have even half his resolve when the time came for her to step down.

She was proud of the work she had done. In fact, it was precisely because she had done so well that the whispers to depose her were starting. They had elected Stone House when she was thirty-eight years old as the Berillai threat had begun to grow in earnest again. For nearly two centuries, the Battle of Strussfaran had settled them, and the Berillai had seemed satisfied with the land they'd stolen from the Mesop.

However, in the past half-century, they had begun to spread their tentacles along the Erril basin. Even if it was through technology — offering to build railways and such — the threat was clear: accept our help...or else. Unfortunately, the trade-off had often been seen as the better choice by her vassal states, especially after the coup in Amoriai. Allegiances had fallen away until her 'empire' seemed to be in name only. Even worse, she couldn't exactly blame them. It was far better for them to be rich than destroyed, surely...

That Berillai threat was why she had been chosen to rule, of course. As keeper of Stone House — and its army — she had been a natural choice for empress. But the others were beginning to forget. Because she had used her powers not to start wars but to prevent them, they were growing soft. But she knew the truth. Any war she began with Berill would destroy her people, a defeat that would change the Continent forever.

So, she had bided her time, avoiding wars she couldn't win while she made her army stronger. They were still unlikely to ever defeat the Berillai again in open conflict, but they should be prickly enough to appear unappetizing to the ever-expanding maw of the western raiders. As Berillai commerce became the law of the land, though, the other houses were growing impatient — and greedy. Her detractors wanted their piece of the industry spreading east, River House chief among them. Speaking of which, she still needed to write a letter to Duchess Shillyen about her recent lunch with the Marquis...

Hiyelleom opened her eyes, turning to her desk. As desperately as she wanted to sleep, there was work to be done. And even as her body failed her, her eyes growing heavier by the year, this single hour in her study was the only time she could be truly productive. There were many things even an empress was forbidden from choosing, and her schedule was chief among them. And after a day bursting with lady's maids and insipid nonsense, this hour was hers, and she would wield the bloody royal pen.

She rang the bell on the corner of her desk, and immediately, one of the guards opened her study door, allowing her butler to enter. He stepped through, bowing low at the waist.

"Mother?" he asked. "How may I serve?"

"A pot of coffee," she said, "and some cherry biscuits. The kitchen is almost out, and I want to have some before we're forced to wait for the spring harvest."

"Right away, Your Majesty," he said, turning toward the open door.

"Thank you, my son," she replied. "Oh, and Dannelei?"

He turned back, bowing again. "Yes, Mother?"

"Send the maids to bed," she said. "I'm afraid it'll be a late night. Tell them I'll undress on my own. I don't want them suffering for my sake."

He nodded and left. Hiyelleom turned to the desk and took out a few sheets of parchment. She pulled over her wax stick and began to melt the end for her royal seal. It was time to meet these rumors head-on. She wouldn't hide in the palace waiting to be deposed. She would face it like the Stone House daughter she was. And if the time came for her to step down, she would at least have everything in place. There were wolves prowling the land, and if she was forced to leave her sheep in the meadow, she'd at least build them a fence first.

2

Itorunai, the sacred breath, leapt from her mother's lungs and rushed across the world, surging as a mighty wind over the land. As she passed above each peak and valley, she came to know her sister's creations and thought that they were good. She saw the mountains and trees and flowers, longing to live among them as she flew overhead.

-Verses 14-16 of the Anushgiar Leyosil

—:—

Erso smoked his pipe, leaning against the rail of the ship. He pulled off his hat and ran his hand through his hair, letting the ocean breeze cool his forehead. It felt good to be free again, untethered, away from the locks and chains of one place. Especially when that place was Berill. He shook his head, turning as his eyes swept across the deck, looking for Sumi. She was near a cluster of deck chairs, chatting with a couple who were on their honeymoon, which was coincidentally the cover story they were using on the ship…

He smiled. She made an art out of being self-deprecating, but she was actually pretty good at making friends. They had already talked to more people on this journey than he had during his last five, and that was only one of a thousand ways this trip was different. With a companion as pleasant as Sumi, it actually felt like a holiday — instead of being on the run for the hundredth time.

This time *was* different, though, wasn't it? As good as it felt to be free, he had to remember that he was *not* running away. This time, he was running toward something instead of away from it. He was taking a chance on someone, really taking them on as a student. And in so doing, hopefully, his life wouldn't feel like such a waste anymore. He just had to hope— Sumi finished her conversation, breaking off in his direction.

"You know," he said, taking his pipe from his mouth, "it's a lot harder to maintain a low profile with you being so friendly all the time."

11

"They talked to me!" she said, pretending to scoff. "It'd be more suspicious if I didn't talk back."

She joined him at the railing, looking out at the water. They were heading east along the coast and still had a few days before reaching Amoriai. It had grown steadily warmer as the coast curved toward the south, and the passengers were spending more and more time above deck. Out of the corner of his eye, though, he caught her looking west. Berill was like a magnet to her, even when they couldn't see it.

"Still thinking about home?" he asked.

She nodded, her smile fading for a moment.

"Leaving felt easier when I could still see it," she said. "But the further I get, the more I think about it." She turned back to him, flashing him a small smile. "Don't get me wrong, I'm grateful. This is the first time I've ever even left home, and I'm trying to enjoy it. But…a part of me is dying to get back too."

"And you will," he said, smiling, "I promise. Once we're done training, you'll be free to go anywhere, even Berill."

His jaw clenched as images of Aelibis in a noose involuntarily floated up in his mind.

"Just don't rush back. You're no good to your people if you can't do this safely."

Hopefully, with enough time, she'd realize she didn't need to go back at all. It would likely always be dangerous there; the Berillai police might keep her description on file forever, for all they knew. But it wasn't his choice either. His students were always free to decide for themselves how to live their lives, and this shouldn't be any different. *She* shouldn't be any different…

Sumi nodded solemnly, looking down at the water. They stayed that way for a while, watching the waves in silence. Even that was pleasant, though. With other people, he was always jabbering away, but silence never felt heavy around Sumi. She gasped, smiling as she pointed at the waves. He looked down, finding a group of arnisoles jumping through the water.

They looked like tumbleweeds with snouts — only silvery in color and slightly more organized. It was a school of ten or so, and they leapt into the air at the crest of each wave, shooting out like arrows as they spun. It cracked him up, the things she found joy in. Back in Amoriai, arnisoles were pests. They liked to crowd around the docks, chewing on nets and things — sometimes even freeing fish someone had already caught. But seeing things through her eyes…it was loads better than his usual company.

"I wasn't sure if they were real or not!" she said, turning to him. "Grandpa swore they were, but we don't have them back home."

"Yeah, it's strange how few animals you lot have, like they can sense how much you hate magic or something. The Continent's drowning in 'em."

Suddenly, a deep-purple arnisole broke the surface, far bigger than the rest.

"What's that one?"

"That'll be the mother," Erso said. "They swim as a family, so the silver ones must be her kids. I can't remember how long they live, but I think they turn purple after five years or so."

"It's beautiful," she said, "like a plum!"

Then, even over the rush of the waves, he heard her stomach growl.

"Thinking about dessert again?" he asked, raising an eyebrow. The dining room had served plum pudding the night before, and Sumi couldn't get enough of it.

"I blame you," she said, flushing. "All this training. But…do you think they have any left in the kitchens?"

"We can check, but I can't just keep rewarding you for your graceful presence. If you can't suppress your pop at all today, I get all the pudding."

She eyed him but finally shook his outstretched hand, nodding resolutely as she marched below deck.

———

Sumi followed Erso down to the third deck, where they'd booked berths side by side. Erso kept calling them 'middle class,' but for someone from the terraces who'd never been on a ship, they seemed plenty comfortable to her. Besides, the way Grandpa talked about the navy, she'd been half-scared they'd be sleeping in hammocks stacked ten high, surrounded by stinking sailors…

They squeezed to the side of the hallway as they passed Mrs. Ulaiyar, an elderly woman staying two berths away. As always, her cat Curimos — who somehow even joined her at dinner — was in her arms. Mrs. Ulaiyar smiled, giving them a knowing wink. It was meant to be friendly, of course, but given the woman's obsession with their 'honeymoon,' it only made her cheeks flush. *Not that Erso wasn't handsome, but—* She forced a smile on her face before her mind raced any further, turning as quickly as she could toward the cat.

Curimos was already purring, but he squeaked when he saw her, offering his little gray head for scratches. He looked just like Amis, down to his jewel-like eyes.

"Ah, he likes you," Mrs. Ulaiyar said. "Don't you, Curi?"

"Well, at least we get to see you both at dinner," Sumi said, smiling again despite the lump growing in her throat. "I just have to grab my shawl," she said to Erso as she ducked into her room, barely getting the door closed as her tears began to fall.

She cursed herself for being a child, but it had been like this the whole trip; every moment of sunshine just a moment away from rain. But if feeling guilty about leaving Berill hadn't been bad enough, it felt like reminders of Amis were everywhere. How was he feeling without her? Was he wondering where she'd gone? She knew he'd be safe, but she just wished there were a way to explain to a cat what was happening and why.

She and Erso had left the bar late that night he'd broken her out of jail, sneaking back up to the terrace. They hadn't lit any lamps, and Sumi had rushed about in the dark, trying to pack and prepare the cottage to be left behind. They'd spent a tense, sleepless night there, Nela's bedroom transforming from a shrine into a guest room in seconds — even if there was no one more deserving of it than the Shapewalker who'd saved her life.

In the morning, after frantically scrawling letters to Mr. Furttenhur and Seriai, Erso had come back with a carriage, ready to take them as far east as they could get — to the eastern wool ports where the boats wouldn't be watched. While Erso loaded up their bags, she'd scooped up Amis, clinging to him as he squirmed. They'd gone to the only place she could think of, a large townhouse in Runa Terrace where Nela's connections could still help them. She'd knocked on the door, her eyes darting to the street every second, terrified the detective would appear. And as Alip Tellemuir opened the door, she'd handed him the cat, stammering through her lie.

A relative in Anushai is sick—need to leave right away—catching the next train. Could he watch Amis?

He'd agreed immediately, of course. She had touched his shoulder, thanking him over and over, but before the rest of the family could see her, she was rushing out the door again. And before she and Erso could tempt fate any further, they were off, leaving the eastern gates of the city as everything she knew slipped away behind her.

Sumi sat on her tiny bunk on the ship, desperately trying to wipe away her tears. Erso would be wondering about her, and after saving her life, he shouldn't be stuck with a weeping mess too. She took a deep breath. She had to stay positive. She was lucky to be alive at all. Everything else would sort itself out, wouldn't it? Besides, she couldn't even shape properly, and if she didn't focus on her training, he would have saved her for nothing…

She went over to the tiny cupboard built into the wall and pulled out her tiny box of things from Berill. It seemed like a paltry pile — you couldn't fit your entire life in a bag, after all. Still, looking at them made her feel better, a small tether back to home. Even being near the box seemed to calm her, her tears finally drying as she lifted the lid. She had brought her favorite of Grandpa's wine corks from her collection, the bottle of Nela's perfume, and Nela's picture from the front hall, which she had removed from the frame and carefully rolled up.

She picked up the cork, rolling it between her thumb and finger. It had a rough, rippled texture and a purple stain at the bottom. She lifted it to her nose and sniffed it, though any trace of the wine was already more than ten years gone. Then, she carefully opened Nela's photo, running her thumb along the edge of the picture. Strange to think she was heading toward Nela's home and leaving it behind at the same time. Could she ever bridge the two?

She took a deep breath, absorbing the box's stillness. One day she'd have to learn to calm herself without a crutch, but this would have to do for now. She tried to imagine Nela with her, even as she knew she'd lecture her for being moody.

"Come, child, you never been on ship. Why no smile?"

And she was right. Even with all the pain and homesickness, there was a lot to celebrate. Traveling was probably nothing special to Erso, crossing the world ten times over every year, but it was incredible to her. There were so many other people to talk to and things she'd never seen. Even getting to talk to Erso — when she hadn't had her own friend since Seriai left — felt like a breath of fresh air. Maybe it was because he'd saved her life, but it felt like she'd known him forever. And for the first time since Nela died, it seemed like anything was possible again.

She took the perfume, spraying a small mist onto her neck. Then, she clenched her fists, taking one last deep breath. She could do this. She hastily grabbed her shawl — almost forgetting her excuse — and rushed toward the door. Training couldn't wait forever, and if she knew Erso, the longer she took, the harder he'd make her work.

3

Essomuai was her mother's blood, and thus, filled every part of the land. But when she pushed toward the sky, thousands of flowers and trees emerged. Essomuai eagerly danced with her creations, entering each to feel its color, each one a reminder of the rainbows of the Void. Essomuai continued to craft the land, forming mountains and valleys in Wellonai. And as she did, the plants changed, with new types thriving in every corner of her Mother's body.

-Verses 7-12 of the Anushgiar Leyosil

—:—

"Relax," Erso said, holding up his fists as he opened them like flowers. He sure liked that metaphor. Apparently, tapping your powers was supposed to feel like a blossom blooming, not a screw being twisted in. Still, she'd never had a flower give her a headache... Sumi nodded, though she spared a glance for the puddings he'd left on the bedside table.

"Maybe just a little bite?" she asked. "It'll help me find my center."

Erso laughed, snapping his fingers.

"No pudding for poppers. Repeat the process to me again."

"Okay," she said, walking through the steps in her mind for the thousandth time. "Find my center, then picture the—"

Erso held up a finger. "Don't forget to breathe."

"Right. Find my center. Breathe. Then picture the cave?"

Erso nodded. The cave was supposed to help her find stillness in her mind, preventing the ripples and pops that led Detective Parimu right to her. Instead of picturing a happy memory like she used to do, the goal was to picture the thing you wanted to be in a calm, still place, like a cave, before easing into its form.

"Soon you won't even need it," Erso reminded her, "but it helps in the beginning to have something to picture. Eventually, it will be just

16

like walking through a door."

He talked about doors a lot too. Sometimes, it seemed like shapeshifting was nine parts metaphor and one part magic. Not that she could blame him… How were you supposed teach someone to fly who'd never left the ground? Even worse, she'd grown up in Berill, where they had no words to describe magic at all. She'd only just discovered Nela's beliefs — Anushai, her ancestors, the goddess Essomuai — and now, Erso had completely different names for everything. He called the goddess Mu'lalat. Or maybe it wasn't a goddess. He seemed to think it was a place — hence the doors?

In Erso's description, it was like every shape you could ever want was in this long hallway, hidden in its own room. Shapewalkers were simply people who could walk between them at will. When the powers first came to you, it was the sheer force of your memories kicking down those doors. But as you progressed, as long as you could find the stillness, you didn't need to barge your way through anymore.

But stillness seemed far away when she felt so awkward. Sitting cross-legged on Erso's bed, she felt like she was all knees, and she couldn't possibly look very cute with her eyes clamped shut and—

Focus! she thought. Why should he care if she looked cute? She was his student — and not a very good one, at that. She took a deep breath, centering herself again. They were starting with forms she already knew to ease the transition, but it was hard to focus on each object without falling back on the crutch of her memories to help her through. She imagined the umbrella again, trying to focus on its shape and texture.

"You know this door," Erso said calmly. "You may have pushed through last time, but it's open now. Don't think about your memory. Think about how it *felt* to be an umbrella."

How did he stay so patient? They'd tried this a dozen times the past few days with no luck. She only transformed into the umbrella once, but she'd forced her way through by accident, causing a giant ripple. Luckily, Erso had already swept the boat, promising her there was no one on board who could sense her. But what about when they reached Amoriai, unable to know who was around them in all the buildings?

She thought back to that night, in the alley, when Parimu's men had chased her. For a time, she'd blocked it out, but as she trained, it was on her mind more and more. She hadn't needed a memory then. How had she done that? It had felt almost like she wasn't even the one doing the transforming, as if she'd stepped back from her own body, realizing it was just one shape among many. It was still hard to tell if Essomuai was a goddess or an idea, but she'd felt real that night.

Forget the umbrella, then. She'd escaped Parimu as a hawk, and if that memory kept calling to her, she would use it.

Essomuai, she prayed in her mind, *help me let go of myself — let me be the hawk again.*

Even if she was only talking to herself, it felt like something. She shut her eyes gently, not blocking out the room but just letting it…drift away. She pictured the cave. She wasn't sure if her cave was enough like the one Erso had described, but at least it was hers. She no longer tried to force herself to imagine it. Like that night in the alley, she just decided to believe there was a version of herself in a cave. A version of herself who could be a hawk.

The stone of the cave was a smooth, deep gray with veins of blue and black running through it. It wasn't dark — there was a small hole in the ceiling where light filtered in — and she could hear waves somewhere, the place somehow connected to the sea. Little plants were growing in the floor's crevices; small, mossy things reaching for the sunlight. Sumi felt herself there, her boots firmly on the stone, and before her was a pool, its water completely still and smooth. She couldn't see the bottom, but the water was clear, her eyes following the curve of the rock as it slipped into darkness. She sat by the water, and when she looked up, she saw the hawk across from her.

The hawk wasn't just a memory; in this cave, it was real. It was a part of her. She was both the human and the hawk, and she could be either if she wanted. In fact, she wasn't just sitting in the cave — she *was* the cave. They were all her forms, and somehow, in that moment, she knew the pool was Essomuai, filled with an ancient power that had welled up over thousands of years. Nela was in that pool, and her great-grandparents too, every form they'd ever taken like a single drop in an infinite aquifer.

When she opened her eyes again, there was a woman in the hawk's place. *She* was the hawk now, and the woman was her human form. The pool began to glow, filling the cave with golden light…

She opened her eyes and saw Erso, his jaw hanging open. Only, he was too large, like the other side of a magnifying glass. She looked down at her arms but found wings there instead. She did it! She opened her mouth to yell in victory when Erso unfroze, throwing up his hands.

"Best to keep the cabin hawk to ourselves," he said, grinning. "I think you'd scare Ulaiyar's cat right off the boat."

She clamped her beak back shut, though she could feel herself smiling — or whatever a hawk's version of a smile was.

"But well done," he said, reaching for a handshake before he remembered she was a hawk. Still, he gently took the talon she offered him. "I knew you'd get it soon enough."

She flew over to his coatrack to celebrate, spinning in a circle as she preened, Erso clapping all the while. But suddenly, she remembered her prize, her head whipping toward the puddings — like a hawk spotting a mouse in a field. Erso followed her gaze, shaking a finger at her.

"Not so fast," he said. "Hawks don't eat pudding — leads to indigestion. If you want one of these, you'll have to shape a human again, no ripple."

She ruffled her feathers, giving him what she hoped was an indignant stare. That most certainly had not been the deal. Still, he had a point. She had to be able to go back on her own, right? She flew down from the coatrack as she closed her eyes, trying to summon the pool again. She imagined the cave, feeling her talons on the stone as she pictured her human form across from her.

I'm me, she thought.

She imagined herself as a person again, trying to remember the feeling from moments ago. But when she opened her eyes, she still had feathers. She tried again, trying to *feel* human, but it was no use. She looked at Erso, finding a smug smile on his face.

She huffed at him, jamming her eyes shut again. She didn't return to the cave, making her mind go blank instead. She tried to imagine being human again, but nothing happened. *Why isn't it working?* All she wanted was a pudding and some congratulations on her accomplishment! She started to picture herself eating pudding, remembering the smooth cream and the tang of the fruit. If only she could— Suddenly, a bright flash erupted in the cabin, her body changing back to normal with a loud pop.

She found herself in a heap on the floor, her dress rumpled underneath her.

"Ugh," she said, squeezing her temples. "I'm sorry, I don't know why I couldn't do it."

"Hey, it's alright," Erso said, springing to his feet with a pudding in his hand. "You did great; it was your first time without a ripple!"

"Yeah," she said, forcing a small smile to her face. "But I couldn't make it back."

"Pshh," he said, handing her the pudding, "you barely popped, like a bottle of wine."

She eyed him, almost rejecting the pudding out of pride.

"Why the sudden change?"

"Cause you look too sad for making sport," he said, "even for me.

And, well, I can't exactly eat two puddings by myself."

She pushed him, and he laughed, sitting on the floor with a pudding of his own. His finely tailored pants hiked up along his leg, revealing brightly striped socks.

"You were *this* close," he said between bites, holding his finger and thumb an inch apart. "You shouldn't have let me fluster you."

"You shouldn't have tried to fluster me! I'm still working this out, you know."

"Hey," he said with a grin, "the world's a flustering place. You should be proud, truly. Your first transformation is a big deal. But I'm always gonna push you. I want you ready, and I want you safe."

She took a deep breath, nodding. "You're right, thank you."

In the real world, there would be far more chases and far less pudding. She'd gotten lucky with Parimu, and she might not again if she couldn't figure this out. She had to keep trying. Even if she hadn't ever been particularly talented at anything in her normal life, she knew she could work hard. But she *had* been close, hadn't she?

"Hey, I just realized," she said, pointing at her pudding. "On my way back, I wasn't using a memory. I was thinking about eating pudding. Does that mean anything?"

Erso scratched his chin, nodding. "That's a great first step, I think it means you're close. Gets you closer to the doors that you design."

Once they were done with smooth transformations, he'd said he wanted her to start shaping with her imagination. According to his lectures, you could find the whole world in Mu'lalat — the past, the future, even things you'd only dreamed of.

"I hope so," she said. "I mean, maybe it didn't count? I knew what the pudding tasted like already. It just wasn't a *specific* memory, you know?"

Erso shook his head. "No, no," he said, pointing at her with his spoon, "that's exactly where you should start. Take my hat, for example."

He pointed to where it hung on the coatrack. It was his usual bowler hat, though now that she looked at it, it was green today instead of beige. She hadn't even realized he had changed it.

"I made that myself," he went on. "Of course, I know what hats are, right? How they fit, how they're shaped. But I've never owned a *green* bowler hat. Your mind can create with things it knows, like bricks on a house, but that doesn't mean it isn't new."

He put his pudding down, turning serious.

"There's no shame in using a form you're used to. Remember, the most important thing is to live another day. It's not worth dying over pride. Imagination can be good, but I'll become a rat nine times out of ten if it gets me away. Just promise me you'll run when you have to. Shaping well takes time, but I only want you safe."

She met his eyes, nodding, though something bothered her about that. His concern was heartwarming, of course — it made her feel much safer to have *someone* in this new world who cared for her — but she still wanted to go home someday. And as terrified as she was of being captured again, there had to be something more to this life than running away. But would she be brave enough to know the difference?

She turned back to her pudding, savoring her last bite. She closed her eyes and let it sit on her tongue, trying to stretch out that last second of sweetness. When she reopened them, Erso was standing, smoothing out his pants. He had finished before her, of course — he ate every meal like it was his last, unlike her who'd been forced by Nela to eat like a queen. As if on cue, though, the ship's clock chimed five times.

"And that's dinner," Erso said, offering his hand. She took it, standing. "Like all my methods, early dessert might be unorthodox, but who said pudding's not an appetizer?"

4

Vilodai awoke, finding herself deep within the depths, confined to the space where great caverns met the land. Despite her captivity, Vilodai discovered her Mother's voice and its incredible power. Not only could she shape the very earth, but she could make powerful storms, which surged forth and covered the land, pouring down rains that formed rivers to the sea.

-Verses 23-26 of the Anushgiar Leyosil

—:—

Parimu sat tensely in a passenger car, his train hurtling eastward. He was a few days into his journey, but his stomach was still in knots, unable to watch the scenery for long as he eyed the other passengers. He'd left the kingdom hundreds of times while he was in the navy, of course, but this felt different. He had no uniform, no ship, no *buffer* between him and the world. Instead, he was on a train full of strangers, just one anonymous face among them.

The further he traveled east, the worse the feeling got, everything around him slowly becoming more…*foreign.* The first night, their train had passed through Strussfaran. Once a part of Luterrin, the westernmost of the Three Sisters, it had been Berillai some two hundred years — though you could hardly tell. The buildings he'd seen from the train car were ancient, done in the Continental style, untouched even by the great battles from the history books. And as he'd stared up at them, the window streaked with rain, it had dawned on him just how far he'd left his home behind.

He was bound for Amoriai, a six-day journey by train. He had booked a sleeper car, but he may as well have forgone the expense for all the sleep he was getting… He'd spent the last two nights rolling around in his tiny bunk, agonizing over every detail of the Shapewalker's escape.

He felt like he was in Ciersein's court, the hall of the dead, every memory pouring through his eyes. Only for him, it was worse. Instead of seeing his life, he only heard that girl's voice, the same words repeating over and over.

"We won't build community by being less of ourselves, by picking out who belongs and who doesn't. If we can't be who we are, how can we be anything to anyone else?"

He'd heard Shapewalkers lie before, had heard dozens give their pleading last words. But this time, to his infinite dismay, some of it *made sense.* Berill was festering, losing its heart and rotting at the core. They *did* need community — to know and be known, cared for by others. The factories, the train lines; they gave plenty, but the people weren't asking what they took away.

He squeezed his temples; he had to get her voice out of his head. Those monsters would say anything to manipulate you. Besides, what could she possibly know about community when she spent every night running around with someone else's face? Of course, she had known the right words to say, knowing a loyal officer of the queen would want the best for Berill. The queen… He gulped, his collar suddenly feeling too tight as he remembered who had ordered him on this train.

The summons from the queen had come quickly, a mere hour after he had written her himself. After a sleepless night searching for the Shapewalker — and using every asset he had before his authority expired — he'd admitted defeat, telegraphing the queen about his failure. He'd thought about resigning, but that would only bring him more shame. If the queen wanted to strip him of his post — or even his head, for that matter — the privilege should be hers. So, for the second time in just a week, his eyes bleary from lack of sleep, he'd found himself walking the gravel path toward the palace.

If only he hadn't failed. He'd ground his teeth, forcing himself to review the details for the thousandth time. The woman, the child, the wicked man impersonating an officer! What a fool he'd been. If only he could sense them when they weren't using their powers. His predecessor, Drekkles, had been wildly talented at finding Shapewalkers. Parimu himself had learned to sense the ripples easily enough, but every time he'd pushed the older man to train him further, he'd been vague, promising his powers would develop with time.

Still, arrests had been frequent then, the department fully staffed. So, for a time, he'd taken Drekkles at his word. But as the population of Shapewalkers dwindled, the other officers had given up their posts until, finally, Drekkles died, taking his secrets — and his clout in the police department — with him. And now, the other officers, the ones who thought him such a fool, would see just what a failure he'd become.

Unfortunately, word had spread quickly, even for a rumor mill like the RPS. He was fairly certain the palace guards hadn't gossiped, but he couldn't say the same about the police. Everyone had seen his arrest at the beach, and even the Peers — always eager to besmirch the queen — wouldn't have had to work hard to hear the story. Everyone had been talking about it that morning — none of them bothering to whisper — though none of the stories had been even close to right. Some had him mistakenly arresting civilians, while others even had him beaten up by the woman and child. Not a single rumor had the truth: they *were* Shapewalkers, and they'd escaped with evil magic.

He'd been hurried through the palace halls, escorted by a rough-looking pair of guards — no longer worthy of a chamberlain to escort him — until they reached a sort of armory. The room was full of ancient things: maces, shields, and plate passed down through generations. Compared to his first time in the palace, meeting in the dining room, it was a very different place for a very different kind of audience. And just as the room was different, so was the woman he met.

Queen Welaya had been waiting for him in a straight-backed chair, perched between two enormous suits of silver armor. She was surrounded by guards, though she may as well have been taking tea, reading calmly from a stack of papers. She looked almost like a statue, beautiful as she was, barely moving as she read. He bowed formally, kneeling on the floor until she spoke.

"Detective Parimu," she'd finally said, "thank you for coming." Her voice was quiet and cool, sending a shiver down his spine. "Please rise and face your queen."

No matter how severe she looked, though, they both knew she could have brought him there in chains if she'd wanted to. Why hadn't she, then? He raised his head and stood, bowing his head in gratitude.

"I appreciate you writing to me so quickly," she said. "It allowed me to have at least a few hours' advantage over my enemies. It also showed me the reliability of your…loyalty, if not your competence."

That had felt like a sword through his heart, but he kept from wincing, simply bowing his head again in acknowledgment. It was his failure, and he wouldn't hide from it.

"Unfortunately, while few seem to know the extent of your failure, my sources tell me that, somehow, Vice Peer Pont'dulairn knows the true nature of your captives."

He'd opened his mouth to swear his loyalty, but she silenced him with a wave of her hand.

"I know it wasn't you," she said. "Pont'dulairn's fingers are everywhere. Still, I took a risk giving you my guards, and this may well cost me my police powers."

He'd looked away, the shame suddenly too much to bear. He felt the bile rise in his throat, a thousand curses forming in his mind for Pont'dulairn. Still, what right did he have to curse his betters? Even children knew Berill had two halves, the crown and the peerage, sharing power since the time of Rummon and his clan chiefs. Still, to think of a peer challenging the queen, fighting her authority…

"I see your contrition is sincere," she said, though he couldn't bring himself to meet her eyes. "But this problem didn't start with you, Mr. Parimu. Men see fit to mock the old ways, accusing me of chasing ghosts. But you may serve me yet."

He'd looked up at that, his vision swimming as he moved his head too quickly. If there was any way to make things right, he would do it in an instant.

"I find myself in a double bind, Detective. I need those Shapewalkers back to show the threat is real, but I also need this dealt with quietly before I lose what little authority I have left. My Thorns are occupied, dealing with all these threats at home. And so that leaves me you."

The room had fallen silent, and he felt himself being weighed, the scales suddenly tipping from the weight of his failure. Still, when she spoke again, her voice was quiet, her anger gone.

"Your predecessor had a jailbreak once. I was a girl then, but my father brought me to his council. Five Shapewalkers escaped, too many to rule out inside help. But Drekkles tracked them down, found them hiding in Maldegurn — a decidedly unfriendly nation at the time. And when he returned, we didn't take them to the docks. We hanged them at the palace, to show the people our resolve."

She closed her eyes for a moment, and a slight smile came to her lips.

"I will give you the same chance at redemption, Detective. My Thorns tell me there's no sign of them from here to Enozeira, which leaves Amoriai. Find them and vindicate your queen."

She'd snapped her fingers then, the grim butler from his past visit suddenly appearing, a leather case in hand.

"Train tickets," the butler said, "and a few other things you may need."

Parimu nodded, taking the case.

"My queen," he said, bowing. But as he'd turned to go, she spoke once more.

"Oh, Parimu," she'd said, absently looking over her papers again. "My Thorns know your face. If you fail me again, they'll find you and the Shapewalkers both, and you can hang together."

5

Vilodai had failed to realize that by using the soil, Essomuai would be within her children. But Essomuai loved mankind, exalting in the power of their passion. Here, in one creature, was such a variety of shape and spirit. She followed them as they traveled to the ends of the earth, seeing with their eyes and hearing with their ears.

-Verses 33-35 of the Anushgiar Leyosil

—:—

The train whistle sounded, breaking Parimu from his reverie. He blinked, taking in the car around him again. It was already evening, the sunlight gold where it glinted off the tracks, and he could feel the train slowing. According to the schedule, they'd be stopping for fuel and passengers before continuing through the night. He stood from his seat, nodding to the woman across from him as he headed to his sleeper for his pipe.

He would need to take advantage of the break to get a smoke in. There were smoking cars on the train, of course, but he wasn't partial to them. They were primarily occupied by men, and they seemed to think the absence of women turned the place into a tavern, with enough cursing and boasting to make a pirate blush. He much preferred to wait for a chance to stretch his legs, even if the time without his pipe made him grind his teeth…

Still, he could certainly use a break from stewing in his own thoughts. Like his mother used to say, only full branches snap during a storm. But aside from worrying about the queen, there was another ghost on his shoulder now, his memories of Drekkles impossible to escape. He'd been grinding himself to a nub, lying awake each night in a kind of trance as he tried to figure out the man's secret to hunting Shapewalkers, reliving every ripple he'd ever felt. Their transformations were hard to

27

miss — like a lightning bolt to the mind — but Drekkles hadn't even seemed to need them. But how?

He finally reached the sleeper cars, where the hallways ran along one side, allowing room for a half dozen berths on each car. Luckily they'd booked him in coach — Umilai forbid he ever squandered the queen's coin — but the cars were still beautiful, the dark paneling and rich blue carpet the signature of the Berillai Royal Line. When he reached his room, he put his ear to the door, making sure no one was waiting for him inside. He had nothing to fear, of course; no one knew him here, and the trains were well guarded. Still, being abroad, with enemies on every side, who could he really trust?

Going in, he pulled his bag from under the bed, breathing a sigh of relief as he found everything still in place. At the top was a thick packet of papers from the Foreign Office — too many to stuff in his coat, but too vital to leave unlocked. But just like his ghostly assassins, he seemed to have gained an irrational fear of losing those letters.

The first was a letter of introduction to the Fida'lalean in Amoriai, that kingdom's Shapewalker-hunting police. He would be looking for a Captain Erlmak, their leader. He nodded to himself. It was good the Berillai influence had grown so much under Amoriai's new crown. The Amoriai were one of the few peoples who'd had enough sense to overthrow their government and start fresh, staging a coup and signing treaties with Berill.

The next document in his case was a writ of acceptance for foreign banks. He had a large purse on him already, but the Foreign Office had given him the writs in case of emergency, another four thousand sovereigns if he had need of it. It was a ludicrous amount of money, but it did drive home the crown's commitment to seeing justice done. Finally, he had some papers to support his cover as a merchant, factory orders for a leatherworks in Amoriai, and a false identity card.

Beyond the papers, though, the most important thing in his luggage, by far, was his silver crossbow. It was taken apart at the moment, but he reached out, gently running his finger along the flight groove. Drekkles had left it to him, and while he tended to avoid using it back home — wary of scaring his own citizens — out here, surrounded by monsters, it was the most reassuring thing he had. He still wasn't entirely sure what it was about silver, but if the collars drained their magic, silver in the body, delivered by an arrow...

There were many parts of this work he'd never understand, but for this mystery, at least, he was grateful. As the queen herself had said, silver was from the gods themselves, given to King Rummon to conquer these wicked lands. And even now, in the age of trains and cannons, it seemed Umilai protected them still from the Continent's dark magic.

The whistle sounded again, the train grinding to a stop. He shoved his bag back under the bed as he leaned out the window, finding the train pulling into Hafanelle. He grabbed his pipe and his tobacco, eager not to miss his precious few minutes at the station.

It was already well into evening as he stepped onto the platform, the city half in shadow as the sun dipped into the water. He remembered Hafanelle. About a third of the way through Luterrin, it had been a common supply drop in the navy. But just like everything on this journey, nothing looked familiar now, every landmark he knew obscured by teeming buildings. The sea at least had a logic to it. You knew where the water ended, and you just followed the curve of the land home. Not so with the trains, built through endless fields, with nothing to guide you but lonely metal tracks.

He looked at the other people on the platform, recognizing some from the dining car. He nodded at a passing woman who he knew to be Berillai, though the bulk of the passengers were from the Continent. Many on the platform wore either Amoriai scarves or flowing Three Sisters dresses. Although, most of the men wore suits, which was quickly becoming the fashion in every kingdom. Parimu nodded to himself — if he couldn't wear his uniform, at least give him the dignity of a suit.

The buildings around him looked old — older than Strussfaran — though at least the train station was new. The platform was open to the air, but there were wide awnings of freshly forged iron and a series of neat brick columns. He leaned forward, looking at the long stretch of their train, where there seemed to be an endless line of cargo. Livestock, coal, ore; all manner of things crossing the Continent for one reason or another. It was certainly interesting — if you could ignore the thick smoke belching from the engine. He'd heard another merchant call it the *smell of money,* but he'd take the clean salt air on a ship any day.

He reached into his pocket for his pipe. Normally, he wouldn't smoke so close to the door where there were women present, but given the cloud of soot surrounding them, the spice in his tobacco might actually be a relief. He began packing his pipe, carefully covering the navy crest on the bulb with his thumb. As he was about to strike a match, a man spoke behind him, making him jump.

"Hello, friend," the man said with a thick Three Sisters accent, "mind if I use a match?"

Parimu whipped around but managed a smile. *Easy, man*, he thought to himself. He was getting too jittery being away from home. The man was smiling back, a pipe also in hand. Perfectly normal.

"Of course," Parimu said, stammering as he handed over the matchbook. He took a deep breath, trying to— Suddenly, there was a strange buzzing in his ears, as if someone had struck a tuning fork. His vision swam, seeming to vibrate with the air, and he blinked, putting a hand to his forehead.

"Sorry," he said, shaking his head as the man handed back the matches. "Did you hear that noise?"

Just then, a train whistle went off a few tracks down.

"Thank you kindly," the man said, taking a pull from his pipe. "You mean the whistle?" He reached into his pocket, pulling out a watch. "Is your train leaving soon?"

"No, no," Parimu said, shaking his head again. "I'm on this train here, I just…never mind. I think I've been sitting too long. I think I'll walk a bit, if you don't mind. Enjoy your smoke."

The man shrugged but smiled again.

"Sure thing, friend," he said. "You as well."

Parimu nodded, turning away. Was the coal smoke getting to him or something? He walked down the platform, forcing himself to take deep breaths — even if it was the same dirty air. When he was far enough away, he stopped, squeezing his temples. He looked back toward the other man, but he was hard to see, a strange glow in the air making him squint. He blinked hard, trying to clear his eyes. Some trick of the light maybe? He looked toward the engine, trying to see if the fire in the boiler was somehow glowing through the haze. He shook his head, knocking out his pipe as he hurried back to his car. The train would be moving soon, and they'd leave this smoke behind. He just needed some fresh air, that was all.

6

—yet this peace could not last forever. The passion of Vilodai was not a match but a forest fire, and it would not be easily quenched. Mankind began to multiply twice over, and as they grew, the valleys and hills swelled with their number. There was abundance on Wellonai, but her people felt uneasy, afraid there would never be enough. So they pushed into new lands with all their might, shaping the world to their will.

-Verses 42-46 of the Anushgiar Leyosil

—:—

Sumi followed Erso up the stairs, making the familiar climb to the fifth-deck dining room. The week had flown by, their time still split between training and taking in the air. After working in the flower shop for ten years, it felt downright lazy, but training *was* important, wasn't it? She just…hadn't expected being on the run to be fun. It felt like something she didn't deserve, but here it was.

She hadn't been able to perfect turning back into herself, but she'd still managed to learn something every day, at least. Just that morning, in fact, they'd practiced sending messages through Mu'lalat, like the ones Erso had used to guide her in Berill. He'd had her change into a trolley token — something about inanimate objects' hazy vision being easier — and held her in his hand. She'd found herself reading his palm, following his love line the way Nela used to do.

It wasn't exactly easy to send messages through Mu'lalat, though, and the most you could hope for were little snippets. What he'd done in Berill, essentially, was send an *aura,* bright and positive, to say yes to her questions. To do so, you picked a color and a feeling you wanted to convey and just…filled yourself — or your pool — with it. Of course, Erso hadn't made that lesson particularly easy either.

"Let's start," he'd said, holding her as a coin. "I'll ask you a question, and you can send me an answer with your aura. Sumi — should I put you on the dresser?"

She'd focused on his hand, trying to fill herself with a bright white light. She'd concentrated so hard, she thought the coin might vibrate.

"Still nothing," he'd said after a few moments of waiting. "Try one more time. You have to focus on your emotion too, the full intent of what you're trying to show the other person."

She tried again, her mind boiling over with light. Her yearning should be enough, shouldn't it? But after another minute, nothing had happened. His face still loomed over her, completely unchanged. He twisted his mouth up, drumming his fingers on his chin.

"Well, guess this coin is a dud. I think I'll just stick it in my shoe for safekeeping."

That time, she had vibrated her coin in annoyance. If she'd had a tongue, she would have stuck it out at him. She pictured a storm cloud in her mind, shouting at him in her head as the cloud rippled with lightning.

"Don't you dare put me in that shoe!"

"Whoa," he'd said, almost dropping her as he jumped. "I actually got something that time! Well done! It was…dark, definitely a no."

After that, they'd managed a yes, though she had to shout in her mind again to be heard. He really was a good teacher — even if most of his lessons involved antagonizing her. And with his guidance, she felt herself getting closer to being a *real* Shapewalker, to feeling like she had a chance at surviving in her strange new world.

As they continued to climb the stairwell, she looked out a window, catching a pair of cranes flying in the distance. Just another sign she'd left Berill behind. You never saw cranes in winter back home. In fact, they'd sailed so far east, she didn't even need her coat above deck anymore. At home, they probably had snow on the ground. She was losing track of the dates without work to guide her, but it had to almost be the middle of Shaffinom, the fourteenth or the— The fifteenth of Shaffinom…her twenty-sixth birthday.

She'd completely forgotten in her panic. Not that her birthday would have mattered if they'd hanged her in Berill… She eyed Erso, deciding to keep it to herself. She was lucky enough to have dinner with a friend, and after everything he'd done for her, she'd hate to have him feel the need to celebrate somehow. Besides, she could always find her own way to celebrate once they reached Amoriai. It wasn't like she'd ever had her birthday on the right day back home.

Nela had always insisted on doing birthdays by the Anushai calendar, which had Sumi's on the seventeenth of Keonnes. It was horribly confusing growing up — with Berill having eleven months and Anushai ten — though sometimes it meant she got presents from Grandpa on one day and Nela the next. But Nela had promised this year, which fell on a Grass year in the Anushai calendar, would be important, a time when new things would grow. And they were: discovering her powers, leaving Berill, all of it part of a new future growing before her eyes.

"I've been meaning to ask," Erso said, looking over his shoulder, "is your name short for anything?"

It was like he'd read her mind — which it sometimes felt like he could — thinking about how they did things in Anushai. He'd been teaching her to look for keyholes, the shimmer of light from other Shapewalkers, and she was half afraid he could somehow hear her thoughts through hers.

"It is," she said carefully. "But it's not a great name. Kind of embarrassing, really."

He scoffed. "Yeah, I'm sure the Berillai kids were completely tolerant of strange names. I only ask because it sounds Anushai, only less…wordy, maybe?"

She chuckled. "That's fair. They sure have a lot of syllables. My grandpa never could say my grandmother's name, either. Probably why they shortened mine."

She pulled to the side on the final landing, motioning for him to come closer. "I'll tell you, but only if you promise not to use it against me in training."

He held up his hands in surrender — though it was noticeably short of a promise.

"It's Sumilnyeon."

Erso mouthed the syllables, chewing on each part before he nodded. "My Anushai's a bit rusty these days," he said, "but does it have something to do with plants?"

"Wow," she said, raising her eyebrows, "I'm impressed — and almost glad I told you. But yeah, it means 'verdant green shoots' or something odd like that. I'm surprised my mother let Nela name me, honestly. She used a Berillai name her whole life, absolutely hated the one they'd picked for her."

"Well, I think it's a great name," he said, "very pretty. You know what Erso means?"

She shrugged.

"Me neither," he said. "But from the way people shout it as I run away, it might be a curse word."

Sumi pushed him, and he smiled. They turned down the next hallway, joining a line of passengers being seated in the dining hall.

"And what was your Nela's name then?" he asked, his voice lowered.

"Essolurei," she whispered back.

Erso mouthed the name again, staring at the ceiling as he worked through its parts. "*Esso...*" he said, scratching the side of his head, "that's like a big building, right? And *lurei* sounds like...green thunder? That wouldn't make much sense, though, would it?" He finally shrugged and smiled. "Like I said, the old Anushai's a bit rusty."

"Your guess is as good as mine," she said. "My Anushai is alright, I guess, but those ancient words they use in names are beyond me."

Just then, the maître d' guided them to their table, and soon they were greeting the other couples seated there, their own conversation forgotten for the moment. Mrs. Ulaiyar was seated already, with Curimos barely concealed on her lap. Like every other night, no one seemed to care. Though, based on the beautiful jewelry she wore, it was entirely possible she tipped her way through the ship, the porters conveniently missing the cat in her arms.

There were six other guests at their table, all from somewhere in their section of the ship. Two of them were couples: the Eldalins and the Rutherams, both from Berill and traveling on business. And the last person at the table was Amoriai, a Mr. Hal'deen, who was some kind of steel merchant. There was certainly an awful lot of business traffic on the boat. Unfortunately, it made them seem like a novelty — the young couple blissfully traveling for their honeymoon on a budget. As they sat down, all eyes turned to them, Mrs. Ulaiyar squealing in delight.

"I caught these two heading to their berths just before dinner," she said, throwing her head back and laughing. "Oh, to be young and in love."

Sumi's heart skipped a beat, but thankfully, Erso jumped in, smooth as ever.

"I love the sea air," he said, "but the sun makes me dizzy after too long."

Nods and agreements filtered from around the table. With no one else at the table below sixty, they were at least in the right age group for that kind of excuse... The server appeared at Sumi's shoulder.

"Wine, madam?" he asked. She assented, turning to look him in the eye as she thanked him. It was still strange to have someone serve all her meals, especially so formally from behind her chair. It all felt a bit too *anonymous* to her, though she had to admit, she didn't miss her own cooking one bit. The others continued their conversation where they left off, comparing different vacation spots and the various ships they'd taken over the years.

It still amazed her how widely they had traveled. Even ten years ago, it seemed like no one ever left home, but now there were trains across the Continent every hour. And tickets weren't even all that expensive anymore. Nela had never so much as hinted at wanting to return home to Anushai, but now she wished she'd forced the matter. Even if she saw the world now, she couldn't help wishing it was with Nela by her side.

She turned to Erso, the size of the table making it easy to have their own conversation. "Do you have a favorite ship to travel on?"

"Well, I don't normally travel in this kind of style," he said in a low voice, chuckling. "Plenty of rats on ships. If the journey is going to be quick enough, sometimes I just stow away in the hold."

"Stop!" she said, laughing. Unfortunately, Mrs. Ulaiyar heard, turning the conversation back to them as she cooed again about newlyweds.

The rest of the dinner continued at the same tempo. They would peel off, having their own quiet conversation until Mrs. Ulaiyar inevitably reeled them back in. The meal, at least, was just as delicious as it always was. They had some kind of baked stork that was apparently native to the coast of Enozeira. Even though the ship didn't stop in every port, the chef seemed to have planned ahead, making each meal local to the place they were closest to on the map. But as they were wrapping up the meal, Erso placed a hand on her arm.

"I hope you don't mind," he whispered, "but there's a special dessert tonight."

Just then, the waiters burst from the kitchen, one of them pushing a giant chocolate cake on a cart. It was covered in a dark, glistening frosting and brimming with candles.

Sumi stared at the cake as it wound its way through the dining hall. That couldn't be what he meant, could it? There had to be someone else on the ship with a birthday. But the cart kept moving until it finally stopped beside her. She shot a look at Erso, but suddenly, everyone was clapping and singing, the waiters urging her to blow out the candles — all twenty-six of them.

An hour later, her face sore from smiling, she found herself on the top deck with Erso, sitting on a pair of deck chairs with a bottle of wine between them. She stared up at the stars, each one shining brightly in the dark. There were a few glowing lights on the shore, where villages dotted the hills, but for the most part, they were moving through a swaying *nothingness.* The dark sea rolled calmly below the ship, the salt wind blowing through her hair.

"Thank you for doing that," she said, turning to look at Erso. "I…didn't think I'd have a birthday this year with Nela gone."

"Of course," he said, picking his head up from the deck chair and smiling at her. "Everyone deserves a birthday, no?" He pulled out his pipe, packing it carefully before he struck a match. "Hope I didn't embarrass you too much. You let your birthday slip when you were telling me about the memories you used for Shapewalking, and the cooks were more than happy to oblige."

"It was lovely," she said. Ever since Grandpa died, she hadn't felt like hosting a big birthday party. She and Nela had a wonderful dinner by themselves the year before, of course, but if Erso hadn't sprung it on her, she probably wouldn't have had a room full of people singing to her ever again. It was beautiful. Mrs. Ulaiyar had a surprisingly good voice, too. It made her think of Nela's, which had only grown richer with age. Nela always sang in Anushai for birthdays, her voice particularly good in her native language.

Zeyel neyom leyal, essom cheang, neyom zeyel zeyel. It meant: *Another year has come, we sing, may another and another follow after.* Sumi took in a deep breath, trying not to cry, especially after such a wonderful night. But as she thought back to the birthday she and Nela had the year before, she was reminded again of Nela's Grass year comment and the strange hint in her letter. *"If anything strange should happen."* It made her wonder what Nela had known and why she hadn't said. The doubt bubbled up in her mind, demanding an answer.

"Hey, Erso?" she asked in a quiet voice. "My Nela told me twenty-six would be a lucky year — something to do with the Anushai calendar. But I got my powers this year, and…I guess I've been wondering if she knew, if it's normal to get them at my age. And if she did know, why wouldn't she tell me?"

He sat up, turning to face her.

"I don't think she did," he said, smiling sadly. "Most people get them when they're young, but it can be…a quiet thing inside a person, like water underground. If you're raised by Shapewalkers, you spend every day knowing you're probably going to have powers, so when you dig a well, the water comes out early. But if you live in Berill, where it's a dangerous thing, and you have mixed blood to begin with… She probably thought if you hadn't shown powers by twenty-five, you weren't going to. I guess I haven't tested the theory, but sometimes your keyhole doesn't appear until you shape the first time."

He looked back up at the sky, letting out a puff of smoke.

"Grief can be funny. When my mother died, I already knew I was a Shapewalker, but I couldn't shape for a month straight. But in your case, losing your grandmother turned that pool into a geyser, pushing it to the surface, whether you wanted it or not."

He looked at her, the same sad smile on his face. But it wasn't pity; it was understanding.

"It could be the powers skipped your mother, too — mixed blood can be odd like that. So, if I had to guess, she probably thought your life would be easier not knowing. But she loved you, and I'm sure she just tried to do what's best."

Sumi looked down at the deck, nodding slowly. It made sense; she'd just needed to hear someone else say it. Nela had kept so many secrets; there was just a part of her that was scared she'd always be in the dark. But as private as Nela was, she certainly wouldn't withhold anything she thought Sumi would need. If Erso was right, and her mother hadn't been a Shapewalker, Nela probably had every reason to think Sumi wouldn't be either.

"Thank you, Erso," she said, "for everything."

"Don't thank me yet," he said, chuckling. "Train with my family for a couple weeks and see how you feel."

She smiled, pouring a tiny extra dram of wine into her glass. If only he knew how much being with any kind of family would mean to her. They could be wild boars for all she cared… She shot a glance at him, his eyes on the sky again as he leaned back in his chair puffing out rings of blue smoke. He talked a big game, but swashbuckling rogues didn't usually go around ordering cakes for acquaintances. His family was probably lovely. She just hoped *she* was good enough for *them*. She sipped her wine as the sea slipped beside them, barely noticing them pass, the future twinkling somewhere up there with the stars.

7

-Verses 53-55 of the Anushgiar Leyosil

—:—

Fifteen Years Ago
Amoriai

Fu'reisim stood at attention in the banquet hall of the royal palace. It was sometime after midnight, and there wasn't a soul in sight. Still, according to his superiors, every room had to be guarded at all hours. He held in a yawn, blinking heavily. He hadn't always been the best night watchman in the army, but he wanted to do better, lucky as he was to have this job. His friend Pulek had pulled some strings, and he certainly didn't want to let him down.

Besides, despite the silence, there was a strange energy to the palace that night. It could just be his new surroundings, but even with his fatigue, something in the back of his mind kept needling him, warning him to stay alert. And it wasn't just him. The captain of the guard had felt it too.

"Strange night," the captain had said as he stopped by on his rounds, handing Fu'reisim a canteen. The captain had stared up at the cavernous ceilings of the banquet hall and shuddered. "Stay wary," he'd said. "Some of the men seem jittery tonight; not sure why."

Fu'reisim decided to walk the perimeter of the banquet hall, anything to keep his blood flowing. Besides, there were only a few lamps lit, and the shadows at the far end of the room were playing tricks on him. If nothing else, it'd be good to prove the boogeymen in the corners weren't real.

As he reached the end of the hall, he came to the head chair where the king always sat. Upholstered in velvet, its back was a head higher than the others, like a second throne. Fu'reisim held his breath as he passed, like a tiny prayer. He hadn't gotten to guard the king yet, but even these tiny things seemed to floor him. He'd never thought of himself as particularly patriotic, but now that he was here, he felt more Amoriai somehow, as if the uniform had changed the man inside.

He reached the end of the hall, starting back on the other side of the table. Perhaps he could take another lap, could—

A scream. He froze, his hand going to his sword. It had come from the hallway beyond the double doors. But as he stood, straining to listen, he found only silence. Had his tired mind made it up? But which would be worse? Hearing things or someone actually screaming in the palace?

He tiptoed toward the hallway. As he drew closer, he could see the glow of torchlight slipping under the door. He pulled it open, finding a mob of men outside. There were at least a dozen, most of them wearing dark hoods over their faces. They stood in a circle in the middle of the hall, facing…the captain of the guard. The man had fallen to the floor, blood spilling from his armor as it stained the pristine tile. Fu'reisim tried to back away, but one of the men looked up, their eyes meeting.

"Stop!" he yelled. "Come out!"

Another man — no hood over his head — stepped from the circle, pointing at Fu'reisim.

"Grab him!" he bellowed.

He knew that man…but he was a cabinet minister, Roilani E'busek, the exchequer.

Men with swords quickly swarmed toward him, and he threw his hands in the air. There was no sense pulling his sword when these men had a dozen of their own. He was a soldier, not a blade master.

"Smart," the exchequer said. "Not all your friends had as much sense. Get him a collar."

Another man — also with no hood — stepped out from the group. He was bald with bushy white eyebrows. He had no sword but carried a large burlap sack. He reached into it and pulled out a silver collar, clipping it around his neck.

"What is this thing?" Fu'reisim asked.

All he got as a reply was the butt of a sword to the gut. He doubled over, but their hands were already on him, dragging him down the hallway toward the throne room.

The room was crowded with people, some twenty or thirty men and women, all in the same robes, with swords in their hands. They dragged him to the center, where a dozen other guards were on the floor, their hands bound with those strange silver collars on their throats. The men carrying threw him down, while others tied him up. They hadn't gagged the other guards, but no one said a word. He looked around the group, but they all stared at the floor, their eyes glazed over. He finally managed to lock eyes with one guard, Piri'soh, but the man just shook his head.

Small groups of hooded men still swirled around them, heading into the other hallways in search of something. Were they looking for other guards? But it would take all night to search them all, the palace like an octopus with all its looping halls. And what would come after? Was this a coup? Would they let the loyal guards live?

He thought of his wife, struggling to hold back a tear. What if he never saw her again? She'd been so happy when he got this job, sure it would be safer than the garrison.

Spirits of Mu'lalat, he prayed, *let me see my wife again. Please.*

He turned, looking at the king's dais. It was a mess, the throne tipped over, surrounded by goblets and things strewn about. And there, in the center, was a body, face down and wearing the king's robes. Fu'reisim gasped audibly, recoiling into the guard behind him. A hooded man came up, kicking him in the ribs. He fell hard, unable to protect himself with his hands bound. He lay in a heap, his gaze forced onto that horrible scene. He couldn't see the king's face, but he was clearly dead, unmoving, his crown tossed to the ground. But if the king was dead, then why let the guards live? These men weren't afraid of the butchery, so what were they waiting for?

The western door of the throne room banged open, and another group of attackers came, a large group of women between them. Some of them were scullery maids, while others looked like courtiers. Regardless, most of them had torn clothes, their makeup streaking down their faces. The bald man with the mustache rushed over to greet them.

"Excellent!" he said, his accent thick. "You've finally found the women!"

Instead of tying them up, the bald man ordered them on the dais, lining them up beside the throne. Then, walking up to the fallen king, he grabbed a fistful of dark hair, lifting the man's head. Only it wasn't the king… It was another scullery maid in the king's robes, her face pale with death.

"Do we have a match?" the man asked, looking up at the line of women. Halfway down the row, one of the women tried to run, but they grabbed her by the hair, dragging her to the ground. She was the spitting image of the dead woman. The bald man walked over, taking her by the chin.

"Yes, yes," he said, "that's exactly right." He turned, calling to the back of the room. "I believe it's time if you'd like to do the honors!"

E'busek marched over, looming over the woman. She spat in his face, receiving a backhand in return.

"Is it really that easy?" the exchequer asked the bald man.

"Usually. I suppose they never thought it necessary with their own kind in power."

The exchequer laughed.

"No, I suppose not. At least those days are over."

E'busek pulled back his coat, revealing a long silver dagger, a sapphire on its pommel. He pulled it, slamming it into the shoulder of the scullery maid. She let out a piercing scream as a bright light flashed. Fu'reisim shut his eyes, but he could still hear the screaming, and it…started to *deepen.* When he looked again, the scullery maid was gone, the king now in her place, panting as blood stained his dress.

"So, we see your face at last," E'busek said. "How fitting for you to wear the garb of a servant. You never once served your own people — only those creatures in the north."

The king groaned but pushed himself to his knees. He looked up at the exchequer, defiance in his eyes. "Do what you came here to do, then."

"Gladly," the exchequer said, smiling. Then he drew his sword and cut off the king's head. A scream escaped Fu'reisim's lips, but it was drowned out by all the others as the massacre began.

———

One Month Later

Erso walked behind his father, barely watching where he put his feet. He was focused on the puzzle box in his hands, looking up just often enough to avoid running into passersby. Well, almost enough… Still, at fifteen, he could walk Amoriai blindfolded if he had to. Even if his father never let him explore.

His inattention didn't seem to bother his father much — not that it was easy to tell with how quiet the man was. Still, he never seemed to get angry. Never got happy either, really… Still, he was solid as a rock, and Erso's mother loved him for it. They may both be Shapewalkers, but

Mum was the interesting one, the source of all the passion and drama in their relationship. In fact, when his parents met, she'd still been acting in a traveling troupe, apparently transfixing his stodgy old father in the crowd.

The point of his latest puzzle box, as far as he could tell anyway, was to get a brass ball from one side of the box to the other. But without being able to see the maze inside, you were meant to guide the ball by memory. He'd been struggling with it for a week, though he could tell he was getting close, putting the box to his ear as he gave it a gentle shake. He redoubled his efforts, focusing only on the box until the street around him fell away. He was so focused that when Pa stopped dead in his tracks, Erso crashed into him.

He'd had been staring at a piece of parchment posted on a lamppost. He shot Erso a stern look but went right back to looking at the poster.

"Can't be that interesting," Erso muttered to himself, brushing off his shirt as he turned away. He had dropped his puzzle box and was stooping down to get it when he noticed another paper on the ground — and dozens more exactly like it. They looked like they had been machine-printed, identical with neat black ink. He frowned, picking one up. It had a drawing of a dark figure looming over what looked to be a scared housewife. The creature had one hand on the woman's purse, while the other held a knife to her throat. On the bottom, it read: *Know who you do business with. Know who your neighbors are.*

He stood, walking back over to his father. A crowd had gathered, all of the adults looking at the posters and whispering in small pockets. Erso climbed up on a sidewalk bench, his eyes widening as he realized the posters went all the way down the street. They were attached to benches, lampposts, you name it, and there were three times as many littering the ground.

"Erso!" his father called sharply. "Come on. We're going home."

He walked off in the direction of their house, leaving Erso to run behind him.

"Pa," Erso said, panting as he struggled to keep up, "what do those mean?"

He had grown much taller over the previous summer, but he still had a foot or more to go to catch up with his father, and the man was taking full strides with his long legs. He turned briefly toward him, seeming to have forgotten he was there for a second.

"It's nothing, son," he said, his mustached face pulling down in a deep frown. "Just keep up. We need to find your mother."

He wanted to press him, but he knew it would be no use. His parents had been strange since the new king had taken the throne. They stayed up late at night, whispering in the kitchen, and they wouldn't let him ask any questions. It was a bit scary that King Ela'imat had been deposed, but to his mind, there was a romance to it too. If anyone could take the throne, then maybe even he could be king someday.

They walked quickly through the market to their neighborhood, where he looked up, catching sight of the lighthouse. They lived just south of it, halfway to the beach. Looking for it was a ritual of his — just as he watched the spinning light before he fell asleep — and it didn't feel like he was home until he saw it. Their house was like all the others — whitewashed wood with sea-green tiles on the roof — built by sailors ages ago to be closer to the port. There were rumors the new king was building a port on the west side of the river, but what would happen to this one? To all the sailors living here?

They approached the house but walked right by, heading to his mother's theater instead. After she married Pa, she'd stopped traveling, taking up with a local troupe out of an old building near the port, selling tickets to tourists who didn't have Shapewalking actors in their towns. While Mum loved to complain about giving up life on the road, he knew she loved the theatre. Commissioned by Anushai royals a million years ago, it was almost as tall as the lighthouse, with huge red oak columns that glowed like marble. And everyone else loved it too. Until recently, they'd sold out every show.

When they reached the theater, Erso sat outside, leaning against the columns as his father went in. He looked up at the wood where it had been carved into familiar little stories. The one behind him had a man climbing a mountain, one hand stuck out, a flame rising from his palm. In the next one down, the man had apparently reached the summit, using his palm to light a bonfire. After looking at them for his entire life, he still had no idea what they meant — and neither did his mother, nor anyone else, for that matter. She said it was some kind of legend from Anushai about acting, but what it meant was anybody's guess. Besides, it wasn't like they could ask, with Anushai patrons a thing of the past.

As he usually did when he sat on the theater steps, he wondered if he should be an actor himself. The plays they did *were* interesting, and with Shapewalkers for actors, they could play anything they wanted. He'd only seen a human play once, but it had felt so…limited, every person stuck in just one role. He wanted to play a hundred roles, to be anyone other than a regular boy from the docks.

Maybe he should ask to try out? Both his parents were giving him lessons now, and he was getting better at Shapewalking all the time — even if Pa never admitted it. Though he might need to get a bit quicker. Some of the costume changes were a matter of seconds, with only enough time to duck behind the curtain between scenes. Still, it had to be a better job than his father's, sulking all day with the other merchants while they complained about the price of beans. Not to mention what acting would do for his love life…

His heart beat faster as he thought of Me'lekona. She was only a couple of years older than he was, but she was already an apprentice in the theater. To make matters worse, she was *gorgeous*. Tall and sinewy, she always had a glint in her eye, like she'd heard the greatest joke that you wouldn't understand. The first time he saw her, he'd felt like his father must have at that first play, like he was dreaming, the whole world falling away except her face. She was obviously perfect for him; he just had to convince her he wasn't a child. But if he learned how to act…

He heard a creak on the steps behind him and spun, finding Me'lekona right behind him. She flashed him a wry smile — could she tell he'd been thinking about her? He forced himself to swallow, trying to regain his cool.

"Oh, hey," he said, hoping he sounded casual. "How's the acting?"

She sat beside him, his neck burning as their thighs touched. That is, before she reached out and tousled his hair. He slapped her hand away as she laughed.

"Oh, it's going alright," she said. "Though I'm not sure if we'll go through with this one. We have the old king in this play, and the cast has been arguing all day about whether it's safe to put on."

She looked out at the water, sighing.

"I'm sorry," he said sincerely. "I know you've been working hard. Mum hasn't been home for dinner in a month."

She turned back and flashed him her dazzling smile, leaving him feeling like he'd just looked directly at the sun.

"That's alright," she said. "The next play will have more roles for me, anyway, so I'm alright either way."

They both looked straight ahead for a while, Erso resting his elbows on his knees, fidgeting with his fingers.

"You know," he finally said, "if you ever have time after rehearsal, feel free to stop by for dinner. There's always extra food."

She stood up, brushing off her dress as she went down the stairs. She walked backward, looking at Erso with that wry smile again.

"You know, I might just do that," she said. "And if you want to ask me on a proper date sometime, just say so." She winked, turning away without looking back.

He started to stammer a reply, but she was already gone, shooting down the street toward whichever sky she'd be lighting next. He sat there in a daze, his mind spinning with new possibilities — and dozens of questions. Was that an invitation to ask her out, or was she just messing with him again? And that smile…it could be taken a thousand different ways. He'd have to ask Uncle Beysal what he thought; he certainly couldn't risk asking Pa.

A few minutes later, his parents finally emerged. His father's face was red, and his mother's mouth had drawn into a thin, angry line. They'd been arguing again, then… Still, his mother leaned down, kissing him on the head.

"Let's go home, dear," she said.

They all started back toward the house in silence. His father had probably been trying to convince his mother to leave again. He kept suggesting they go to Anushai until things cooled down. His mother didn't speak Anushai very well, though, so she was terrified it'd mean the end of her career. They'd traveled through the north plenty of times to put on shows, but apparently that was different from living there, competing with local actresses for roles. They'd been having the same argument nonstop since the coup, but there was no end in sight.

He personally would have been fine with leaving just a year earlier. His father had spent plenty of time in Anushai in his younger days, and he'd taught Erso enough to get by. But what about Me'lekona? That wink at the end could mean he was finally getting somewhere.

"I vote we stay," Erso said, speaking to his parents' backs as they plowed ahead, their shoulders stiff.

"Keep out of it," his father said, whipping his head around sternly, but Mum turned to him and winked.

After a tense dinner — in which no one but Erso said anything more than a grunt — he was finally excused to do as he pleased. He didn't feel like being inside with his parents shooting wounded looks at each other, so he decided to head into the back yard. There was a government road running to the lighthouse behind their home, so they were lucky enough to have a long stretch of grass, and there was always something to collect. It was usually just rocks and bottle caps and the like, but one time, he found an old necklace, a heart-shaped locket tucked in a thicket of grass.

He was creeping along the right side of the fence, about to pick up an interesting slug, when he heard the back gate open. He looked up, finding Beysal coming across the yard. He had a bottle of whiskey under his arm and a serious look on his face, though he smiled when he saw Erso.

"Uncle Beysal!" Erso yelled, jumping to his feet and running over. Beysal tossed the bottle to the grass just in time to grab Erso under the arms, spinning him around. Even though he was getting older, Beysal was still built like a giant, and he spun him twice before forcing him to the ground and twisting him into a chokehold. Erso laughed, fighting with all his might to escape. Beysal had been teaching him how to wrestle, but he could still only escape when the older man let him. Finally, Beysal released him, and they both leaned over, breathing heavily, smiles on their faces. Beysal tousled his hair before stooping to pick up his bottle.

"Whiskey again?" Erso asked.

Beysal shrugged.

"Hard times call for hard conversations, I guess," he said with a sheepish grin, "and even harder drinks." He winked, heading into the house. When he opened the kitchen door, Erso heard shouts from inside before his parents realized they had company. He sighed. It was probably going to be another long night. He turned back to the yard, eager to find more slugs — and put his family's worries from his mind.

THE END OF PART ONE

PART TWO

8

Essomuai took a piece of her heart, a well of pure gold, and shaped it into children of her own, making them look exactly as the humans did. Yet Essomuai's children could take any shape they wished, and their hearts were full of their mother's memories: the lives of plants and bugs, beasts and men. She caught Itorunai's wind, breathing life into her children, and as they blinked awake, they laughed with joy. "This is life," she sang to them, "sing with me of its many colors."

-Verses 73-76 of the Anushgiar Leyosil

—:—

Sumi closed her suitcase just as Erso knocked on her cabin door. She glanced in the mirror as she passed, but more fussing with her makeup wouldn't save her. She kept waking up during the night, and she was starting to get bags under her eyes. She'd been having strange dreams, though they were hard to remember. Lots of flying…and *falling,* which was probably why she jerked awake so often. But it was her first time away from home; strange dreams were to be expected, right?

She opened the door, stopping to stare at how different Erso looked. His suit had been traded out for workman's clothes, just a simple vest and white shirt, his bowler hat substituted with a gray woolen cap. His mustache was still long, but it was no longer waxed, sitting on his upper lip like a caterpillar. Most jarring of all were the work boots, tall and covered in mud — and in the place where his fine leather shoes used to be.

"What did you do with Erso?"

He took a deep breath, shaking his head sadly. "I know," he said, clutching his heart. "I've been dreading this day. You've grown accustomed to me being the finest of gentlemen, and now, it appears I'm

48

no different than all the rest."

"I wouldn't go that far," she said, laughing. "You're still fancy somehow, just not quite so…*bespoke.*"

"Thank you, miss," he said, taking off his cap as he bowed. "You, at least, can still see the real me."

He stepped into her room and took her luggage, leading her out into the hallway.

"So, why are you really wearing that?" she asked. "Are you trying to lay low for the customs check?"

"More or less. Since we'll be going through the silver arches today, I've been forced to wear my real clothes. The customs officers probably wouldn't like it if my clothes burst with light and turned back to normal."

"Wait," she asked, her jaw dropping. "You mean you *shape* your clothes? Like all of it? Every day?"

"What better way to stay up on the latest fashions than to make them yourself?"

He continued down the hallway, but there was a spring in his step, clearly pleased with himself.

"Isn't that, I don't know, incredibly hard?" she asked, hurrying to catch up.

"I am, luckily for us both, extremely talented."

"Humble too," she said, smacking him on the shoulder as he laughed.

"Careful now," he said, "I wouldn't want to accidentally drop your bag."

They reached the middle of the ship, turning into the stairwell.

"But really," he said, "it's not so bad once you get used to it. It's all about reducing resistance. Take this hat—" He put down his bag for a moment, handing her his cap. "I make sure whatever I shape is the same size as this one, and I use wool for both. Even though I change it to a bowler hat — and give it a stunning color — it takes way less energy when the base is close."

Sumi turned the hat every which way, trying to study it. She'd have to notice a lot more about fashion if she was going to shape her own wardrobe. She hadn't ever thought much about fabrics and cuts, only buying a new dress every few years and mending it until it fell apart. She glanced at Erso with a grin, popping his hat on her head.

"How do I look?" she asked.

"Like you have something to hide," he said dryly.

"Well, maybe if it was fancier…"

She took it off, gently putting it back on his head. Just then, they reached the top of the stairs and came out onto the deck, the port of

Amoriai stretching out before them.

The customs house blocked them from having a complete view, but it was still obvious they'd entered a completely different world. Berill was…well, *organized,* to say it politely. Here, everything seemed to thrive on chaos. Even the shoreline was more crooked than in Berill, and as far as she looked in either direction, she could see the land zigzagging in and out of the water. And just beyond the narrow strip of beach, the city was *everywhere,* pushing at its boundaries as it threatened to spill into the sea. Berill had been so carefully planned over the years, it seemed almost like a museum exhibit of a city, even with the new electrical wires running everywhere. Amoriai looked more like a forest, its rooftops jutting out like trees, desperately searching for their own patch of sun.

"There's…so much…everything," she said to Erso.

"We had a couple thousand years' head start on Berill," he said, smiling. "There are pros and cons, of course. It's a good deal more fun here, but it's basically impossible to give directions. It's like describing the location of a rock on the beach. If you want the apothecary, people in Amoriai want to know what it's next to and what park it's near. And forget about street names — they change every two blocks."

They crossed the deck, reaching a line of passengers waiting to descend the ramp into the customs house. She kept trying to steal glimpses of the city while they waited. Wandering through Berill had seemed like an adventure, and she'd known every street by heart. What would it feel like to be somewhere completely new? It was still hard to believe she'd left home so far behind.

"Just don't leave me," she said to Erso. "I'd probably never find my way."

"I think you'll find plenty of people eager to help a cute Berillai woman. But don't worry, if I don't come home with a guest, I doubt they'll let me in the door. I'm always in a bit of hot water when I haven't visited in a while."

"How long has it been?" she asked. If she had had any family left, it'd be inconceivable to never see them — not that running around the Continent saving Shapewalkers wasn't a noble enough reason.

"Well," he said, counting on his fingers, "before Berill, I was in Alara, and then I went downriver to Mesopyn — just to get my feet wet before your people tried to kill me, of course. So…two years?"

"You haven't been home in two years?!" she asked, her mouth open. "How has your family not sent out an army to drag you back?"

"Well, I *am* the rogue of the family, remember," he said, scratching the back of his head. "It's part of my appeal. Besides, they have their hands full with their son."

"Who is this we're seeing again?" she asked. He'd mentioned an uncle so far, but he was so tight-lipped about his family, if she didn't ask now, she'd walk in without a clue.

"Well, you can never know exactly who you'll see — bit of an open-door policy — but we're staying with my Uncle Beysal, his wife E'loseir, and their son Kel."

That was already more people than she talked to in a month back home — not to mention all Shapewalkers! More importantly, Erso had assured her his uncle was the best teacher there was. Even if her progress was halting on the boat, he would apparently help her find a breakthrough.

"Uncle on whose side?" she asked, hoping it wasn't too much prodding. He hesitated for a moment, fiddling with something in his pocket.

"Uh, my ma's side," he finally said. "More of a family friend, really. But Beysal raised me, so we just go with uncle."

Sumi nodded. There was no shame in being raised by someone other than your parents, of course. The family you made for yourself was all that mattered in the end.

"And all of them can shape?"

"Oh, yeah," Erso said. "As you know, Beysal's one of the best there is. But even Kel — who's five — can manage a few forms."

Her eyes widened. To think of having your powers that early! It had taken her two decades longer than that, and she still wasn't sure if she would get it. When had Nela started? For all she knew, Anushai was the same as Amoriai, with children changing forms days after learning how to walk. She wanted to ponder that more, but they reached the docks, the customs building looming up ahead.

It was a new building, with neat brick and glass windows reflecting the sea. Still, as they moved toward the giant entrance, it looked more like a monster keen on swallowing them whole.

They don't know who you are, she repeated to herself. *You're just another tourist.*

Not that it was helping soothe her nerves… The silver arches Erso had mentioned were the main thing worrying her. Built into the ground at every entrance, if a person stepped through them while shapeshifting, they'd be forced back into their original form — right in front of dozens of agents.

Erso seemed to sense her nervous energy, touching her shoulder.

"You have *nothing* to worry about," he said in a low voice. "Remember, we're just a happy couple from Berill."

"And the rings?" she asked.

"Nothing to fear," he said. "I promise. We're both wearing real clothes and holding our own forms. Just walk tall, and they'll never know."

"Why silver, though? I've been meaning to ask. Why can they use it against us?"

"That's a good question, honestly," he said. "I've heard a few theories. Some of the old-timers used to say that all metals have a special room in Mu'lalat. The old temple had shrines dedicated to them, I think, but they say the silver door was always locked. Anyway, that's just one example. Take the Anushai, *obsessed* with gold. If we go north, you'll see. I think they applied a metal to each of the three goddesses? Can't remember what Itorunai is, but I'm pretty sure Vilodai was silver and Essomuai was gold. Though why silver hurts us is anybody's guess."

Sumi nodded, thinking of her necklace where it was hidden beneath her blouse. It had a gold chain and gold backing beneath the flower. Hopefully it really did connect her to Essomuai somehow. Real or not, having a goddess looking over her made her feel a bit better.

They merged with the mass of passengers from the other ships, pushing through the doors where officers were barking orders and grouping people based on which country they were from. They were pointed to the Berillai line at the far end. It was the most crowded line by far, though it was moving quickly.

"Is this line moving faster than the others?" she asked.

"Courtesy of Her Majesty Queen Welaya of Berill," Erso said, shaking his head. "You get double the customs officers — part of the trade agreement. At least I'm pretending to be with you today; the locals' line is almost as bad as the one for Anushai. 'Why'd you leave the kingdom? Who did you meet? What have you brought back?' They assume anyone who travels anywhere but Berill is a criminal."

"Well, at least you *are* a criminal, right?"

"Ha-ha," he laughed sarcastically. "So are you now, missy."

She gulped. He was right about that, actually…

"Just how dangerous is Amoriai? Or any of the other kingdoms, for that matter?"

"It all depends," he said in a low voice, jerking a thumb over his shoulder to the east. "Relimora's at the end of the train line, and they basically couldn't care less what anyone does. Ekosinar is split — the south of the peninsula is aligned with Berill, so they're threatening to outlaw Shapewalking there. Amoriai isn't the safest, but they're not great at enforcing it either; I'll explain that later."

He scratched his chin, looking at the ceiling.

"The Three Sisters are done for, though they have too many princedoms to enforce it consistently. I guess the only other notable place is Mesop. After they lost the war with Berill, they blamed the Shapewalkers, so they have these shamans who hunt for children with keyholes." He shook his head. "Pretty grisly stuff."

"That's awful!" she blurted out before remembering where she was. Still, no one looked her way, everyone focused on moving ahead and through— *The silver arches.* A shiver went up her spine. They were ten feet wide, each arch flowing seamlessly into the next. If she hadn't known their true purpose, she'd think they were sculptures, the gleaming metal rising and falling like ocean waves.

Suddenly, their turn was up. She felt her shoulders tense, but she kept walking, keeping her eyes straight ahead as they went under the arch. Thankfully — as promised — nothing happened, but it still took everything in her to look normal as they approached the desk. She forced a smile on her face, slipping her arm through Erso's. They had to be newlyweds now. And happy newlyweds were relaxed, carefree. They had nothing to be afraid of, right?

They had agreed that she would do the talking. Erso's Berillai was basically perfect, but with his slight accent, the less talking he did, the better. Still, her heart thumped in her chest, and she wanted to shrivel into a tiny speck the moment the customs agent laid eyes on her. The man looked like a rat, his eyes peering from beneath his cap as if they'd personally ruined his day.

"Nationality?" the guard asked in Amoriai. Her Amoriai was basically nonexistent, but Erso had at least prepped her on the standard questions they would ask.

"Berillai," she said, trying to keep her voice steady.

"Good," the man said, smiling as he suddenly switched to her language. "You wouldn't believe the amount of people who try to jump the lines. Welcome to Amoriai. What brings you east?"

"Our honeymoon," she said, smiling warmly at Erso. He smiled and nodded along. "We just got married."

"Congratulations!" the guard said, smiling wider than either of them. He looked down, hurriedly filling out the customs form — which somehow took twice as long in the other lines. "I hope you don't mind me making a suggestion," he continued, "but Har'kerat's in the Western Park District has a lovely candlelit dinner, perfect for a honeymoon."

"Oh," Sumi said, forcing her rigid smile even wider, "that sounds lovely. We'll be sure to do that."

The officer winked, slapping a large ink stamp on their forms and handing them to her. And just like that, it was over. They moved quickly toward the exit, the light beyond beckoning them into the city. Erso immediately dropped his smile, his face like a storm cloud, but all she could do was breathe a sigh of relief. For now, they were safe.

9

Essomuai came into a village, on the edge of the Erril Sea, hiding her spirit in an ancient tree. She lived amongst the humans there, breathing their air and drinking their rain. She saw babies laugh, couples dance; she even watched an old man die. Vilodai's power was strong in them, and each one had its own color, fierce and bright. They spoke different words and sang different songs, like an orchard with many kinds of fruit. But despite their variety, the humans were somehow of a whole, and she knew then she'd have to join them in their world.

-Verses 64-69 of the Anushgiar Leyosil

—:—

As they stepped out of the customs house, Sumi had to squint, shielding her eyes from the sun. She'd known the Erril Basin was warmer, but with the breeze from the water gone, it was like winter in Berill had been a dream. She pulled at her collar, feeling the sweat beginning to pool on her back and under her arms. Hopefully, Erso wouldn't notice — not that he'd think twice about a sweaty shopkeeper…

As her eyes adjusted to the light, she stopped, staring at the palace where it sat gleaming in the sun. Berill's palace was imposing, but it was flat, practical — more of a fort than a castle. This one was enormous, a spiral of vertical towers topped in silver shingles, the metal sparkling in the light. She turned to Erso, but he was already down the steps, looking at a line of cabs.

"What are you looking for?" she asked, quickly hurrying to his side.

"In Amoriai," he said, his face serious, "you need the right kind of cabby. Especially where we're going. Come on."

He started down the sidewalk, passing a half-dozen cabs, though the drivers all looked the same in their black top hats, calling as they passed.

"Ho," one shouted, "get a driver for the pretty lady, sir!"

"Too warm for walking!" cried another.

Erso paid them no mind, pushing forward until he reached the end of the row. The cab there looked like the others, open to the air with perfect velvet cushions. The driver had the same uniform, though he'd tucked a tiny white flower into his hat band. She'd thought Erso might be looking for a Shapewalker, but the man had no keyhole — as far as she could tell, anyway.

The driver turned his head, nodding as he touched his hat.

"Looking to rent a cab?" he asked, his voice gentle compared to the others.

"Long as you know how to fly," Erso answered.

She cocked an eyebrow at him. What was that supposed to mean?

"Quick enough to beat a spider," the man said, smiling.

"This one will work," Erso said, putting their luggage on a small rack at the back. The cabby climbed down, helping her up onto the seat with a gloved hand. She tried to catch Erso's eye, but he was already talking to the cabby, slapping him on the shoulder as he worked his charm.

She looked at the city while she waited, a gigantic park across from the customs house giving her an open view. The whole place had been built in a circle, with every road heading toward the palace, and everything glistened, the brand-new buildings surrounded by more manicured parks. This area, behind the customs house, seemed infinitely more planned out than what she'd seen from the boat. But did that mean all of this was built after the coup? She frowned, watching Erso as he climbed into the cab. It must be so hard for him to look at this part of the city, and here she'd been, gawking at it.

"Everything alright?" she asked in a low voice, looking at the cabby as he turned his horses into the street.

"Definitely," he said, smiling. "But in a place like Amoriai, it's good to double check you've got a friend on your hands." He jerked his thumb toward the driver. "You're a proper king's man, aren't you, C'erun?"

"Surely am," the driver said, laughing, "though I can't say which one."

"As you already know," Erso said, "Shapewalking is illegal. But unlike Berill, everyone knows what a fellerhurn is, and not many officers would admit to their abilities. So, while they officially rely on the silver arches and things, it doesn't mean you're safe either. They might not say as much, but a cabby who doesn't like the look of you — or your keyhole — might take you somewhere very different from your destination. C'erun isn't like us, but he's a good east-sider, and we can trust him."

"Well, thank you, C'erun," she said. "We're lucky to have you."

"My pleasure," he said, tipping his hat to her. "They gave me this fancy suit, but I remember where I'm from. Me and your friend here were actually just joking about the old days. Turns out I had a cousin who lived in his neighborhood back when."

"Yup," Erso said, "one of the neighborhood beauties, too. Everybody knew her."

"As you can probably tell," C'erun said, "the looks in my family weren't divided up all that equally. In fact, maybe we were second cousins?"

They laughed, and he turned back, working them through the traffic. They rode on, the men chatting on an off while she looked at the landmarks, trying to get her bearings. They passed a row of statues and what looked like a military garrison before they finally reached the river. The Ko'lesta was famous, something even she could recognize, and it surged through the center of the city, crowded with grain barges and a dozen other kinds of boats heading for the sea. There were bridges all along it, where traffic hummed across. And as they reached the nearest bridge, the carriage went down to a crawl, joining the throng of carts and people going east.

Compared to the other landmarks they'd sped by, the traffic at least let her appreciate the bridge. The whole thing was intricately carved, as if they'd made it from a giant block of marble and dropped it over the water. It had two raised walkways for pedestrians, the railings covered in miniature flames, and every ten feet or so, there was a column topped with a statue of a fire hawk.

"These are gorgeous," she said in a reverent whisper.

"Pride of the city, miss," C'erun said, overhearing.

"Even better," Erso said, "they were a gift from Anushai."

"That's right," the cabby said. "From Empress Solmiyae, if I recall, gave 'em to us after the second war with Anushai."

"You had wars with Anushai?" she asked, her eyes widening. Everything she'd learned growing up had been Berill first, their books ignoring almost everything before King Rummon landed on the Continent. But now that she was here, with only eight hundred years of history in her head, she felt...lost.

"Plenty of wars," the cabby said, "and the second wasn't even the last. The Amoriai don't like answering to anybody too much — unless you come east with a train and a pocket full of money, of course."

They crossed over the center of the bridge, and she looked across the river, where she could see all the other bridges as they arched over the water.

"There's so many!" she said. "And these were…a gift…for going to war with you?"

"Well," C'erun said, "I think they burned down all our other bridges. So, it was a bit of a reparation, I suppose. Hard to say what the old bridges looked like, but the ten they gave us were probably a good deal prettier than the ones we had before."

"Used to be ten, anyway," Erso said, frowning.

"What happened to the tenth?" she asked, trying to count them as she passed, but the river was full of bends, making it hard to see. Still, the water was nice to look at, perfectly blue — and far cleaner than she'd expected, though the current likely helped.

"The Berillai tore it down to build the train line," Erso said. "Guess we'll see how that turns out."

"Good luck getting paid back if it doesn't," C'erun said.

The men laughed together, but Sumi frowned, looking at the bridges again. What *hadn't* her people done to Amoriai? If only she had known. She couldn't have changed it, of course, but it felt like she should have been mourning this city and its stolen past. At least she had friends to teach her now.

"Seems like you know everything about the city," she said to C'erun. "Sure you wouldn't rather be a tour guide?"

"Thank you, miss," he said. "Though I suppose the jobs aren't that different at the end of the day. You learn it over time, pick something up from every passenger. Unfortunately, that means I have ten different stories for every place and no way to tell what's true."

"Well," she said, chuckling, "tell us whichever one you like, and we'll believe you."

Finally, they were over the bridge and into the east end of the city. The traffic picked up as the carriages fanned out from the bottleneck, and she was back to trying to catch what she could as they hurried past. But where the west side had been rigidly planned — especially around the palace — the east was…an explosion of *everything*. The streets were narrower, and they branched out at random, each corner brimming with buildings of every possible design. There were tiled roofs and wooden homes, squat pubs and cafes with metal siding. She turned her head as quickly as she could, though she only caught a glance at each street before they zipped away.

But the best part was the people. On the west side, it had been hard to tell it was a city at all, with only soldiers and a few stray businessmen walking around. On the east side, people lined the streets, with fashions she'd only seen in magazines: patterned dresses from Relimora, Ekosinaran leather, and plenty of fancy hats that would look at home on Erso's head. She glanced over at him beside her. He was smiling now, his shoulders seeming to relax the moment they'd crossed over.

"Are they all like us on this side?" she asked. She kept looking for keyholes, occasionally catching a glimmer in the air, but it was hard to pinpoint in the crowds.

"Not everyone," Erso said, "not in that way, at least. But they're certainly our kind of people. You end up here if you can't prove your bloodline is 'pure,' which basically just means you don't have good connections."

"Not that I see why you'd want to be on the west side," C'erun said. "Bad pubs, and even worse women."

"Hear, hear," Erso said.

They passed a few more dense blocks, when abruptly, the left side of the street opened up, devoid of buildings. It stretched out like a large field or park, but there were still patches of paving stones and old shells of buildings, charred and blackened where they stuck through tall thickets of grass. What was left of the buildings was falling apart, looking like jagged, broken teeth.

"What in Velloni's name is that?" she asked. Erso glanced in that direction before looking forward, his hands squeezed tightly at his side.

"Su'selo'mae," the driver said, shaking his head sadly. "Means 'the burnt bones.'" He took off his hat, bowing in respect.

"Bit of a sore subject," Erso said, forcing a sad smile to his face. "I'll tell you some other time. Better yet," he said, pointing down the next street, "let's look at something else. That's the old palace down that way."

"Okay," she said gently, doing as he asked and craning her neck, looking down the diagonal street. It ended in a large stone wall, and above it reached a beautiful, ornate building. It was divided into multiple wings, at least three from where she could see. It was shorter than the other palace, but still imposing, its dark limestone walls capped in the soft green of old copper.

"It's beautiful," she said, "such an interesting shape."

"Made to honor the halls of Mu'lalat, miss," the cabby said. "Sort of looks like an octopus, no?"

"It does," she said, laughing, "but a beautiful one."

"Better than a spider web, at least," Erso said, nodding to the west, where the Silver Palace was. "That's what east-siders call the other side."

"Fitting name, that," C'erun added, "and not a good place to be a fly.

That web can catch you something awful if you aren't careful."

Soon, they were past the burnt bones and into a more built-up area, with homes bunched up around warehouses. They turned off the main road, and it suddenly dawned on her that they were getting close. Her heart beat faster. What if Erso's family didn't like her? What if they turned her away and left her to fend for herself? She started patting down her hair, though it was twenty-six years too late to start working on her appearance. She looked down at her skirt. What had possessed her to wear this old thing, anyway?

She took a deep breath, trying to calm herself. *Erso tolerates you*, she thought, *his family will do the same.* This was her chance to start again. Still, she found herself wishing she could have met them in some other form: a hawk, a coin, a more beautiful woman. But regular old Sumi was all she had. If only she could be sure that were enough…

10

They lived that way for generations, until Vilodai sensed the gold growing in her people's hearts. She had laid in the earth for aeons, and knew every stone of her mother's breast. She knew of its iron and coal, and of stones so precious men would one day kill to possess them. But she knew of silver, too, the metal which could tell only truth. She recognized the gold immediately for what it was, and her anger boiled over, shaking the earth in her rage.

-Verses 92-96 of the Anushgiar Leyosil

—:—

Parimu woke in his berth, his sheets soaked with sweat. It had been growing warmer as they traveled east, and he'd foolishly slept with all the covers on again the night before. By the time they reached Amoriai, it would be downright tropical as far as he was concerned. He sat up, rubbing his eyes. He couldn't remember when he fell asleep, but it didn't feel like he had gotten much.

If his late-night thoughts of Shapewalkers weren't bad enough, he'd started having strange dreams. They weren't nightmares exactly, but they left him unsettled, like he wasn't in his own body. He had vague memories of flying, or was it swimming? He could vaguely remember these odd lights, white and gold, but he always woke with a start and couldn't remember much beyond that.

He shook his head, pushing himself to his feet; he may as well get a start on the day. The best thing he could do on this train was be consistent. The other passengers had seen him in the dining car every morning for breakfast, and he wouldn't be late now. Even a businessman — as he was pretending to be — would be expected to keep regular hours.

He stepped over to the narrow window in his berth, pulling back the curtain as he got his first real glimpse of the sea. Sometime during the night, they'd crossed the first branch of the Kolbenz River, entering the chicken claw-looking delta at the heart of Enozeira, the middle of the Three Sisters. There wasn't much to see yet — they wouldn't be in Cötthurn, the capital, until midday — but he felt so much better by the sea. He pulled the window up, letting a rush of wind into his room. He breathed in deeply, sucking in the salt air.

After shaving and fixing his hair, he started dressing. It was just a plain suit, one he'd bought himself some fifteen years ago, but it still felt like a disguise — and one he wanted to get right. After so many years in uniform, though, it felt strange to have use of it again. He'd certainly been a very different man when he had bought it… His tie half tied, he leaned over, pulling his badge from beneath his pillow. He ran his thumb over it before returning it to his valise.

Perhaps it was a bit sentimental, sleeping on your badge like that, but he could use the reminder of who he really was. Especially when he was chasing an evil thing like a Shapewalker, always ready to put on a false face. At least he was traveling in his own body… Besides, it wasn't his choice to pretend; it was in service to the queen. The Foreign Office had made very clear the need for caution when sending police abroad, and he would honor that order, no matter how it chafed him.

He made his way to the dining car, where the porter showed him to his usual table. It was near the back, and there were decent views of the coast from his side of the train. He picked up one of the newspapers on the table, flipping through it. He couldn't read Trierlien, the language spoken across the Three Sisters, but there seemed to be at least one newspaper in Berillai in every city along the railway now.

He started with the crime section, of course. Nothing major back in the city, thankfully, though there was the usual cargo theft and the like on the railway. It was incredible how honest men took just one step forward while the crooks took two. It was probably unbecoming of a merchant to growl at the crime section, but he couldn't very well hide every facet of who he was. He was so engrossed, he didn't hear another passenger sit across from him. But when the man started to speak, Parimu jolted, flipping the paper down onto the table.

"Sorry to startle you, Jenrell," the man said, offering his hand, which Parimu shook hastily. "I didn't realize you were such a news man. I did try to say your name before I sat, but I don't think you heard that either."

He'd have to get better about that. If he didn't start answering to the name he'd given everyone, his false identity wouldn't serve much purpose. Horicus Jenrell — a strange name, though it hadn't been his to choose.

"Apologies, Herrell," Parimu said.

They'd been seated together for dinner the first night of the trip. The man was from Maldegurn, the easternmost of the Three Sisters, and was heading back home after some business in Berill. He was friendly enough; he just tended to ask a lot of questions — questions that could trip him up if he wasn't careful.

The server appeared, setting coffee in front of Herrell and tea in front of Parimu. How marvelous it was to be on a Berillai train! He doubted a foreign rail service would memorize what drink you took in the morning. They ordered their breakfast, giving Parimu a blessed minute of not having to make conversation. Once the waiter was gone, they sipped their drinks for a moment before Herrell spoke again.

"So, it looks like we'll be stopping in Cötthurn today, eh?"

The train would be stopping for a much longer stretch that afternoon, with enough time for passengers to wander into town if they wanted.

"I'll be getting off for good, of course," Herrell continued. "I'm heading up to Miedaral by boat."

"Ah," Parimu said, nodding for a moment as he thought of what to say. "Well...it's been nice traveling with you. I hope the rest goes smoothly."

"Same, though the pleasure's been all mine," Herrell said. "I'll have my boat to catch, but I've done a fair bit of business in Cötthurn if you'd like a lunch recommendation?"

Parimu was tempted to try his luck on the train. There wouldn't be a normal dining service, but he wouldn't mind a moment's peace without the other passengers around. Still, it was probably easier to listen to the man's suggestion, whether he took advantage of it or not. He assented, and Herrell sprang into action, talking a mile a minute as he scratched out a map for Parimu to a place called the Lilakelz.

They talked for another twenty minutes, Parimu focusing as intently as he could on his porridge. Finally, the man left, heading to his berth to fetch his luggage. He wasn't a bad chap, really, and maybe Parimu could have been friendlier, but he was all nerves from hiding his identity. And if he was honest, it had been a while since he'd really spoken to anyone outside of an official capacity. He had neighbors he would say hello to, of course, but without any real friends at the station… He shook his head, leaving a tip — another practice he was getting used to — as he headed back to his cabin.

He sat on the small chair in his room, skimming through his book without paying much attention. He supposed he ought to enjoy it more. He usually worked from sunup to sundown, and it didn't leave much time for reading. The book he'd brought, *Elkor's Allumin*, had been his favorite in the navy, devouring the old stories in his free time. But most of them were love stories — a subject that seemed particularly beyond him now. He sighed, just another problem he could do nothing about. He settled back in his chair, forcing himself to refocus on the book.

But not even an hour later, when the train whistle blew to signal their arrival into Cötthurn, he found himself staring out the window. Cötthurn sat at the top of the delta, right where the middle branch of the rooster's claw began to split apart and flow into the sea. There were hundreds of giant windmills poking between the branches of the river in all different colors — something about the owners of the mills competing. How any of them made their businesses work was beyond him, though, piling onto the same patch of land and fighting to mill as much Amoriai grain as they could.

He got up and sat on the bed, turning toward the window so he could watch the city approach. Maybe he really did need a break from the train, staring out the window like a boy. He pulled out his watch and looked at it; they'd have three hours in the station before continuing on to Amoriai. He *could* step out for lunch. Herrell wasn't Berillai, but he was a businessman, after all, and maybe the Lilakelz wouldn't be such a bad place. Besides, he clearly needed practice using his false identity in public. He made his decision, putting his coat back on as the train whistle sounded the final approach.

Parimu stepped off the train, his face flushed from pushing through the scrum of passengers. Or perhaps it was the humidity, the warm delta air feeling foreign in the winter months. He clutched his bag tightly in his hand. It probably would have been safe on the train, but he didn't like the thought of leaving it unattended for so long. He followed the crowd, going out the station's northern exit into Cötthurn.

To his left, he could see the city wall — and the gap where the old gray stone had been blasted open for the tracks. In other places, the wall had giant lifted grates where the river passed through on its way to the coast. Even as it split, the water flowed quickly, surging northward from the mountains in the south. He could see the windmills more clearly now, whirling on a stretch of hills in the center of the city.

He set off, following Herrell's directions, which were surprisingly easy, given the chaotic layout of the city. Everything depended on the prongs of the river, allowing him to safely ignore the teeming buildings and winding streets. He went east, crossing into what seemed to be a nicer part of town, the streets lined with well-lit shops and townhomes.

And he quickly realized why, the gleaming dome of the capital rising up above the neighborhood.

It was difficult to keep the rulers straight in the Three Sisters, crowded with princedoms as they were. But he recalled some sort of governor, chosen by the other kingdoms to govern Enozeira. That sort of chaos was probably what led them to be so easily defeated at Strussfaran all those years ago. He nodded to himself — a strong backbone had always served Berill nearly as well as its armies had. Which was all the more reason his queen needed him to succeed now.

He turned toward the dome, keeping the river in sight. He followed it as it snaked to the north, the street curving with the water. After a block or two, the river split again, forming an island in the delta. Interestingly, the island was like any other part of the city, new buildings sprouting up again as soon as the water ended, while the street continued on a bridge.

The instructions said to stay with the right branch of the river, following it until he passed the fifth bridge, where the restaurant would be on the north side of the street. He kept moving at a brisk pace, though he tried to spare a glance at the shops he passed. Cötthurn wasn't as orderly as Berill, but the buildings were still pleasant enough to look at. Known for their dense forests in the south — and the woodworking to match — the roofs all had dark-stained cedar shingles, making a striking contrast with their whitewashed timber walls.

He passed by one shop full of finely carved dolls, fanciful things like clowns and animals. He stopped, suddenly remembering a toy he'd had just like it. His father had bought it for him — a wooden lion. What had he named it? Their village, Emillon, had been fairly far to the east, and his father had sometimes gone to Strussfaran with his smithwork. Money hadn't been tight exactly, but he only now realized what a sacrifice his father had made to buy it for him.

He smiled sadly. If only there were someone waiting for him back home, a family he could bring his gifts to. He thought of Jalicyne suddenly, her beautiful face and her wavy hair. How it would have felt to have her open the door for him, their children running to greet him, their eyes sparkling just like hers had. If—

He shook his head. How could he have let his mind wander so badly? He thought he'd put those memories away. Of course, he still dreamed of Jalicyne some nights, but that was out of his control. He squeezed his temples, pushing the thought from his mind. He could get sentimental when he retired. For now, he was still in enemy territory. He tightened his grip on his valise, moving down the street.

He stopped at the next bridge, marveling at how strong the flow of the river was. The Kolbenz, after all, was just another branch of the mighty Eltimeir River that ran through the east of Berill. They were all fed by the mountains of Vilodai's Heart, far to the southeast. It was strange to think of all the kingdoms being connected by one river. He'd never felt that way at sea — even with most of the kingdoms on the coast — but maybe the ocean was just too large, too powerful. The rivers were like a busy road, teeming with life wherever you went. As he watched, a grain barge glided past on its way to the mills.

He passed the capitol building next, staring up at it as he passed. The edge of the roof was covered in bronze eagles, their wings wide as they guarded the golden dome. He'd seen foreign capitols before, but it was strange to consider it up close. He was here for his queen, but there were probably men just like him, serving this kingdom. But where did their loyalty come from? He at least knew his was the nobler cause, but the other kingdoms had only recently joined the side of commerce and reason. He supposed you couldn't blame a man for staying loyal to his homeland, but there had to be a way to help them see the light, right?

As if on cue, as he crossed the next bridge, a giant ripple from a Shapewalker tore through the city. It rang out like a lightning bolt in his mind, a cannon going off at close range. He looked around, afraid he'd imagined it at first. He was getting so used to his nightly meditations, it almost felt like Shapewalkers were everywhere. But he finally felt its afterglow, the dark magic drifting over from the west side of the river. He almost took off running, his instincts gnawing at him, but he wasn't here for chasing magic. He had a single quarry, and one he needed for his queen.

He stopped, taking a deep breath as he leaned against a lamppost. He just had to stay the course. After all, he was abroad, where his people's laws didn't always apply. Looking around, no one else on the street seemed to be reacting to the ripple — though whether it was because they couldn't sense it or didn't care wasn't clear. He nodded, moving on. He could do this. After all, the queen had sent him to the bear's cave, and he wouldn't run at the first growl he heard.

He continued up the street, though he found himself blinking as he walked. His vision had gone funny after the ripple, and the light seemed to be playing tricks on him. Some of the people he passed almost seemed to be...*glowing*. In fact, it was just like that man in Hafanelle. Surely, it was just the stress. Before, there had been all that smoke from the train. And now he'd felt the ripple, keenly aware of how deep he'd ventured into enemy territory.

Finally, he reached the Lilakelz. It was a cozy little building, wooden framed with flowerboxes in the window, each one filled with lavender. He walked through a garden to reach the door, which was propped open for the breeze. He stuck his head inside, finding a dozen or so diners in wooden booths along both walls. A server emerged from the kitchen, a young woman with thick braids. She smiled, greeting him in Trierlien.

"Molenurg!" she said in a bright voice.

He smiled awkwardly and nodded. "Erm…yes…*Molenurg.* I'm from Berill, and, uh, I thought I might get some lunch?"

A few people looked at him when they heard him speaking Berillai, though they all quickly looked back at their food.

"Oh, yes," she answered, her smile widening. "We have travelers from all over; I think you'll find our restaurant most comfortable."

She beckoned for him to follow her as she glided across the floor to a table in the back. She poured him some lavender tea before walking him through the menu, translating quickly as she pointed out all the dishes with lamb — no doubt thinking it was all his people ate. He ended up picking a fish stew. He'd had enough 'crate meat' in the navy for one lifetime, but near the water, fish was always fresh.

He delicately bit off a corner of the flatbread the server had left as he sipped his tea. Looking around the room, he let out a grateful sigh. No one was glowing. Everything was okay. Perhaps it had just been a strange cast to the light, the sun reflecting oddly off the humid streets. The server brought his stew, and he tucked in, forgetting his troubles for the moment. It was heavily spiced, and the sting on his tongue was a welcome distraction. Besides, he was always more at ease during a meal. Ever since the navy, struggling to find someone to eat with in the mess, he knew he could always focus on his food, finding whatever sweetness the gods had saved for him in life.

He'd made it to the last spoonfuls, about to scrape up the stew with his flatbread when the serving girl called out again. He looked up, finding three new customers coming through the door, and they—

He dropped his spoon, flinching as he realized two of them were glowing. He clamped his eyes shut, hoping the illusion would pass. But if it was a trick of the light, why was it still happening in the dim restaurant? He slowly lifted his eyes, watching where the men had sat. They were laughing, already drinking wine, but the glow was there, unmistakable. He winced as a buzzing filled his ears, like the ripple from the street, only fainter. It was almost…*rhythmic,* only just faster than the pounding in his temples. His palms began to sweat. Were the two connected somehow? Were those…Shapewalkers?

It took everything in him not to bolt from the table, his mind racing.

How could he see them? There hadn't been another ripple, so there hadn't been a transformation. Suddenly, he thought of Drekkles. Was this the ability the man had never taught him? The older man had often gone abroad, so perhaps he'd just needed more exposure to the creatures. Unlike the explosions of the ripples, this was subtle, hardly even there.

His heartbeat finally slowed, his calm returning as he considered the information in a new light. He'd always hoped he'd someday measure up, finding even a fraction of Drekkles's ability.

He paid the server and left, hurrying back toward the train. He saw more of the glows on his way back — a disturbing number — but he no longer felt afraid, the possibilities multiplying in his mind. Most of them looked like people, which was the problem, of course, but if he could find the monster within… Even if they could hide their glow, he heard their buzzing now, would *feel* them when they drew near. He felt reinvigorated, hope blossoming in his chest. *Where men had courage, the gods left silver.* This was a gift, and when the time came, he would be ready to use it.

11

She carried her children to the north, to the great mount Seongbelm,
which means 'the Wall of Life.' It was far from the eyes of Vilodai,
and she made a home for them there. She called the place Anushai,
which means 'the true home' in the tongue of the goddesses.
> **-Verses 80-81 of the Anushgiar Leyosil**

—:—

Erso knocked on the door to his family's house and stepped back. Sumi stood on the curb, her hands balled tightly at her side.

"Keo'lose! Keo'lose!" someone called from within.

The door finally opened, and a bear of a man stood there, a thick beard on his face. His eyes landed on Erso, wide as saucers, before he yanked him into the house, babbling in Amoriai. Sumi hesitated for a moment before stepping up to the threshold, where she found them wrestling on the floor. That would be Beysal, then… At least they were both laughing, Erso wrapped in a chokehold as his uncle rubbed his knuckles through his hair.

A woman — presumably E'loseir — rushed over, her mouth hanging open, though she quickly had to start smacking them with a towel, the fight showing no signs of ending. Sumi carefully stepped through the doorway, looking around the room as she waited. They were in an enormous kitchen with a roaring fire and a table that could easily seat a dozen guests. To her left, stairs went up to another floor, and out back, the windows looked out at a beautiful garden — though the view was partially blocked by pots and pans of every shape and size hanging from the ceiling. Basically, it was just about the coziest place she'd ever seen.

But as her boots clicked on the floor, all three of them suddenly looked up, freezing in a strange tableau. Even Erso looked like he'd forgotten she was there in his struggle to breathe.

"Um, hello," she said in a small voice, raising her hand in a tiny wave. Just as quickly, they all sprang into action, switching from Amoriai to Berillai as they swarmed around her.

"Of course, you'd finally come home over a girl!" Beysal said, dropping Erso as he stepped up to Sumi. They shook hands, his palms like furnaces as he rapidly pumped her arm. "I'm Beysal. Not sure if he mentioned me — the lad's a touch ashamed of us — but I'm very glad to meet you."

"I'm Sumi," she said, smiling, "and he mentioned you, I promise."

"I'm E'loseir," the older woman said, somehow maneuvering around her husband and giving Sumi a tight hug. "It's so lovely to meet you."

She shot a look over her shoulder at Erso.

"Somebody doesn't like to write, so we spend most of our time worried sick, not knowing if he's dead or alive."

"I…uh…thought you liked surprises," he said, scratching the back of his head. "Sumi's my newest student, and we had to come quickly. Berill's not exactly a place for making plans."

"A student!" Beysal roared. "Now *that* makes sense. The kid couldn't keep a woman if he tried. Lucky for you, I taught him everything he knows. But please, get comfortable. You're a guest here!"

A fresh flurry of activity started, the men taking the luggage upstairs while E'loseir rushed around the kitchen making tea. Sumi offered to help, but she was forced into a giant chair and presented with a plate of cookies. She bit the end off of one, finding them delightfully elden flavored. So, she hadn't missed all of Alomidiar after all! Finally realizing how hungry she was, she quickly ate two cookies before pushing the plate away. She couldn't make a bad impression now — not that these people would even mind, lovely as they were. In fact, it felt like she'd been worried over nothing.

The kettle finally whistled, and E'loseir joined her at the table, carrying a tea tray laden with mugs.

"These cookies are incredible. Did you make them? I'm sorry I already took a few…"

"Oh, thank you, dear," E'loseir said, smiling as she took a cookie of her own. "I made them this morning, actually, must have felt Erso coming in my halls — they're his favorite."

She finished her first cookie and took a second, giving Sumi a wink.

"And don't you worry, have as many as you'd like. They'll last about a minute once the boys come down."

As if on cue, the stairs rattled with thunderous footsteps as the men reappeared. Erso now sported a small boy on his back, who was bouncing up and down as he held onto Erso's shoulders.

"Uncle Erso, Uncle Erso, Uncle Erso!" he yelled in sing-song.

When they reached the bottom of the stairs, Erso lifted the boy down, and he immediately climbed into his mother's lap, snagging a cookie from the plate. He took a big bite, finally looking at Sumi, his eyes widening.

"Are you Uncle Erso's Berillai friend?"

"Sure am," Sumi said. "I'm Sumi. Thank you for having me."

"We are glad to have you as our guest," he said formally. "You can call me Kel."

His mother laughed, tousling his hair. "He's been desperate to try out his Berillai on a real live person from Berill," she said. "It's a huge part of their schooling now."

"Ah," Sumi said, nodding. "Well, your accent is very good, Kel!"

"It's his Amoriai accent I'm worried about," Erso said, taking his own turn at tousling Kel's hair as he grabbed a seat at the table.

With tea to pass around, everyone finally relaxed, slipping into the rhythms of family as they bounced between topics — and interrogated Erso. It felt like a holiday, sitting with so many people around a table, and her face began to hurt from smiling. Even though she'd never had a big family, somehow it felt familiar too, the constant flood of jokes and stories like Grandpa — especially as they tried to tell her a lifetime of embarrassing things about Erso.

Still, it wasn't long before they were satisfied by the account of their prodigal nephew, and they turned on her, their questions rushing in.

"Oh, you'll have to help me in the garden," E'loseir said when she heard about the flower shop. "This is the first house we've had with enough room out back, but it seems neither of us was born with the green key."

"I'm happy to help," she said, eager to repay even an ounce of their kindness, "though I can't make any promises. We sell flowers at the shop, but my garden is abysmal."

"Sumi has an issue with being too humble," Erso said. "We stopped by her house on the way out of town, and I've never seen so much squash!"

"We have squash!" Kel said with a laugh, pushing his chair out as he ran into the garden. With the boy out of earshot for a moment, Beysal leaned forward, rubbing his hands together.

"A friend of Erso's is family as far as we're concerned, so stay as long as you like. But it sounds like things got a bit dicey back home, eh?"

"You could say that," Erso said. "You know what Berill is like."

Sumi bowed her head quickly in gratitude. "Thank you," she said, "truly. I don't know what would have happened to me without Erso. But I don't want to put you out. You're sure it's alright if I stay here?"

"We'd be angry if you didn't," Beysal said. "Right, Elo?"

"Absolutely," his wife said, smiling.

"Even if you came in bad company," Beysal said, shooting Erso a grin.

"Didn't have much choice," Erso said. "Promised her I'd find her the best teacher in the basin — even if it meant going in the bear cave."

"So, that's why you're here!" Beysal said. He slapped Erso on the back, splashing his face with tea. Erso laughed — when he was finished choking — and twisted in his chair to fight when E'loseir cleared her throat.

"Right, right," Beysal said sheepishly, smiling, "no wrestling at the table. We've broken a few here or there. Anyway, my boy can be hardheaded, but at least he brought you to the right place. We'll teach you up in no time!"

"What about a demonstration?" Erso asked. "She's learned loads about Mu'lalat, but I'm sure she'd love to see a run down the halls."

Beysal scratched his chin, glancing at his wife.

"I think we could do a little show."

He got up, moving around the kitchen as he closed the shutters facing the street. He also cleared a space by the fireplace, moving chairs out of the way. She didn't know what 'a run down the halls' meant, but it looked...*physical.* As Beysal busied with his preparations, Kel came back from the garden, handing her a bunch of squash blossoms.

"Pretty!" she said, holding them up. "I can't believe you have blossoms already. It's still winter back home."

"You can wear them in your hair if you want," Kel said, so she did, tucking one behind her ear.

"We're lucky to have the warm weather here," E'loseir said, "but I'm afraid we don't do much with it. Once the squash is done, the sun isn't good for much but wheat. Not like—"

Beysal clapped his hands together, standing like a showman in the center of the room.

"So," he said, "Mu'lalat. As I'm sure you know, it's the hallway of the spirit realm, connecting us to everything that *is* and everything that *can* be."

Sumi nodded, almost wishing she had something to take notes with.

"Well," Beysal continued, "Shapewalkers — Mu'amashdar in our language, or 'people of the halls' — just use them as the gods intended:

for walking."

He strutted to the fireplace and back, Kel giggling at his swaying arms.

"The key to this magic is embracing that freedom. It's not a train, forced to go from station to station. Running the halls is about opening your mind, knowing you can go through any door you like."

"There's no rush to get to this point," Erso said, turning back to Sumi, "but this is the goal. Finding your pool and knowing you can be anything."

"That's right," Beysal said. "The pool is peace, and peace is freedom. When you stop pushing, the halls can pull you in. Now," he said, tipping an imaginary hat as he took a bow, "a drum roll, please."

They started drumming on the table, Kel standing in his chair to bang his tiny hands with all his might. Beysal began to do a little dance, swaying side to side as he moved his arms like a metronome, back and forth in front of his face. Sumi began to laugh with Kel when the shaping began, and her mouth fell open.

It was like fireworks in miniature, right before her eyes. There weren't flashes — not like she'd produced back home — but the room grew brighter all the same, like the glow of an electric lamp. And from that glow, shapes began to burst out in a continuous stream, the light only slightly fading as Beysal joined the shapes together.

First, he appeared as a robin, fluttering in the air. But just as quickly, the bird flipped backward, reappearing as a butterfly. The butterfly made as if to land, when suddenly, it changed into a sunflower, reaching up from the ground. Each change appeared in the already glowing air, like a hot coal at the center of a fire. Just as suddenly, the sunflower was gone, and an actual tower of flame appeared where it had been, the heat glowing on her face. The glow grew brighter, and a bear appeared before them, standing on its hind legs as it roared. Sumi actually flinched, her heart pounding, even knowing it wasn't real. And then it ended, Beysal standing before them as he took a bow, the glow disappearing as quickly as it appeared.

Sumi leapt to her feet, clapping with the others. Kel danced around the room, growling like a bear.

"Incredible," Sumi said, her breath catching. "How did you ever learn such a thing?"

"Beysal used to act in his spare time," E'loseir said, her face glowing with pride. "But he wouldn't play a character; he'd be the background: plants, animals, whatever they needed. Eventually, he got fast enough to play them all."

"Lucky for me," Beysal said, "Elo has an eye for detail. Otherwise, she would've dated the leading man and not a shrub in the background."

"Well, the first night I saw him perform," E'loseir said, "he actually came out as a bear, which isn't that far from his usual self. It was a good advertisement."

They all laughed, and Beysal took a deep breath, reaching for another cookie. He looked exhausted, like he'd just run all the way up Fort Hill, the way she often felt after just one or two forms.

"Is it okay to ask questions?" she asked as they sat back down.

"Ask away," he said.

"Always question the great master," Erso said with a wry grin. "Can't let all that clapping go to his head."

Beysal cocked an eyebrow at him, but it didn't turn into a fight.

"Well…" she started, "when you were a bear, you were *huge*. This might be silly, but when I was in Berill, I started wondering how big one Shapewalker could go. Could you, say, be the size of a boat if you wanted to?"

"Very good question," Beysal said, shooting Erso a look. He took another cookie, placing it on his plate. "Take this cookie. Let's pretend it's a Shapewalker. It has a certain shape, right? And it only covers a little of the plate. But we can stretch it."

He looked at his wife, flashing a nervous smile.

"Sorry, honey."

He smashed the cookie with his fist, Kel laughing as E'loseir rolled her eyes. But a moment later, he'd spread it out, covering the plate with crumbs.

"See? One Shapewalker covering the plate. It's the same with me — one Beysal can be a bear. But if you tried to, say, put enough cookie out to cover the table, it'd be too thin. Same idea with your boat. Maybe you could get there, but you probably couldn't hold the form long — assuming you didn't hurt yourself trying."

Sumi nodded, tapping her chin.

"But," Erso said, butting in, "luckily for us, we aren't limited to just one cookie."

"Let the teacher talk, eh?" Beysal said, elbowing him in the ribs. "Excuse my boy, but in this case, he's also right. So Elo doesn't kill me, I won't break any more cookies, but if you had enough crumbs, you could cover the whole room if you wanted to — and it's the same with us. If your connection is good enough, you can shape together, and with two or three? You could make a boat no problem."

"Could you teach me that?" she asked. Only a few weeks ago, she'd thought she was alone with her powers, but now…

"We'll certainly try," Beysal said. "You have to get the basics down first, but I'm sure we'll get you there in no time."

"One time, when he was acting," E'loseir said, "he even made a mountain. It took four of them to do it."

"That was a long time ago," Beysal said, shaking his head but clearly proud. "And I was sore for a week!"

"I can't believe you used to act," Sumi said. "Why'd you stop?"

The room suddenly got quiet, everyone finding something interesting in their tea. She remembered the coup, suddenly feeling foolish.

"I'm sorry—" she started, but Beysal waved a hand in the air.

"It's okay," he said, smiling. "A lot has changed. In fact, I used to be a carpenter, in the Woodworkers Guild and everything, just like my father. But they moved it across the river, along with everything else. They outlawed the plays, jobs dried up. Heck, I don't even know where you'd do a play now, with the theater gone."

"But hey," he added, smiling at his wife, "what do I need to act for now? It got me what I really need."

"Don't worry about this old goat," Erso said, slapping Beysal on the back — with only a bit too much force. "He's got plenty to do. Elo's business keeps him busy — and mostly out of trouble."

"Oh?" Sumi asked, turning to E'loseir.

"Yes, well, we run a sort of informal guild for Shapewalkers. It's all hush-hush now, obviously, but we keep our kind in touch, help anybody in trouble, that sort of thing. With all the official guilds over the river, we just try to take care of our own."

"She's being modest," Beysal said. "She's always had a brain for politics — her father was a guild boss in the old days — and she put the whole thing together herself. All I do is drop off groceries."

That sounded just like Nela's work, only for Shapewalkers! Maybe — even on the run — she'd still be useful after all...

"I'd love to help if you'll have me," she said eagerly. "I guess I don't know my way around yet, but I'm sure I could drop off groceries if you drew me a map."

"Light your halls, dear," E'loseir said, touching her arm. "Don't feel obligated — you *are* a guest — but there's always something to do. Especially for Beysal; he's getting lazier with age. In terms of a bear's life, he's approaching hibernation."

Beysal started to protest as Elo looked up at the kitchen clock.

"Speaking of groceries," she said, "I'm sure you're both starving. We should be getting dinner started."

They all stood, suddenly moving around the kitchen. E'loseir moved to the window and looked out into the garden to see what she could harvest, while Beysal started knocking around the cupboards, promising to make bread.

"Let us help," Erso said. "I feel bad I didn't warn you. Why don't I go to the market and pick up some meat for dinner?"

"Oh, that'd be lovely, sweetheart," E'loseir said, sticking her head back in from the garden.

"And what can I do?" Sumi asked. It was a little nerve-wracking to test her paltry cooking skills on them, but it was better than sitting idly by.

"You go with Erso," Beysal said, turning from his mixing bowl. "If you can keep him out of a pub, you'll have done more than all of us combined."

Sumi laughed; they all moved so fast here, one quip coming after another. That must have been where Erso got it from… He stuck his tongue out at Beysal's back, and they quickly gathered their things, heading back into the street and off to the market.

12

*But Essomaui could see all things, even the goodness in the humans'
hearts. And she knew if they could see the beauty of the world, they
would change. She tried to sing them her many songs, but she found
she could not reach their ears. The humans only heard the chirping of
birds or the rustle of the wind. They lived only so many days on only
so much of the earth. She came among them to watch more closely,
eager to know how to speak to their hearts.*

-Verses 56-60 of the Anushgiar Leyosil

—:—

Sumi followed Erso from Beysal's neighborhood, taking the shopping
basket from his shoulder.

"So," he asked, "ready to run away yet?"

"No!" she said, whacking him on the arm. "They're lovely, far too
nice to be your family."

"We'll see how you feel after training with the bear."

They passed a shop, and Erso slowed, looking in the windows. "Know
what you want for dinner?" he asked.

"Anything," she said. "But it's your welcome home dinner. Is there
anything Amoriai you crave when you're away?"

"Good point," he said. "I guess I forgot I had tastebuds after all that
bloody squid."

He rubbed his hands together. "Hopefully Beysal makes his baked
rice — almost as good as my mum's. But we're out for meat, so maybe
wood ox? It comes from Anushai, but we cook it better in the south."

She eyed him. His parents were coming up more in Amoriai, but he
still talked around them, like a hole in the ground he didn't want to fall
into. Should she ask about them? She wanted to listen, to support him,
but the way they talked about the coup, those burned buildings… If he

77

wanted to be happy, to celebrate being home, she didn't want to spoil it.

"Sounds good to me," she said lightly. "What's the market like? Is it like Wembly?"

"Oh, much bigger than Wembly," he said. "There's not as many shops on this side of the river these days, but the market more than makes up for it."

They followed the main road back toward the old palace, its copper roof baking in the sun.

"Want to see it?" Erso asked, following her gaze.

"Sure," she said. "I mean…it's safe, right? They won't assume we're Shapewalkers for walking by?"

"Oh sure," he said. "It's still open, houses diplomats from the east — a reminder not to cross the Berillai, I guess. But people still come and go, workers to maintain the grounds and such. Just don't stare. People used to mourn there after the coup, and that ended…predictably."

She nodded, her chest suddenly tight. If she had one vice, it was staring at buildings. But here, it suddenly seemed like a dangerous hobby. She'd have to remember to keep asking what was safe to look at.

They snaked around the outside of the palace grounds, following the curving streets as she peeked through the fence — careful not to stare. Eventually, they reached the front, emerging onto a large plaza. Surrounded by ten large buildings, it had a huge green with a clock tower in the middle. It had to be at least six stories high, and it had Anushai numbers on it — another gift, perhaps? — but the windows had a dull look to them, like they were covered in dust.

"What is this place?" she asked.

"The old guild buildings," he said, shielding his eyes from the sun as they stopped to look. "Like Beysal's old Woodworkers Guild, yeah? They used to have a voting council under the king. Some of them helped in the coup, so they got invited over the river — though they purged all the members who couldn't join them."

Her jaw clenched looking at all the empty buildings. It was terrible what those people had done — what *her* people had done. She felt so helpless, torn between wanting to cry and feeling guilty for not knowing, and maybe even for *contributing* to their loss; a Berillai Shapewalker, with one foot on either side. She hoped she could do *something* while she was there, even if it was just delivering some food.

"Come on," Erso said gently, waving for him to follow. "It was a long time ago. And if we don't get that meat, they'll think I took you to a pub."

"No pubs," she said, finally smiling as she pointed a finger at him. "Don't make me fail my only job."

Still, she felt better, his kindness always right on time — even if it made her feel like even more of a burden. But maybe that was why Erso laughed so much. How else could you keep from crying?

They crossed the square, entering the market. It wasn't marked in any way, but as they crossed the last street, it just *began*, spilling in every direction, a hundred different smells drifting on the air. There were clothes and books, piles of spices, and people roasting meat. Each little shop had an awning to block the sun, but they didn't seem organized in any way; fruits sold next to toys, baskets next to onions, everything mixing like it had fallen from the sky.

Erso let her lead, and she flitted about like a child, drawn in by everything she passed. She kept looking back, worried she'd make them late, but he only smiled. Eventually, after watching a man make glass, she stopped at a scarf stand run by an elderly woman, who smiled when she saw Sumi, forcing her hand open so she could feel the silk.

"He'ayr emto noseelei," the vendor said in Amoriai as Erso joined her. *"Zelowem jesh'em weilen."*

"She says I should buy my pretty wife a scarf," Erso translated. "Since the nights are still chilly."

"We must be too good at acting," she said, laughing.

Erso pulled out some coins, but Sumi grabbed his arm.

"You don't have to do that! After my ticket and everything else…"

"Well, it suits you," Erso said, winking as he paid the woman. "Besides, these are some of the only real coins I carry — other than a bit of Anushai — and I like to help the vendors."

She looked at the vendor, who was watching them, trying to follow their conversation in Berillai — no doubt worried they'd change their minds.

"Okay," Sumi said. "Thank you. But only if you're sure."

Erso nodded at the woman, picking up a green-and-gold scarf. He wrapped it around her, the fabric even softer on her neck.

"Jesh'em," Sumi said to the shopkeeper — *beautiful* — the only Amoriai word she'd recognized.

The woman bowed her head in thanks. They walked away, but she paused a few feet away, pulling him aside.

"Thank you," she said, "seriously. But I can't keep taking your money. Between you saving my life and staying with your family… You have to find some way for me to pay you back."

"I can understand that," he said, nodding. "It killed me being taken care of by Beysal when I was young, always feeling guilty — probably why I hit the road so soon."

He sighed, grinning. "But don't feel too bad. For a vagabond like me, money's easy come, easy go. It's all from odd jobs and hustles, anyway — when I'm not outright stealing."

She opened her mouth to protest, and he raised his hands in defeat.

"And — *for you* — we'll find a way for you to help. I'm sure you'll be plenty useful, helpful as you are, but try to enjoy your training too. Having you alive is payment enough."

"Okay," she said. "Thank you."

He jerked his thumb behind him at a meat vendor. "Now, let's get that meat. Don't want Elo thinking you're as bad as the rest of us."

Erso started haggling with the meat vendor while she looked at some parasols. For all the bad in Amoriai, the market, at least, felt free. You could almost forget where you were. Like you—

She looked up, seeing a police officer coming down the next aisle. She must have jinxed herself, like naming Ciersein herself, the goddess of death appearing in the dark. The officer, a middle-aged woman, looked almost exactly like the Berillai police, wearing a dark-blue uniform and a silver badge. She was glaring at every vendor she passed, when, suddenly, her eyes fell on Sumi. Her heart stopped, her legs suddenly frozen. She'd been caught; it was over.

"Just keep shopping," Erso whispered in her ear, suddenly at her side as he took her by the elbow. He guided her to a nearby row of cabbage, babbling about the produce. It took everything in her not to look back, but eventually her heart slowed, and she shook her head.

"Sorry," she said. "They just look so *familiar*. I thought for sure she'd know what I was."

"I hear that," Erso said, chuckling. "I don't think I'll ever feel the same about the color blue. But you're safe. Like I said earlier, any police with abilities aren't likely to admit it. Amoriai's not a great place to be a fellerhurn."

He pulled the meat from his coat, handing her the wax-paper package. "Let's go," he said. "I'll let you do the honors, start getting you some credit."

"Did you get the wood ox?" she asked.

"Of course. Best meat in the Continent. You ever try it? You must've, with an Anushai grandmother."

She shook her head, chuckling. "I never did, actually. We always seemed to eat Berillai food. But one time, my Nela shouted at my grandpa, 'it's always sheep with you people!'"

Erso laughed. "I think she would have been my kind of lady," he said. "Not sure how she did it, eating all that chewy stuff."

He reached into his other pocket, pulling out a book. "Speaking of which, thought you might want to brush up."

It was a book on Anushai, the same drawing of the temple on its cover.

"Where'd you get this?" she asked, flipping through it.

"By the meat," he said, pointing over his shoulder. "Right where you'd expect it, eh? But don't worry; it was practically free. Besides, you might need it if we go north."

"It better have been free! But thank you, really. I promise I'll study up. I can be your tour guide."

"Deal," he said, chuckling. "Now, let's get back, eh?"

They started back the way they came, Erso babbling about dinner and the meat he swore would taste like butter. She kept looking over her shoulder, but the police officer was nowhere to be found. They kept walking until the market was behind them, hidden by the guild houses and all their abandoned history.

13

Vilodai was enraged, discovering her sister had meddled with her creation. Humans were to have been her great revenge, free of the bondage she lived with, driven only by their passion and limitless in their ability. But now, Essomuai, the freest of them all, had tainted her own flesh and blood. So Vilodai summoned the greatest king of the land, Elomikarus, to the southern mountains, to the Heart of Vilodai. She brought him to her caverns, showing him her metals and teaching him their uses.

-Verses 99-103 of the Anushgiar Leyosil

—:—

Fourteen Years Ago

Relsenair Parimu, first mate of the *Runai,* climbed to the top deck, taking a deep breath of salt air — which never failed to put him at ease. But it was more than just the smell of the sea; it was the smell of a well-maintained vessel, of freshly applied lacquer and new wood where the boards had been replaced. He had always taken pride in working on the Royal Fleet, but now it was his job — his sacred responsibility — to give the ships what they deserved.

And he was especially fond of *this* ship. His captain, Admiral Heller, was the most decorated in Berill. Not that awards meant anything — his father had always warned him against being a ladder climber — but in this case, the captain's medals were deserved. He ran a tight ship, and that was its own worthy battle, the first victory that allowed for all the others.

He hadn't ever thought he'd make first mate. His father's service had earned him first cadet when he enlisted, but the rest had been an accident.

82

He never shirked his duties, but it seemed to have come down to intuition. He *understood* his ships, knew what they needed to thrive. Take the rope loops, for example. If you kept them oiled, you'd ensure the lines didn't snap in a storm. And if you coiled the bights correctly, you knew your sailors wouldn't trip or fall overboard at night. He just needed to understand the meaning of a task, and he would never fail to see it done.

Not that he was completely immune to the benefits of rank... He thought of the picture hidden at the bottom of his trunk, a miniature of Jalicyne he'd had painted at the fair. With his new commission, he might just be able to afford a cottage in Berill. Jalicyne had always dreamt of moving to the city, and as an officer, he might actually be able to give her the kind of life she deserved.

Assuming, of course, she could ever love him in return. He hadn't said anything before he left. What if he was just a neighbor in her eyes, a childhood plaything she could cast aside? Of course, *she* would never be just some village girl to him. He loved her, and even after all his travels, she was the most beautiful thing he'd ever seen. His mother still wrote about her, seeming to know the truth without needing to ask. But at least he knew she wasn't married yet. He just had to do his duty and hope he'd end up worthy in the end.

He shook his head. *Get it together, man!* he thought, disgusted with himself. He already allowed himself ten minutes each night of staring at her picture, and now he had a ship to run. He set off across the deck, mentally going through his checklist. He started at the bow, looking for their sister ship, the *Elisor*. It was gliding along the coast on their landward side, safe and sound. Besides the two frigates, they had two cutters for scouting and two civilian ships in tow, but they were otherwise alone, and he couldn't help but watch for danger.

Their fleet usually worked the southern Erril Sea, but they'd received a special duty carrying gold and silver for the treasury, and they were traveling down the Golden Coast. There was a new royal mine past the Itros Cape, which meant they were sailing crown-less waters. They'd be stopping in Anushai to resupply before they sailed the Gap, but until then, pirates were a very real possibility. The *Runai* had long-range cannons, which is why they'd put the gold — and the *Elisor* — along the coast, but pirates were like storms; the sooner you spotted them, the better chance you had at living.

Not that spending the night in Anushai would feel much safer... The men grew restless there, kept on the ship and forced to look out at a port they couldn't visit. Apparently, it hadn't been that way in his father's time, but like all rules, he understood this one's purpose: you simply couldn't trust a kingdom full of Shapewalkers. They used their passphrases carefully enough in other ports — something the men seemed to think should apply here — but the risk was too high. If one of his men had their face stolen, they'd be halfway out to sea before the demon showed its teeth.

He passed by a crew doing maintenance on the cannons, and they snapped to attention as he passed. He nodded at them, stopping briefly to check their work on the fuses before moving on. The men hadn't taken to him easily. Not one for politics, he'd never been popular per se. But luckily, after getting them safely through a few scrapes on their last deployment, he'd finally earned their respect, if not their fondness.

The rest of the day sped by, and before he knew it, Parimu was eating dinner below deck with the other men. He ate quickly, impatiently spooning in the mouthfuls, eager for the sustenance, if not the tedium of taking it in. He normally ate quickly — partially to take the pressure off the men once he left the mess hall — but tonight, he also had more to do than usual. It was the night of their weekly conference, when the captains of all their sister ships came aboard. He had to get a bottle of whiskey from the quartermaster, extra biscuits from the cook, and still find time to brew the tea exactly how the admiral liked it.

Half an hour later, Parimu approached the admiral's cabin, pushing a serving cart in front of him. He heard voices inside already, so he quietly opened the door and slipped inside. It was a cool night, and a brazier had been set in the middle of the men, flames crackling against the metal grate. He set the whiskey and biscuits on a table in the center before pouring tea for each of the men. There were eight of them in all, with a captain and first mate from each navy ship.

With everyone served, Parimu silently slipped into his chair and took a measured drink of his tea, trying to catch up on the conversation. He often took notes after the meetings, and the admiral had taken to perusing them. Tonight, though, it was mostly talk of Anushai. As of that night's docking, they were only fifty miles west of the city. They went over supply manifests and requisition orders, occasionally detouring into talk of politics or old war stories. Still, he couldn't put his finger on it, but something seemed off about the room. There was…a *tension* he hadn't noticed before. He listened more carefully, taking stock of each of the men in turn.

Finally, he found the source of the odd feeling: Captain Cornerall of the *Elisor* was acting strangely. It had taken time to notice because it was the *absence* of the man's usual talk that finally stood out. Cornerall was a careerist at heart, and he usually never missed a chance to butt in.

But tonight, he seemed absentminded, nervous even. He sat hunched forward in his chair, his eyes narrowed. At one point, Admiral Heller even asked him if he was alright, but the man waved him off, saying he was worried about the weather. Nothing more came of it, and eventually, the men were making their goodbyes.

Parimu lingered for a moment to ensure the admiral had everything he needed before hurrying away. He'd make a note on Cornerall in his report, but there wasn't time to worry about it at the moment. The next day would be a hectic one, and he intended to be fresh. Still, he followed protocol to a tee, returning the remains of the whiskey to the quartermaster and washing out the tea things before rushing up to bed. But as he climbed beneath the covers, he had a sinking feeling, and it was a long time before he drifted off.

Parimu woke in the middle of the night to alarm bells, footsteps pounding on the deck above. He bolted upright, stumbling into his clothes as he sprinted topside. He emerged into a bright moonlit night, men crawling everywhere as they shouted instructions, setting sails and pulling the anchor. But the men who weren't running seemed caught in a daze, frozen in place as they stared toward the coast. He followed their eyes to where he spotted the *Elisor*, some five hundred yards away, its hull smashed onto a stretch of rocks and its deck in flames.

He ran for the bridge, shouting orders to the wheelman as the ship lurched forward. How in Ciersein's bloody claws had the *Elisor* drifted off their anchor? And what had dashed them on the rocks like that? The seas were still calm, and none of the other ships had drifted a hair.

They raced toward their sister ship, trimming sails just in time to glide next to it as they worked to put the fires out. The scout ships weren't far behind, and soon, they had bucket lines and pumps going, men zipping between the ships. Parimu raced across the gangplank with the others, when the admiral appeared, the men's panic lifting as he organized the chaos. Parimu redoubled his efforts, pushing on with his bucket, time slipping away until the fire was finally out.

When it was done, they stood, stunned, blinking the smoke from their eyes as they tried to assess the damage. The deck had been horribly burnt, and a few of the rear berths were completely destroyed. Parimu felt dizzy as he considered the men who'd been sleeping there, but at least they weren't taking on water. As he slowly led the *Elisor* through a roll call, a pit formed in his stomach; they'd lost nearly two dozen men. As he ran through the tally once more, he realized two glaring names were missing:

Captain Cornerall and his first mate, Morisan.

"Men!" he yelled out. "Your captain is missing! Search the ship!"

The men, who'd seemed like sleepwalkers a moment earlier, sprang into action, their grief forced to wait as they took off running through the ship. He followed them, a human stream surging in all directions. As they reached the bottom deck, he finally heard a shout.

"Admiral!" one of the sailors yelled. "We found them!" Parimu didn't see the admiral with him, but he ran down the hallway as fast as he could. He found a thick knot of men around the hold, the door hanging open. As some of them recognized him, they parted, letting him through.

Why is the hold unlocked? he thought, slowly picking his way to the front of the crowd. Inside, he found Captain Cornerall and his first mate gagged and hog-tied in the middle of the floor, their clothes stripped off. Their faces were red as they writhed on the floor, their eyes glassy with fear. Parimu stepped up to them, blinking in confusion. He looked up at the shelves in the hold and gasped, realizing the gold and silver were gone.

More than a week later, Parimu was crossing the deck, hurrying toward the admiral's cabin. They were finally in Anushai, though it had taken an eternity to tow the damaged *Elisor* to port. He ignored the city lifting up around them, his bleary, sleepless eyes intent on his destination. They had sent word for help from Berill, and after days of tense waiting, they'd finally received a visit from a royal investigator. According to the admiral, they'd sent the Director of Reality himself. But didn't that mean…Shapewalkers?

He slipped into the cabin. The admiral was speaking, but he noticed Parimu, nodding to the chair next to him. There were two detectives in the middle of the room, writing in small notebooks. One was older, bald, with a thick white mustache. He wore a standard uniform, while the younger wore the colors of a palace guard. Could he be a Thorn, then? Of course, the man would never reveal it if he were, but sailors did like to whisper about the queen's secret guard… It was good to know the Crown cared, but it sent a shiver down his spine all the same.

The older man glanced at Parimu as he sat. He did a double take, narrowing his eyes, seeming to see right through his skin and down to his bones. It was only a moment, but Parimu felt his body tense until the man returned to his notes.

"This is my first mate," Admiral Heller finally said. "He was first on the scene in the hold. I trust no one more, so ask him anything you need to know."

With that, the admiral excused himself, and suddenly, Parimu found himself alone with the two men. They seemed almost casual, flipping back through their notes for a time, muttering to each other as if they'd forgotten he was there.

"Squadron First Mate Parimu," the older man finally said, reading his official rank from his notes.

Parimu nodded, unsure if he was meant to confirm the information.

"My name is Detective Drekkles, Director of Reality. This is Corporal Jeonnes from the palace. We're hoping to get to the bottom of this…tragedy. Just a few formalities; what is your third-tier passphrase?"

Parimu racked his brain. He knew all his passphrases by heart, of course, but suddenly, he was terrified to get even a word of it wrong.

"Er…where goes the ocean goes the waves," Parimu said, finally forcing out the words.

"Good," Drekkles said, not looking back at his paper for reference. Had he memorized their passphrases? "And the fifth?"

It was hard to do them in random order, whether he knew them by heart or not. He was forced to start from the top, thinking through each one in his mind.

"Alomidiar brings rain to Emillon," he said quickly, not wanting to look like he was dithering.

"Very well," Jeonnes said, "thank you for that. If you could tell us what you saw in the hold that night. Every detail."

He told them everything: the men bound and gagged, the treasury shipment gone. They continued to ask questions, probing deeper and deeper, prying loose fragments of memory he hadn't even realized he'd remembered. They even asked what he had smelled in the hold, reminding him of the stench of sweat and urine coming off the men. He hadn't put the pieces together before then, but that had to mean they'd been in the hold for some time, right? But he had seen them in the admiral's cabin only hours before…

The questions finally stopped, the men conferring with each other as they left him stewing in his chair. His mouth went dry, and he felt like there was a bucket of eels in his chest.

"You can go," Drekkles finally said. "Thank you for your time."

Parimu blinked, standing as their instructions finally reached him. He started toward the door but stopped, needing to ask the question, even though he felt he already knew the answer.

"Sir," Parimu said, turning toward the detective, "if I may, do you…really think this could be Shapewalkers?"

Drekkles looked up from his notes, narrowing his eyes. The intensity of that stare made him thankful he'd never done a single thing wrong in his life.

"I'm afraid so," the older man finally said, letting out a deep sigh. "Not uncommon in these parts of the world, as I'm sure you know. There's a pirating network we've been following, though we've never seen them do anything this brazen. We likely wouldn't have even known they were connected if they hadn't crashed the ship."

He closed his notebook and stepped up to Parimu, putting a hand on his shoulder. He suddenly seemed fatherly, the wolf become a shepherd.

"I promise you, son, the queen will see her justice done."

Parimu nodded eagerly, his eyes widening in gratitude.

"Thank you, sir," he muttered.

The detective nodded once and released him. Parimu turned to go, his hand on the doorknob as the detective spoke again.

"You said in your notes you thought Captain Cornerall was acting strangely. Those are good instincts, son; make sure you act on them in the future. This is a dangerous world we live in."

Parimu spent the rest of the day trying to be about his tasks, busy overseeing the repairs to the *Elisor*. But no matter how much he tried to concentrate, he couldn't stop thinking about what the detective had said. He found himself looking up each time the cabin door opened, trying to catch a glimpse of the investigators. He also felt his anger welling up, his mind going through the list of every sailor who'd died over and over. Before today, he hadn't even really known if Shapewalkers were real, and now they'd done this. They'd killed his men.

A few hours later, when Detective Drekkles finally emerged from the cabin to leave, Parimu was hot on his heels.

"Detective," he called out just as he reached the gangplank, "if I might have a word."

He almost lost his nerve as those cool eyes landed on him again, but the man nodded, pulling off to the side.

"Thank you for coming," Parimu said. "But um… Well, sir, my commission is up in about a year. And I was wondering you'd ever hire a sailor. It doesn't sit right with me, what happened here, and I'd like to help if I could."

The detective peered at him again, sizing him up anew. He looked at him for a long time, until Parimu wondered if he should say something. Just as he opened his mouth to apologize, though, the detective finally spoke.

"I think you might actually have what it takes," Drekkles said. "Write to me when you're home. If you stay as loyal as you are now, I'm sure we'll have a use for you."

With that, the detective turned and left the ship, disappearing into the horrible city. Parimu watched him go, his chest tight. Still, part of him felt relieved too. If there was justice in this world, that man would find it, and someday, maybe he could help.

14

Elomikarus began to conquer the world. Humans had always fought each other, but only with rough spears and iron swords. Elomikarus was given steel stronger than any other, and by channeling Vilodai, he could shake the ground itself, rending the earth beneath his feet. He fought with the bloodlust of his mother, and before long, he took great swaths of territory in her name.

-Verses 113-116 of the Anushgiar Leyosil

—:—

Erso and Beysal leaned against the short wall in the alley behind the house, nursing their pipes after dinner. It had been a wonderful meal, probably the best he'd had since he last left home. More importantly, everyone was getting along swimmingly — not that he'd had any doubts they'd like Sumi, of course. For once, it seemed there was a lot to be thankful for. As the smoke from his pipe drifted up into the sky, he followed it with his eyes, watching as it broke apart and disappeared.

The last bit of sun was reflecting off the highest sliver of the alleyway, the rough brick turning gold against the deep-blue sky. He tilted his head back and closed his eyes for a moment, basking in the light. When he finally reopened them, he turned to find Beysal looking back at the house, a satisfied smile on his face. He was watching the women in the kitchen as Kel ran circles around them, repeatedly dashing upstairs to bring something down to show Sumi.

"Pretty nice life you've made for yourself," Erso said, elbowing Beysal. "I'm surprised an old bear like you pulled it off."

Beysal laughed, shaking his head.

"I guess we lived pretty rough back in the day, eh? Wish I could make that up to you."

"Never! We lived like kings. You know how bad every fifteen-year-old boy wants to live like that? Drinking whiskey, eating cheap meat out of tin cans. It was like camping every day. Plus, you let me get away with basically whatever I wanted."

"I suppose I did that," Beysal said, stroking his chin. "Let myself get away with pretty much anything then too." He sighed. "If Elo hadn't come and found me, I'd probably still be in some pub. That or the gallows, I guess."

"You'd do well in a pub," Erso said, poking one of Beysal's giant arms. "Be a bouncer, drink for free."

Beysal laughed.

"Why do I get the feeling you'd get your hands on most of those free drinks?"

Erso raised his palms innocently. "Hey, it was my idea. I should at least get a finder's fee."

Beysal met his eyes.

"Listen," he said, turning serious. "I know you don't like talking about old times, but I really have been meaning to apologize. Now that Kel's around… Well, I know I could've done better by you. Especially when you ran off, I just—"

"Beysal," Erso said, cutting him off, "nobody's ever done more right by me in my whole life, and you know it. You're like my father and brother in one. You didn't ask to be handed a kid, but you gave me everything you had. And you *deserve* what you have now. Kel's amazing."

Beysal frowned, searching his face for something. Finally, he nodded.

"Alright," Beysal said. "I guess it couldn't have been that bad if you still want to visit. But it'll break Elo's heart if it's another two years, you understand?"

He looked back at the house for a moment before shoving his pipe in his mouth.

"And—" he said, locking a giant hand on Erso's shoulder, "you're gonna be a good uncle, yeah? You ever tell Kel about me letting you drink at fifteen, and you'll see how good a bouncer I'd be."

Erso laughed, puffing a cloud of blue smoke into Beysal's face. "You'd have to catch me first, and you know it."

He glanced down at the hand on his shoulder. He was already caught, by the looks of it… He raised his hands in surrender.

"Look, I promise, alright? On my own key, I'll only tell stories that make you look good."

"Smart lad," Beysal said, slapping him on the back before returning to his own stretch of wall. He was an earnest man, the best one Erso had ever met, certainly, but neither of them could bear being serious for too long — and nothing chased away the past like laughter. If you didn't make a joke every five minutes, the things you'd rather forget might just catch up with you.

"You know," Beysal said after a time, "you could have this kind of life too if you wanted."

Erso rolled his eyes. Elo had been trying to set him up with women for years, probably just to tame him.

"Oh, boy," Erso said, "not this again—"

"No, no," Beysal said, pointing a finger at him. "You're gonna hear me out this time. I didn't think *I'd* ever have this; didn't think I deserved it, to be honest with you. I let my friends die, and we all just rolled over when the Crown fell. But if I can find a way to live again, so can you."

"I'm happy for you," Erso said, "really. And Elo's cousins are very pretty, believe me. It's just…"

He looked up at the sky and flicked his hand toward it, trying to summon whatever it was he felt on the road, that feeling he'd been chasing all those years.

"Doesn't have to be here," Beysal said. "I know you're happier out there — wherever *there* is. Just give yourself the life you deserve, whatever that looks like. Maybe there's someone who wants to be out there with you. Or maybe that some*where* is really a some*one.*"

Without meaning to, he looked back at the kitchen, where Sumi was holding one of Kel's toys, smiling that lovely smile of hers, like distilled sunshine.

"See?" Beysal said, poking him in the ribs. "That stare says it all. She's too good for you, but she doesn't know that yet."

If Beysal could see it too, then maybe it was true. But he was right about one thing: she was *far* too good for him. Besides, as soon as she was trained, she'd want to go home — or at least head north to Anushai. Wherever she ended up, he certainly wouldn't warrant any space in her wonderful new life.

"Yeah, yeah, old man," Erso said, tapping out his pipe. "Let's get you back inside. I know you lose your grip when you're away from your wife."

"Whatever you say," Beysal said, laughing as he led the way back to the house. Erso followed him, grumbling, but as the kitchen door opened and Sumi's voice drifted out, he felt his chest tighten. Too good by a mile.

He shook his head. He was just here to help her, and when she was trained, that would be it. He just had to keep reminding himself of that. They'd be off to bed soon, and that would give him one less day with her. But that didn't mean he wouldn't enjoy every single second he had left. He forced a smile onto his face and stepped inside, eager to join the fun.

15

She gave Elomikarus the power to conquer the land and take every people for his own. The only thing she asked him in return was to destroy the children of Essomuai.

-Verses 107-108 of the Anushgiar Leyosil

—:—

Sumi was soaring, her wings wide, gliding without ever needing to flap. She wasn't sure what kind of bird she was. She looked at one of her wings, finding it covered in gold feathers. It seemed natural, though, so she looked back down, focusing on the rolling hills beneath her. It felt so good to glide above the plains, their golden grass waving in the wind. It was neither night nor day, but a kind of strange, permanent sunset.

How had she gotten here, anyway? She could smell the sea but still had no idea where she was. How would she get back? She started to flap, pushing higher. But when she finally made it over the hills, she recoiled, horrified. The grass was gone, and the fields below her were a deep red, like a sea of blood. She gasped, and suddenly, she was a human again. She was falling, rushing toward the ground and that horrible lake of death. She screamed, but right before she made contact with the ground, there was a brilliant emerald flash.

She jolted, gasping as she sat up in bed, sweat soaking through her nightgown. She looked around the room, her heart pounding. Where was she? This wasn't her room. She— Beysal and Elo's house. She took a deep breath, clutching a hand to her chest. Just a nightmare, then. She shook her head, flopping back down on her pillow.

What in Velloni had that been? Trouble sleeping seemed normal enough when you were away from home, but why did she have to see such horrible things? She'd been having strange dreams ever since they left, but that was the most vivid one by far. It was hard to shake, like it'd been real, and sitting there in bed was the dream. Couldn't she have a normal nightmare, like walking around town with no clothes?

She wiggled her shoulders, settling back under the covers. She was still boiling hot, but she pulled the sheet over her, trying to feel some sense of security. She sighed out another deep breath and shut her eyes. There was too much training to be done to lose sleep over nothing. Trying to think of something happier, she pictured Nela, imagining her with them in Beysal's lovely house, surrounded by his little family. She smiled, and before long, she was gone, floating away on another current of sleep.

16

-Verses 105-106 of the Anushgiar Leyosil

—:—

Parimu quickly packed his bag as the train approached Amoriai. He locked his valise before he started tidying the room. They had people to clean the berths, surely, but he just couldn't leave a mess in good conscience. Luckily, he knew how to make a bed in a hurry from the navy, because he wanted to be off the train the moment it stopped. He felt weeks behind instead of days, those vile creatures far too many steps ahead. If he couldn't find them here, would he ever get another chance?

As the brakes let out their last squeal, he was standing by the exit, jumping down on the platform the moment the conductor opened the gate. He needed to get to police headquarters. They were apparently eager to help — everything arranged by the Foreign Office — but the sooner he got the girl's information out there, the better chance they had of finding her.

The city, at least, was well organized, and it was relatively easy to find his way. Everything led toward the Silver Palace, its beautiful turrets rising in the sky. Now this was a place designed around what mattered! If only Berill put its Crown first. Sometimes it felt like commerce owned the throne back home. And while business had clearly been a useful guiding force here in Amoriai, he couldn't help but wish they had a river of their own, a place to cross over and start anew. There just had to be enough loyalty, enough conviction, enough…*something* in the world to bring his people together again.

He reached the second ring road, following it to the northeast in search of the courthouse complex. He passed a pair of vacant lots — one of the only signs the marble city was barely a decade old — where he finally saw the river. But as he looked across the rushing water, he finally saw the east side of the city, the crowded buildings sprouting like a fungus. Those poor people. He thought of the factory slums back home, the people in squalor even as they worked themselves to death. But even worse, the east side of Amoriai supposedly still had Shapewalkers, doubly trapping the city's poor.

So, was the west side all just a facade? A pristine palace for the rich? He hoped not. He hoped such monuments could inspire men to find their inner angels. But there was only one way to find out. As he turned into the courthouse plaza, he stopped, taking a breath. There wasn't much he could do for the Amoriai, but he could seek justice, and if he rid this city of one more Shapewalker, hopefully the rest would follow.

After what felt like hours of checking himself in — showing his badge, singing his name again and again — Parimu finally found himself across from the captain of the Fida'lalean, Yad'mur Erlmak. He was a large man, sweating profusely despite the cool of the morning, and continuously wiping his face with a handkerchief. Above all, he seemed nervous — albeit eager to please. Erlmak reminded him of the ladder climbers back in the navy, the men who would say one thing to their superiors and another thing entirely to the men beneath them.

"You will, of course, have men," Erlmak said in his thick accent, pointing again to their patrol maps, "though it will take time."

Even with his description of the girl, the captain was convinced they'd have to search the entire city, casting as wide a net as possible. That was helpful, of course, but with so many men in the Fida'lalean, he'd hoped they could make quicker work of it. He was on his own in Berill, and the only one he knew who could sense Shapewalkers. Wouldn't it be easier to just search out the strange glow of the creatures instead of combing through each neighborhood?

"Captain," Parimu said, cutting the man off mid-sentence. He looked up at him with his beady eyes. "Wouldn't there be an easier way to root them out? Can't your men track the ripples of the creatures? These two must have continued their criminal activity now that they're in your kingdom."

The man blinked slowly before narrowing his eyes at him.

"Ripples?" Erlmak asked. "No, nothing like that, Detective. We have a clean office here, no one as impure as that. It wouldn't even be worth it. They're like *rats*, those things. Impossible to say how many there really are in the city these days. Anyone clean enough to join a guild and come west already did so. And in the east…well, it doesn't matter now; you can assume there's an enemy on every street. We track illegal activities, of course: fleecing, bootlegging, unlicensed production, things like that. That's usually enough to sniff out their disloyalty and hang them. The rest takes care of itself. In fact—"

It was Parimu's turn to narrow his eyes in confusion. He let the man drone on as his mind turned over what he had said. What did tracking Shapewalkers have to do with purity? He was the most loyal of all the officers back home, and he could still sense them. It was an ability, nothing more. They must not have recruited the same way Drekkles had. Perhaps they put loyalty first, which was admirable enough, but to not even be able to sense the ripples? The city really must be crawling with the things if they could let that much activity go…

He returned his attention to Erlmak as he realized the man had asked him a question. The patrol map had been turned toward him as well as the list of officer units. He shook his head, recalling the question. Which…patrol would he like to start with?

"I'll take whichever starts their shift the soonest," Parimu said. "And I was hoping you could have an officer take me by your armory. I'll be needing a sword — they thought I'd be less conspicuous on the train without one. But I'd like to begin as soon as possible. I've lost enough time as it is."

"Yes, of course," the captain said, rising from his desk. He obviously would like this to be over with, special relationship with Berill or no. That was fine by Parimu; he'd sooner have the monsters in nooses and be on his way as well. He stood, following the captain out of his office, eager to pick up a patrol and get started.

THE END OF PART TWO

PART THREE

17

They began with the land, making tools from the stones of the earth and tilling the soil. They conquered both forests and mountains, hunting the animals and trampling the flowers. These children of Vilodai were true to their namesake, shaping the very earth to their will. While Essomuai wept at the loss of her oldest companions, she saw still the beauty of the humans. In the place of the plains, they planted many new flowers, and as their wheat and corn grew, there were new seas of green to enjoy.

-Verses 47-52 of the Anushgiar Leyosil

—:—

Three Days Later

Erso walked into the back courtyard at Beysal's with Sumi close behind. Carrying a sack of flour over one shoulder, his other hand had a finger looped through a jug of ale. Beysal was going to start training Sumi tomorrow — Erso's lack of warning leaving him and Elo with meetings they couldn't get out of — but instead of sightseeing, Sumi, saint that she was, demanded they fill their days with helpful chores. They'd cleaned the house twice, weeded the garden, and even given Kel some Berillai lessons. But somehow, he was having the time of his life.

He looked over his shoulder at Sumi and grinned. Hopefully, she was enjoying herself as much as he was. He knew her well enough by now to know her constant smiling could be a defense, but she really did seem to be opening up. The family had dinner together every night, and she was even starting to make her own jokes — which received roars of laughter, of course, since they usually came at his expense. But he

100

couldn't blame her; making fun of Erso was his family's common language, and she was quickly getting fluent.

If there was anywhere on Wellonai that he could call home, it was here. A tiny part of him was still needling him to stay on the run, but he was successfully ignoring it for now. He had gotten good at that part of the dance, at least — ignore the fear, have all the fun you could, live another day. Your tears would be there waiting for you, so you might as well rollick while the sun was out.

To that end, today, he and Sumi were making pretzels. Having cleaned everything in sight, she'd asked for suggestions on what to cook for the family. And since he was home, how could he not make his mum's famous pretzels? He took no credit for the recipe, of course, but they were better than Beysal's, and they were an Amoriai delicacy besides. Even better, after how much Sumi had liked those pretzels in Berill, this might finally give him a chance of converting her away from all that mutton and squid...

Sumi hurried to open the door for him, unlocking it with the key Elo had given her. The kitchen was blessedly cool, the sun already well over the house, with a strong breeze coming from the water. A perfect day for boiling the house with baking. He set the flour and ale down on the counter and started rolling up his sleeves.

"So," he said hanging his hat by the door, "you ready to take on the legendary Milak'erat pretzels?"

He probably shouldn't call them that, actually, seeing as they came from his mother's side, but still...

"It's going to be far harder than any training you've done before, I'll have you know."

Sumi laughed. "You probably should have let me carry the flour, then. I wasn't exactly the baker in my family. You won't turn me out if I fail, will you?"

He took an apron from the coat rack and tossed it to her.

"As much as I'd like to," he said, "Beysal and Elo wouldn't have it. They already prefer you to me by far."

He put his own apron on and turned back toward the counter, just catching her smile. He tried to slip in whenever he could how much his family liked her. Even after days of them gushing about her, she still seemed to find it surprising. Even if she was the most pleasant person he'd ever met, she just couldn't seem to let go of seeing herself as a burden. He may not have a lifetime with her, but he'd have to break her of that, no matter how many subtle compliments it took.

"Alright," she said, coming up next to him at the counter as she rolled up her own sleeves. "Show me the way, oh wise one."

"I thought you'd never ask," he said, rubbing his hands together. "The first step is extremely important, so I want you to pay extra-close attention."

He reached into the cupboard, taking out a bowl for mixing and two small cups. He put the cups side by side, filling them both halfway with ale.

"Why two cups of ale?" she asked, raising an eyebrow at him. "Couldn't you just fill the one cup all the way and get the same measurement?"

"Patience," he said, raising a palm. "The student does not question the master." He took one of the cups, tossing back the ale in a single gulp. He nudged her to do the same, and she gave him a look before drinking hers too.

"You must always test the ale," he said, sighing with satisfaction. "Failure to do so could ruin the pretzels. Luckily for us, this ale is very good, which means we can begin."

She arched her eyebrows even further, past the point he thought eyebrows could go.

"You seem skeptical of the wise words of your teacher. Maybe you should be taking notes?"

She replied by throwing a towel at him.

They fell into the rhythm of the recipe, Sumi measuring the flour and yeast while he stoked the fire. There was still a decent enough flame from breakfast, so he got it roaring again in short order. He came back to find her holding the measuring cup in front of her face, carefully leveling off the flour on top. If he knew her at all — and he liked to think he was starting to — she was probably *actually* worried she'd be kicked out if the pretzels weren't good.

"Don't worry," he said, coming up beside her, "you can't break these pretzels." He pointed at the ale and the flour. "The magic's in here. I've made them without even measuring sometimes, and they were excellent, some of my best work."

Sumi combined all the ingredients — this time measuring the ale. "Is that everything?" she asked.

"Yep," Erso said, picking up the whisk. "Unless… You have a full day tomorrow, but do you want to add a little Shapewalking?"

"As…your whisk?" she asked, chuckling.

"It's never too late to learn."

Her smile faded, and she stared at the whisk, considering.

"Are you sure it's safe? Your family's been so kind to me, and my ripples. I just…"

"It's alright," Erso said, gently touching her shoulder. "You're doing great. And they don't investigate ripples here, not like in Berill. There's too many of us, and not enough fellerhurns with the police. Kel's still learning, and he hasn't been dragged in yet."

"Okay," she said, taking a deep breath, "I'll do it. But this isn't an excuse for locking me in a drawer so you can go to the pub, right?"

"I find that offensive," he said, handing her the whisk. "I don't think I've ever once been in a pub in my entire life."

She held the whisk in front of her, looking at it every which way. She even held it up toward the ceiling and looked at it from the bottom. Apparently satisfied, she put it on the counter and closed her eyes. Erso leaned back, folding his arms as he watched her, trying not to rush her in any way. Finally, she started to glow, and a moment later, she was on the floor as a whisk.

"Very nice!" he said, clapping as he stooped to pick her up. He shook her a bit — making sure there wasn't any dust on her — when a buzz shot into his hand. He felt a strong aura, almost like laughter with a distinctly *pink* color. He laughed. Incredible. She might struggle at first, but if you taught Sumi anything once, she'd quickly apply it to a hundred different situations. Maybe pretzels would have to be a regular part of his training regimen, even if his usual students didn't look quite so cute in aprons…

"You laugh now," he said to the whisk, dipping Sumi into the flour. He started whipping the ingredients together, spinning her quickly in the bowl, the clinking of the ceramic reminding him of childhood. He'd watched his mother make pretzels as a baby, and started helping her the moment he could reach the counter. It had been their own little ritual, something only the two of them had done. He sighed; if only he could make them with her now. Wherever she was in the halls of the dead, hopefully, she was proud he still remembered.

Just then, the front door flew open, and Beysal came stomping into the house.

"Well, well, well!" he roared. "Look what we have here!"

Erso jumped, not expecting him so soon, causing the Sumi whisk to fly from his hand. As she hit the ground, there was a huge flash of light, and Sumi reappeared, a dazed look in her eye and flour in her hair.

"I should have known," Beysal said, laughing. "Of course, you wouldn't be making pretzels yourself, you lazy oaf." He walked over to Sumi and offered her a hand, easily lifting her from the ground.

"How did I do?" she asked with a sheepish grin.

Erso looked into the bowl. The ingredients were mostly mixed — certainly well enough for his style.

"Exceptionally well, if you ask me," he said, laughing. "You're certainly ready for this old geezer to teach you tomorrow." He handed her a tea towel. "Just wipe the rest out of your hair, and we'll have you fully human again."

They all laughed as they started a three-person assembly line to twist the dough into pretzel shapes. Beysal poured more of the ale into proper glasses, and they all got to talking. His mother wasn't there, but her pretzels were, and he was surrounded by friends. Maybe Beysal was right — maybe there was something to this kind of life. If he had to put a color to the moment, he was sure it'd be pink.

18

The humans arrived in droves, each assigned to an elder according to their needs. The ten had learned every shape in Essomuai's heart, though they all excelled in different realms. Geomon knew strength, having spent many years studying to be a stone. Heyal loved to swim in the River Leyolcheom and had learned to be every kind of creature from its banks. Saldal loved watching things grow, so she had often taken to the grass, watching the circle of life unfold.

-Verses 120-124 of the Anushgiar Leyosil

Sumi woke early the next morning, the light filtering through the shutters in her room. She lay in bed, staring at the ceiling as she remembered yet another dream. It had been about flying again, though the details were already slipping away. Or had she been swimming? Suddenly, she heard a buzzing in her ears, like the vibration of a keyhole. She bolted upright, looking around. It seemed to be coming from outside, though she'd never felt one from far away before. She got up, opening the window, but there was nothing there. She closed her eyes, trying to follow it, but it was already fading, as if it were moving away from the water.

"Strange," she muttered, "must be half-asleep."

She shrugged, lying back down. She closed her eyes, listening to the sounds of the neighborhood outside. Compared to the quiet birdsong of the terrace, Amoriai never seemed to stop moving. But crowded in the brick buildings and surrounded by Shapewalkers, it sounded like *possibility.*

She stretched, climbing out of bed. The days started early in the house, and she wanted to help with breakfast. She'd never really left home, but she hoped she was being a decent houseguest. They all seemed to be getting along well, but she couldn't get complacent, especially if she blundered her training today...

As she was dressing by the armoire, she looked down, spotting Erso on the patio.

"Early for him," she said to herself, trying to see where the sun was at. It was so bright in Amoriai, it was hard to tell what hour it was, but if Erso was up, she must be later than she thought. She laced up her boots, flying down the stairs, but when she reached the kitchen, there was no one there, the fire not even lit. She went out on the patio, spotting Erso again as he went around the corner. She frowned, shutting the door behind her as she followed.

As she came onto the main road, Erso was already halfway up the next hill heading east, a cloud of pipe smoke trailing behind him. At least she could always follow the smell if she lost him.

"Erso!" she called, but he didn't turn around.

The hill climbed through an empty field, and the wind was blowing hard off the water. He probably couldn't hear her, but she didn't want to yell any louder, lest she wake the neighbors.

She hurried up the hill, her boots clicking on the stone. But when she reached the top, he was nowhere to be seen. To her left was a huge hedge, like a castle wall, the evergreens towering over the street as they ran toward the sea. Had he gone in there? She caught a whiff of his pipe and ran along the wall, finding a small iron gate built into the trees. Was it some kind of park?

She went through, closing the gate behind her when she stopped, staring. If it *was* a park, it was the strangest she had ever seen. There were thousands of tall obelisks made of wood, standing in random clusters as gravel paths wound through them. It looked almost like a forest, except the pillars had no leaves at the top, their wood stained a deep black color. They were about as high as the hedges, looking like each one had been carved directly from a tall tree.

She followed what looked like the main path, slipping between the rows of wood as she scanned the horizon for Erso. As she passed the first cluster, though, she noticed they were covered in small, round bumps. She leaned closer, gasping as she realized faces had been carved into each circle. They were incredibly lifelike, exactly like a person's head, only half the size.

She stood there, staring at the intricate carvings until another whiff of pipe smoke reached her nose, pulling her deeper into the park. She tried to follow the smell, winding along the path until she finally caught a glimpse of Erso's suit, his light jacket standing out against the dark wood. He was standing completely still, staring intently at one of the timbers in the middle of the field. She marched forward, almost reaching him, when his head snapped around, hearing her on the gravel. He looked tense, but then he recognized her, relaxing as he waved.

"What is this place?" she asked, joining him.

"Mu'na'sokar," he said, sweeping his arm around him at the thousands of obelisks, "the hall of the dead."

She looked around, seeing the place anew. The Berillai always scattered their ashes. She knew other kingdoms didn't, of course, but she'd never thought about what that meant — until now.

"So, this is a...*cemetery?*" she asked, remembering the word.

"More or less," Erso said, smiling. "Guess you lot don't have those, eh?"

She shook her head, suddenly feeling very foolish.

"These aren't exactly graves like in Relimora," he said, turning back to the obelisk. "More like memorials, though we do add a bit of ash and such to the pillars."

Sumi followed his eyes, tilting her head back as she ran her eyes along the carvings. There were dozens, with three or four on each row until it reached the top, where there was only one.

"Is this your family?"

"Yeah," Erso said, "or a couple hundred years' worth, anyway. When someone thinks they're important enough, they start their own tree."

He pointed to the single face crowning the top of the pillar.

"That there is my great-grandfather times a few. He was some kind of well-to-do cloth merchant, so he left his family's tree and started his own. That one there is the pillar he left behind."

He pointed to another not far away in the clump, which had even more faces on it.

"It's incredible," she said. She had Nela's picture, but hardly knew her family before that. And to think he could see them all together. "Do you come here often?"

Erso sighed. "Not as often as I should. Though I guess no amount of visits will take away the guilt of being the last one left."

She followed his eyes to the bottom row of the pillar, where there were only two faces.

"Your parents?" she asked quietly.

He nodded, giving her a sad smile. On the right was a beautiful woman, her eyes bright and her head covered in a waterfall of curls.

"She was gorgeous," Sumi said, barely above a whisper.

"I think the sculptor got her pretty close," he said, wiping a finger along the carving's cheek to clear away the dust. "They have expert carvers do these. Not many photographs back then, but I had an old playbill with a drawing of her. I don't think they quite got my pa, though."

She turned to the man on the left, realizing he had a mustache just like Erso's.

"Still pretty handsome," she said, smiling.

"The Milak'erats did alright, I suppose," he said, scratching the back of his head.

They were quiet for a while, looking at all the faces on the pillar.

"I'm so sorry, Erso," she finally said, forcing the words past the lump in her throat.

He turned to her again, his usual smile slipping back over his face, masking whatever he'd been feeling.

"It's alright," he said. "I think you and I have both had our fair share. But it's good to remember every now and then. Halls know I don't do it enough."

She nodded. Outside of Nela, it wasn't like her own parents came to mind very often. With the new regime, with so many things destroyed, at least he still had this place.

"How do they protect this place? If there are Shapewalkers buried here…"

"Unfortunately, the Amoriai only like to hurt the living," he said, turning to look at the forest of pillars around them. "Though I guess superstition doesn't hurt. The way we see it, Mu'lalat and Mu'na'sokar connect, like wings of a house, and I guess the bastards in the spider web don't think it's worth a haunting."

She imagined the hallway in her mind, connected to her pool, and she imagined traveling deeper, looking for the doors that hid the dead.

"Even humans," he continued, "who can't touch the halls themselves, believe our dreams are from that world. It's why in dreams, you can believe you're anything. *Do* anything."

He ran a finger along his mother's face again, as if there was already new dust collecting on it. But she looked perfect; all the carvings did.

She looked out at the sea of black columns, so dark they almost looked like they'd been burnt, like Su'selo'mae, the burned-out section of the city.

"Erso," she asked quietly, "what happened to your parents?"

He looked at her, his mouth opening before he shut it again. He seemed to be sizing her up, deciding whether he could slip away with a joke or if it was time to tell her. He took a deep breath.

"Things were messy after the coup," he finally said. "They call those years 'the Hardness,' and a lot of people died as the city changed. Anyone who could move away did, but the rest of us were trapped. Without work, some starved, others got sick. People lived on the streets, their houses burned by mobs. There was a lot of death that first year especially, and…my family isn't any different. Just two drops in a sea of death."

She reached out and touched his shoulder, instinctively knowing there was nothing she could say, nothing that could make his pain any smaller. Words would only trivialize what was in his heart. Still, he softened at her touch, making her glad she'd taken the risk. If only she could help him, help this city, even a little. But at least she could stand there with him. She could bear witness and refuse to look away. They stayed that way for a long time, silently looking at the carvings, her hand on his shoulder.

"Anyway," Erso finally said, turning from the pillar, "that's enough of the dead. Breakfast should be on. Why don't we get living, eh?

"Let's do that," she said, smiling.

As they walked away, he started joking as he always did. And somehow, she found herself laughing — *really* laughing. Life and death were so mixed up; you couldn't ever hope to keep them apart. All you could do was live, laughing when you could, and crying when you must.

19

She gave them everything they would ever need: fields of flowers, streams teeming with fish, and forests filled with trees. There was ample rain and the flow of seasons, all to give her children the fullness of life, the palette of color Essomuai treasured so.

-Verses 82-84 of the Anushgiar Leyosil

—:—

Thirteen Years Ago

Parimu worked his way down the street in Berill, keeping a careful eye on the buildings he passed — while trying to avoid being run over by the throng of people. He still wore his uniform. It was the only presentable thing he owned besides his suit, and, if he was honest, he wanted to save that for his wedding day. At least his officer's coat earned him a bit of respect in the traffic, though his head was still swimming. After being on a ship of only a hundred men for so many years, it was overwhelming to have so much…*everything* surrounding him. Still, he kept moving. He had been to two addresses already with no sign of Jalicyne, and he wouldn't rest until he found her.

He'd rushed back to Emillon, feeling like he might burst after holding in his love for ten years. But when he'd arrived at the village, she wasn't there. He'd gone straight to her house, not even stopping at his own. Jalicyne's mother, clearly confused, had told him she'd been gone a year already, moving to the city for a factory job. Even worse, her mother hadn't approved, and they didn't write anymore, though she at least gave him her address. But why hadn't his mother told him? What if he'd been able to get out early, to find her before she'd left?

He'd taken the first train back to Berill, but when he arrived at her address, it seemed she didn't live there anymore. He'd talked with two gruff landlords already, and both of them had sent him on to another place. According to the first man, she'd moved out because the rent was too high. The second place had been subsidized by her factory, but the business had folded, forcing her to move on. He was starting to worry. The second place wasn't a hovel by any means, but it was hardly a home. And this third address… The further east he walked, the worse it got, the stench of crowded squalor filling the air.

He almost missed the third apartment, the numbers barely legible on the wall of a broken-down tenement. There were three buildings in all, crowded together in a knot, though it was a wonder they could stand at all. Someone showed him to the landlady's door — little more than a plank of wood — and he knocked.

"What d'ya want?" someone shouted from inside. The door opened just a crack, revealing a woman bent over with age, her beady eyes narrowed.

"Oh," she said. "Apologies…sir."

She opened the door wider. It was lucky he'd worn the uniform after all.

"Excuse me for bothering you, madam," he said, nodding in respect. "I'm looking for a woman, and I was told she lived at this address. Her name is Jalicyne Ulterinne. Does she still live here?"

The old woman blinked, furrowing her brow. "The tall beanpole girl? Stringy hair?"

He wouldn't have put it that way, certainly, but that had to be her. She was noticeably taller than any other woman back home, and she did have beautifully long hair. He nodded eagerly. "Yes, that's her," he said, "is she in?"

The woman sniffed. "I should say not." She eyed the insignia on his uniform pocket. "Hope she didn't owe somebody money or nothin'. Died months ago, middle of Ewannin, I think."

He recoiled, shaking his head as his stomach clenched. "D-died?" he stammered. "You must be mistaken." He reached out unconsciously, grabbing the door frame for support.

She raised an eyebrow at him. "No, I'm sure," she said. "I was here when they carried her out. Whatever factory she was at sent somebody to look for her. Sleeping sickness was bad then, they thought that was what done it." She held up a finger. "Wait here. They gave me her papers; didn't know where else to send them."

He stood there, mouth hanging open as the woman disappeared into her house without waiting for his reply. This had to be some kind of mix-up. He had been on a goose chase the whole morning in this absurd city.

There could be thousands of tall women in a place this size. Besides, Jalicyne had never had so much as a cold growing up; there was no way she could have been pulled down so easily.

The woman came back a moment later, handing him a stack of papers tied with string. They were forms, work writs and bank letters. It took him only a second to find the name at the top of the first page. *Jalicyne Ulterinne*. His hands clenched the stack, feeling like he'd been kicked in the chest. He kept his feet under him somehow, barely managing to form his next sentence.

"Did they…say…where they were taking her…body?" he forced out, finally tearing his eyes away from that name, a name he should have never found on those awful pages in this awful place.

"Pauper's Gardens, if I had to guess," she said. "That's where they take all the factory girls. Scatter the ashes and whatnot." She narrowed her eyes at him again. "Look, I barely knew the girl. If she owed you money, that's none of my business."

"No, no," Parimu said, already turning away, "nothing like that. Thank you for your time."

He was already down the steps as the door closed behind him, the woman muttering something inaudible. His mind was racing. Her ashes scattered? How in Velloni's name would he ever find her? What would he write to her mother?

He made it to the curb just as the strength left his legs. He dropped down on the spot, burying his face in his hands. For once, he didn't care how he looked, crying there in his uniform.

She had been gone this whole time, all alone, tossed to the wind without him there to mourn her. And he'd been living his useless little life, pining for the day he'd see her again. What if he *had* come home earlier? What if he'd been there to nurse her back to health, gotten her out of that factory? Did any part of her know how much he loved her? Did any part of her call to him at the end? The traffic continued flowing by, no one seeming to notice him as grief buried him inch by inch.

———

Two days later, Parimu stepped out of a post office, everything that needed doing finally done. His eyes ached from the lack of sleep, but what else did he have to hold on to? He'd failed Jalicyne while she was alive, but he wouldn't fail her now.

He'd gone to Pauper's Gardens first, finding the giant field on the outskirts of the city. There was a royal crematorium there, its chimney reaching high into the sky. He'd arrived in the late afternoon, the sky turning gold as a thin line of smoke lifted from the chimney. He'd brought a dozen roses, though the workers seemed puzzled when he asked if he could pay his respects. He still wore his uniform, though, which helped. They eventually let him wander into the field, though they warned him there was no way to know where she'd been scattered, the men shifting the spot every few days so the ash didn't pile up.

He wandered to the center of the field, hoping that would put him close. The place had been cleared from the forest at the foot of the mountains, and pines loomed overhead. Birds sang from the trees, but otherwise, it was silent, just him and the wind blowing through the waist-high grass. It was knocked down in places where the workers had cut paths, but with all that ash, everything was lush and full of flowers.

When he felt like he was somewhere near the middle, he knelt down and prayed for her, asking the gods to look out for her and begging Ciersein to keep her safe. Then he talked to her directly, rambling about everything and nothing — memories from childhood, of how much he loved her. When he had no words left, he'd put the flowers in the grass, walking back to the city.

The next day had gone by in a blur. He rented a room, realizing he couldn't face going back to Emillon. Then he'd spent the rest of the night writing the letters he just dropped off. The first was to his mother, but written in a way that it could be shared with Jalicyne's family. He spared them the details of how she died, how alone she'd been, but he told them about the flowers he'd left for her, leaving out the awful emptiness of Pauper's Gardens.

The second letter he wrote was addressed to Detective Drekkles. After Jalicyne, there hadn't been a single doubt left in his mind. There was nowhere for him to go back to now, nothing to keep him from working with the police. Besides, now, he knew exactly what he was fighting for: the very soul of this kingdom. They had been too quick to spring forward, desperate for commerce at the expense of human life. And the anonymity those creatures used was the same that left his love to die, her landlady not even remembering her name.

Nothing could bring her back, and there was nothing that could make him whole again, but he didn't need to be whole to fight for justice. He turned from the post office, facing the street where people hurried by, too lost in the rat race to realize what they left behind. But there would be time to save them, time to give them a kingdom worth having. It was only a beginning, but it was something worth fighting for.

20

She kept the ten eldest in Anushai, singing the songs of wisdom as a beacon of hope. "Teach them of my love," she urged the ones who left. They did as their Mother asked, living amongst the humans. And they did find joy there, learning to love them as their Mother did. They spread Essomuai's blood through all the kingdoms, marrying and having children, creating new generations to continue their Mother's work.

-Verses 85-88 of the Anushgiar Leyosil

—:—

After the largest breakfast of her life, the family split up, Sumi going with Beysal to train, while Erso and E'loseir took Kel out on guild business. She followed Beysal from the neighborhood, unsure of why they were training outside — and too afraid to ask. She caught his eye, but he only smiled, marching forward with his huge legs and leaving her to scurry after. When they reached the river, he finally stopped, leaning against the railing as he looked down at the water.

He patted the railing, so she joined him, watching the river go by. It seemed like an awful hurry just to stare at the water — not that she was complaining. It was beautiful.

"What kind of kid were you, Sumi?" he finally asked.

She looked at him, but he kept his eyes on the river.

"Quiet, I guess," she said slowly, thinking back to how afraid she'd been when her parents died, always on her best behavior.

"I mean on the inside," he asked, looking over at her. He tapped the side of his head. "In here."

That question was easier, at least. Even as an adult, she hadn't changed — her mind constantly racing, worrying about too many things.

"Nervous," she said. "I was an orphan, so I think I was afraid I'd be thrown out if I wasn't good."

"I was an angry kid," he said, turning to face the street. "Might not surprise you, big brute that I am. But my pa — a woodworker like me — was a drinker, and he'd get rough with me and my mum. Taught me how to fight, I guess, in a roundabout way. Never set him straight, but I fought plenty of other kids around the neighborhood."

Sumi eyed his tree-sized arms. She certainly wouldn't fight Beysal, but he was so gentle now, a totally different person. *Something* had changed for him. Shapewalking wasn't just about changing your outside, after all. She'd at least learned that much back home.

"Thing is," he continued, motioning at the crowds, "there's a lot in life you can't solve by fighting. This city is proof enough of that. I worked in the guild 'til I couldn't take it anymore, and that's when Sa'le'rein — Erso's mum — found me and set me up at her theater, building sets."

He shook his head, grinning at unseen memories.

"Those were the days. If you think Erso has a spark, you should have seen his mum. She knew everybody, too, kind of person who'd fix your problems before you even told her."

Sumi thought of the beautiful woman from the cemetery. If only she could have met her too.

"She was like the sister I never had — brought me over for dinner, tried to set me up with her friends, things like that. Ended up becoming real good friends with Erso's pa, Mishkal too. Anyway, she got me into acting. 'Be a tree, Beysal,' she'd say. 'Try a flower. Come on, Beysal, come on.'"

He laughed, scratching the back of his head.

"Thing is, my ma never taught me too well, and I had a lot of trouble holding my forms. I think I was *too* angry, holding on to too much, you know?"

She nodded, thinking back on all the times she'd failed to transform, struggling to find a happy memory.

"She broke my block, doing exactly what we're doing now: walking around the city, talking. Helped get the waters calm in my pool, you know? I had to learn to see myself through all that noise. She taught me about Essomuai too. Even if she couldn't speak much Anushai, she loved philosophy, picked it up while she was working there. Erso tells me you have family there, so we can mix that in too. But I wanna show you something first before we practice. Come on."

They followed the river south, though they thankfully stayed on the east side of the city. He told her random stories, pointing at the buildings they passed and what had happened in them.

"I know it's a lot of talking," he said, "but for whatever reason, it works. Shapewalking isn't something you do, it's something you *understand.* And one day, maybe even today, you'll just get it, and *poof,* you're free. Even if that's only the start of a lifetime of change."

They passed another bridge, this one carved with tiny diamond shapes. It also had statues on its columns, though these were topped like large bears. They looked like the grizzlies they had in Mesop, only with thick plates of bone sticking out from their backs, and claws shaped like shovels.

"What are those?" she asked, unsure if any topic could count as training.

"Granite bears," he said, chuckling, "distant relative of mine. I heard the Berillai hunted 'em clean out of the west — not that I blame 'em. They're territorial buggers, that's for sure. Wouldn't mind seeing one of their dens, though; heard they collect those blue stones you lot like so much."

"Speaking stones?" she asked. "They're beautiful. We have them at the library."

She tried to imagine a bear sneaking in to steal the stones. She'd already seen so many new things since leaving home. It was like stepping into Pallinayum's book, only nothing on the Continent was how she'd imagined it.

"You know," Beysal said, "the one time I visited Anushai, everybody kept calling me one of those things. I'm big, I guess — even for Amoriai — and they all kept yelling *'hagelnyeong'* and slapping my belly. It was the darnedest thing."

Sumi giggled. She certainly couldn't picture Nela smacking a stranger's belly. Although she had been one of a kind. Maybe she'd been reserved even for her own country.

At the next bridge, this one carved with arnisoles, they turned left, stopping just short of the market. They were directly east of the palace now, and it felt like the whole city was passing by, with workers streaming east and west. Although, the people from the palace side looked more well-to-do, no doubt making it into the new guilds, and there were plenty of police officers coming east with them. There was a chorus of noise too — drivers calling to their horses, snippets of conversation, shouting market vendors. Beysal pulled her to the side, where they leaned against a brick wall in the shade. It was like being on a riverbank, sitting just outside a surging river of humanity.

"So," Beysal said after a moment, "your first lesson, courtesy of Sa'le'rein. You're gonna learn to still your pool."

"Still my pool," Sumi mouthed. "In Mu'lalat, right?"

"That's the one. Still your pool and still your mind. It's about taking the thoughts that hold you back and letting them go."

He made a fist and slowly opened his fingers, just like Erso liked to do when they were training.

"For me, that was anger. But for you, it might be worry. Sometimes, you might even be in danger, but you still need to let it go."

She thought of running from the detective again, the night she turned into a hawk.

"That would be good," she said. "But how do you ignore danger?"

"It's not ignoring, exactly," Beysal said. "It's more like shifting your focus. All of you is inside Mu'lalat, but you still get to choose where you look."

He took his hands, pulling them apart until they were separated by about a foot. "Our pools are deep, full of good and bad, and they're both there all the time. You don't have to get rid of the bad to change; you just use the part of your pool that makes you *you*. Even if you're using a memory, the good times don't take away the bad, right? But they make it all worth it. And someday, you'll even learn to use the bad, recognize it as a part of you too. If you can do that, you'll run the halls no problem."

She narrowed her eyes, thinking, but Beysal only laughed, patting her on the shoulder.

"Enough of my blabbing, eh? Let's start."

He held up his hands in a triangle shape with a gap in the center.

"Make your hands like this, then pick something on the street and look through."

The first thing she saw was a streetlamp, and she held up her hands, closing one eye so she could focus on it.

"What do you see?" he asked.

"A streetlamp."

"But the rest of the city's still there, right? You *know* it's there. It isn't like you forgot; you just decided to focus on one part of it."

"Makes sense," she said. "But how do you do that in your head?"

"Well, you can sit somewhere quiet — people in Anushai do it all the time, sitting in the parks, just breathing. But since I'm a big brute who can't sit quietly, Sa'le'rein brought me here, where it's more obvious. Eventually we'll use your thoughts, but we can start by ignoring *things.*"

Now that he mentioned it, Nela used to sit in the garden like that. She and Grandpa would always watch her, wondering what an old woman was doing sitting in the grass.

"My Nela used to do that," she said, "but I thought she was just avoiding my grandpa."

"It's good for that too," Beysal said, chuckling. "Actually, speaking of your Nela, this might be a good time for some Essomuai. She's the goddess who's in everything, right? Well, they mean *everything*: plants, animals, even cockroaches. So, keep that in mind. Even the bad parts of your life; she wants it all."

She nodded. Maybe that's what was keeping her from transforming back into herself. Even if her heart was full of hidden things, Essomuai would know them all.

"Embracing the scary parts of a thing can also help you take its shape," Beysal continued. "Let's say you're a mouse. You'd know what it feels like to be chased by a hawk; you'd have the instincts for it. So, when you want to be a mouse, you don't ignore that, you tap into it. But just like you, a mouse isn't just its fears; it's many things."

Just then, he laughed, pointing at a rat who was scurrying across the street with a piece of bread in its mouth. "See? If they thought about hawks all the time, they'd never have any fun."

He let out a deep breath, shaking his head. "Sorry. Let's do another exercise before I confuse myself with all the gabbing."

He had her close her eyes, standing there on the street. At first, the blackness felt wrong, like anything — especially the police officers — could attack her at any time. She felt her eyes darting behind their lids, her ears latching on to every sound as she tried to keep tabs on her surroundings.

"Now," he said, as if shutting her eyes wasn't hard enough, "I want you to think about something that bothers you. A memory, a fear, anything. Just focus on it."

Without trying, she pictured herself back home, standing in the kitchen. No one was there, not even Amis. She was completely and utterly alone.

"How do you feel?" Beysal asked after a moment.

"Alone," she said. "And afraid."

"Good," he said. "Now, picture your cave and look at the pool. Imagine your fear, pretending it's a leaf. I want you to picture yourself putting that leaf in the pool. Just let it drift down. Essomuai is in the pool, and she's taking it, absorbing it."

She did so. She took the image in her mind of the empty house, and watched herself fold it up until it was a leaf. She placed it in the water, watching it sink down into the darkness. She stayed in the cave, watching until the ripples in the water smoothed, the calm finally entering her mind.

"Fear is only a tiny part of your experience," Beysal said. "It doesn't define you. There's a difference between feeling alone and believing you deserve it. Just like me — feeling angry with my pa didn't mean I had to be an angry person. Take a deep breath."

She did so as he joined her, motioning with his hand as they sucked in the air, holding it for a heartbeat until they sighed it out again. As she breathed, she somehow felt lighter, and she realized he was right. Even at her loneliest, she had Nela inside her. She wasn't cursed or unworthy. She was the same Sumi, even with everything she'd lost. And she'd found new things, too: her powers, Essomuai, Erso. She would be okay.

"Well done," Beysal finally said, smiling. "You survived your first lesson."

"How do you know I did a good job of it?" she asked.

"I've been doing this a long time," he said, chuckling, "but not everyone's willing to take that first step. So, I know you didn't run away; that's a start. Besides, I watched your face, and it looked like you really found something. Ready for your next lesson?"

She nodded, closing her eyes again.

"Wow," Beysal said, "you really are a good student. Couldn't get Erso to close his bloody eyes on the first try."

She laughed but kept her eyes closed. Those two men, never missing a chance to rib each other, even if it was bursting with affection.

"This time, we're gonna practice looking past what's in your mind. Ignore the street, ignore your thoughts, just listen to your breath. In...and out..."

She took another deep breath and really tried to listen. She was vaguely aware of the bustle still, the shouting and the horses, but when she truly focused on her breath, the street just...faded away. But how had she ignored breathing her whole life? Wouldn't you notice if a storm passed through your body every second?"

"Good," Beysal said, "keep it steady. You can even count 'em if you want, or just mark them in and out."

She did the latter, losing track of everything else as she muttered *in and out* under her breath. She wasn't sure how much time had passed, but eventually, he tapped her on the shoulder.

"Another job well done," he said. "That one should come in handy. I like to think of these exercises as long- and short-term. Putting worries in the pool is for the big things, the hurts that take years to heal. But this can help you in the here and now to look past the things in front of you.

Sometimes that's all it takes to shape, to push out the thing that's holding you back."

"Thank you," she said.

"Don't thank me yet," he said with a grin. "While we walk to the next place, I'm gonna make you share some memories, things we can use."

They continued on, winding through the city as they found a sort of rhythm. They would move to a different corner, finding an area humming with activity. And while they walked, he pried a bit more out of her each time: memories from childhood, things that stuck with her. He told his own stories too, helping her to open up. And each time they stopped, they'd lean against a wall, recalling the things they'd just discussed as she gave them to Essomuai.

Some of the memories were harder to let go of than others. Before the third stop, he asked her about Nela, her mind clinging to the freshness of the pain. She stood by the pool for a long time, unwilling to let go of the leaf. But then she thought of what Erso said, about the spirits living in the halls. She pictured Nela with her there, taking the leaf from her hand as she hugged her. Then she watched as Nela drifted to the halls, a smile on her face. That's what Beysal meant about anger, right? Letting go of sadness wouldn't make her love her Nela any less. You learned to put down the pain, but the love was still there, waiting behind it, ready to fill your heart again.

And after each memory, they'd use the street itself, shifting her focus not just to her breath, but to all of her senses. When they got to sound, he even had her *listen* to the crowds instead of ignoring them. According to Beysal, it wasn't just about what you heard, but the sensation of hearing itself. Still, it was hard in practice, her mind wanting to process every snippet passing by.

"Just let it wash over you," Beysal said. "Notice it, but then let it go. Don't focus on your own understanding, but the sounds themselves, watching them come into your mind and float away."

At one point, when he asked her to feel her own feet, the lesson finally clicked. Your feet were always there, but she finally watched herself pay attention to them, the sensation filling her mind. Of course, you'd notice your feet if you stepped on something sharp. Just like a worrying thought: it poked at you, forcing you to look at it. But if she could put her mind into her feet, then she could put it anywhere, even past her fears.

Finally, as they passed the sixth bridge — this one covered in blue jays — they pulled into a quiet street near a park. The buildings were shorter there, filled with shops with handprinted signs and brightly colored awnings. A gentle wind blew through the park, cooling them after their walk in the sun. He had her close her eyes, telling her to focus on her breathing again. After a few minutes, though, he spoke again, telling her to see what she could smell. She inhaled sharply through her nose, smelling…bread.

She cracked one eye open, laughing as she found a sandwich in front of her face. It was wrapped in wax paper, with just the end exposed where he held it under her nose. He had a matching one in his other hand, a mountain of ham between thick slices of golden Amoriai bread.

"Where did you get these?" she asked, taking one.

He was already chewing, but he pointed at a shop across the street, its windows open to the breeze. *Ka'bayas* the sign read, with a picture of a sandwich underneath.

"Best meat in the city," he said. "How about a lunch break in the park?"

"Sure," she said, "I'm starving. It's surprising how much thinking takes it out of you."

"What's my excuse then?" Beysal asked, smacking his belly with a laugh. "I just stood there."

The park sat on a triangle between two streets, where it was fenced in and filled with flowers. But the gates were open, so they went in, sitting on a bench. There were two old women kneeling in the grass, doing battle with the weeds between the flowers.

"Poor lot, them," Beysal said in a low voice, pointing with his chin. "The old palace used to pay to keep the gardens, but the Growers Guild moved west. So now the old palace workers do the work, tough old birds."

"How do you know they're from the palace?"

Beysal had just taken a bite of his sandwich, but he ran a finger along the front of his shirt, which she took to mean their clothing. She looked again, noticing their long green tunics, the cloth covered in a diamond pattern. Beysal finally swallowed, taking down more sandwich than she could have eaten in five bites.

"New king lets 'em stick around — on a shoestring budget, mind you. Unfortunately, Elo doesn't have much sway here, or I'd find some blokes to do the work."

"What neighborhood is this?" she asked, running her eyes over all the beautifully painted shops. At least something on the east side was maintained…

"Tu'kilat," Beysal said, "means Tailor Street." He pointed down the way. "Bunch of tailors and cloth merchants over there. They're in with the 'good' folk over the river, but they couldn't move the cloth mills, so here we are, hoity-toity folk east of the Ko'lesta."

Sumi scanned the crowds; the people *did* seem to be well-to-do, with more suits and fewer shirtsleeves. It didn't seem fair, but she suddenly found it funny, Erso rubbing off on her.

"At least Erso doesn't need a tailor," she said. "He gets fancy on his own."

Beysal laughed, shaking his head. "He certainly doesn't need any help with that, does he?" He sighed, finishing his sandwich. "Now that we've lunched, you ready for the real lesson?"

She gulped. "This wasn't the real lesson?"

"First half," he said, waving a hand. "Important, yeah, but you can do this anytime. Now you need to shape, and more than one at a time."

Her eyes widened. Would she have to shape like he had that first night?

"Easy, girl," he said, patting her on the shoulder. "Don't wanna lose your eyes now. You don't have to do the big dance yet; we're just gonna get you fluid."

"Okay," she said, nodding, "I trust you."

"Good," he said, raising a finger. She waited as he ran back to the sandwich shop, returning with two more. He went over to the gardeners, handing them to the women.

"Alright, missy," Beysal said, offering his hand as he helped her off the bench. The gardeners smiled as they left, sitting on the grass with sandwiches in hand. If she would learn from anybody, it'd be from someone like Beysal, someone kind. And maybe there was a lesson in that too. It couldn't solve all her problems, but like a shift in focus, sometimes life was nothing more than a sandwich and a smile.

21

Itorunai surged with power as she flew over her mother, shaping all the creatures of the world. And while they had her breath, they had the soil too, and Essomuai with it. The goddess ran among them, delighting in their variety. As Itorunai's power spread, stretching into sea and sky, Essomuai went with her, feeling the waves on the fish and the wind beneath the birds.

-Verses 18-21 of the Anushgiar Leyosil

—:—

Beysal and Sumi walked north from the park, moving at a leisurely pace. Instead of training more, they just chatted — while trying to walk off the boat-sized sandwiches, of course. They walked until they almost reached the water, where they stopped beside a stretch of row houses. It was another interesting neighborhood. While the houses had been built the same — tile shingles for the salt air and squat brick walls — each one had a *personality* — doors painted different colors, gardens bursting with flowers, no two alike.

"I brought Erso here once," Beysal said, leaning against a garden fence. "His parents trained him pretty good, but he still had a few kinks to work out when I took over. I'd never taught anybody before, though, so it was mostly babbling — not unlike what I put you through today."

Sumi smiled. She loved the way he taught, but she didn't interrupt.

"Anyway," he continued, "he was having trouble holding more than one shape, but when we turned down this street, it all clicked."

He nodded toward the houses, pointing at three of the closest doors. The one on the left was a dark blue, a round glass panel in the middle. The middle was soft pink, no doubt to match the roses in the garden. And the third was a dark green, its wooden panels framed with iron.

"In Mu'lalat," Beysal said, "you can open any door, but how's that supposed to help a kid? The hard part is starting small, taking just a few to show you all the rest."

Sumi nodded slowly. It was sort of like her memories again. You had a lifetime of moments, but you started Shapewalking by using the most powerful ones, narrowing down the infinite possibilities. She could have been anything in Berill, but an umbrella or a coin — even a cat — had made more sense.

"Don't worry," Beysal said, chuckling, "I'm not done rambling yet. What I realized is that starting with similar things is the key. These doors are *almost* the same, but they're still different. Helped Erso not rip the doorknobs off in Mu'lalat — if you get my meaning."

"Uh…sure," she said, laughing.

"I'll work on more Berillai sheep metaphors later. For now, just close your eyes and think about those doors."

She did so, holding them in her mind.

"What color were they?" he asked.

"Blue, pink, and green."

"Exactly. And what shape?"

They were all the same…right? They had different trimmings, but they were all a half-oval shape. Was it a trick question?

"They're all the same," she finally said.

"Right again. What about the roofs?"

"All the same," she said.

"Mm-hmm. Now, give me the colors in reverse."

"Green, pink, blue," she said.

"Alright, open your eyes."

She raised an eyebrow at him. She wasn't going to have to be a door, was she?

"When you're changing quickly, you have to stop treating yourself and the thing you want to become like two different things. Everything you want to be is a version of you, just with different colors on the doors. Essomuai already knows all things, right? So, between you and something else, there isn't that much difference. When you run the halls, you just open the door, and *boom,* you're something new. And if you start with similar things, something next door, it's that much easier."

"I think I get it," she said slowly.

She kept thinking of *Sumi* as something she had to go back to, but the way Beysal put it, she could just keep *running.* Every door was in the hallway, and none of them were locked. Take this street. If she walked from door to door, she'd still be herself, just walking through a different door. And when she was done, all she had to do was walk back out.

"I want to practice," she finally said. "Before I think so much it doesn't make sense anymore."

Beysal's face split into a wide grin. "I knew you were smart. Took Erso the whole walk home to get it — called me a batty old man too. Let's go. I think you're ready for the final lesson."

They quickly covered the handful of blocks back to the house, coming through the alley and into the courtyard. Beysal pulled a well-worn piece of paper from his pocket, placing it on the patio wall. It had three butterflies drawn on it, each done in the same rudimentary way: a 3 on each side of an oval-shaped body. One had stripes on its wings, another had dots, and the third had little spirals.

"Did you draw these?" she asked.

"Unfortunately, yes," Beysal said, shaking his head. "I know it looks like Kel's work, but I'm not that kind of artist. Still, hasn't failed me yet. Just like those doors I showed you, these three are similar but different — and you're gonna use 'em to get your shapes."

She picked up the paper at his urging, studying the three butterflies.

"Imagine each in turn. In your halls, your cave, doesn't matter. Picture them flying together, and remember, they're real, so give 'em some personality. Even if you make them up, they're real to you, and that means they're real to Essomuai."

She nodded, taking a deep breath as she closed her eyes. She started at her pool, imagining herself walking down the halls of Mu'lalat. She tried to feel the *realness* of it: the cool damp, the gentle breeze from an unseen sea. And as she walked, she found doors on her left, the same ones from the row houses, built into the smooth stone of the cave. Those doors had always been there, of course, just as they'd never been there either. It felt real. Or...it *was* real.

She went up to the first door — the midnight blue one — where a soft light glowed from within. She knocked before laughing, wondering why she would knock on a butterfly's door. She pushed it open, finding another pool. Cut into the stone floor, it was almost identical to hers, save for a skylight placed above it, a hazy light filtering down. She found the butterfly floating there, its wings the same color as the door with the white dots from Beysal's drawing. She beckoned to it, and it followed her to the hallway.

She did the same at the next two doors, returning to her own pool with all three butterflies in tow. As she reached the water, they went across from her, dancing in the air like leaves in the wind. They swirled together, a cyclone of impossible colors.

"I'm ready," she whispered to Beysal, keeping her eyes closed. "What now?"

"Just keep 'em flying," he said, his voice quiet but full of excitement. He almost sounded far away. "Remember they're real, so fly *with* them. Don't miss a beat."

Essomuai, she thought, *let me dance with them.*

She watched the butterflies, the pink one catching her eye. She watched it climb and fall, studying its movements, not worried about anything but the rhythm of its dance. *Flap, flap, flap.* How good it would feel to have wings like that! She'd had wings before, hadn't she? *Flap, flap, flap.* Essomuai knew those wings, *remembered* all those wings. All she had to do was walk through the door. *Flap, flap, flap.* She began to nod her head, circling to the rhythm of the butterfly. She felt a lightness in her chest, and when she opened her eyes, the courtyard seemed *bigger,* magnified through bug eyes as she floated in the air.

She kept the same rhythm for a moment, her wings still attuned to the butterfly in the cave. It felt…natural, even though she'd never held this shape before. She had truly let go. There was no shock, no surprise, only a rightness to being in this form. She flapped harder, spinning in an arc as she rose through the air.

"That's it!" Beysal called from below. "Now the next, right through the next door!"

She pictured the cave again, but now she was floating with the others. She saw the shape of Sumi on the other end, watching with her legs pulled up beneath her, transfixed by their dancing through the air. She saw the blue butterfly in front of her and flew after it, taking on its pattern. She could be that butterfly too, just as she had always been. The lightness returned, lifting from under her wings, and when she looked again, she was blue.

"Again! Again!" Beysal yelled. "Don't quit now!"

She did it again, and not a moment later, she was spinning through the air with green wings. Beysal laughed, clapping as she danced with joy, cartwheeling through the air. She did it! All three, just like that! She looked down, finally noticing the potted flowers in the courtyard, their buds flashing at her like gemstones. If she could fly like a butterfly, then she could celebrate like one too.

She dropped down on a long stalk of foxglove, using her tiny legs for the first time as she scrambled to the nectar. Or had she used these legs before? A memory that wasn't hers flashed into her mind, of being a caterpillar, staring at the sky as she built her own cocoon. She remembered the taste of leaves, her *excitement* for the change to come.

Where did that come from?

But there was no time for thinking. There was only the flower, her snout unfurling as she drank the nectar. It was incredible, the sweetest thing she'd ever tasted. She could drink forever, she could—

"Alright, don't get drunk now," Beysal said, chuckling as he gently shook the flower. Or what he thought was a gentle shake, anyway. It felt like an earthquake to her, the tiny clamps on her legs digging into the stalk. She glanced longingly at the nectar, but he was right. She had to go back — had to prove she *could* go back.

She shot into the air, pushing through her fear. She could do this. She wouldn't let Beysal down. She had just done three shapes; she could do anything!

Essomuai, she thought, *thank you.*

Suddenly, she felt calm, her worries disappearing. Like Beysal had taught her, those fears were still *somewhere,* but they were deeper in her pool now, and all she needed was an inch, enough to feel her joy again.

She went back to the cave, finding herself still sitting there. She swirled in the air, and her human form danced with her, her dress rippling as she spun. She was a butterfly *and* she was herself, her spirit in the pool, a shape that could take on any other. She danced like she had as a girl, doing pirouettes to Nela's phonograph. And then, without needing to try, a glow filled her eyes, and she was human again. She was still spinning, but she could feel her legs, and she finally stopped, opening her eyes to find Beysal.

"A dance to go with it, no less!" he said, clapping for her.

She laughed, shaking her head.

"I can't believe it," she said. "Thank you. Thank you so much."

She ran up and hugged him, his chuckles shaking her as they spilled out from his barrel-shaped chest.

"My pleasure," he said, smiling. "Besides, I should be thanking you. You learned faster than Erso, and that's something I can use against him for the rest of my life."

He sat on the ledge, patting the spot beside him. The brick was warm from being in the sun, and it felt good to sit. She was suddenly very tired, like she had run for miles.

"The moment I saw you, I knew you'd get it," Beysal said. He tapped the side of his head. "Still waters run deep, you know?"

"I wish I'd been so sure myself!" she said.

He pulled out his pipe started packing it.

"Well, if you had, you wouldn't be needing me, now would you? This magic isn't just for changing things; it's about how you see the world. And like I said this morning, you can see it in an instant, but there's always more work to do. Accepting yourself — *freeing* yourself. It takes a lifetime. But now you know, and someday, maybe you'll teach someone else."

"I hope so," she said. "And I hope I keep learning too. I want my whole life to feel like that."

"It will," he said, smiling at her over his pipe. He took his free hand, gesturing at his hulking frame. "Just look at me. I went from a big, angry bear to having a family fit for a king. Just keep letting go, and you'll find your way."

Just then, the clock tower by the market let out six long tolls. Sumi looked up, realizing for the first time how low the sun had gotten. Even Beysal looked surprised.

"Wow," he said, standing, "I better go. Promised Erso I'd meet him on the west side — guild business."

He opened his arms, giving her another hug. "Thank you for training with me," he said. "You were great. Go on and celebrate with Elo, and when I'm back, we'll all sing your praises."

"Alright," she said, smiling. "And thank you again, for everything. Keep Erso out of trouble, will you?"

"Always," he said with a wink before he took off down the alley, a cloud of smoke trailing behind him.

Sumi smiled, tilting her face up to the golden glow of the sky one last time. This was what freedom felt like. Her fears were still there, but she felt like she could see beyond them now, where the rest of her was full of hope. She finally stood and crossed the garden, heading into the kitchen to find E'loseir.

22

Elomikarus sailed across the Erril Sea, hunting for the Shapewalkers. Essomuai felt the pain of those who ran from his wrath, ordering her children to protect them. And so they joined as one, meeting on the shore to turn his armies back. They danced together, taking many fearsome shapes: swimming as sea monsters, raging as storms, and forming an ominous sigil in the sky.

-Verses 125-128 of the Anushgiar Leyosil

—:—

Erso hurried down a street on the west side of the river, his jobs for E'loseir almost done for the night. It had been a long day, and the dozens of transformations were starting to make his neck feel tight. Still, it was good work, *satisfying* work. Elo and Beysal had really built something here, and it felt less…futile than his normal gig — with the exception of training Sumi, of course. Besides, even if he was just guilty about not visiting, it was nice to help his family for once. He'd never clear his debt with them — who could with family? — but you had to nudge it in the right direction.

The sun was getting low in the sky, but it was still hot, and he lifted his hat to wipe his brow. His hand came back a good deal sweatier than his vanity would like, but what else could he expect after traveling for two years? He turned off the east-west palace road, grateful for the sudden shade. Bloody bastards and their 'urban planning.' The circular shape of the spider web ensured 90 percent of the streets were shrouded in darkness and the main avenue got baked by the palace's silver windows. At least the king had enough light to read his bloody death warrants.

He finally reached the High Court, his teeth already grinding. Built into a giant marble square, it was like a chopping block for the heads of gods. Looking at the white stone, though, you'd never know how much blood they'd spilled there. How many 'suspected' Shapewalkers had they killed in the first few years of the Hardness? Neighbors turning on neighbors, business partners stabbing each other in the back. He almost wished the blood had left a stain, just to have some memory of all the magic they'd wasted.

He shook his head, crossing the street. He wasn't here to get himself worked up. He headed for the police buildings where they sat on the other half of what they unironically called the 'justice pavilion.' His last job of the night was intelligence. Even purged of fellerhurns as they were, it wouldn't do to let the police surprise you in this town. And while he didn't want anyone else in his family taking the risk, swinging by the station was the least he could do when he was home.

He walked around the grounds to where the police offices stood, the twin buildings tall and skinny like wheat stalks. He went to the one on the right, where the Fida'lalean worked — pompous fools. The name meant 'Silver Eyes' in Berillai, though at least it wasn't as terrible a name as the 'Department of Reality.' On his way to the entrance, he had to pass a statue of Roilani E'busek, disgusting rat of a man. He'd died a few years back — an occasion for an immense night of raucousness on his part — though his son had managed to cling to the crown with Berillai support. He was tempted to spit at the statue's feet, though that wouldn't bode particularly well for his disguise.

He reached the entrance, unconsciously smoothing the lapels of his jacket. He'd shaped a dark-blue postal uniform, which should be perfect for infiltrating the snake pit of an office. The police looked down on everyone in Amoriai, of course, but postal workers drew a special brand of disdain. Even if they'd made it to the west side, they still had to deliver letters in the east ends, after all.

He came around the side of the building, taking a narrow alley to the basement mailroom, where there was only one policeman standing guard. Erso tipped his hat, but the man didn't even nod, opening the door without meeting his eyes. Must be awfully hard to guard things when you were looking down your nose at everyone. Like trying to protect your cupboards without recognizing the existence of ants. He'd rather be the ant, of course, but not everyone was happy with crumbs.

Stepping down into the basement, he found it nearly as bright as the outside, with another hundred tons of marble lit by bright electric lights. Luckily, this wasn't his first time, so he managed to take a right without being blinded. He passed the electric lifts — which was a type of dark magic he certainly wasn't used to yet — and ducked into the mailroom.

Thankfully, there was no one there, the cavernous room empty save for a fleet of mail carts and an endless row of shelves. Funny they thought their work warranted storing 'evidence.' Didn't those blokes know they didn't need it? Any judge in Amoriai would order anyone they wanted to the gallows, but he supposed everyone liked pretending in their own way. Still, this was the beating heart of the building — and his ticket upstairs. You couldn't risk being a fly in a place like this. Even if the white walls didn't give you away, how could you be sure the Fida'lalean wouldn't squash you out of spite?

Stepping into a blank spot by the other mail carts, he pulled a letter from his pocket. Stolen the last time he was here, it was addressed to the Fida'lalean, hopefully speeding his way to the top floor. His first time had been…inefficient, to say the least. He began to glow, appearing as a gleaming mail cart, his fake letter perched neatly on top. That was the key to his disguise, of course. He could shape a letter, but it would turn back eventually, and he would hate to have them tighten up security.

Now that he thought about it, this would have been a good exercise to have Sumi try. He wasn't quite as good — or *insistent* — as Beysal at making up metaphors, but this would still be a good way to learn how to carry objects through the halls.

After making a mental note to tell Sumi later, he sat there blankly, letting his mind drift. He left his field of vision open, waiting for someone to come, but he didn't *yearn* for them. He would have to maintain this form for a while, and the calmer you were, the easier it was to hold. You had to really *be* the mail cart. If you were just a man masquerading as a mail cart, itching to get back to your own body, you'd turn back quicker than a hat turned into a house. A mail cart wouldn't give two licks about how long it sat in the basement; that was the height of its existence — other than carrying mail, of course.

He wasn't sure how much time passed, though it could be that way with objects. It was as if without breathing, life lost its hidden tempo. Eventually, though, the door opened again, and a clerk entered with a box of letters. He placed them on a table before disappearing into the shelves. The man was whistling a tune, and Erso started humming along in his mind. He knew this one, though… A memory came to him of his parents dancing to the song. It was a dockside jig, but one he hadn't heard since the Hardness. Maybe the man had been from his neighborhood, though he'd clearly had more luck than the Milak'erats.

The man finally returned, carrying a new box filled with files. He stopped by Erso, picking up his letter. He muttered to himself — something about the other porters getting sloppy. Luckily, he dropped his box on Erso's back, wheeling him out into the hallway. They took a right, slipping down the marble floors toward the lifts. The man had stopped whistling — at least he had *some* sense — though he still hummed quietly as he rang the bell.

With a great groan, the lift on the right began its way downward, a wheel turning just at the edge of his mail cart's hazy vision. With its pulleys whirring, it only took a moment until the lift appeared, an operator inside opening the gate. The mail clerk asked for the top floor — thank the halls — and they began lurching upward.

Finally reaching the sixth floor, they exited into yet another marble hallway, though the Fida'lalean at least rated wooden paneling on the walls. Giant windows looked out at the east side of the city, like a giant hawk perched above its prey. Still, the sheer artisanship of the police offices always struck him. The arches around the windows had little mosaics in the brickwork, and the windowpanes had silver in their joints. They must have had their pick of guildsmen in the Hardness — probably working for free to boot. Even with the Berillai, how else could the king have paid to put up a new city overnight?

The clerk went halfway down the floor, leaving Erso in the perfect spot. Next to him were the desks of the commerce department, the branch of the Fida'lalean most responsible for harassing the people on the east side. Even better, he was only a few feet away from the large blackboard the detectives used to plan their routes. He stared at them for a long time, trying to memorize them — along with the color coding the officers used to divide their shifts. At least Beysal could confirm the information with a few days of scouting.

Finally, he found a list of merchants from the east side the police thought were suspicious. Not everyone was in Elo's guild, but at least she could warn the ones who were. Funnily enough, he probably couldn't have read the words from five feet away if he hadn't been sitting there as a mail cart, but luckily, with a bubble of awareness, if the words were close enough, you could sense where the ink was on the page. Too bad the Fida'lalean wanted his kind dead. He'd have made a very useful policeman.

Eventually, the clerk came back, wheeling him back the way they'd come. Hopefully the man would take his tea break instead of wheeling him around the whole night, but it hardly mattered now. He had what he needed, and if it put his friends even one step ahead of those bastards, it was worth every second as a mail cart.

An hour later — and freed from his life as a mail pony — Erso walked toward an upscale tavern on the west side. He was meeting Beysal and had changed into something more dapper — not that it would matter to his highly bear-like companion. Now he was really stiff from all his shaping, and he kept stopping to stretch his neck. Still, it felt good to be free. And it would feel even better with a drink.

Luckily, he wasn't running late yet, giving him plenty of time to enjoy the sun on his face. The place they were meeting was just a few blocks from the court, making it — despite the dodgy company — the perfect place to eavesdrop on military types. As he reached the tavern, he found the windows open to the breeze, the divine smell of flowers floating over from Pe'ritrine Park. Named for the spring goddess, they said the flowers never stopped blooming, with something for every season.

Bloody vultures, he thought, shaking his head. What were they doing worshipping the old gods anyway? Shouldn't they have moved on to the Berillai god of the sea nonsense by now? Not that his own gods made much sense… How *had* the Amoriai come up with the halls? They'd been ruled by the Anushai for long enough, you'd think they'd worship Essomuai. Not that his scowling would make much sense of it.

He went into the tavern, looking for an open booth. Like everything on this side of town, the place was thoroughly modern, with black and white honeycomb tile and silver fixtures on the walls. They must be hell to polish every day, but the officers probably tipped well. Beysal still hadn't arrived, so he took a booth in the middle, hanging his hat on the attached coatrack. Then he headed to the bar, eager to get a drink before his neck knotted permanently.

The barmaid had her back turned, allowing him to appreciate the fashionable cut of her dress. She had long hair and—*and a voice he recognized. A'lufell.* His heart stopped. He could still run, could be halfway across the park before she realized it was him. But for some insidious reason, his legs wouldn't move, and a smile — a smile! — came to his face as she turned around.

He was such a fool. Of course, that was the real reason Beysal had chosen this place — A'lufell was one of the guild's eyes and ears on the west side. Not that the bear would bloody care that she'd also been Erso's first real love. Actually, there had been that girl, Me'lekona, but the coup had put an end to that. No, A'lufell had been the first proper woman in his life, and he'd abandoned her for a life on the road. It had been, what, ten years? Not that he hadn't heard things, like Elo having to keep her from hunting him down with a crossbow…

She smiled at first — leaning against the bar chest-first, about to ask him what he was drinking. But then, as recognition filled her face, her mouth narrowed to a thin line. Still, somehow, a moment later, a small grin appeared, and she started making a drink.

"Heard you were in town," she said, filling a shaker with whiskey as she sprinkled in some herbs. She shook it up, pouring it into two glasses. She pushed one toward him, shooting back the other in a single gulp.

"Thanks for the drink," she added.

"I suppose that's fair," he said, chuckling as he put a piece of silver on the bar. It was enough for ten drinks. She eyed it for a moment, but left it there, starting on another round.

"Heard you brought a Berillai girl too," she said, focusing on the cocktail as if she might bore a hole through the shaker with her eyes.

"Just a student," he said, taking a careful sip of his drink — and keeping his eyes on her to avoid an ice pick to the neck.

"Sure," she said, pulling a muddler from behind the bar, "just like how I was a student, right?"

He winced. That was a cheap shot. He had technically been a student at that point, too, sort of… During the Hardness, Beysal had more and more requests from parents to train their kids — hoping they could keep them safe. The overflow had started going to Erso. But he and A'lufell had been the same age, and they'd spent most of their time walking around, talking. And then the walking turned to holding hands, and the rest was what it was.

He watched her as she moved smoothly around the bar. She was intent on her ingredients, perfectly measuring and pouring each one. If he hadn't known her better, he'd have said she was working out a way to poison him, but she had been like that with everything — pure intensity. She was just as he remembered: stunningly beautiful, frighteningly focused, and surprisingly soft once you got past that shell of hers. He felt a sharp pang of regret. Suppose he could have stayed? Though, of course, that would have only made things worse.

Not that leaving had anything to do with her. Their first summer was perfect, a chance to kiss in the sunshine and forget all the wretched awfulness around them. But then the months turned into a year, and something changed. Every time he pictured marriage, all he could think of was his mother, dying in a pool of blood. So, he ran. But leaving her had broken him, making him question every feeling he had — especially love — and whether he was worthy of them. At least alone, he couldn't hurt anybody else.

She slapped another drink in front of him, the amber liquid sloshing against the glass. He blinked, not realizing how lost he'd been watching her. He hastily finished his first drink and picked up the second. He took a sip, rolling it over his tongue. There was something floral about this one; lavender, maybe? *Of course...* Her mother had been an herbalist, and she was always teaching him about plants they saw on their walks. This was a tour of their past — and one she probably hoped would be adequately painful for him. Still, she didn't meet his eyes, automatically starting on another round.

"Listen," he said in a low voice. She froze for just a moment before busying herself again, peeling another lemon. He spoke quickly, afraid if he didn't get it out, he never would. "I'm sure it doesn't do any good to say this now, but...I'm sorry. You deserved better; still do. This is probably obvious to you by now, but my leaving didn't have anything to do with you."

He paused, sucking in a breath. "Life had just become this awful, terrible thing. And when you were on the outside of my life, you were a ray of sunshine, but inside... I guess I realized you couldn't take the dark away, and I made that your fault. But you were *good,* at a time I didn't think I'd ever have anything good again. So, thank you, A'lufell. I mean that, thank you."

They looked at each other, the bar disappearing around them. It was like they were seventeen again, if only for a moment. Then a soldier called her name at the end of the bar, demanding another round, and the spell was broken. Still, she smiled, some sort of acceptance of his apology, however small.

"Maybe you finally learned something with all that traveling," she said.

She put the third round in front of him, flying down the bar to her other patrons. He slowly let the air out of his lungs. He had said the words at least. Now he just had to heal the scar again. His heart was like a dark room, one he preferred to keep locked so all the rubbish he'd stored inside wouldn't crash down on him. But maybe this apology would leave the room a little cleaner. Maybe it'd even let him crack the door again someday. He took a sip of his drink, almost choking on it as a giant hand clapped him on the back.

"Look at you!" Beysal roared. "Early for once and starting without me!"

He took the other drink A'lufell had left, shooting it back.

"I don't think I'm early. I think you're getting slower in your old age."

"I was training Sumi, thank you very much," Beysal said, grinning.

"And she's mighty talented, I might add. Still, I'm glad you could catch up with an old friend, lad. It's good to mend fences, especially before starting something new."

So, it was a set up after all. Erso sighed, drinking what was left in his glass.

"Hey!" Beysal called to A'lufell, waving.

She motioned for Beysal to take a bottle of wine from behind the counter, so he did, also grabbing the small envelope next to it. He left a coin of his own on the bar before turning toward the booth where Erso had left his hat — apparently uninterested to see if Erso followed.

Erso shook his head, giving A'lufell a final glance as he stood — his legs wobblier than he expected. Still, he wasn't ungrateful, at least not in retrospect. He had to face his past. He'd promised himself things would be different this time. And even if he wasn't foolish enough to think Sumi was anything like A'lufell, she still deserved a better teacher. He'd made enough mistakes for one lifetime; now he just had to hope he really had learned something after all.

23

The Elders taught the humans of their mother, showing them the many worlds in her infinite eyes. Essomuai sang songs of joy to them, joining them to her family. The humans and the Shapewalkers lived in harmony, laughing, crying, marrying and having children. Each new generation held the sacred blood of both sisters, creating something new. Peace and prosperity settled over the land, and they rejoiced in the bounty of their home.

-Verses 140-144 of the Anushgiar Leyosil

—:—

Sumi walked into Beysal's, finding E'loseir at her little desk by the fireplace, writing a letter.

"How was it?" the older woman asked, motioning toward a nearby chair.

"Incredible," Sumi said, sighing as she eased into the chair. She still felt like a butterfly, like she might just float away. Remembering herself, she bowed her head in thanks. "Thank you again for having me. Beysal was such a good teacher; I don't know if I would've figured it out without him."

Elo laughed.

"I don't know how he has that effect on people. But I'm glad it helped. I had a good feeling about you."

Her eyes flicked toward the back door.

"Where is the old brute anyway?"

"Oh," Sumi said, looking out at the garden as if Beysal might reappear. "He said he was meeting Erso for guild business. Was he…"

Elo rolled her eyes.

"I told him to pick something up for me, but I didn't mean tonight. He just wanted to meet Erso at the pub, I'm sure."

"Ah," Sumi said, biting her lip. "Sorry, I—"

"Don't blame yourself," Elo said, chuckling. "I swear, those two are more like brothers sometimes. I honestly should have known they'd sneak off drinking. Happens every time Erso's home."

She shoved her letter into an envelope and hastily addressed it. She stood, adding a stamp with perhaps a bit more force than necessary.

"If we're going to mail this *extremely* important letter, we'll have to stop by a pub for some reconnaissance of our own."

"Only seems fair," Sumi said, chuckling. "What about Kel, though?"

"Oh, he can come," Elo said, throwing a scarf over her neck. "This is Amoriai. Besides, you did well today; we should celebrate."

Sumi stood, looking down at her dress. It was the same one she always wore, though it looked a little drab as she considered a night out on the town. Maybe if she grabbed her new scarf.

"Kel!" Elo yelled up the stairs. *"Al'delat keo'loseman!"*

"Coming!" Kel called back in Berillai, his footsteps thundering down the stairs.

It suddenly dawned on her that she hadn't had a female friend since Seriai got married. Even worse than her dress, would she be any fun to talk with? She was hardly interesting compared to E'loseir. Apparently, though, she was good enough for Kel, the boy barreling into her.

"Sumi!" he cried, hugging her knees. "Are you coming too?"

"We're all going," Elo said. "Get your shoes."

Kel ran to the door, his face scrunched in concentration as he laced his boots.

"Wait," he said, standing. "Do I get to hold the letter?"

"Only if you don't crinkle it," Elo said. "Remember what we talked about?"

"I won't," he said, snatching it from her hand. With that, he wrenched the door open, bounding into the street.

"A'besera ullinh!" E'loseir yelled after him, pulling out her key.

Sumi stepped outside, the other woman grinning as she locked the door.

"Five-year-olds," she said, shaking her head. "You're good with him, though. Have you ever thought of having children?"

"Uh…" Sumi hesitated, but Elo had already started down the street, hurrying after Kel.

Sumi caught up, watching as Elo grabbed Kel's hand, the little boy dragging her forward despite his size. She'd loved working with kids with Nela, but she'd never thought she'd have the chance to have her own. After all, if no one ever fell for her, how was she supposed to start a family? And now, on the run and away from home, how would she ever manage it? Or maybe that was selfish. Look at what Amoriai had been through, and they still found a way. Maybe that's what happiness really was, carving out a place for yourself regardless of the circumstances.

But what would she do next? Even if she made it home — assuming she *could* go home with the detective chasing her — what would her life look like? Would she have to stay in hiding? And even if she didn't, what would her life mean with no one in it? She wasn't sure she could go back to her lonely life before, when all she had was her job and an empty cottage.

There had to be another way, a way to build something like Beysal and E'loseir had, to *do* something for her people. Still, could she really change Berill? Could anyone? She looked up, catching a glimpse of Su'selo'mae in the distance. There was so much pain, so much suffering in the world. It felt impossible for someone as small and insignificant as she, but how could she not try? Like Nela used to say, you should never let tears be shed for nothing. No matter what her life looked like, she couldn't just survive. She had to fight.

After a few blocks, they reached a mailbox, and Kel whooped with joy as he got on his tiptoes to push the letter inside. It was a particular magic of children to get excited over nothing, but it felt like an answer to her questions too. Life, *any* life, was always worth it, even when things got tough. And to that end, the mailbox — basically just a giant iron rectangle — was there for Kel, even if it looked like it had been painted over too many times, the dark maroon of the new regime dumped over the top.

"Well," Elo said, "that's our big job done. But Kel, you look thirsty. Do you want to stop for something?"

"Let's go to Uncle Re'humal's!" he cried. "It's right over there!"

"Sure," Elo said, "lead the way, my love."

"Okay!" Kel said, running ahead as he ricocheted from one interesting thing to the next.

"Men," Elo said with a wink. "Have to make it sound like their idea, you know? Improves our alibi."

They walked slowly after Kel, Elo only calling out to him when he got too far ahead — and once when he tried to poke a dead rat. It was a beautiful night for walking, though Sumi couldn't help but feel a nagging in her mind.

"E'loseir?" she finally asked. "How *did* you start your guild? I know

Beysal mentioned your father, but... I guess I was wondering how you did something so *huge.*"

"It's really not so much," Elo said, smiling sadly. "Though it's better than nothing, I suppose."

She ran a hand through her hair, looking at the sky.

"It just came naturally, I guess. My father ran the Ironworkers Guild, and there were always people at our house. My poor mother; sometimes he had her making biscuits at midnight while he argued in the living room. And I hated it sometimes, always entertaining other people's kids. But when he was gone...I missed it. So one day, I just took out his address book and started writing. It wasn't supposed to turn out how it did — so *big* — but... Well, we need each other, especially now, and I'm glad my father taught me that."

She made it sound so *easy.* Or, maybe not easy, exactly, but...natural. But it wasn't so different from her, trying to fill the hole in her life that Nela left behind. And she *had* gone back to the women's group. If she hadn't had to run, if she could make it home again...

"Enough about me, child!" Elo said, pushing her on the arm. "This was supposed to be my night to hear more about you. You have a gift for avoiding the spotlight, you know."

"Oh, sorry," she said. She didn't mean to be withholding, she just didn't know how else to have a conversation. Peppering other people with questions seemed like the natural thing to do. Besides, Elo was just so much more *interesting* than she was.

"Don't be," Elo said, putting her arm around Sumi and giving her a quick squeeze. "And don't look so horrified, either. I won't make you talk when you don't want to. It's honestly refreshing. We have too many actors in this family as it is, always competing for attention. I suppose that must be what makes Erso like you so much."

"Erso? And...me?" she asked, her cheeks flushing. E'loseir must have gotten the wrong idea. Erso was simply doing her a kindness, nothing more. Besides, why would someone so handsome and interesting ever fall for her?

"I don't know," Elo said, giving Sumi a sly look. "Haven't seen him bring home a beautiful girl before now. So, it stands to reason—"

Just then, Kel called out to them. He was standing outside a pub, waving. It had a sign with a key on it, and its name — *The Errant Locksmith* — in both Amoriai and Berillai. Squeezed between two larger buildings, you'd hardly notice it if you weren't looking.

Kel opened the door for them — even though it took his whole body weight — and Sumi smiled at him, grateful he'd saved her from having to explain herself to E'loseir. Inside, the place was lovely — and surprisingly long, running back some thirty feet as it made up for its narrowness. To the right was a wooden bar, gleaming in the light from dozens of bronze lamps. There wasn't a single patron, but somehow, it didn't feel empty. It was more like a dozen people had been there only moments before, having just gone out the back.

Kel had already run up to the bar, scrambling onto a chair as he talked to the bartender — presumably his uncle Re'humal. The man seemed to be in his sixties, with a bald head and a short white beard. He was leaning forward, nodding at whatever Kel was saying, when she noticed the shimmer of a keyhole around him. She felt the buzzing in her ears, and oddly, it almost sounded…*musical,* though it could have been her imagination.

"Welcome," he said, waving them over. "I see we have a friend from Berill, if I'm not mistaken? Not many keyholes in your people."

"I'm Sumi," she said, joining E'loseir at the bar. "And I just got in from Berill a few days ago, actually."

She'd noticed his keyhole, of course, but she still had to get used to others knowing what she was. Re'humal reached under the bar, setting two glasses in front of them.

"Well, we're glad to have you," he said, "and with the Guild Chair, no less! To what do we owe the pleasure, Elo?"

"Erso's in town," E'loseir said, "and Beysal seems to think they have their own tavern business to attend to."

"Ah," Re'humal said with a knowing grin. "I thought I saw him the other day, but I was worried I'd gone senile. Still, in my bar with no husband, sounds like a celebration to me."

He turned, running his finger along a row of bottles until he grabbed one at the end, made of dark-green glass with a tulip-shaped cork.

"Knew I had some cloud wine left; glad I saved it for a guest of honor."

"Rehu," E'loseir said, her eyes wide, "you can't waste this on us."

Sumi looked between the two of them. She'd never heard of cloud wine, but if it was too much to waste on E'loseir, then it was definitely too good for her.

"It's from Alara," E'loseir said, noticing her look. "Grows in the mountains by the Nyfatsi. But it's impossible to get east of the river these days. Don't think I've had it since my father's last guild elections, what, fifteen years ago?"

"I was at that guild election," Re'humal said, "and I vote we drink it."

He pulled the cork, taking out a third glass as he filled them with a golden liquid. Sumi stared at hers, watching as thousands of bubbles danced in the light. Re'humal even pulled a thimble from his apron, pouring a tiny dram of wine in it and handing it to Kel.

"I wouldn't even have a bar without Elo," he said, "so let's drink to her health — and to new friends, of course."

"To E'loseir," Sumi said, taking a drink. It was…*delightful.* She hardly remembered the wine from Seriai's wedding — aside from the hangover it had given her — but this was like drinking sunshine. The bubbles fizzed on her tongue, starting out tart but finishing like honey. She hadn't realized she'd closed her eyes, but when she opened them, she found the others with dreamy looks on their faces.

"The first five seconds says it all," Re'humal said, staring into his own glass.

"Well," he finally added, shaking his head, "Elo doesn't meet guests without something important to discuss, so why don't you take the nice chairs in the back. I'll bring some snacks and leave you be."

Both women made lengthy thank-yous as they stood up, wandering to the back corner, where there was a circle of green suede chairs. She'd only had one sip, but it already felt like there were bubbles inside her head, trying to pop out through her ears. It was strangely similar to Shapewalking, actually.

They settled into a pair of chairs while Kel wandered the bar, muttering to himself as he played pretend. A few moments later, Re'humal brought the rest of the wine, along with a basket of pretzels.

"See?" E'loseir asked. "We can have more fun without those boys around."

"You were right. You must be the one who taught Erso to be so entertaining."

"That's one thing you could call him," Elo said, grinning as she swirled her wine. "Don't think I've forgotten, by the way. I still want to hear more about you and your plans."

She'd been hoping Elo would forget, but you probably didn't run a guild without a good memory. Still, unworthy as she was, this felt distinctly like an interview with a prospective mother-in-law. It made her think of Seriai's marriage tea with Ekkel's parents — and how it had ended in tears after his mother's endless sniping. It was a wonder they'd gotten married at all.

"There isn't much to tell," she said carefully. She took a sip of her wine, trying to buy herself some time. "But I don't want to overstay my welcome. I promise I'll come up with a plan as soon as Beysal thinks I'm ready."

"I din't mean like that," E'loseir said, smacking her on the arm. "Our home is your home; stay as long as you like. I meant in general. What do you *want* out of life?"

Sumi frowned, nodding. "I guess I haven't really thought about it before — or no one's ever asked. But everything happened so fast, it's hard to remember I still have choices to make. It's been so lovely being here, traveling, but…eventually, I'd still like to go home. I want to make a difference there, even if that sounds silly."

"It sounds like the opposite of silly," E'loseir said, smiling. "I didn't think about what I was doing when I made the guild, I just…*ached* for something of the life we'd lost. Most of my father's guild fled to Anushai, basically rebuilt the neighborhood abroad. I guess, I had to decide if I wanted to recreate the life I lost or start a new one in its place. And that wasn't even my only choice. Lots of the people who stayed wanted to fight back, to stand against the coup — though they're all dead now, of course."

She sighed, sipping her wine.

"I guess I picked the middle path. I've found peace here, and I have a beautiful family. It's an incredible life, but was it the right choice? I guess I'll never know. But if I have any advice for you, it's to not rush your decision. Enjoy your travels, go see Anushai. You'll learn your powers, and I'm positive you'll help people. But there's a million paths you can take. Life is a lot like wine. You'll drink it all down in the end, but you might as well savor it."

E'loseir was right, of course. She couldn't plan her whole life from the outset. Even a year ago, she couldn't have predicted any of this if she'd tried: Nela dying, discovering her powers, leaving home. Still, she had to do what was right, to answer the ache in her own heart. After all, even if it couldn't change the city, what would the Shapewalkers in Amoriai have done without E'loseir's guild? Or maybe that *was* changing the city. Just look at everything Erso had done, the people he'd saved. Every life was a world of possibility, a hallway with infinite doors. And even if she wasn't as strong, even if she wouldn't accomplish a tenth of what Nela or E'loseir had, she'd never forgive herself if she did nothing.

"That's good advice," she finally said. "It just feels so far away from where I am now."

"You'll get there," E'loseir said, squeezing her hand. "But you start here, learning your powers. Today, you took a huge step. So, celebrate. There'll be plenty of worrying to do later."

She raised her glass, clinking it against Sumi's. And then they talked about happier things, sharing stories — especially about Erso — and sipping the rest of their wine. And as they talked, Sumi found herself staring at the bubbles, wondering if any of life's questions had answers inside those tiny dancing spheres.

24

The humans and Shapewalkers joined on the beach, dancing and singing in a festival that raged for many nights. With the war over, the humans could return to their fields and villages, though many decided to make Anushai their home. Each of them swore an oath to one of the Elders, vowing to sing the song of Essomuai, humans and Shapewalkers alike. Each house was gathered according to its gifts and bore the sigil of its Elder: Stone, Sky, Grass, Flame, and River; Earth, Shadow, Ocean, Forest, and Rain.

-Verses 135-138 of the Anushgiar Leyosil

—:—

Two Weeks Later

Erso woke up to bright morning light in his bedroom, an image of Sumi just disappearing from his mind. The dream was already fading away, but he thought he'd been standing with her on a beach. Or maybe it was a field? He couldn't remember much besides her face; but there had been the sounds of waves, hadn't there? It wasn't the first time he'd dreamt of her since they arrived in Amoriai, though hopefully — if he knew what was good for him — it'd be the last.

He groaned, pulling a pillow over his face. Bloody Beysal and his bloody ideas about family life. He should be preparing for when Sumi left, not daydreaming. If he did his job right, she'd be well trained and ready to have the kind of life she deserved. The new year had come and gone, and he should be figuring out how to spend his days without Sumi to fill them.

He pushed himself out of bed. Hey may be a fool, but no one could accuse him of doing his job poorly. The past few weeks had been a blur, with Sumi getting better every day. After her big breakthrough with Beysal, the three of them spent every day in the courtyard until her transitions were nearly perfect — even turning back into herself. They even found time to do his lessons on moving objects through the halls: coins, house keys, even a frying pan. She'd learned to change those objects too, and even if there had been…an incident with his hat, he was just *proud*. He'd never had a better student and probably wouldn't ever again.

On New Year's Eve, she'd even shaped her clothes, coming downstairs in a low-cut silk dress, like a waterfall of midnight blue.

"Where did that come from?" he'd asked, forcing himself not to stare.

Apparently, Queen Welaya had worn it to a parade once. Fit for a queen indeed… Luckily for the rest of them, she'd been feeling festive and decided to wear it all through dinner. New Year's wasn't as much of a holiday as it was in Berill, but at least the whole family's calendar had lined up. They'd cracked some wine — even if it was swill compared to the bloody cloud wine Elo had found without them — and cooked a giant dinner. The rest of them shaped their clothes too, though Kel still had to run upstairs for his tiny brown suit.

"Enough," he said to himself out loud as he threw on his clothes. He could torture himself with memories when she left. They had a long walk out to the forests today, and he shouldn't keep them waiting with his misery. He and Beysal had trained out there when he was younger, and the old bear apparently had some kind of surprise training for her today. Even better, away from the city, she could finally stop worrying about her ripples — even if they weren't even an issue anymore.

Still, as he hurried from the room, he caught an unfortunate look in the mirror. He was in need of a shave and had bags under his eyes. Frankly, he looked a mess, but what could be done? Like the fool he was, he'd spent the night by his parents' pillar, drinking until the moon was gone. He hadn't planned on sleeping late, of course, but Kel hadn't jumped on him that morning — even if it was his own fault for using a five-year-old as an alarm clock.

Dressed for the hike, which was casual even for him, he went down to the kitchen, finding the rest of the family there. Sumi looked up at him over her toast with a smile, and he found himself grinning like a fool. Kel launched out of his chair for his morning attack, scrambling onto Erso's back as he made his way to the kitchen counter.

"Mum said I can't wake you up anymore," he whined.

"Sorry, pal," Erso said, "but rules are rules."

He turned to Elo, mouthing his thanks. She rolled her eyes at him, pointing to the coffeepot on the counter. Beysal was by the cutting board, putting the finishing touch on some sandwiches for their hike.

"You're lucky Kel's the only one who wakes you up these days," Beysal said, laughing. He looked over his shoulder at Sumi. "Used to have to pour water on the lad to get him up."

Erso shuddered at the thought. As if it had only been water! There was the one time with the frog, and then the wheat worm. It had taken him a year living on the road to stop being afraid in the morning.

Erso rushed through a quick breakfast, and before he knew it, the three of them were standing in the courtyard, ready for their journey. Sumi wore her usual dress and boots, only adding a hat for the sun. It actually looked like one of E'loseir's, made of straw, with lace violets sewn on the side. It was a bit large, but it framed her dimples perfectly. It— *It was just a bloody hat.* He shook his head, clenching his fists.

He did admire her practicality, though. She was so sturdy, so *reliable.* She woke up every day and put on her dress, ready to work in a flower shop or travel the world. It was absolutely foreign to him. Growing up around so many theatrical people had taken its toll, of course, but he'd never seemed to have any kind of practicality in his life. It was a good thing to have some flair, but someday it'd be nice to put on clothes without them needing to be a costume.

They headed south, going behind the palace — and the royal graveyard, Mu'na'raelomae. It was almost as large as the one that held his family, only far less populated, reserved for direct descendants of the first king. The obelisks were twice as tall too, made of marble with metal faces. During the Hardness, people said that the entire two-hundred-person palace staff had slept on the grass, desperate to protect the graves.

"So, there was this pretzel maker," he said, starting a joke to draw Sumi's eyes off the graves. She'd seen enough sad things, and today was about her, about celebrating her accomplishments. "He worked in the palace, and he'd been making pretzels for years."

"Oh no," Beysal said, grimacing, "not this one."

"So, the old king dies one day," Erso said pointedly, giving Beysal a sharp look, "and the new king says he wants biscuits now. He tried them in Anushai, and he *loved* them — flaky, buttery, everything he was missing in his afternoon tea. But see, the pretzel maker only has the same old ingredients, but even so, at least he tries. So anyway, the next day, the king comes in for tea, and when his servant delivers his tray, he opens it to find — more pretzels."

He stomped his feet and puffed out his chest, acting out the part of the angry king.

"The king stomps through the palace and sentences the pretzel maker to death. And with his head on the chopping block, the king asks him, 'Why didn't you just make the bloody biscuits?' And you know what the guy says?"

"What?" Sumi asked innocently.

Beysal just sighed, but Erso wasn't about to give up on his joke now.

"'Sorry, Your Highness,' the guy says, 'but the pretzels were ingrained.' Get it? *In—grained*?"

Sumi stared him, but then, luckily, she started laughing.

"I don't know how you translated that damned joke into Berillai," Beysal said, chuckling despite himself — even as he shook his head with disapproval, "but it didn't get any better."

For a moment, he felt like a genius. Unfortunately, Amoriai — and its awful history — was always there to pull him back down. After passing Raelomae, they turned left, the burned-out husk of the old temple looming up ahead. Maybe he should have planned their route better… Just southeast of the palace, it had been used by Shapewalking priests to explore the halls, performing whatever rites and rituals the king had thought would keep him safe — lot of good that did him, of course.

Built into the same octopus shape as the old palace, the temple's wooden interior had been completely burned away, with only its stone shell remaining. The empty window frames showed the remnants of the bronze dome, melted at the edges from the fires. Sumi's eyes never left the building as they passed, though she said nothing. He hoped she wasn't saving her questions for their sake, but what was there to say? Every burned thing in this city was from the Hardness, and the Amoriai had done it to themselves. Still, when she finally turned back, their eyes meeting, he forced himself to smile. She was a *good* thing in their miserable little lives, and she should know it.

They turned south again, finally passing under the train tracks. They passed some nurseries run by the Gardener's Guild, but eventually, the city just…disappeared. There weren't any walls around Amoriai or anything — they'd been under Anushai's thumb too long to build them — and as they came over the top of the first hill, it was like they'd been transported miles away. Wheat fields stretched as far as they could see, the golden waves following the contours of the hills as they rolled toward the sea. There was birdsong and the smell of hot earth as the sun burned away the morning fog. And at the edge of the horizon was their destination: a dense forest sticking out above the wheat.

Some said that the entire eastern bank of the Ko'lesta had been forest once. Founded by the legendary conqueror Elomikarus, the capital had been north of the current city, on the Vulneran Peninsula, where it stuck out into the sea. He'd visited it once with his parents, though, and there hadn't been anything there, just fishing towns and an inn by the beach. When Amoriai itself had been founded, the farms had pushed all the way to the Alaran border, the old crown preserving these last stretches of forest for their hunting. Luckily, it seemed the new crown was too busy counting their money to hunt much, leaving the forest here for them.

They took the road until it turned to the west, walking directly through the fields as they followed the cart paths generations of farmers had etched into the earth. A few men stood to wave as they passed, but no one gave them any trouble. The farmers, at least, still held to the old ways, their guild getting one of the rawest deals when trade with Berill opened up.

Eventually, about halfway to the forest, they took a break by a stream, sitting on some rocks and sipping from their canteen. The wind rippled through the wheat, pulling at the ribbon on Sumi's hat. If he wasn't careful, he could lose the whole day staring at her like a rube.

"This is lovely," she said, smiling. "I feel like I haven't walked enough since leaving home. I think my body misses the climb up to the terrace."

"*My* body doesn't miss it," Erso said, chuckling. "I climbed that hill more than once looking for you, I'll have you know, and my legs still regret it."

"Excuse the lad," Beysal said. "Now that he's fancy, he's not in the same shape he used to be."

There hadn't been any farmers around for the last half mile, so Erso closed his eyes and glowed, changing into Beysal. He sat like the other man, his elbows on his knees with his beard hanging down.

"I'm in good enough shape," he said with Beysal's voice. "It's just the beard that slows me down. Drags me backwards in the wind, it does."

"Alright," Beysal said, laughing as he lifted a leg to forcibly kick Erso off of his rock. "Watch yourself, or I'll give Sumi your sandwich."

Erso changed back into himself, bowing low.

"I formally apologize," he said. "There's no need to take things so far, my good man. Withholding a sandwich is just cruel!"

"I don't think I could take his sandwich," Sumi said. "If he gets any skinnier, he'll disappear."

"Not you too!" Erso shouted, but the two of them were already off their rocks, continuing up the path and leaving him to run behind. It seemed Sumi had learned more than just Shapewalking in her time in Amoriai, but it was too late to stop her now. And he wouldn't want to either. Even as he grumbled to himself, he smiled. His regret could wait. This day, at least, was perfect.

25

With so many new children, the Great Houses began to shape their sacred home. Forest House began to harvest trees, building homes for all the new arrivals. River House made their boats, sending their children to trade with the other kingdoms. Grass House searched the fields for medicines, healing those who had been hurt in the fighting. And between the houses, they chose one among them to lead the people based on what they needed most.

-Verses 145-149 of the Anushgiar Leyosil

—:—

They reached the woods a little past noon. Having eaten their sandwiches by the tree line, they worked their way through the forest along a narrow, winding path. The day had grown hot, but it was still cool beneath the trees. Beysal led the way, and they moved in single file, leaves and sticks crunching underfoot. Erso was in the back, and he smiled as he watched Sumi's head eagerly shoot from side to side, always trying to take in every single thing around her.

After a mile or so, Beysal suddenly turned into the bushes, leaving the trail behind.

"You aren't taking us to a bear cave, are you?" Erso asked, looking around. "You might look like one, but that doesn't mean they'll let us in."

"That's why I brought you to offer as a snack," Beysal answered without turning around.

They worked their way up a hill, climbing around a huge rock face where the land suddenly leveled out. Ahead, the shade gave way to a sunny clearing. He froze, realizing where they were.

"I can't believe it!" he yelled, running ahead. He stood at the edge of the clearing, staring in awe. "You really kept it?"

"Why tear it down?" Beysal asked, chuckling. "It's not like anyone comes this way these days."

Sumi stepped up beside him, scanning the canopy.

"Um, what are we looking at exactly?"

"This," Beysal said, his arms wide, "used to be our clubhouse, where I trained the lad when the city was too dangerous."

"I guess it's actually kind of hard to tell," Erso said, pointing at the trees, where branches crisscrossed the clearing at odd angles, "but we built an obstacle course."

"We still use it sometimes for kids in the guild," Beysal said, "but I thought it could be fun to bring you here, give you an initiation trial."

"Do I get a badge if I pass?" Sumi asked, pulling off her hat.

"You can have Erso's hat," Beysal said, moving deeper into the clearing.

"Oi!" he yelled as the others left him behind again.

While Beysal walked Sumi through the course, Erso found a log, pulling a bottle of whiskey from his pocket.

"Just like old times, eh?" he asked Beysal as the old man stomped back over.

Beysal stopped, his eyes bulging as if he'd pulled out a snake.

"Or not," Erso said quickly, suddenly feeling a twinge of guilt. Beysal was fine hitting the pub with him some nights, but a full bottle of liquor during the day? It was enough to give anyone flashbacks of the Hardness. He thought of their conversation in the garden, the night he'd come home. Beysal must regret those days more than he let on.

"I suppose a nip won't hurt," Beysal finally said, joining him on the log. "Long as I'm fit by dinner, mind you. I'm not having Elo blame me for your mess."

Erso crossed his heart, handing him the bottle.

"I'll keep you on the straight and narrow. Besides, we're in the company of a lady."

"That hasn't ever stopped you before," Sumi said, coming over.

Beysal took a sip, but he immediately coughed, giving Erso a sharp look.

"Sure doesn't taste like a gentleman's drink," he said, tossing Erso the bottle. "Come on, lass," he said to Sumi, "let's get you started on the course."

Erso chuckled, taking another drink as he closed his eyes, leaning his head back in the sun. This was about as close to paradise as he was ever gonna get.

Beysal took Sumi to the starting point, a tree with a few boards nailed into a makeshift ladder. The goal was to Shapewalk your way across the course, where a sort of makeshift track ran through the canopy. Beysal had built it as a joke, but it wound up being a halfway-decent way to learn. There were different obstacles and things along the way, forcing you to think on your feet.

After talking with Beysal for another minute, Sumi nodded, starting up the ladder. There was a tiny platform at the top, about ten feet in the air, just wide enough to stand on as you took your first form. Beysal came back, sitting on the ground.

"Alright lass, let's see what you got!" he called up to her. "And remember, nothing with wings!"

Sumi nodded — her face serious — as she began to glow, reappearing as a squirrel.

"Not a bad choice," Erso said, nodding. "Won't make it past the second obstacle, though."

"That's the idea," Beysal said, grinning. "Everybody always thinks they'll make it as a critter — you did a rat your first time, remember?"

Beysal took out his watch, watching as the second hand ticked around to the top.

"Alright," he called out, "in: five, four, three, two—"

On *one,* the Sumi squirrel took off, dashing across the first branch. The first obstacle was a flat board, forming a perpendicular wall. With her claws, Sumi made it over easily enough, though that was precisely the point. The first obstacle always lured you in, making you overconfident.

As she came onto the next length of the track, the branches suddenly stopped, interrupted by a five-foot length of twine. Sumi froze at the edge, her tiny head bobbing as she tried to guess whether or not the twine would hold her weight — it wouldn't, of course. Beysal looked at Erso with his eyebrows raised, pulling a tiny slingshot from his pocket. So, the old man still had some tricks up his sleeve… The first time Erso had run the course, Beysal had started throwing sticks at him. But this was an advanced form of cruelty.

Beysal loaded an acorn, hitting the branch just below Sumi with a thwack. She jumped about a foot in the air but somehow kept her cool, glowing in the air and landing as a ladybug. She was just barely visible from where they sat, and both men stood unconsciously, walking closer to watch her run across the twine. Technically, ladybugs *did* have wings, but if she didn't use them, they wouldn't dock her for it. She made decent time, but the trick was shaping quickly on the other side. Sumi seemed to realize this, shining as soon as she reached the other side to take off as a squirrel again.

She reached the halfway point, approaching the third obstacle where the branches ended again, a half-dozen tin cans hanging down on string. As she jumped toward the first one, Beysal shot another acorn, taking her in the shoulder. She squeaked, falling from the branch. But just before she hit the ground, she glowed, appearing as a dandelion fluff.

"Not bad!" Beysal yelled out. "Keep at it!"

A dandelion fluff didn't have wings, after all, and according to the rules, you were allowed to fall as long as you got back up without the ladder.

"She really is a wonder," Beysal said as the dandelion Sumi floated back toward the branches.

"I'll drink to that," Erso said, taking a swig.

They'd done a few drills earlier in the week, having her jump off a chair in the courtyard repeatedly, forcing her to Shapewalk in the air. Beysal hadn't told them why, of course, but it was certainly coming in handy now. Besides, you didn't always have the luxury of time when you were shaping. It wasn't like that bloody fellerhurn Parimu would ask politely next time he chased their kind.

As Sumi landed on the branch again, flashing back into a squirrel, Erso eyed his own watch. There was only one more obstacle, but she'd have to be quick about it — and she couldn't be a squirrel, either. The final stretch had a thick branch hollowed out into a tube. The hole was narrow, and the top had been covered in sharp sticks, making it impossible to run straight across.

Sumi looked at them with her tiny squirrel eyes, her eye-roll clear even from fifteen feet away. She probably knew her time was short, but if she turned into a bug again, she'd never clear the tube in time. Suddenly she glowed, reappearing as a snake as she slithered into the branch. Beysal hollered in support, clapping Erso on the back.

"What did I tell you, the girl's a natural! I spent a month digging out that bloody branch for you, and it took you all summer to think of something decent for it."

Sumi made it back to the start, the second hand just over the minute mark. She turned back into herself, and they both cheered, clapping as she took a tiny bow.

"Did I do it?" she called down. "That felt longer than a minute."

"Only just," Beysal called back. "I think you could get it next time. Just can't use the same form twice in one day."

"What?!" she said, her jaw dropping. "You didn't tell me that!"

"Did the same to me growing up," Erso said, raising the bottle in solidarity.

"Don't think you're any better," she said. "Sitting there without saying anything."

She stuck her tongue out at him, but a second later, she was looking at the course again, sizing up her options, ready to begin again.

By the time they finished — with Sumi finally victorious after ten more runs — the sun had touched the trees, making the clearing glow with golden light. They still had a few hours until dinner, though, so Beysal lit a fire, dragging a few large branches to the makeshift fire pit they'd made more than a decade earlier. Sumi joined them on a log, looking tired, though she had a wide smile on her face.

Erso leaned forward, handing her the whiskey — though he earned a look from Beysal when the firelight made it clear a quarter of the bottle was gone already. He shrugged, turning back to Sumi as she pulled the cork, looking into the bottle before she took a careful sip. Immediately, she began to cough, though she laughed between her sputters.

"Don't say anything," she said, pointing at him. "I earned it."

"That you did," Beysal said, waving a hand in refusal as she offered him the bottle.

They all stared into the fire for a time before Beysal spoke again. "You know, I wasn't going to tell you this — Elo wanted it to be a surprise — but we're having a guild dinner in a few days; have the families together, show off their kids, that kind of thing. But I thought — and this is the only reason I would ruin her surprise — you might want to show off a few shapes for them, seeing as how you've passed your training now."

"You want me…" she said, trailing off, her eyes wide as she looked between them.

"Don't worry," Erso said, "I can help with a routine. But I agree; I think you're ready."

"Is this something people normally do?" she asked. "Isn't it strange to Shapewalk for a room full of Shapewalkers?"

"Not at all," Beysal said. "People do it all the time — like when I run the halls. Besides, by now they've all heard about you, and we always have our students show their stuff."

"How many days do I have exactly?"

"Well," Beysal said, chuckling, "by a few days, I meant two."

Sumi shot Erso a look, but he just smiled reassuringly. That was plenty of time to work up a quick routine — just string together a few of her favorite forms and call it good. Still, as he looked back at the fire, he felt a lump form in his throat. He wouldn't be doing a routine, of course, but he still hated guild parties. They were lovely people, presumably, but they had almost all known his parents, and they always found a way to corner him for their interrogations. *No, he wasn't back for good. Yes, he'd write them if he ever got married. Blah, blah, blah.*

"Alright," Sumi said, squaring her jaw, "I'll do it." She pointed a finger sharply in Erso's direction. "But don't go thinking you can wriggle out of helping me."

Beysal laughed, slapping his knee.

"She's known you two months, and she's already got your number, boy."

"Not so fast," she said, turning on Beysal. "You're not off the hook either. If I have to perform for the guild, you two have to perform for me — right now."

"Look out, lad," Beysal said to him as they shared a look. "Either the whiskey's already gotten her, or your luck's run out."

"What exactly did you have in mind?" Erso asked wryly.

"Well," Sumi said, "the first day I arrived, we talked about using more than one Shapewalker to make a boat. I'm probably not ready yet, but I want to see it done. I want you two to show me something big."

"So, the student becomes the master, eh?" Beysal asked, humming in appreciation.

"It's a lovely idea," Erso said, "but you see, Sumi, Beysal is *already* something really big."

He got a stick thrown at him for that, but Beysal was already standing, rolling his shoulders.

"We're really doing this?" Erso asked, standing up himself.

"You heard the girl," Beysal said. "Besides, she's earned it. But first, a bit of history."

"Please," Sumi said, leaning forward on her log.

"Back in Anushai, they used to have performers join together. They'd make huge dragons and the like, things from their storybooks. They say that in the olden days, when they needed to make something big — to protect the kingdom, say — Essomuai would join them all together. The legends say they could be anything — any size — and even a bunch of soldiers who didn't know each other could do it."

He reached over and grabbed the whiskey bottle, taking a quick pull.

"But," he continued, "even if that was true in the old days, it's nowhere near as easy now. When you shape with someone now, you have to know them really well, or you'll make it about as long as an eyeblink. It's about trust, since you're not only letting go, you're letting someone pull you with them. Otherwise, it's pretty simple. You hold on to someone, and they walk you through their halls."

"Simple if you're the one leading," Erso grumbled.

"Exactly right," Beysal said with a laugh. "My boy here is referring to the fact that I usually lead. Now, without further ado."

Beysal took a few steps back from the fire, and Erso joined him. They stood side by side, locking arms.

"Start with a deer," Beysal whispered.

Erso shut his eyes, breathing out as he let himself slip into the form of a deer. He began to glow, and he could tell that Beysal was glowing too. Suddenly, he felt a tugging in his mind, and the glow grew brighter behind his eyes. As their transformations overlapped, he let himself go, picturing himself as a leaf pulled along by Beysal's current.

When the glowing subsided, they were standing there as a deer. It was a strange feeling, shaping with Beysal. Even though a deer had eyes, he was somewhere in the back, like an inanimate object, while Beysal was the deer itself. Still, he could feel his energy fueling them even as they followed Beysal's will. If he hadn't been calm, this was the moment most lost their transformation.

Beysal reared them up on the deer's hind legs, flicking his hooves in the air, and just as quickly, they were glowing again. Erso kept his mind focused on the leaf, pouring his energy through Beysal. They reappeared as an elephant, this time more than twice as large as they'd been as a deer. Either of them could probably manage an elephant on their own, but it'd be draining. Together, though, it felt…effortless. Beysal trumpeted with their snout, and Erso could make out Sumi at the campfire, her eyes wide as she started clapping.

Beysal stepped their elephant up to the edge of the campfire, taking Erso's log and launching it into the woods. He buzzed with annoyance, but he couldn't stop Beysal from doing what he wanted to — short of halting the transformation completely. They stomped around for a few more minutes as Sumi oohed and ahhed. Then, Beysal marched them back to where they started, and they began to glow again. This time, he felt Beysal's energy pulling away, the bright light fading away until they both stood again, clutching their arms in their original forms.

They took a bow, and Sumi clapped again as they walked back over to the fire.

"That was incredible!" she said, standing.

"All in a day's work, miss," Beysal said. "Though it's much more fun with a quality audience."

Erso went over to where his log had been and looked out into the woods. There was a path of broken foliage where Beysal had thrown it, but the log was nowhere to be seen.

"It's alright, lad," Beysal said, coming up and slapping him on the back. "Just jangling your keys a bit. It's probably time we got moving anyway."

"Then I'm sure you won't mind me driving next time, eh?"

"Whoa now, son, let's not get carried away."

Erso shook his head, smiling as he walked back to the fire. Beysal was a bloody menace, but he wouldn't have it any other way. They prepared to leave, dousing the flames and covering their tracks as best they could. They set out of the woods with the sun heading for the horizon, the buzz from the whiskey still glowing inside him. He took the rear again, but he kept looking back toward the clearing until it was completely out of view. He missed this place — maybe even missed home if he was honest, and it was a good reminder that not all of his memories were sour. Even if it left him as an elephant's butt, it was good to be back for a little while.

26

Finally, Elomikarus felt his courage fail, realizing there must be goddesses and monsters of even greater power than his mother, Vilodai. He turned his ships, contenting himself with his dominion in the south. He built his palace on the Cape of Yinel, where Itorunai's wind did not blast, in the land called Amoriam, which means, 'The Dancing Grain.'

-Verses 131-133 of the Anushgiar Leyosil

—:—

Fifteen Years Ago

Erso jerked awake, shooting up in bed as his ears strained to listen. Was that a scream he'd heard? The wind was knocking against the windows, making it hard to hear anything beyond the shutters rattling. He rubbed his eyes and lay back down. Maybe it was just a nightmare. His parents were only getting tenser, and every morning, he'd woken up with his sheets a mess like he'd been tossing and turning. His parents looked no better, rings under their eyes, the sound of their arguing carrying up the stairs late into the night.

After a week of bickering, they'd finally agreed to leave for Anushai — though now they were arguing over the specifics. His father wanted to be gone six days ago, while his mother wouldn't leave until she arranged for the entire theater to go. She said she felt bad enough abandoning her city, and she wasn't about to abandon her actors too. Beysal had been coming over every other night now, and he was running dozens of errands, trying to get things closed up. Still, Beysal wouldn't be joining them. With no family to worry about, he saw no reason to leave.

Erso wasn't sure if he wanted to stay or go anymore — not that they were giving him a choice. At first, he'd been for staying, obviously, hoping he could steal a kiss or two from Me'lekona. But if the whole theater was leaving, she'd probably go too, wouldn't she? Besides, things were getting scary now. There had been fights breaking out in the market, mobs ripping apart stands with signs of loyalty to the old crown.

He looked around his room. It would just be so strange to leave this all behind, knowing he would never see these walls again. Every memory he'd ever had took place here. His father had promised they could come back — they owned the house, after all — but he was old enough now to recognize the voice adults used when they lied to you. They both knew they wouldn't see Amoriai again for a long time.

Erso rolled onto his side, letting his eyes wander around the room. He looked at his trinkets on the wall, the knickknacks on his dresser, the little desk where he did his schoolwork. How were you supposed to put your whole life in a single piece of luggage? His mother kept chiding him to pack, but every time he went to start, he just couldn't decide what should stay and what should go.

He was running through lists of things to bring, just starting to get drowsy again, when he heard another scream. *That was no bloody dream.* He leapt out of bed, crossing to his door in a heartbeat. He opened it, finding his father already on the landing, heading down the stairs. His mother stood at their bedroom door, worried eyes looking into the darkness. She turned, realizing he was there.

"Go back to bed, dear," she said, "I'm sure it's nothing. We have a busy day tomorrow."

He was about to do as she said, when they suddenly heard a bunch of shouting from somewhere down the street.

"Mishkal," Erso's mother called down to his father, "maybe we should go to Beysal's."

Beysal lived near the Woodworkers Guild, where there hadn't been as many problems — especially since some of the mobs seemed to be *from* the Guild Houses. But his father paid her no mind, opening the door and stepping onto the porch. As soon as the door was open, they could make the shouting out for what it was — *chanting.*

"Ha-da-lab mu-sei-kal, ha-da-lab mu-sei-kal," the voices rang out, low and ominous, like thunder shaking the sky. *Get out, monsters*, they were saying. If this was like one of the mobs at the market, they'd need to leave as soon as possible. Erso ducked back into his room, pulling on

his clothes as quickly as he could. He heard his mother's footsteps pound down the stairs to pull his father back inside. He had his shirt over his head when he heard the sharp sound of glass breaking somewhere up the street, horrifyingly close.

Suddenly, it seemed like the whole city had descended on their tiny street. The chanting drew closer, growing louder until it sounded as if it was in his bedroom. He heard shouting in front of his house, and he thought he heard his father's voice. He turned to run outside and help when the front door slammed. He ran down the stairs to find his mother with her back to the front door, her eyes wide.

"Run!" she screamed at him. He froze, looking at her in confusion. But it only lasted a moment, the stillness broken as rocks came hurtling through the windows, fists pounding on the door. "Run!" she screamed, this time her voice breaking as his legs suddenly worked again. On instinct, he shot back through his room, reaching his window just as the front door splintered. But where was his mother? Shouldn't she be running with him?

He turned back to look for her when another scream rang out below. He ran back to the landing, his heart pounding. He found his mother on the floor, unmoving, dark blood glinting in the streetlight through the open door. But she was alone…what had happened? He started down the stairs to go to her when he heard the sound of plates breaking in the kitchen. He finally noticed the torchlight bouncing off the walls, the sound of men's voices from below. He ran, flinging open his bedroom window and jumping to a narrow roof below. He grunted, rolling off the shingles as he landed in a heap in the garden.

He pushed himself up in an instant, sprinting across the yard toward the garden fence. The chanting sounded even louder outside, the voices of the mob filling the night from all directions. As he jumped the garden fence, he noticed flames lapping the curtains in his kitchen, but he didn't spare them another glance, running down the alley as he headed for the water.

The wind was still whipping down the street, and smoke drifted toward him, pushing into the alley from every building on the block. The sky glowed a dull red from hundreds of fires, reflecting off of low-hanging clouds. The bloody wind was pushing the flames into every building on the block! If the rain didn't come soon, they'd never salvage the wood. But what would they even have to salvage?

He finally realized that he was running *away* from Beysal's place. But the mob had been going south, so he had gone toward the water on instinct, desperate to get away. He stopped, pausing in the alley. He found a gap in the fence between two houses and crept along it, trying to get a look at the street. The houses on either side were engulfed in flames, so he covered his mouth, staying low to the ground. He stuck his head out, finding dark shapes still moving in the fire's glow, hundreds of shadows moving from house to house. But there were stationary shadows, too, person-sized and littered across the ground. He squeezed his eyes shut, thinking of Pa running out into the street. And Mum—

He shook his head. He had to think. What if Pa escaped somehow? His parents always said to meet at the theater if they split up. He would head there first, and if his father wasn't there, then he could go to Beysal's? But he'd have to go as far east as he could to get away from the neighborhood. Erso turned and crawled back to the alley, continuing toward the water. He saw no one else as he ran, though he still heard screams pierce the air every so often. Hopefully, some of his neighbors had escaped, too — though if they had, they hadn't run in his direction.

He couldn't think clearly anymore. He could only move, though one question kept creeping into his mind. *Why?* Why them? Why this place? Why now? There was all that rubbish floating around about Shapewalkers, but the city had to be at least half and half, right? His neighborhood was known for the theater and the docks, people coming and going, but was that enough to burn it down? It was just a simple place, and now there wouldn't be anything left of it. Tears stung his eyes, mixing with the smoke and salt air.

He finally reached the end of the block, rounding the corner at a run. But as the theater came into view, he froze. It was a column of flame, the wood erupting in a blinding glow. The paving stones in front of him were shining as if the sun were overhead, and the glass on the windows was already gone, melted away. Erso stood there for a long time, just staring at the fire.

Finally, thunder from the thick clouds cracked overhead. Raindrops began to pelt his head, and he looked up, blinking as the water hit his face. He finally moved, drifting like a ghost back the way he'd come. But he didn't head toward Beysal's — wasn't sure he'd even know the way in his current state. He walked toward the lighthouse, the only stone thing in the neighborhood. Its light was off, the tower lifting into the dark. Had the lighthouse keeper fled?

Erso went up to the base of the tower, worming his way under the porch. The rain continued to pelt the ground in front of him, splashing onto his legs. He felt cold, shivering as he pushed himself flat against the stone. He could still see the glow of the neighborhood, the flames pressing on despite the downpour. He prayed the rain would continue on, even if it only saved the scraps. He hugged his knees to his chest, wishing he could disappear. Every muscle in his body was tense, but in spite of himself, he somehow drifted off, the pounding of the rain at least drowning out the crackle of the house nearby.

______

Erso woke early the next morning, predawn light filtering into his hiding place. His skin felt clammy, and his clothes were damp. He blinked his bleary eyes, and for a brief, beautiful second, he forgot where he was and how he'd gotten there. Then recollection swept in, despair knotting in his chest. He rolled onto his knees, clambering from beneath the porch. His legs were stiff from holding them to his chest, and he felt unsteady as he headed up the street. It was deathly quiet now, so he headed for the main street.

The first thing he saw was the theater. Or what used to be the theater… There was nothing left but the foundation, just a few black splinters sticking up at odd angles like they had sprouted from the rock. In fact, as he turned up the street, there wasn't much of anything anywhere. Almost every single building had burned down, only a handful of brick houses with anything left at all. He could see clear into the next neighborhood, with only a short wall here or there to block his view. There were several dozen people combing through the wreckage, same as him, drawn by first light and hoping for something that clearly wasn't worth hoping for anymore.

He made his way down the street, trying to find his place. There wasn't much to go on, though, with all the usual landmarks charred beyond recognition. He wasn't sure if it was a blessing or a curse, but most of the bodies from the night before had been pushed into the flames. It was better than walking past them, but it also meant there was nowhere to look for his father. If he hadn't seen him by now, there was no reason to believe he escaped the mob. And his mother… A pit formed in his stomach as he realized what he already knew: They were both gone.

Still, he forced his feet toward the house. He went slowly, using the clock tower in the market to guide him. Finally, he found a beech tree that he recognized. Burnt as it was, with huge swaths of bark missing, he could still place it as his next-door neighbor's. He stepped carefully over the remains of his family's fence, walking up the stone steps of their porch. There wasn't much left of the house's frame, just huge heaps of ash.

He went to where the front door should have been and took a deep breath. He knelt down, picking through the ash until something gleamed with a milky whiteness. He wanted to vomit and run in equal measure, but he forced himself to pick it up. A piece of bone. It was small, about the size of his finger, and it had a curve to it. His mother's bone. He didn't want to think about which bone it was. He pulled off his shirt and tore a strip from it, wrapping up the bone before he put it in his pocket.

He stood, looking around one more time. He looked up to where his room had been, finally realizing why his mother hadn't followed him. She'd been blocking the door with her body. Not that it had held for very long, but she'd only cared about the one second he needed to escape. Why hadn't he blocked with her? He wished he had dragged her to safety or at least died by her side. He closed his eyes, listening to the wind as it blew down the street, rushing past with no houses to block it for once.

"I'm sorry, Mum," he said, his hands in tight fists at his side, his eyes shut. "*Lu'meset rikalan mu'na'sokar*," he whispered. *A good journey to the hall of the dead.* "Please visit my dreams," he added, wondering if she could really hear him.

He opened his eyes, walking from the house without a second glance. It was time to find Beysal and tell him what had happened. Maybe they could still run to Anushai with the others, rebuild some fragment of the life they'd had — assuming any of the others were still alive. Though as he walked, he felt the piece of bone pressing against his leg, and he knew the life he had was gone. Tiny fragments were all that was left for him now, reminders of a life turned to dust.

27

"How will I know them?" he asked. "For these creatures can take up any form." Vilodai laughed. "You will know them by their weakness," she said, "for their hearts were formed by my sister. As you conquer, they will reveal themselves, for they can bear no suffering. They lack your heart of steel, filled with nothing but the softness of clay."

-Verses 109-112 of the Anushgiar Leyosil

—:—

Two days later, Sumi woke in a heap, her covers knotted. She sat up, squinting in the morning light as she listened to the house around her. She'd been sleeping deeper lately — no doubt tired from all the practice she'd been doing for her performance — but thankfully, it didn't sound like anyone else was up yet. It would be a busy day preparing for the party, and she'd hate for the others to have to wake her. Just imagine how mortified she'd be if Erso burst in on her looking so bedraggled...

She shook her head, pinching her forehead. Burst in on her, would he? She had to get a hold of herself. As if he would care two bits about what she looked like, even on a good day. She pushed herself to her feet, hurrying to the washbasin to clean her face. With that, she walked to the wardrobe, looking at her dress. It looked rather plain, hanging there. But should she shape it like she had on New Year's Eve?

"They'll just have to get to know the real me," she said to herself, pulling the dress over her head. After all, she was no princess, and they shouldn't be expecting one. She tied her boots, hurrying to the kitchen to get started.

An hour later, she found herself elbow-deep in flour, rolling dumplings with Beysal. It didn't seem like they'd have even a second to spare, and even Erso was awake, dutifully following Elo around as they

165

rearranged the furniture. Kel was helping too, his hair looking particularly neat as he wandered around the kitchen, filling vases from a basket of flowers his mother had given him.

The hours flew by, and before she knew it, she was washing her hands and hanging up her apron. She turned around, leaning against the kitchen counter as she took it all in. The house was…*transformed.* It was like a tea house; dumplings roasting by the fire, flowers everywhere. There was even music, Beysal having pulled an old phonograph from the basement. When was the last time she'd been to a party? It had to have been when Nela was still alive — though that probably meant it had been one of her horrible singles' mixers.

Hopefully, today would be more fun, though she was only mildly intimidated by how many people were coming. She hadn't seen a guest list, but they'd prepared enough dumplings for a small army, bringing every chair in the house downstairs.

"Beysal," E'loseir said, looking up as she poured wine into a punchbowl, "I've got the raspberries. Where are those plums I asked you to buy?"

Beysal kept cooking, but he froze, his back completely still.

"I…uh…didn't buy them just yet," he said. "Got to keep 'em fresh and all, you know?"

Elo's mouth formed a thin line, but she said nothing, pouring the raspberries in the bowl.

"Sorry," Sumi said quickly, "it's my fault he had to train me so much."

"Oh no, dear," Elo said, suddenly smiling warmly. "Don't ever let this lout lay the blame at your doorstep."

Erso finished his centerpiece, wiping his hands together.

"I, for one," Erso said, "have spent a lifetime taking the blame for that lout. We can grab plums at the market and dash right back."

"But the guests will be here any minute," Elo said, looking up at the clock.

"All the better," Erso said. "Warm them up for Sumi, and we'll arrive dramatically, the guest of honor in tow."

Sumi shot Erso a look. She wasn't sure about that guest of honor business, but it would certainly be easier to slip into a party already underway…

"Fine," Elo said, "but come straight back. And if you pick up extra whiskey, I'll kill you myself."

Erso slowly backed away, jerking his head toward the garden door. Sumi smiled, following him, and before long, they were out of the alleyway and heading for the market.

She looked around as they walked through the neighborhood, surprised by how different everything looked after just a few weeks. She had really fallen for this place, and she found that she knew most of the streets in the neighborhood now. Not to mention how much she'd changed herself! She may still be on the run, but after all her training, she didn't feel quite so helpless now.

"Hey," she said as they approached the market, "why don't we buy them from a Shapewalker? I can practice on my keyholes."

"Sure," Erso said, "though you don't *have* to practice, you know. You passed your training already."

"Well, at least we'll keep the money in the family."

"Lead on, then, Professor," Erso said, bowing his head.

She rolled her eyes, turning back toward the stalls. She paused for a moment, taking a deep breath as the buzzing filled her ears. When she looked again, the market itself seemed to glow, like a sky full of twinkling stars.

"There's so many…" she said, her eyes wide.

"Can't kill us all," Erso said, grinning.

Sumi smiled sadly. Was that all they could hope for? Clinging to life, hosting the occasional dinner party? Even that was a gift, of course, but something still felt wrong about it — not in the Shapewalkers, but in the world. They shouldn't have to hide. She shook her head. At least she was here, even if all she could do was buy some plums.

They walked between the vendors, trying a Shapewalker with plums. They walked through the whole place, and she was about to suggest they give up when they found one at the southwest corner of the market. They were the biggest plums she'd ever seen, their dark purple shining in the sun.

Sumi smiled at the vendor, reaching for the fruit and—

Suddenly, she was yanked backward. She let out a yelp, her eyes rolling wildly as she realized Erso had her by the shoulders. A silver crossbow bolt cut through the air exactly where she'd been. It ripped through the vendor's stall, fruit exploding in a shower of color. For a moment, everything around her seemed to freeze. She turned in a daze, her mind feeling far from her body. But then time jolted into motion again, and they were running, Erso pulling on her arm.

"Get them!" a voice yelled in Berillai, and Sumi's eyes widened as she recognized it. She would never forget it as long as she lived — Detective Parimu. Somehow, he was here, come for them. And judging by the crossbow, he wasn't here to ask questions.

They sprinted down the cobblestone street, the market exploding around them. Everywhere, people were running. A tidal wave of police had crashed into the stalls, the navy tunics struggling with vendors — some of whom were fighting back. Creatures of every kind flew into the sky, all Shapewalkers trying to escape. More arrows ripped after them, with screams and yells filing the air. Sumi tried to block out the chaos, focusing on running, her heart pounding against her ribs.

Suddenly, an officer appeared out of nowhere, bursting from a nearby aisle. A light flashed around Erso, and his cane became a sword. He let go of her hand but didn't break his stride, leaping into the air as he swung into the officer's head. The steel sheath made a crunching noise as it landed, the officer falling back.

"Keep running!" Erso yelled, dodging under the nightstick of another who'd appeared. Sumi ran straight ahead, the other officer crying out in pain. Within moments, Erso was at her side again.

"We need to get out of here," he said, his breath coming out in rasps. "Do you think you can shape?"

Sumi reached into her mind, desperately searching for the stillness of her pool, but all she could feel was her racing heart, her blood throbbing in her temples.

"I don't know," she said. She thought back to the last time Parimu had chased her; she still wasn't entirely sure how she'd managed the fire hawk that time. Still, she should be able to, shouldn't she? After all her training, all those obstacles in the woods. But that had been exhilarating. Now, she felt only fear, *terror* even. She knew she had to let go, had to separate from those fears, but if she tried and failed…

Erso didn't answer, pulling her forward as they reached the square, the old clock tower ahead.

"We just have to hide," he said, stopping as he looked behind them. "I'll see if I can distract Parimu. Once I do, sneak back to Beysal's."

He pulled her by the hand toward the tower. At its base was a giant steel door. He tried the handle, which turned, but the door wouldn't budge. He rammed his shoulder against it, the hinges starting to groan.

"Let me help," Sumi said. On a count of three, they both slammed into the door, the ancient metal finally opening. Pain spiraled down her arm, but she paid it no mind, stumbling into the darkness of the tower.

The first floor was dusty, the high ceilings disappearing into shadow. Whatever the base of the clock tower had been used for, it was just storage now. There were dozens of crates, and behind, a staircase ran along the wall, circling the tower to the floors above. Erso forced the door back shut, taking her by the arm.

"We can hide you in here," he said. "Then I'll head back out and lead them off. Wait five minutes and then run."

"What about you?" she whispered, looking back at the door. "I can't leave you."

"I'll be fine," he said. "I can still shape. Besides, this isn't my first dance."

He flashed her a tiny grin, though his eyes were tense. He turned away, dragging her up the staircase. The second floor was much the same as the first, only with lower ceilings. He pulled her behind another row of boxes, pushing her into hiding, despite her protests. Then he disappeared, running back down the stairs.

Sumi sat in hiding, counting out the seconds as her heart thundered in her ears. The dust made it hard not to cough, so she held her breath, desperate to keep quiet. Still, she burned with shame. If only she could shape! She had gotten Erso into this mess, and now he couldn't get away because of her. What if he didn't manage to escape? How could she live with that? Still, she stayed where she was, terrified she'd put him in even more danger if she disobeyed him now.

As she reached a count of fifty, she heard shouting through the grimy windows. Suddenly, Erso appeared beside her. She jumped, but he covered her mouth, holding in her scream.

"The police are outside," he whispered. "Showed up just as I made it to the door. They're fanning out to check the square. Hopefully they'll leave, but I couldn't risk them seeing me run off without you."

He cursed under his breath.

"I don't know what Parimu can see, but if he's learned to spot keyholes... We can't both hide here. If they come in, stay put, and I'll try to lead them higher. After they pass, you can run out the front."

With that, he disappeared again, and she shut her eyes, straining to listen to the sounds below. Some of the shouts of the police grew more distant. Like he said, with any luck, they'd just pass by. Even with Erso and her pushing it open, the door would be hard to open, and maybe the police would think they hadn't managed it.

A minute later, though, she heard the awful shriek of the old hinge. Voices drifted up to her, but it didn't sound like many. Suddenly, she heard footsteps slapping on the stairs.

"Get him!" roared a voice below. *Parimu.* Someone ran past the second-floor landing, flying up the stairs, the stomp of boots behind them. That had to be Erso. *Oh no,* she thought, *oh no, oh no, oh no.* Her nails dug into her palms.

She crawled from her hiding place, creeping toward the stairs. She could hear the sounds above more clearly now: more shouting and what sounded like metal against metal. *Were those swords?* Her mind raced. She looked at the steps below her. He had told her to run, but if they had swords, and he was fighting them… Why hadn't he just flown away at the top of the tower? She set her jaw, turning toward the third floor. If he was in trouble, she couldn't leave him, no matter what he said.

She followed the sounds, climbing as quietly as she could as she made her way around the tower. After the fifth floor, the ceiling opened up, revealing the giant mechanism of the clock. The gears were turning, some slow, some frantic, but she paid them no mind, climbing to where she saw the light filtering down. Finally, she reached the roof, the sound of swords clanging above the turning of the clock.

She poked her head onto the roof, her heart leaping into her throat. Erso stood with his back to the edge of the tower, sword in hand. It had blood on it, and two of the officers were on the ground, unmoving. He was breathing heavily, but was he hurt? She couldn't see any blood on his coat. Parimu faced him, his own sword in hand, his crossbow at his side. That must be why Erso hadn't run. If he took a silver arrow while he tried to fly away, he'd be finished. Unless he was still distracting Parimu for her sake…

Her mind raced, trying to think of some way to help. Maybe Erso wouldn't have time to transform on the roof, but what if he could jump off the edge? All he needed was a second out of sight, and Parimu would never hit his shot. She slipped back down the stairs, working her way across the walkway until she was just under Erso, where she found a grimy window. She pulled the latch, and after a hard push, it creaked open. She poked her head out, gulping at the drop. Was she really considering this? Yes, she was. For Erso. She closed her eyes.

"Essomuai," she whispered. "Please. You have to help me save him."

She took a deep breath, picturing herself in the cave, the pool beside her. She could see a golden light in the distance. That hadn't always been there, had it? Why had she imagined that? She felt a warmth coming from that distant glow. Somehow, a strange confidence filled her; she could do this. Before she could think too much, she put her foot on the ledge, stepping out the window. The ground was still there, mocking her with its pull, but she didn't look down. She took another breath, shouting as loud as she could.

"Erso!" she yelled. "Jump!" And then she leapt out the window.

As soon as she did, she began to glow, appearing as a fire hawk. She saw a shadow from the corner of her eye, and Erso flashed above her, suddenly falling as a rat. She pointed her wings toward him, grabbing him in her claws. She banked hard, swooping to the right just as a streak of silver passed her. She plunged toward the ground, gaining speed. Officers swarmed below, drawn back to the tower by the yelling. She shot out from the base of the tower, flapping as hard as she could as she flew to Beysal's house, the only place she could think of.

They crashed into the courtyard, flashing to their normal forms as they burst into the party. Two dozen faces turned toward them, greetings pouring out. But as they saw the wild look in their eyes, the smiles began to fade.

"Police," Erso croaked out.

The room exploded, guests pouring out the front and back. Beysal sprinted down the basement stairs, reappearing with a bag in hand. Then, he grabbed Kel, scooping him up with his other arm.

"Get her safe," he said to Erso. He told Elo to hurry before running out the door. Elo ran over to her desk, pulling out two stacks of papers. She threw one in the fireplace, putting the other under her arm as she ran after Beysal. Erso had disappeared, but she heard his footsteps above. Sumi finally unfroze, rushing toward the stairs, but he was already coming back down, their suitcases in hand. She reached out for hers, and he let her take it, pushing the front door shut before he dragged her toward the back.

He took her by the arm, running down the alley. And not a moment later, she heard shouts from the direction of the house, a loud bang sounding on the door. Erso led her down two more blocks before he pulled her down another alley, the pines of the graveyard rising behind them.

"Okay," Erso said, his chest heaving. "He knows our faces; we need to be somebody else, anybody else."

Sumi nodded. Somehow, she still found the stillness from the tower, and glowed, turning into Seriai. Erso appeared as a man she'd never seen before, but he looked at her and nodded. Then, he was pulling her down the alley again, toward the north where the old docks were. She was glad to have his hand on her arm. Otherwise, she might have never moved again.

"Oh my goodness, Erso," she said, her throat tight as she finally realized what she'd done. "I led the police there. I didn't think. I'm so sorry."

"It's alright," he said quickly, his eyes on the street. "There was nothing else you could have done. But it's fine; they've planned for this.

We got them out."

He finally looked at her, his eyes wild. Still, he softened for a moment. "Plus, you saved my life. Thank you."

She shook her head, but he didn't see, already turning away. He was the one who'd saved her. Erso kept pressing forward, his head swiveling as he scanned the street. She jogged behind him, desperate not to fall behind. As they reached the docks, he pulled them to the side again, looking at the boats.

"Where will they go?" she asked. She didn't want to distract him, but the look on Kel's face was frozen in her mind.

It was a while before he answered. "They always have two places," he said. "It's set up through the guild. I don't know where, but there's an apartment they can go to. And there's nothing at the house with their name on it, no pictures. Everything they have is in the desk and Beysal's bag. They'll be fine."

She nodded, still in a daze. She had to cling to those words. Even if Parimu caught them now, all she wanted was for the others to be okay.

"Alright," he said, pointing to the docks. "I think I see my friend's boat. We need to head for Anushai."

"Okay," she said, nodding.

"I never would have thought he'd follow us," he said, shaking his head as he looked back at the street, "not in a million years. All this for one Shapewalker? But it'll be safer there than here."

"Will it really?" she asked, holding tightly to his arm. "Is anywhere safe? Erso, you can put me on a boat if you want, but you don't have to come. I've put you in enough danger as it is."

"No," he said, shaking his head. "I'm getting you out of here."

"But what will we do over there?" she asked. "He'll still find us eventually."

"Maybe," Erso said. "But there's no Fida'lalean in Anushai. Maybe you have a relative there still, I don't know. But we have to go."

He took her by the hand, pulling her toward the docks. She hated what she'd done, but there was no way to fix it now. She let him drag her to the boat, the city falling away. But she kept looking over her shoulder, certain that death would reappear, like a shadow in the sky set to sweep them both away.

THE END OF PART THREE

PART FOUR

28

"Hiyyeon paiyel kalyeon bollom, shelmmes reyyelm nelek jeyon."
**"The ocean sends a thousand waves, but only the deepest stand
before them."**

-Hiyyeongiar yal Chelmun
The Anushai Ocean House Motto

—:—

Sumi sat with Erso on the boat to Anushai. As promised, he'd had a friend who put them on a ship. There hadn't been time to book berths — or even get physical tickets — a porter showing them to the sitting room seats as the boat left port. But it was good enough for her, and it was better than prison — or worse… According to Erso, with Anushai just across the Erril Sea, it was only a one-night trip. They were on the top deck, in a room with windows on all sides, sitting on benches with some thirty passengers in all.

The sea was dark outside, the boat rocking as it pushed forward, waves coming over the sides. They'd been on the boat for hours already, and the sun was disappearing. She and Erso hadn't spoken, mostly looking out the windows — their silence broken only by the occasional awkward glance. Despite the calm on his face now as he looked out at the water, he seemed tense, his foot bouncing as his hands gripped his knees.

Sumi sighed, looking at the portrait of the empress again. Hung between the doors to the bow and flanked by Anushai flags, she looked like a stern woman. She didn't know her name — Nela had never mentioned her, though she'd presumably been her subject once. She wore a diamond circlet in her hair and flowing purple robes, and her eyes felt like they were staring back — possibly with contempt. She certainly had enough contempt for herself after what had happened.

Her guilt flooded up again, threatening to choke her.

"I'm so sorry," she said, breaking the silence. "I just can't believe I brought this on your family, especially when…they're all you have left."

Erso shook his head, grabbing the top of her hand.

"It's not your fault," he said firmly, meeting her eyes. But it only lasted a moment, his eyes drawn back toward the storm. "I'm sorry I'm so tense, but it's got nothing to do with you — or even Beysal. I *know* he'll be fine. This isn't the first time they've had to move, and it won't be the last. They were ready — you always have to be in Amoriai."

It seemed he was right about that, at least — they *had* been ready. They'd had a bag packed and managed to leave in under a minute. Though that didn't mean they'd be happy at being forced to leave their home behind…

Erso shut his eyes, taking a deep breath. When he opened them, he looked down, letting go of her hand suddenly, as if he hadn't realized he'd been holding it.

"Sorry, for stewing," he said, rubbing his eyes. "I'm just…*angry*, though not at you. It's just those *bastards*. No matter how many years go by, nothing ever changes."

He looked at her again, his jaw tight.

"But none of us could have known Parimu would find you. And even if we had, I'm sure my family would have helped you anyway. We just have to look forward now. We got you out, and the police will calm down once they realize we're gone. Give it a month or two, and everything will be as it was."

He swallowed, forcing a smile to his face.

"Besides, I promised you we'd go to Anushai. This isn't the way we planned it, but let's make the most of it, eh?"

She nodded. Erso turned back toward the water, looking calmer, though when his hands fell on the bench in front of them, he gripped it tightly, his knuckles bulging.

They'll be alright.

She had to hold on to that thought, even as her thoughts raced and her shoulders knotted up. Even if it didn't dull the ache in her heart, that thought was all she had. After all, it was the first time she'd felt at home since Nela died, and the police had blown it to pieces. Even worse, Erso had risked his life for her — *again* — and it was his family she'd put in danger. Worrying about them must feel like losing his parents all over again. She'd known grief in a small way, but her family hadn't been *stolen* like his had. How could you live with that kind of fear? That kind of anger? And even now, forcing himself to comfort her.

"Just don't pretend things are okay for my sake, Erso," she said, staring at the floor, the shame boiling in her chest. "You can be angry with me — *should* be angry with me — even if they'll be alright. You've lost enough: your parents, your neighborhood, so many people you've tried to help. You should have left me back home instead of letting me screw everything up. You don't owe me anything else, promised or not."

He leaned forward, putting his forehead in his hands. "Don't do that," he said, his voice strained, coming out more like a growl. He turned quickly, pointing a finger at her. "Don't you *ever* let them make you think that you're the problem. This wasn't. Your. Fault. And I refuse to be angry with you for it."

He let out a dark laugh, shaking his head. "I'm angry alright, but not at anyone who wants to live. I'm angry at the killing, at having to run away my whole life, for the games they play with our lives. Maybe next time we won't get away, but this time we *did.* And that's enough. I would never leave you to die just so my life could be easy. They've taken enough, and I'm done. They can't have you; you're worth too much."

He took a deep breath, grabbing both of her hands, seeming like it was an accident again.

"Just promise me something."

She nodded. Anything he asked, anything to give something back to him, however small.

"If we see Parimu again, promise me you'll run. Don't come back for me. The next time I see him, I'll kill him, even if I have to drag him to Mu'na'sokar myself."

"No, Erso, I—" she stammered, but he shushed her.

"It's alright," he said, forcing another smile on his face as he let go. "I'm sure it won't come to that; just getting carried away. Anushai is different. I just…need to know you'll listen. You saved my life today, but it's okay to run when I tell you to."

He stood, offering her his hand. "Come on, we can't sit here and stew. It won't change anything. They have Anushai sweets in the canteen, and I, for one, mean to try them all. I bet there's ones you've never even seen."

"Okay," she said, taking his hand. Even if it wasn't okay, even if she could never agree to let him die, she owed him this much. Owed him her own smile, and whatever he needed to forget — if only for a moment. Besides, she *hadn't* had many Anushai sweets. Nela had always made Berillai cakes for some reason. And somehow, even with all this death around her, thinking of Nela made her feel lighter. He was right; they had to look ahead. There was still part of this world that was theirs, and as Erso would put it — even if she couldn't say it out loud — they couldn't let the bastards take their joy.

As they turned toward the canteen, holding on to the benches as the boat rocked, she promised herself that she'd keep fighting. Even if they had to run, for now, she had to believe there was a way to make things better. All these people had risked their lives for her, and she had to honor that sacrifice. She didn't know how, but she wouldn't simply hide in Anushai. If this was really the home of her people, then there had to be someone who could help them. She wanted more than safety; she wanted a way to *live*.

29

In the 47th year of the reign of Emperor Sorinae II (1231 N.E.), a horrid pestilence devastated the crop in Amoriai, which came to be known as the Great Wheat Blight. A jewel of the empire, Amoriai and its grain were crucial for feeding livestock and warhorses alike. The Houses convened, electing Empress Temmasil of Earth House to the Golden Throne. She was nominated by Lord Peortinae of Fire House with eight in favor and two in abstention.

-Voting Records of the Anushgiar Leyosil

—:—

Sumi woke early on the boat, her back stiff from sleeping on the bench. Most of the people around them were already awake, the bow crowded with passengers. They were all looking in the distance at…*Anushai.* She hurried toward the window, pressing up against the glass. It was *beautiful.*

Seongbelm, the giant mountain Nela had always talked about, rose into the sky, disappearing into the low, misty clouds. Around its base, thick forests crowded the slopes, and more mountains stood in the distance, rows upon rows stretching to the north. And just before them stood the city, still dazzling despite the rain.

Built onto the slopes, the city climbed upward from the port. It wasn't as steep as Berill, of course, but you could see almost everything, each building just a touch higher than the one before. And at the highest point, near the edge of the mountain, stood the palace. It covered an entire hilltop, its wide wings covered in tiles that somehow glowed despite the clouds. Steep stairs led down into the city, where there was a huge patch of green, like some kind of royal garden. And in its center was a bright-blue line, a water way running all the way to…*the Temple of Essomuai.*

Sumi's breath caught, her eyes wide. Even knowing it would be there, it shocked her all the same. How long had she dreamed of visiting that place? Even though it had technically only been a few months since she first read about it, it felt like a lifetime ago. In some ways, it felt like home. A place she could be safe, a place where she *belonged.*

"Not bad, right?" Erso said, stretching as he joined her. "Even with no sleep, it's quite the view."

All she could do was nod, no words coming to mind to describe what she was seeing.

"Saved you the last pastry," he said, holding up a bun. "Something to eat while we wait."

He tilted his head toward the docks, where passengers were already lining up.

"Thank you," she said, popping it in her mouth as they went to get their luggage. The Anushai pastries were fantastic, strangely herbal but with just the right touch of sweetness. More importantly, they'd saved her last night — saved them both — finally letting go of all the tension they'd been holding. They'd worked through an entire tray of them while they talked — *really* talked — staying up late into the night.

He'd told her all about Anushai, of course: the Royal Houses, their strange government and how all ten houses ruled. But then, as the other passengers went to sleep, he'd told her about himself: about growing up in his cottage, living with Beysal. His voice had been quiet, transfixing her as it mixed with the sound of the ocean. And finally, his voice no more than a whisper, he'd told her how they died. At the end, she'd unconsciously gripped his hand, and they froze there for a moment in silence. When the spell broke, Erso pulled his hand back, clearing his throat as he suggested they try to get some sleep.

He was back to his old self now — pointing at things in the harbor and joking under his breath. Before long, their turn was up and they were on the docks, swallowed into the throng of arriving passengers. She followed him toward the shore, trying to appreciate the city around them. But a part of her still felt under the spell from the night before, unable to wake from the dream of talking with Erso — and the nightmare of knowing what had happened to him.

"Come on," he said, nudging her shoulder as they reached the gates into the city. "I know there's a lot to see, but let's get to the inn and get out of this rain."

She nodded, trying to keep up in the crowds, but there was just so much to see. There were people everywhere — with an impossible number of keyholes — and she even saw a man playing the sellomaera, its mournful wail rising above the traffic. Even ignoring all her memories of Grandpa saying it sounded like a dying bird, it was the strangest instrument she'd ever seen — like a large wooden potato covered in gold horns, played by blowing into a tube on one end. She chuckled, digging into her bag to toss a coin in the man's hat.

"*Sheyol nulshem,*" the musician said, taking his mouth off the sellomaera for a moment. *Thank you, miss.*

"*Buyel siom deloss,*" she replied, smiling. Thankfully, her Anushai — which she'd feared would be too rusty — was coming back to her. She could even understand the snippets of conversation around them, words she'd thought forgotten swirling all around her. She nodded at the man once more, scurrying after Erso.

Not that she kept up for long… Without the benefit of the carriage they'd taken in Amoriai, she couldn't help but look at everything. Even the shops they passed were like sculptures, the wooden eaves decorated in different splashes of color. As she looked closer, she noticed little patterns in the paint. One butcher shop they passed had tiny blue stars painted on it, hundreds of them crowded like a night sky.

"What are these?" she asked Erso. He slowed, turning to look back. The butcher shop was crowded, men who looked like sailors in uniform waving their hands and pointing at the counter.

"It's the houses," Erso said, walking on as she caught up. "They all have their own little kingdoms. Ocean House controls the navy, Stone House controls the army — things like that. But every shopkeeper pledges their loyalty to one, sometimes for generations. Keeps the business in house, I guess. Like our innkeeper — who you're gonna love — is a Fire House devotee, and he lives to talk about it. Anyway, I think that butcher shop is Ocean House, with the dark blue and all."

"That explains all the sailors, I suppose."

"Exactly," Erso said. "They all have their little areas. Fire House, for example, supports all the theaters, so actors always stay at our inn. My parents even stayed there back when they used to travel."

"That's amazing!" she said. "Does the innkeeper remember them?"

Erso shrugged.

"He says yes, but he's one of those blokes who says he knows everybody. I'll bet you a copper crown he claims he's had royalty visit recently."

"Deal," Sumi said, reaching out to shake on it. "But anything less than royalty, and I win."

They kept walking, though they had to stop briefly to pull their coats out of their luggage. The temperature was milder than Berill, but it was still plenty cold once the rain started soaking in. As she shrugged her coat on, she looked up, finding herself face to face with a giant house. Standing behind tall walls, it still loomed above the street. Made of alabaster, the white stone gleamed through the rain. It seemed like it had been carved from a single piece, the roof sweeping in waves like a seashell.

"What is *that?*" she asked, pointing.

"That," Erso said, gently taking her arm, "is a royal manor house, for one of the big families."

As he pulled her down the street, she finally noticed the guards staring at her, no doubt displeased to have her pointing at their giant house. She bobbed her head in apology, and they looked away, though they never smiled.

"Is that Ocean House?" she whispered, afraid to look back at the seashell roof.

"You got it," he said, chuckling. "And don't worry, it's not a crime to stare. But they all look like that, some motif about their namesake. This dock is close to the navy yard, so that's where the house head lives. I'm sure we'll see more on the way. We can even do a tour if you want."

"I'd love that," she said.

Which house had Nela been devoted to? She had almost always worn simple black frocks in Berill, never showing a particular affinity for any color. Unless one of the houses' colors was black? Her necklace had an emerald on it, though. Did that mean something?

They walked another block or two before coming to a wide boulevard. In the center ran a stream — flanked by grass and trees — with dozens of bridges crossing over it. Remembering the temple again, she ran ahead, stopping on the nearest bridge to look. The temple was directly in front of her now, only a few blocks away.

"It's so big," she said to herself, her eyes wide.

Erso joined her, leaning on the railing of the bridge.

"It's exactly like the book back home," she said.

Without that book, without Essomuai, she never would have made it this far.

"It's a really special place," Erso said. "But I can't even imagine how it must feel for you. I always knew what I was, and it still blew me away the first time. Even having Mu'lalat, this place feels…*important*, somewhere completely dedicated to our kind — especially with our own temple gone."

He frowned, a momentary cloud, though it didn't last long. He turned back to her, smiling as he wiped the rain from his face.

"Let's go see it as soon as we're settled at the inn — assuming we can dry off first."

They crossed over the bridge, heading into the western half of the city. It was still quaint and cozy, albeit noticeably less fancy; fewer shops, more apartment buildings, narrower streets. Still, everything looked well cared for. They didn't pass any other manor houses either, though she could see a giant lighthouse in the distance.

"That's Sky House," Erso said, pointing. "Most of the rich blokes are on the east side, but Sky and Grass are out this way."

"Do you know why?" she asked, looking around as if Grass House would be equally visible on the horizon.

"Who knows why rich blokes do anything?" Erso said with a shrug. "Money's worse than booze; goes straight to your head."

As they reached the inn, the rain began to slow, a gentle breeze blowing in from the water. The place looked like a fairytale dropped in the middle of the city. Set behind a lush garden, it was squat and wide with window-filled towers sticking out across its roof. Was that where the rooms were? A sign hanging on the porch read *Jeansil Yeom*, the…*Something* Flame. Eager? Persistent? Either way, there was no doubt they'd pledged to Fire House. And as they climbed onto the porch, she found paintings on the eaves again, deep scarlet flames painted all across the wood.

They stepped through the doorway into another time, like the medieval lodge of some old Berillai warlord. Filled with rugs and tapestries — and a roaring fire in a stone hearth — the inn instantly swept away the cold of the rain. Above the fireplace was a painting of a stern-looking woman in a red dress, and to the side was a doorway to the tearoom, where dozens of tables were covered in fine porcelain. As the door closed behind them, a stout old man with long hair emerged from behind the front desk, smiling.

"Kelam!" he shouted in Amoriai as he recognized Erso before switching to Berillai. "It's been too long, Mr. Milak'erat. I didn't realize you'd be joining us."

As strange as it was to have someone speak Berillai to Erso on purpose, it seemed to be quickly becoming the shorthand for travelers. He turned to Sumi, his eyes blinking through his half-moon spectacles, looking like the type who never let a coin escape him.

"But it seems we know why you're back! A beautiful Anushai wife. A pleasure, dear. Does this mean we'll be seeing more of you?"

"If only I could be so lucky," Erso said smoothly. "This is my business partner, Sumi Elerair. Sumi, Mr. Leyelbeon."

"Pleasure," she said, swallowing as the innkeeper looked at her anew.

"Fascinating," he said, stroking his chin. "You know, I never forget a face, and you look familiar somehow. You have a Berillai surname, though, eh?"

"My grandmother was Anushai," she said. "Though I guess I'm just common enough to look familiar."

"Hardly! A most *uncommon* beauty. That curve to your nose…" He leaned closer, narrowing his eyes. "I'd almost call it a Saldalgiar feature."

He shook his head, chuckling. "I'm sure I'll think of who you look like by the end of the week, I stake my reputation on it!"

"Sorry about the short notice," Erso said, clearing his throat, "but do you think you could squeeze us in?"

"Oh, certainly," Leyelbeon said, pulling over a thick ledger. "We're prepared for anything at the Jeansil Yeom, though we are very nearly full."

He paused his thumbing through the pages to look up at them over his glasses. "In fact, just two weeks ago, completely out of the blue, the princess, Lady Zayelhom Huwalgiar, bless her name, came to greet some performers from Maldegurn. And all I had was five minutes' warning from one of her retainers! You'll never believe the ruckus it caused in our kitchens. But we're all fire men and women here; you'd have thought they were polishing the china for the empress herself!"

As the innkeeper returned to his book — though he kept right on talking about the princess — Erso looked at her out of the corner of his eye, grinning. She rolled her eyes, fishing in her purse and tossing him a small coin. Erso liked to spin a tall tale, but he certainly hadn't been exaggerating this time. Finally, the innkeeper apparently found the page he wanted and looked up, frowning.

"I'm afraid I've only the one room on the top floor of the western spire," he said. "It does have two beds, though."

"Certainly understandable given the short notice," Erso said. "Perhaps you know another good place nearby, where we can—"

"Don't be silly," Sumi said quickly — her neck suddenly very hot from the fireplace. "We'll take it."

Erso gave her a look but signed the guest book as Mr. Leyelbeon turned it around. They took the key, and promising they could find their own way, escaped up the hallway.

"You know," Erso said once they were out of earshot, "it's really no problem if you want me to stay down the street."

"No way," Sumi said, shaking her head firmly. "You've already paid for enough, and I won't have you renting another room just for my sake. Now that you've saved my life twice, I think I can trust my honor in your hands."

"That you most certainly can," he said, clearing his throat.

"Besides," she added, "if this place is good enough for a princess, I'm sure the rooms are enormous."

Erso chuckled.

"What did I tell you? The man can't resist."

"I'll win that copper back somehow," she said, sticking her tongue out at him.

"I'd like to see you try," he said. "Beysal's still trying to win back a fiver I won ten years ago."

They finally reached their staircase — a narrow, metal spiral — and started up. It was a strange design for carrying luggage, but as they came to the first landing, she saw why. They were already inside one of the towers, and the rooms were arranged around them in a circle, with four identical doors around the staircase.

"All the way up for us," Erso said, starting toward the next floor.

The tower narrowed around them as it rose to its peak. The next floor had only two rooms, and at the top, there was only one, the floor basically just a landing and a wall with a single door. Maybe she'd been wrong about the giant rooms, not that she was afraid of sharing a room with Erso… In fact, it was quite the opposite; she was more worried about *him* being stuck with *her*. Still, those thoughts didn't last long as he opened the door, revealing the view.

The round windows she'd seen from below were much bigger than she'd thought. Theirs took up half the wall, flooding the room with light. They were facing west, and she could see Sky House in the distance. Even the edge of Seongbelm was visible, towering over the city. They'd climbed far enough to make it over some of the surrounding rooftops, and she could see the beach, the land slipping away into the Erril Sea.

"Wow," she said, stepping into the room behind Erso.

The inside was only about ten feet wide, but the ceiling ran all the way to the peak of the tower, making the room feel larger than it was. There were indeed two beds, at least, and they were on either side of the door with drawers at their feet.

"Not bad, eh?" Erso asked, leaning against a small desk under the window. "So, which'll it be? Left or right?"

Sumi put down her suitcase, looking between the two beds. In her books, the women always tried to face their beaus with their good side. But did she *have* a good side? And besides, it was ridiculous to think Erso would care which side of a frumpy shopkeeper he woke up to. Thankfully, the bedspreads were different, giving her something to go on. The left side had little orange suns stitched into the quilt, and the right had tiny fire hawks.

"Right," she said, putting her bag on that dresser.

"As you wish, my lady," Erso said, bowing.

She popped open her bag and— She froze. Her underclothes were on the top. She glanced at Erso, but he wasn't looking, so she quickly stuffed them in the top drawer. Suddenly, she had a horrifying vision of having to pass him in her nightgown later. What had she been thinking, sharing a room with him?! And more importantly, where was she meant to change in the first place?

"Keloseera, inshelo," Erso sang quietly, humming to himself as he put his socks in his drawer.

Sumi smiled despite herself. Actually, maybe this would be lovely. Even if she changed in the alley — or shaped her clothes the next few days — it was nice to be here. She was lucky to be staying with Erso, and she'd probably enjoy every minute if she didn't get in her own way.

Erso shut his suitcase, turning toward her. She slammed her drawers shut, looking up.

"Wanna have a look around?" he asked.

"Yes, please," she said, swallowing.

She'd enjoy it alright. She just had to survive it first.

30

"Myeol et myeol, reolan guyang lessem guyang. Dyeol sheng et myeol, bulgyeong shaldeom elshim."
"Let the earth be the earth and the light be the light. The soil is a secret, but the grass always shows."
-Saldalgiar yal Chelmun
The Anushai Grass House Motto

—:—

Sumi followed Erso back through the garden, heading to see the temple. As they reached the street, he paused for just a moment, scanning the street. It had taken her a while to notice — it only took a second — but he seemed to do it everywhere they went. Always looking for danger — danger she'd been too naive to realize was all around them. It made her heart ache anew, Beysal and his family rushing back into her mind.

They'll be alright, she thought quickly, her mantra the only thing keeping her from being sucked under by worry. She had to stay the course. Erso had a plan, and once they found somewhere safe for her, she could see what came next — and hopefully find a way to repay Beysal for all his kindness. She knew for certain if she ever found a home again, she would never hesitate to offer it to anyone in the guild. But what about *her* home? What about Berill? Was she really ready to give it up so easily?

Of course, her dreams of going back were before she'd realized Parimu would hunt her anywhere she went. She ought to be grateful, no matter where she ended up. Erso's family had found a way to live, after all, building a life for themselves. Who was she to question that? Not even a month ago, she'd had no one. What did it matter if she made it back to Berill? What made her think she could change this world? Wouldn't a safe place with people she loved be enough? Wouldn't it—

"What?" she asked, realizing Erso had spoken to her.

"I could watch you look at a city all day," he said, grinning as he shook his head. "It's like you disappeared into a dream."

Normally, it was that simple, wasn't it? Good old Sumi sees a few pretty buildings and completely forgets what she was doing.

"I was asking if you wanted to walk along the stream to the temple," Erso said, pointing.

"I would love that," she said, forcing herself to smile. Being here was good. Being with *Erso* was good. She just had to trust she'd find her way.

They retraced their steps, heading back to the canal. Erso led her onto the stone that lined the stream, following it north. The temple was enormous, somehow even larger than she'd imagined, easily ten stories tall. At first, she was nervous someone might tell them off for walking on the wall, but she quickly noticed others doing the same. None of them seemed worried. In fact, most of them were staring at the water, barely watching where they were going, their eyes glued to flowers spinning in the current.

Her book had mentioned that, hadn't it? Putting flowers in the fountain and letting them flow out into the city. But what was it supposed to tell you? Had Nela ever done that, looking for some kind of sign from Essomuai?

After a few more blocks, they came to an enormous stone square where the temple sat. It felt like the center of the city, with streets running off in all directions. It seemed to devour the horizon, with only the top of the palace and the mountains standing higher. They stopped unconsciously, staring at the building. As beautiful as the drawing in her book had been, it could never do justice to what she was seeing now. The stained-glass window burst with color, like the sun had set inside, each petal of the sacred flower in a different hue. And unlike her necklace, each one had a different symbol, circles filled with strange shapes.

"What are those?" she asked, pointing.

"Sigils for the houses," Erso said.

He pointed to one on the left, in the center of a bright-green petal. The symbol had three triangles in its center, just like her necklace, but with a jagged line running down the middle and a sort of blossom at the top.

"That one's Grass House, I think?" He shrugged. "I'm no expert, but they're definitely old. I think I heard somebody say once that the houses were here before the city."

They started toward the entrance, unable to resist its pull any longer.

The massive doors — each one large enough to be the hull of a boat — were propped open, though it was still difficult to see inside. She squinted, trying to catch a glimpse of the fountain, when she noticed someone waving from the corner of her eye. She turned, finding a man standing in front a flower-laden cart. And he wasn't the only one… A dozen carts lined the square, loaded with enough blossoms to fill Mr. Furttenhur's store twice.

"Flower for the fountain miss?" the first man called in Anushai. "Half off on another for your hair!"

She bowed, waving her apologies, but Erso turned, heading for the cart. She scurried after him, catching up just as he reached the flowers. He was already joking with the vendor, though she hoped he wasn't planning on buying her one, especially after all the money he'd already spent.

"I don't know," Erso said, folding his arms as he looked at the flowers. He turned to her, winking. "I think they'd all look great in your hair, but you're the expert."

"Smart man," the vendor said under his breath, chuckling. He took a bunch of golden flowers, holding them up for her.

"These sunbursts are fresh from the farms, miss; they'll last a week, easy. Great for floating too."

"Thank you," she started, "but—"

"—but she much prefers lilies," Erso said, cutting in.

"Excellent choice," the man said, smiling. "Three keyeols for three. Maybe one for your lapel, sir."

Her mind whirred, trying to remember how to count Anushai money. They'd learned them all in school — something about jobs with the train lines — but the denominations were fuzzy. There was the rumen, the meyon, the keyeol, and then…the julen? She gulped. If she had the order right, three keyeols would be worth a half-sovereign, at least a whole week's groceries back home.

"No, sorry, that's far too much—" she started to say as Erso handed the man the coins.

"I like him," the merchant said, laughing. He held the coins to his ear for a moment — checking them for keyholes maybe? — before dropping them in his pocket. Then, he got to work on the flowers, trimming their stems according to their purpose: one with a long stem for her hair, a shorter one for Erso's lapel, and one with no stem at all, presumably for floating in the pool.

"You didn't have to do that," she whispered as they walked away. "I'm sorry I got us dragged over there."

"I'm not," Erso said, lifting up the lily on his lapel so he could smell it, "and you shouldn't be either — I get to look at you with that flower in your hair all day."

"Save it for the pretty girls," she said, rolling her eyes.

"If I see one prettier than you, I'll double our bet from before."

He pulled her copper from his pocket, flipping it.

"But really, don't think twice about it. Like I said back home, I like spending my real coins on our kind; makes the work feel worth it."

"I suppose that's true," she said.

She tried to picture living in Anushai — working, finding new shops where they would learn her name. It would feel good to help other Shapewalkers, wouldn't it? But what about Berill? Even if she never earned more than a few coppers, she *liked* buying her vegetables from Alip Tellemuir, donating what she could to Nela's charity. You could do good, no matter whose face was on your coins, couldn't you?

As much as she would have liked to keep dwelling, they walked into the temple, and her fears just…slipped away. The silence and shade seemed to sap the noise from her mind, leaving an awed stillness in its wake. The temple was like a giant empty shell, the size of the library in Berill without any of the floors, the walls uninterrupted save for the spray of color from the windows. In each of the four corners, there was a long rope descending from the bell towers, and the only other thing in the giant space was the fountain.

The fountain. She walked toward it as if dreaming, staring into the dark ripple of the water. It was like her necklace had come to life, the ten petals made in stone, rising to her waist where the water pooled before it overflowed, feeding the streams throughout the city. Above the petals was a giant pistil where her necklace's emerald would be. Made of crystal, it seemed to glow as its hundreds of facets caught the soft light from the windows.

Looking down into the water, she finally noticed the poem, its words engraved into the stone. The poem of Essomuai. Its words had saved her back home, giving her meaning when she'd lost hope. She mouthed the words under her breath, slowly following them with her eyes — and saying them from memory when they hid behind the center of the fountain. And somehow, lost as she was, as she finished, she felt the same power she had in Berill. Only this time, it wasn't the lightness of bubbles but the unshakeable calm she'd found in the clock tower in Amoriai. She could feel it in her chest, like a second keyhole, filling the empty spaces in her heart.

"Essomuai," she whispered, "I feel lost. I don't know where I'm going, but help me keep feeling like this, like everything will be okay. Help me find the way."

She wasn't sure if Essomuai was really there, but 'talking' to her had always helped somehow. And here, at the fountain… Without realizing what she was doing, she reached out, dropping her lily in the water. It spun as it hit the surface, like a star swirling in the darkness. It circled once around the basin before it dropped over the side, sliding over a retaining pool and into the western stream. She followed it, walking along the edge as it danced through the water, until it slipped under a grate in the wall and into the city.

She turned back to find Erso smiling at her, walking over from the fountain.

"How did it feel?" he asked.

"Good," she said, nodding slowly. "*Surreal.* But I feel…*better.*" She smiled. "I don't know if my Nela ever had a single doubt in her life, but I wonder if she did this too."

"I'm sure she did," Erso said. "And I bet she got to do the next part too."

He cocked his head toward the rope that hung from the bell tower.

"Once you send your flower, it's your turn to ring the bell."

"Really?" she asked, looking around the room. There were a few other people milling about, talking in low voices, and one or two others approaching with flowers of their own. Her book had said the temple had no priests, and it didn't look like there was anyone who'd yell at her…

She went up to the rope, gently putting her hand on it. It was thicker than her arm and *heavy,* like it was made from steel. She looked back at Erso, and he nodded encouragingly. She pulled it, and it started to sway, though not hard enough to ring the bell. She used both hands, her shoulders straining as she swung it harder until a deep gong sounded overhead. There was a hole directly beneath the bell, and it felt like the sound was pouring over her. It felt like the pool again, like a giant keyhole, the vibration shaking her from head to toe. She closed her eyes, letting it wash over her as the bell grew still.

"Did you feel that?" she asked, finally opening her eyes.

"Feel what?" Erso asked, raising an eyebrow.

"The vibration," she said, shaking her head as she looked up at the bell. "It felt…familiar somehow."

"Must be just for the person who rings it," Erso said, joining her as he followed her gaze.

"Must be," she said, nodding slowly. She forced herself to let go of the rope, following Erso back out into the light. As they passed through the square, the vendor waved at them again.

"Which way did it go?" he asked. "I hope you got your answer."

"Sorry?" she said, pausing, thinking she hadn't understood the Anushai. "My…answer?"

He rubbed his chin, nodding as if he finally understood. "You're Anushai, but not *from* Anushai, no? I just noticed your accent." He pointed to the southern stream flowing past them toward the ocean. "People ask the water — ask Essomuai — when they need an answer on something. The way it flows tells you what she thinks."

He pointed to the north, where the palace was. "Toward the empress is greatness. Maybe you want to be a poet, a general; the north confirms your ambition."

Next, he pointed to the south. "The ocean is adventure, change, running from all that ties you."

He pointed east, where the manor houses were. "The east is wealth. Like ambition, but more cunning. Maybe you want to open a shop, be a merchant, whatever your dream may be."

"And the last?" she asked, looking to the west where her flower had gone.

The man nodded, smiling. "The west is for the people. Some say it means the people you care most for, like family. Others say it represents duty, not what is owed to yourself, but to others."

He laughed, shaking his head. "Don't look so worried. They say Essomuai loves all things, so the choosing is still yours in the end. There's no soil in the field that cannot grow a flower."

He tapped the side of his nose the way Nela used to. "Next time, you'll know to ask your question."

She looked over his shoulder at the buildings crowding the west half of the city. *The people.* It seemed she'd already asked her question without realizing it. But if her fate was duty, to what and to whom? If only Essomuai could answer that question for her…

"Thank you," she said, smiling at the vendor one last time. "I hope I'll get my answer soon."

"Come on," Erso said, pointing at the closest bridge. "Let's take a different way back, see if we can find Grass House."

They wove through the surrounding neighborhood, taking their time as they passed the shops and apartments. Eventually, they reached a huge building surrounded by a gate. It certainly *looked* like a manor house, though there were no guards like the others. Set back from the street, the house stuck out above the ivy-covered gate, the grounds covered in flowers and trees. Still, looking closer, it seemed decrepit somehow, the masonry falling apart in some places while the roof was covered in moss. And yet, it was beautiful too. Tall stained-glass windows ran along the sides of the building, depicting lily pads, fields, vines — everything in vivid greens and blues.

"Do you think it's this place?" Sumi asked, looking at Erso as she stopped outside the gate.

"I don't know. I've never seen it, though everyone says it's over here. But maybe it's a hospital?"

He pointed through the fence at a sign above the door. *Yelyeon*, it read. *Hospital.*

"Ah," Sumi said, smiling, "that would be a good clue if I actually looked, huh? Still, it's beautiful."

Suddenly, something shifted just inside the fence, moving through the brush. She started, looking down as a cat emerged from the leaves, meowing. Or was it *part* of the leaves? It was twice the length of a normal cat but half as tall, like a cross between a bobcat and a salamander. As it stood up fully and stretched, its underbelly was covered in white fur, but its back had plants growing directly on its coat. From the top down, the fur started to look as if it were dyed green like it'd been soaked in algae.

"What on earth is that?" she asked.

"A grass cat!" Erso said, sticking his finger through the fence as the cat rubbed its whiskers along it. "They're supposed to be friendly — and I guess they are."

Sumi smoothed her dress, carefully kneeling down. She stuck her hand through the bars, giggling as the cat pushed his head into her hand, purring. A tiny squeak came from another part of the garden bed, and a kitten-sized grass cat stood up, bouncing toward the larger cat. The adult licked the tiny one's face, meowing in return.

"This must be her baby!" she cried, cooing. The kitten climbed onto its mother's back, nestling into the plants that grew there. Sumi carefully offered the kitten her finger, which it sniffed before giving her a lick. It had a coarse tongue, like Amis, though instead of pink, it was a dark green. She was so engrossed in playing with the cats, she didn't notice a woman approaching the fence from the inside.

"Hello," she said in Anushai, "can I help you?"

She scrambled to her feet, bowing. "Sorry," she said, pointing, "we just saw the cats and…"

"Ah, yes," the woman said, smiling, "they're awfully cute. I was just worried you were having trouble with the gate; it tends to jam. You don't need any medical help?"

"No, thank you; just passing by."

"No problem," the woman said, smiling again. "They do need the attention; we're always so busy inside."

"Are the cats…part of the hospital?" Sumi asked.

The woman looked down at the cats as she reached into her pocket, pulling out a clump of herbs. She tossed them in front of the cats, where they eagerly gnawed on them.

"Sort of," she said, laughing. "This building was donated to the hospital by Grass House some forty years ago — Essomuai light their spirits."

She looked at the sky, touching her forehead in reverence for a moment.

"The cats came with the house. The family used to raise them for new medicines. But when Grass House left, the cats stayed. This pack has already been breeding for nine generations."

"Wow," Sumi said. Now that she knew what to look for, she could see dozens of foliage-covered humps in the garden beds. "Well, thank you for letting us look," she added.

"Take your time," the doctor said. "If you ever need help, though, we're free to the public."

She pointed back to the house, where a large covered porch led to a door with more stained glass.

"The gate is unlocked — when it works. Just come to the front door there."

She waved farewell, wriggling her fingers at the cats before walking back to the house. Sumi and Erso stayed at the fence for a while longer, playing with the cats until Erso's stomach let out a growl louder than their purring. Then, they quickly headed back to the inn to see what Mr. Leyelbeon had in store for lunch. If Fire House princesses really did pop in out of the blue, hopefully, the food would be extraordinary.

31

-Voting Records of the Anushgiar Leyosil

—:—

They reached the inn just as lunch was being served, the servants scurrying about under Leyelbeon's watchful eye. Erso led Sumi to the dining room, taking the table the innkeeper pointed at. Normally, you might want to freshen up before lunch — especially after traveling hundreds of miles — but it was for the best as far as he was concerned. He needed to keep moving, keep busy, anything to keep his mind off of what had brought him here. And there was nothing better to stave off despair than a constant flood of fresh excitement.

Besides, despair or not, taking Sumi to the temple was a treat. Watching her eyes light up always gave him hope that he was doing *something* right. Not that the temple wasn't a relief for him too. Even if he would never be completely safe — hazard of his profession — it gave him peace knowing there was something those bastards couldn't touch. They might have burned down the Temple of Mu'lalat, but they'd have to level Anushai before they touched a single stone on this one.

Their table was by the window, the breeze at least trying to push back the blazing fire those bloody Fire House men seemed so keen on. Someday, he should try staying at an inn affiliated with another house, but the food here just kept bringing him back. Surely nostalgia for his parents was important, but the stomach was stronger than the heart. On top of everything else, the houses all had their own culinary style, and he'd take the spices of Fire House over the pickled cod of Ocean House any day.

Before they even ordered, one of the serving girls wheeled her cart over, piling their table with pastry — though how the Anushai could see that as an appetizer was beyond him. It seemed to be their only true love as a people, and the only thing truly uniting the houses, even if the fillings changed. Actually, that was probably what attracted them to it — besides their old colonial love of stealing grain from Amoriai, of course. Something intricate like pastry would let the houses compete, their chefs tripping over themselves to outdo each other.

"Ooh, cherry!" Sumi said, taking one of the red jelly pinwheels. "We almost never have that back home."

He almost warned her about the spice but decided not to, leaning back with a grin as he took a pink cream horn for himself. It took her a few bites, of course, but finally, her eyes widened.

"These are awfully spicy," she said, panting as she fanned her tongue with her free hand. He started laughing, and she balled up her napkin to throw at him.

"Sorry," he said, putting up his hands in defense, "couldn't resist. What the Berillai call a spice rack, the Continent calls a salt shaker."

She took a long gulp of her tea, finally grinning.

"I have no regrets. But you better watch yourself. I'm gonna train my tongue until I can sneak enough spice in our food to do you in."

She winked, taking another big bite, though her smug look only lasted a few seconds before she had to repeat the cycle of drinking tea and fanning her tongue.

A few moments later, the serving girl returned, and he did Sumi the favor of ordering a few of the inn's...*milder* dishes.

"Is this much heat normal?" Sumi asked, pointing to the pastries as she refilled her tea. "The ones we had on the boat were perfect, so...*herbal*. These feel like they could clean chamber pots."

He chuckled.

"Only at Fire House. The boat probably had a different house affiliation. River, maybe? I met the chef here once; makes the rounds in the dining room sometimes. He said he trained under some big-time so-and-so in the Fire House manor. He said something like, '*fire in the mouth, fire in the heart.*' I think it's supposed to build character."

"Well, you'd better have another, then," she said, raising an eyebrow.

He smiled, innocently taking one from the platter.

"So, aside from burning your tongue off, what else do you want to do while we're here?"

"I honestly haven't thought about it yet," she said. "We came in such a rush. But I guess we'd better start looking for somewhere for me to stay, right? I don't want to keep you from getting home."

"No rush at this point," he said, taking a deep breath. "I'll want to check on them eventually, but I might as well let the air clear. The Fida'lalean saw my face, after all. I'll reach out to a few contacts here in Anushai, but we might as well sightsee while we can. If we have to stash you with some long-lost great aunt in the countryside, you'll regret not seeing the city."

"Right," she said, biting her lip. "Any clues you can dig up would certainly be appreciated. My Nela never once mentioned a sibling, cousin, nothing. But don't feel like you're stuck with me, either. My Anushai seems fair enough, and even if I just find a job somewhere, I'm sure I'll be able to make ends meet. And then—"

He held up a palm, smiling warmly as he stopped her. Once she started with her worries, they'd swallow her up quicker than a rat in a pretzel shop.

"We'll do this together," he said, "don't worry. Besides, Beysal might have let you graduate, but I still have one more thing to teach you — how to enjoy yourself, even when things are awful. This isn't an easy life we have, but you have to laugh when you can. Even if the cat's on the prowl, the mouse wouldn't skip his last piece of cheese, you know?"

The serving maid came back with their meals as the innkeeper approached with a bottle of wine. It was an Anushai white, nothing fancy, but well suited to everything on the menu. He took his, swirling it around before taking a sip. Sumi looked thoughtful but took up her own glass and raised it.

"To every last piece of cheese," she said.

"Hear, hear," he said, clinking her glass before draining his. "I wanna take you to the seafood market by the pier — you'll love it, they sell sharks. And then we should go up the mountain too, maybe tomorrow, and we can see some of the other fountains connected to the temple."

Sumi nodded eagerly, looking as if she were tempted to pull out her little notebook to jot it all down. They went on like that, talking about everything Anushai had to offer as they ate their food. What else could you do but laugh? They would always be mice, and the world would always side with the cats. Even when his mind was spinning, worrying about Beysal. Even as a thousand what-ifs floated through his mind —

a phantom scrap of paper, a clue for the Fida'lalean, anything that could rip his family apart again — he had to laugh.

Maybe he was lying to Sumi about not needing to worry, but it was a good lie, a *worthy* lie, designed to protect her from all this. The only lie that really bothered him was the one he told himself, the one he'd lived every day of his life — that you could somehow plan enough to keep death from swooping in and snatching everything you loved. Even with all his little rules — never break a Shapewalker out of jail, never stay in one place for more than six months, never…fall in love.

He shook his head, pouring another glass of wine. He'd write Beysal at one of the guild addresses, telling him where they ended up. But everything would be fine…wouldn't it? If Beysal couldn't have the beautiful life he deserved, what could the rest of them hope for? There had to be something more. And as much as he hated himself for it, he was letting himself believe there would be. Sightseeing with Sumi, keeping her safe, it all felt *noble* in a way his work never had before. She wasn't just a comma between bouts of traveling. She was the whole damn sentence. And this could be the last time he ever spent with her.

He downed his second glass, putting a giant smile on his face. Let him enjoy these last few days of happiness. The wolves would come — they always did — but he'd still be laughing when they arrived.

———

Sumi shot up in bed in the middle of the night, breathing hard as she stared around her in the dark. Where was she? What was she—

She saw Erso, a dark lump under his covers, his breathing slow and steady. Right…she was in Anushai. They'd spent a full day sightseeing, and she'd nearly collapsed into the bed — even as mortified as she'd been, pulling the covers up to her chin after Erso gave her the room to change. But she'd had another dream, jarring her awake.

She'd been a hawk again, flying — only, there had been another one flying with her this time. It'd had dark feathers, and it had been…in pain? They were flying over that same golden sea, only it had been more like grass, rippling with waves moving outward from the center. It was almost like a spring, pouring out liquid gold. She'd flown closer, to see if she could help the other hawk when it *attacked* her. That's when she'd woken up and—

She felt a powerful buzzing again, the phantom keyhole back, pushing against her mind. It felt closer this time, like the vibrations from the temple. She looked around, but just as quickly, it was gone.

She lay back down, pulling the covers back over her. Just another strange dream. She looked at the ceiling, tracing the shadows with her eyes where the moonlight didn't reach. She listened to the sound of Erso breathing, closing her eyes. His breath was heavy with sleep, drifting in and out like waves against the shore. It was soothing, pushing her nightmare away. Unconsciously, she synced her breath with his. How long did she have left with him? She turned over, watching his chest rise and fall until, finally, her eyelids felt heavy again. She let sleep take her, knowing there was nowhere else in the world she would rather be.

32

"Jeowelm et relonae beyesh jildel, kelshem et yeonmol shuyan leyosil."
"The one who boasts has their name recorded, but the one in the shadow decides the history."
-Yeonmolgiar yal Chelmun
The Anushai Shadow House Motto

—:—

Parimu sat in the telegraph office of the Amoriai police, his foot tapping while he waited. Finally realizing he was slumped over, he forced himself to sit up straight; he was a representative of Berill, after all. Still, he let out a heavy sigh, his frustration growing at the delays. He'd lost so many days chasing those creatures, and now, as they slipped through his grasp again, he was waiting on a bloody telegram!

He stood, pacing the hallway — anything to keep from screaming. Even now, could he even really be sure the Amoriai would tell him when his telegram arrived? Useless Fida'lalean. For all the officers he'd had in tow, two of them had died on the tower, and the others had taken ages to catch up as he chased after the hawk. There'd been nothing at the house they tracked them to, stripped bare by the creatures as they fled. And when he'd suggested they fan out to track the monsters by their light, the officers had feigned ignorance, saying they 'didn't know of such techniques.'

For a city full of spies, you'd think they'd have something useful! It had taken hours for them to hear back from their informants at the docks, and by then, their quarry was long gone. Someone had seen a couple board a boat to Anushai, which had to be them, but given their destination, how was he to follow them? Even if he got permission to dive into the lion's den, how was he supposed to find the creatures in their own bloody capitol?

"Detective Parimu," one of the telegraph operators finally called out, "message for you."

He sprang to his feet, rushing over — even as it took every ounce of restraint he had not to rip the paper from her hands. He scanned it quickly: *Phrase received; winter fall honey dusk.*

Finally, he had the next part of what he needed. He understood the need for safety, but these endless bloody protocols were stealing hours he didn't have. His instructions upon leaving Berill had been very clear: he was not to risk going to Anushai without permission from the Berillai Embassy there. The problem was, receiving said permission required seemingly endless steps to ensure he was who he said he was.

First, he'd had to telegraph the home office in Berill, requesting permission to telegraph Anushai. Once he received that, he'd reached out directly to Anushai with the daily code word from Berill. That, however, had only proven he was authorized to be reaching out in the first place. Then, the Anushai office had responded with a code word of their own. He had passed that along to the Berillai office, confirming it wasn't a Shapewalker on *their* end at the embassy. With that done, he only had to pass along this final authorization code, and he could finally proceed with his actual request.

It was enough to make his head spin, but at least he was nearly finished. He grabbed a sheet from the writing table near the telegraph desks and scrawled out his response to the Anushai Embassy. The poor telegraph operators were probably sick of him pacing the halls, but it was too late to be worrying about things like that. Hopefully, the next response would have him on his way. Every second he lost could prove decisive, especially now that he'd lost the element of surprise. Anushai wasn't anywhere near as powerful as it had been, but it only took one rock on the beach to hide a crab.

Finally, half an hour later, he received the message he'd been waiting for: *Request approved, book passage immediately.*

He grabbed his valise, taking off at a run. He already knew from his briefing which ships he would be allowed to take and where to go once he arrived. All he'd needed was this blessed permission. The only thing that mattered now was speed. He was the arrow the queen had chosen to slay these monsters, and he would fly after them with all he had.

———

Queen Welaya, daughter of King Talmun and forty-first sovereign ruler of Berill, sat in her sunroom enjoying a brief moment to herself. Her father — Umilai bless his spirit — had left her with an ascendant Berill, an incredible gift. Never had their position been so secure or so dominant. However, that gift of dominance also came with the burden of constant vigilance. As their rail lines stretched over the world, it required a firm hand to control all manner of chaos: banditry, graft, rebellion. As Father always said: "Become a giant, and the dogs will forever nip your heels."

If only he hadn't been so right — and she hadn't been so alone. It was a heavy burden for one. She had the navy, of course — thank the gods that blade remained hers — but she had few allies in the peerage, and even fewer friends. She shook her head, returning to her book as she sipped her tea. Her troubles shouldn't follow her into the sunroom. This was a sacred place, and the only one that was truly hers. Her servants knew bothering her here would bring swift punishment, but if she squandered the time herself...

She had just settled back into her book when there was a knock on the door. She closed her eyes, putting a hand to her forehead as she took a deep breath. She needed those little moments to keep her anger in check. Unfortunately, the anger that men had tolerated in her father only made them think her weak. At least she could still demand the moment of privacy between knock and admittance, her one chance to keep the wolves at bay.

"Enter," she finally said in a clear voice.

A small man stepped through the door, and her anger subsided. Commissioner Kollenail was an important official with the Crown, and if anyone had the right to disturb her, it was he. More importantly — and a fact still known to few — he was the leader of her Sterling Thorns. Their spying had kept her family in power for generations, and they were by far the sharpest knife in her belt. Kollenail was a simple-looking man, his dark hair and goatee cut like a sailor's, but ignoring his presence could be fatal.

He came in almost casually, though he finally bowed properly before wandering to the windows to look out at the garden. Unfortunately, he was also the type of man who found great pleasure in impropriety. But she was happy to let him think he could do as he pleased. He wasn't a perfectly loyal dog, exactly, but she was happy to let him preen before he went to gut her rats.

"To what do I owe the pleasure, Kollenail?"

He turned back from the window, folding his hands behind his back. He wasn't yet presumptuous enough to take a chair uninvited in her presence, though he probably wasn't far off.

"I've just picked up some information from the Foreign Office. You think they'd be more careful with their secrets, as deep in Pont'dulairn's pocket as they are. Anyway, our friend Parimu has telegraphed for permission to go to Anushai. It seems he missed his target in Amoriai. My informants in the city say it's the talk of the town amongst the higher-ranking officers; quite a stir over one Shapewalker. At any rate, there's been a flurry of traffic on the wires on his coming to Anushai."

Welaya put down her book, sitting up in her chair and folding her fingers together. The anger bubbled up again, but she kept her composure. If everyone in Berill knew Parimu's whereabouts, then it wouldn't be long until the northerners knew the same. It was a delicate situation, to be certain, sending her police into an enemy kingdom, but she was also sick of walking on eggshells with the Anushai. More importantly, she couldn't allow Berill to seem weak. A single Shapewalker escaping her own agents sent abroad…

"We cannot let him fail," Welaya said. "Especially once this girl is known to Anushai. If we cannot instill the most basic respect for our laws, we will never bring order to the Continent."

"I agree, of course," Kollenail said, "though we may need to take a more…active role. In my opinion, Ambassador Yeilorn is an Anushai sympathizer. It's a dangerous posting; men are easily corrupted at that embassy. But if any criminal believes they can simply race off to the north, it certainly won't improve respect for the crown. The vice peer seems to think he simply needs to lay the rails, but he forgets that it's your sword keeping those trains safe."

Kollenail's jaw tightened at that last bit. He had hinted at assassinating Vice Peer Pont'dulairn before. A loyal dog, indeed… But another thing her father had made clear was to move very, *very* carefully against the Peerage — and to do so only as a last resort. There was still more to be lost than gained killing Pont'dulairn at this point, certainly. Still, she wasn't about to let this creature escape. This girl was a wanted criminal in Berill, and she would be hanged here under her laws.

Besides, she 'd been itching to put Hiyelleom in her place. She'd met the so-called empress twice, and both times, she'd been smug and superior, as if her 'empire' weren't teetering on the brink. And while she'd played coy as the Anushai always did, her Thorns told her the truth: Hiyelleom was moving quietly, expanding her control over the Golden Coast and rekindling her bonds with Ekosinar. Unfortunately, the trains only held so much sway, the further east they ran. It was time to draw a line. So what if it led to war? The Peerage always worried for their coin, but she had her people's honor to defend.

"Have a telegram sent from my office," she said. "Parimu is to be given whatever support he needs. Tell them the queen is involved, the vice peer be damned. Hiyelleom will know that I demand the return of this criminal, and any failure to do so is as good as an act of war."

Kollenail actually smiled. It sent a shiver up her spine, but at least she had his agreement.

"As your will requires, Your Highness," he said, bowing as he left the room.

Welaya paused, looking down at her book for a moment before shaking her head. There was work to be done now. She stood, walking toward her office. The admirals would need to be gathered. If you were going to make a bet, you'd better gather your ante first.

———

Kollenail continued down the hallway at a quick pace. He would obey the queen, of course, but he still hoped Parimu would fail. It was time for a change in the kingdom, and he had no shame in admitting himself an opportunist. He would see Welaya firmly on the throne for now, but to do so, he'd need his Thorns to have more control. The police — and departments like Parimu's — were only an impediment to that.

Still, it was odd how toothless the Department of Reality had become. He had hardly known Drekkles, but the man had been a legend in his own right. Especially the coup in Amoriai; clever bit of work, that. But somehow, the man had been cowed into essentially mothballing his own department. Parimu had been the last man he recruited, and forces within the police had done their own work to shrink it from there. It wasn't as though men with the gift for hunting Shapewalkers couldn't be found. He had offered to take over that work for the queen with his Thorns on multiple occasions, yet she refused. She was a half-decent ruler, but she had a lot of nonsense from her father about keeping everything just as it had always been.

You could never trust an ideologue to get things done, he supposed. Parimu, and the queen herself, for that matter, were obsessed with Shapewalkers nearly to the point of madness. He had a few on his own staff — though he'd never tell Welaya that. *Very* useful for gathering intelligence, wearing any face you chose. Once he had Parimu out of the way, he would gladly offer the queen a few Shapewalkers to hang every year, but she was chasing a few stray magical creatures while Pont'dulairn ate the kingdom whole. He could stomach serving a King Pont'dulairn, of course, but for that, he'd have to survive the coup first…

Ironically, what he and Pont'dulairn wanted wasn't so different — except for the end result, of course. The vice peer was a dangerous man, but in many ways, he was too soft. Pont'dulairn wanted flowery things like trade and peace treaties, but what really mattered to this kingdom was strength. They had taken this land by spilling blood, and if they showed weakness, the other kingdoms wouldn't hesitate. If you asked him, the army never should have stopped at Strussfaran. The Treaty of Trilathdrei was nothing more than shackles on the Berillai, and every rail they'd forged should have been a sword. But he would leave this kingdom stronger, whether or not House Berill was on the throne.

He checked his pocket watch, quickening his step. The queen was right about one thing, at least: their enemies were many. Unfortunately, that left him with much to do, and time was always shorter than he'd like. He would send her telegraph, and then he had actual work to be about. A kingdom was nothing but a pincushion, and it took a sharp edge to hold it all together. Luckily for him, when it came to knives, he always knew just where to stick them.

33

-Voting Records of the Anushgiar Leyosil

—:—

Two Days Later

Sumi pulled on her stockings, rubbing her feet before she had to put her boots on. Erso was waiting downstairs, giving her the room to get ready, but her feet were just so sore — even if it was in a satisfying way. They'd walked *everywhere* in Anushai, each day like a dream. They were having a wonderful time, and finally, it felt like she was truly learning Erso's final lesson. Even when it felt impossible, you had to enjoy this life. It wouldn't take away all her questions about what came next, but she was learning to hold them in her mind at the same time as her joy.

She laced her boots and stood. Crossing to the window as she smoothed her dress, she was looking out at the city when she noticed a giant spider crisscrossing the ceiling overhead, weaving a web. She gasped, jumping back as the hair on her neck shot up. She had no idea where she'd picked it up, but she'd always been deathly afraid of spiders. Her memories of her mother were spotty, but Nela hadn't been afraid of anything, of course, and Grandpa had always said she'd never survive the navy with the masts all full of webs.

Maybe she would have only had a passing distaste for them if she'd been allowed to squash them like everyone else, but Nela had banned the practice. If Sumi wanted one out of her room, Nela would make her capture it in a jar and take it to the garden. Capturing them had been much more difficult than killing them, of course, forcing her to get much closer than she'd like. It had always led to a mountain of shrieking — and peals of laughter from Grandpa.

"Never kill spider," Nela would always say, "you not know him well enough for that."

Carrying countless spiders down to the garden at arm's length, she'd had always wondered what that meant. Now that she knew her family's secret, it must have had something to do with Essomuai, though knowing that wouldn't make this particular spider go away any faster... After Nela had died, she'd smacked a couple with the kitchen broom, but mostly she'd just run from the house, hoping they'd be gone by the time she came back from the flower shop.

She stood, her back against the door, watching as the spider spun its web. In the morning light, the threads were sparkling, and it was actually sort of beautiful — if you could ignore the thing hanging from it. Part of her wanted to run downstairs and get Erso, as mortifying as that would be, but she took a deep breath, shaking her head. No, this was her problem to deal with. And based on the giant web it was building, she couldn't exactly expect it to leave while they toured the city.

Without taking her eyes off the spider, she lifted one foot and unlaced her boot. She slipped it off and crept toward it, her leather weapon in hand. She didn't want to smack it from directly below; that would only risk it falling on her head. She pulled out the little writing chair in the room and stood on it, holding the boot in front of her as she watched the spider move across its web. With a snap, she launched the heel of her boot upward, hitting the spider dead-on with a crunch. It let go of its web, falling to the ground in a heap.

She let her breath out slowly, stepping to the ground to return the chair and relace her boot. But when she looked again, she found the spider on the floor, its legs still wriggling. As it curled up and died, she heard Nela's voice in her head: *You not know him well enough for that.*

Suddenly, she felt very sad. Suppose it *had* been a Shapewalker she'd needlessly smacked? And even though she knew it wasn't, Essomuai was the light in *all* creatures. And if the goddess were real, wouldn't she have felt the spider die? As the adrenaline slipped away, there was only regret budding in its place. She'd let the fear drive her to violence, and it was hard to see now how her situation with the detective was any different. If the Berillai weren't so afraid, the Shapewalkers wouldn't have to suffer so either.

She looked up at the web, its intricate design still glowing in the sun. It was still unfinished, the spider only halfway through when she'd killed it. She couldn't take back what she'd done, but maybe she could leave a bit of its beauty in the world…

She picked up the spider with her handkerchief, putting it on the desk. Then, she glowed, reappearing as the spider on the floor. Suddenly, the room seemed like a diamond, the light hitting all eight eyes at once. She almost lost herself in it, but she had work to do. She walked up to the wall, hesitantly sticking her front legs to it. But as soon as she touched it, she *knew* she could climb it, and that confidence willed her forward, going up the wall as if it were a ladder.

She headed for the corner where the web began. She'd appreciated its beauty before, of course, but now that she was a spider, she saw a logic to it too. Each thread now seemed perfectly placed, and the spaces the spider had yet to fill in stood out to her, begging to be completed. She scrambled onto the web. Surprisingly, the spokes on the web weren't sticky, and she was able to quickly cross them, like a dance her body knew by heart.

She was eager to finish it, but how would she lay the fibers? She put her awareness into her body, trying to feel for the source of her webs. She seemed to find it in her abdomen, a sort of…*fullness* where the webs would be. She moved along the empty spaces in the pattern, imagining she was laying a track behind her, and eventually, the threads actually came, pulling gently on her as she spun them. She worked at it furiously, losing track of time, until eventually, the web was complete.

More confident in her abilities, she attached a new length of thread to the center of the web, lowering herself halfway to the ground. Staring up at it, she felt a deep satisfaction, a *rightness* to how it looked. There was only one last thing to do. Lowering herself to the desk, she scurried to where she'd left the crushed spider. Now that she was the same size, the sadness of seeing what she'd done hit her anew. It was crumpled up, its legs bent at odd angles. What if her own body had been mangled in that way?

She started wrapping the spider in her webs, working from instinct as she threaded the silk over her legs. Finally, it was folded into a sort of burial shroud. Suddenly, an idea came to her, a sort of sailcloth she could attach to it, giving it the sendoff it deserved. But where had that come from? She could feel dozens of designs in her head, some of them far more complex than the web she'd just finished. It was like in Amoriai, her strange memory of being a caterpillar when she became a butterfly...

She shook her head, getting back to work. She laid out her design, keeping the sailcloth firmly in her mind as she wove. Finally, when it was done, she connected it to the shroud. Then she crawled to the floor, returning to her human form. Opening the window, she picked up the sailcloth and released it into the wind, watching the spider float away.

"I'm sorry," she said quietly. "Sleep well, little friend."

She watched it for another moment before closing the window. As she turned to go, she felt another buzzing in her ears. She stopped, looking around the room. It felt like it was level with her, but they were on the top room in the inn. Then again, it felt distant somehow — in a building nearby, maybe? She closed her eyes, trying to follow it with her mind. She turned, opening her eyes to find herself facing north. But as she stepped toward the door, it disappeared. She supposed it was normal enough to feel keyholes in a place like Anushai, but she never felt this sensitive as she and Erso walked around. Maybe she should ask him, and he—

Erso was waiting for her.

She rushed about the room, gathering the rest of her things. She'd gotten so caught up in her spider, she'd completely left him waiting. Still, even as guilt lingered, the spider *had* taught her something about Berill. She was the spider, and her people were the boot. She wasn't sure how — or even *when* she'd get home — but she had to help her people face their fear. Just like the spider's web, Shapewalkers were beautiful when you looked close, and if she could make them see that, maybe her kind would have a chance.

———

Erso sat in the dining room, reading a newspaper while he waited for Sumi. Actually, where was she? She was usually quicker at getting ready than he was, simple — yet somehow elegant — dresser that she was. He could go check on her, although, that would probably only horrify her more. He chuckled. Better to wait. She was shy enough about sharing the room; the last thing he wanted to do was spoil the mood, especially after the past few days they'd had.

It had been...*marvelous,* as if the honeymoon they'd made up was actually happening. If only he could be so lucky. They'd seen the whole city, and while some of it certainly took his breath away, he could have watched Sumi looking at it all forever. Of course, there were moments every day, especially over meals, where they'd both go quiet, grappling with what they'd left behind. And it was a subtle reminder of what they both knew: this time would have to end.

But he couldn't just leave her anywhere. He was fine sleeping in a ditch, of course, ever the lone wolf, but Sumi needed — no, *deserved* — more. Just look at the way her eyes lit up every time she recognized a new part of the city, or how she made friends as easily as breathing. He may be a wolf, but she was a tree — lush and bountiful, but in desperate need of roots.

With that in mind, he'd woken early to see if Leyelbeon could help. They had to at least try to find some family she still had, and knowing the Anushai and their record-keeping — the old timers in Amoriai still talked about the 'bloody grain tax' — there had to be something he could use. And apparently there was. Leyelbeon had given him directions to the municipal office where family records could be found — not that he hadn't been smug about it…

"I suppose you *could* find something useful there, though if it's anyone of note, you may as well ask me."

Charming. Still, of note or not, he hoped he found someplace good for Sumi, if only to protect her from herself. She didn't talk about it openly, but when Berill came up, there was still a sort of *longing* in her eyes. It was heartwarming, of course, caring for your people that much — it wasn't as if he had no affection for Amoriai, even if the city he'd loved was dead — but he couldn't let her go back there. He'd promised her, of course, in that bar back in Berill, but it was too dangerous, too hateful for her to ever be truly safe there — not with Parimu still alive, at least. But if he could offer her flesh-and-blood relatives in Anushai, something she could hold on to…

"Morning," Sumi said gently, even as he jumped like someone burned him. He smiled, jumping to his feet as he motioned for her to sit.

"Everything alright up there?" he asked.

"Uh…yes," she said, taking a hasty sip of the tea he'd ordered her. "Strange…but good."

"I'll keep my curiosity to myself," he said, chuckling as he slid Leyelbeon's map across to her. "This is our plan for today."

She studied the little map, following the lines with her eyes. Apparently, the municipal offices were east of the temple, just down the hill from the army barracks.

"Alright," she said, handing the paper back to him, "we've seen everything west and north; what do we have today?"

"Well," he said, staring hard into his coffee. "I thought we might stop by the records office, start looking for your family."

"Oh," she said.

He looked up, catching just a moment of her frown before she smiled. "That's a good idea, thank you."

Was he imagining things? Or did the thought of leaving him really make her sad? *Impossible.* She was probably just nervous. There was no way she felt even a fraction of what he was feeling. But he certainly didn't want her to worry. He would never leave her somewhere awful; she had to know that.

Just then, their pastries arrived, giving them a moment to fill their plates in silence. He watched as she took her first bite, her eyes lighting up like they always did. Maybe he'd stolen too much caviar in his life, but he wished he could feel as much joy as she did over a simple breakfast. After a few bites, she put down her pastry, taking a deep breath.

"Thank you," she said, meeting his eyes. "For everything. For saving me, for showing me Anushai. It's probably time to get me out of your hair, huh?"

"I'd rather be bald," he said, earning her most beautiful smile. "But seriously, the pleasure's been all mine. I'd be your tour guide anytime."

Even if it meant guiding her away from him…

"I can't think of anyone better," she said. She glanced at the map again. "Do you think we'll really find my family, though? It's a bit embarrassing, but I only know my Nela's given name."

"We can try," Erso said. "I don't know if you've noticed, but the Anushai love record-keeping." He cocked his head toward the front desk, lowering his voice. "I think Leyelbeon could tell you the last thirty princesses of Fire House without looking."

She laughed out loud, slapping a hand to her mouth as she tried not to choke on her pastry. She forced down some tea, balling up her napkin as she pretended to throw it at him. But he only laughed. She could throw rocks at his head if she let him see that smile.

───

An hour later, they finally reached the municipal block — though it felt like it took another hour to find the right place. There were dozens of identical buildings on the block, all of them made of dark stone — apparently in honor of Shadow House, who ran the offices. Strangely, though, as they walked into the Records Office, they found it impossibly bright. The interior was completely white, and a giant atrium flooded the place with sunlight. He looked up, spotting workers on the other floors, zipping by with carts full of documents. It was like a library and a palace had decided to have a baby.

There were already people queuing in front of a line of desks, while others sat at tables, leafing through the documents they'd just received. Moving toward the line, they came across a giant book set up on a dais in the middle of the room. It was like a huge piece of luggage bound in gold, and it looked to have thousands of pages — though it had been left open a bit past the middle. He squinted at the looping Anushai script, trying to make out the words. There were entries with names and dates, and a short sentence after each: 'Helped with sickness,' one read, 'achieved rank in the navy' — little things like that. Sumi looked up at him with raised eyebrows, but all he could do was shrug.

"Never seen anything like it," he said. "Beautiful, though."

They took their place in line, watching as even more workers dashed about behind the counter. There was a forest of stacks behind the desk, the mountain of records disappearing into shadow. The way they ran about, it was no surprise they only had to wait ten minutes before someone called them to the front.

"Hello," Sumi said, smiling as she took the lead given her far better Anushai. "We're looking for birth records."

Erso never had high hopes when it came to government offices, but the man actually smiled back at her. The man did have a keyhole, though. So, this was what it felt like when your government saw you as more than an insect... Or it could have simply been Sumi's lovely smile. The man was a bureaucrat, after all, Mu'amashdar or not.

"We have lots of birth records here, miss," the clerk said. "Do you happen to know which reign the person was born in?"

"Oh, um, I'm not sure." She glanced at Erso, but all he could do was shake his head. "I'm looking for the records on my Nela; she was born about sixty-five years ago."

The man looked up at the ceiling for a moment, mumbling the math under his breath before nodding. "That would have been Emperor Shaolmesun of Fire House." He started shuffling through a stack of index cards in front of him. "Did you need royal records or common?"

"Oh, common," she said quickly, shooting Erso a grin. He certainly thought she was pretty enough to be a princess, though she'd never believe it if he told her.

"Alright," the man finally said, looking up with a card in his hand, "just fill out this form."

He handed them a sheet that Sumi quickly filled out. She handed it back, and the clerk copied some of the information from it before ringing a bell. One of the workers behind him dashed over and took the card, running back through the stacks.

"Feel free to use the tables behind you," he said. "They'll bring the records to you."

"Thank you," Sumi said, giving him a little bow. "By the way," she asked, pointing to the dais, "what is that book in the center there?"

"Oh, those are the imperial grants. People from all the houses petition the crown at the east end of palace, and every night, a scribe comes down from the palace to record the ones they granted. Believe it or not, that book is just for Empress Hiyelleom; she's done quite a bit over the years."

They both did a double take back at the golden dais. It would certainly take a lot of entries to fill a book that size… He couldn't imagine rulers in any other country complying with even a fraction of all those requests. Just then, the runner returned with the book of birth records, and the clerk laid it on the counter in front of them. It was a stout book, as thick as his forearm and clad in dark wood.

"Thank you again," Sumi said, nodding to the clerk.

Erso reached out to help, but Sumi had already picked up the book with both hands, heaving it into her arms as she led him to the tables. She picked one about halfway through the room, just to the side of the dais, dropping the book with a thump as Erso sat across from her.

She gently opened the book's cover, though — despite being older than both of them combined — the binding opened without a sound. As Sumi leaned forward to look through the pages, her necklace fell out, hanging over the table as it spun on its chain. She hadn't gotten comfortable enough to wear it on the outside of her clothes yet, but there was nothing to fear in Anushai, so he didn't mention it. She flipped through the book for a while before leaning back, turning it around to face him.

"So," she said, pointing at numbers on the top of each page, "it looks like it's organized by birth date. Unfortunately, the years are based on Shaolmesun's reign, so we'll need to translate it to the Berillai calendar."

"Okay," he said, nodding, "we can figure this out, right? Hiyelleom has been in power for thirty-five years. So…maybe we go to the end of the book and see what the last year of his reign was?"

Sumi stood, coming around the desk to sit beside him — while he suppressed an audible gulp as their knees touched. They flipped to the end of the book, where there was a huge drawing of the Essomuai symbol, just like Sumi's necklace. Underneath, it read *Kuyel shelm Essomuai Silmelnen Geommes Ulkyull.*

"You're a genius," she said, looking up with a smile. "This says something about him…leaving the world in the…forty-fifth year of his reign."

She looked back down, drawing out imaginary math on the table with her finger. "If we can combine that with thirty-five years for Hiyelleom and Nela dying this year, that makes her birth…the thirteenth year of Shaolmesun, right?"

Erso wiggled his fingers in front of him as he tried to do the math.

"It, uh…seems right," he said, grinning. "But my education was a bit…informal, let's say. I trust you."

"Well, I sure wish I'd learned Shapewalking instead of math some days."

They flipped backward through the book together, both leaning over the pages. They finally got to the end of the thirteenth year, where they found the last month, Semennes, at the top.

They started poring over the names, finding a surprising amount of information. Each birth was recorded with the location, both parents' names, and several extended family members. On the far end of each line, they had even gone back and written in the future children of each newborn. If only record-keeping could win against the Berillai…

They took each page slowly, scanning the entries for an Essolurei. He was looking as carefully as he could, but it was also hard to concentrate with Sumi right beside him — her breath, the rustle of her skirt, her fingers on the page. He shook his head, refocusing. He was officially a fool; the least he could do now was make himself useful. Still, as carefully as they looked, they reached the twenty-fifth day, and there wasn't a single entry with an Essolurei. They went back through once more for good measure, and Sumi even redid her math again, starting with the years and then the months.

"I don't know where I could have gone wrong," she said. "The math still seems right to me."

She pulled out her notebook, reworking the numbers with a pencil. When she went to do it a third time, though, he put his hand over hers.

"I'm sure it's right, but don't beat yourself up over it. Maybe she wasn't even born here; I think these records are only for the city. It used to be a big empire. At least we tried."

He gave her his best smile, which she mirrored back, though there was a sad crease at the corner of her eyes. She sighed, looking around the room as if the answers could be written on the walls somewhere.

"It's okay," he said again. "I promise I won't leave you until we have you somewhere safe. I know we'll figure something out."

"Wait," she said, pointing at the imperial requests in the center of the room. "Why don't we go to the palace? He said anyone can make a request. What if the empress can help us, and…I don't know…intercede on my behalf?"

He bit his lip. It wasn't just some simple misunderstanding the Berillai had with Shapewalkers; it was an extermination they were eager to finish. But when she turned around with that excited look on her face, he felt like he couldn't say no.

"Well," he said, "I'm not sure what they can do about Berill, but I'm sure they have better records than this office. Or maybe they have somewhere people like us can go."

His parents had thought to flee here, after all. And if they had lived just one more night… Well, it was absurd to go petition an empress, but not totally absurd given the way the Anushai seemed to run their kingdom. The grounds to the palace weren't even locked.

He stood, offering his hand to help her up.

"I guess we're off to the palace. If nothing else, this will be the best tour of Anushai I've ever given."

34

"Guyane siom feolem, chelan siom delyes. Geom siom kulnang,
seljem delas lelman. "
**"The light has many forms, but strength only one. Even a single
stone can bear the weight of the entire world."**
-Geomongiar yal Chelmun
The Anushai Stone House Motto

Sumi followed Erso past the army barracks, winding their way toward the royal gardens and the giant staircase leading to the palace. Maybe she was kidding herself — there was no reason for the empress to help her, after all — but she couldn't help but feel a measure of hope, like everything she'd hoped for might take shape somehow. She was just one normal person, but a ruler? Those were the people who really made things happen. Maybe the empress could find her relatives, but what if she could even get her home? It might be naive, seeing the way her kingdom treated Shapewalkers, but what if the empress could convince the police she wasn't a criminal?

If nothing else, she had to find an answer, about what she should do with her life, about how she could do right by her people. Beysal, the Shapewalkers Guild, Erso; they all deserved more than a lifetime of living on the fringes. If she could answer the questions about her own life, maybe she'd have an inkling about how to help them too. And if anyone could help her, shouldn't it be the most powerful Shapewalker in the world?

They finally reached the gardens, passing through a tunnel in its huge wall of evergreens. On the other side, they found a sort of city unto itself, only inhabited by plants of every kind. The gardens were divided into huge sections, some fifty in all, seemingly separated by the type of plants they held. Her eyes widened, struggling to take it all in. Even in the cold weather, there were flowers she'd never seen before and clumps of strange-looking vegetables: pumpkins shaped like watermelons, and strangely striped squash. There were even rows and rows of cherry trees, though they hadn't blossomed yet.

They walked toward the center, where the temple stream ended in a wide pool. An army of workers converged there, pulling out buckets of water as they fanned back out to water the plants. They turned toward the stairs, finding the top of the palace visible above them, as if it were just another peak on the long sweep of mountains surrounding Seongbelm.

"Well," Erso said, meeting her eyes at the bottom of the stairs, "here goes nothing."

"Right," she said, staring at the tile roof above them. "Just petitioning a powerful ruler, like any normal day."

They nodded to each other, starting up the steps. Still, it was a tall hill, and by the end, their resolve had mostly eroded into being out of breath. At the top, they found a gate flanked by two guards, but as promised, it was open, and the men only gave them a cursory glance as they walked past. They crossed into the grounds, where flowers dotted lush lawns in a space almost as large as the royal gardens below. Some people strolled about, and one couple was even picnicking in the grass. She certainly couldn't imagine doing that in Berill...

They followed a gravel path to the right, heading toward the east side of the palace. The building was even larger up close, built with sweeping wings around a tall central one. As they came around the side, while they still saw a few stray walkers, it became clearer where the public space ended. There were a half-dozen guards posted at every entrance and a few patrols roaming around.

Finally, reaching the eastern entrance, they found an ornate set of steps leading to a wide glass doorway. There were four guards on the steps, with two at the base and two just outside the door. Sumi slowed her pace and looked at Erso, but he only nodded encouragingly. Right, she was to do the talking again. This was her idea, after all. She took a deep breath. As unbelievable as this Anushai system was, asking an empress for help probably wasn't meant to be easy. She set her jaw, walking toward the nearest guard.

"Excuse me," she said in Anushai, "we're here to...uh...make a request to the...empress?"

The guard's eyes turned toward her, but otherwise, he was completely still. He gave her a once-over, pausing near her neck. She looked down, tensing as she realized her necklace had dropped out somehow. He looked back at her, narrowing his eyes.

"Are you a house emissary?" he asked. She struggled over the last word for a second, finally sounding it out in her head.

"Erm…no, just me. Sumi Elerair."

He raised an eyebrow at that but seemed otherwise unfazed. "Wait here, please."

Turning, he whispered to one of the guards at the top of the stairs before slipping through the doors. She waited there for ten minutes or so — though it felt much longer with the three remaining guards so close. Still, she stayed where she was by the stairs, too nervous to move back toward Erso, though she looked at him over her shoulder a few times. He was looking around the grounds, looking far calmer than she felt.

Finally, the guard returned, holding open the door behind him as a man in fine livery walked onto the steps. A butler, maybe? He was balding and looked old enough to be a grandfather — though his face wasn't quite so kind. He only came to the bottom step, towering over her.

"You have a request for Empress Mother Hiyelleom?" he asked, his voice nasally. He looked like a hawk who'd just discovered the existence of worms.

"Yes, sir," she said, "my name is Sumilnyeon Elerair, and I was told anyone could ask for help here."

"Of course," the man sniffed, "though there are proper channels for such things. You must first address your house affiliation. If they can't help you, then the house secretary can fill out the proper forms on your behalf, and an emissary can come here for an audience. Do you think the empress takes requests willy-nilly off the street?"

"Oh," she said, suddenly feeling the sweat under her arms. "I'm so sorry, I…uh…suppose not. Though, I'm afraid I don't…*have* a house affiliation."

The man blinked, cocking his head as if he'd misheard. "You don't even have a house affiliation?"

She heard Erso's footsteps as he slowly moved behind her. He didn't say anything, though she felt supported all the same to have him close at hand.

"No, sir," she said, "I'm from Berill, and—"

"Berill?" he asked, chuckling as he cut her off. "That is certainly a new one. I would have thought you were at least an old Grass House acolyte or something. That would at least explain the lack of forms — though most put their requests through Sky these days…"

He shook his head, nodding toward her neck. "Tell me, girl, where'd you get that necklace?"

"It was my grandmother's," she said simply. "She was from Anushai."

"And her name?"

"Essolurei Elerair," she said, though she didn't risk telling him she didn't know her Anushai surname, condescending as he was. Still, what did her grandmother have to do with this? Maybe Nela's old house affiliation would help her get an audience? Though if Nela had one, she hadn't ever mentioned it.

"Well," he said, frowning, "I don't like wasting the empress's precious time, but the necklace is most unusual. She certainly wouldn't be pleased if I let a house pendant go unmentioned. Wait here, though I don't want you to get your hopes up."

He went back into the hallway, the guards silently pulling the doors open for him. She turned away and moved back a few feet to wait this time, Erso following her to the side.

"Everyone's focused on the necklace," she said under her breath. "What do you think it means?"

"I guess we'll find out," he said, shrugging. "Couldn't hurt if it gets us in."

They waited longer that time, some twenty minutes, the silence only broken by Erso occasionally pointing out an interesting plant to distract her. Finally, she heard shoes coming down the hall, the butler coming through the door again. Without even a glance, the guards seemed to pull open the doors just as he reached them. The butler still looked down his nose at her, but his eyes seemed sharper, as if seeing her for the first time again.

"The empress mother will see you now."

She shared a look with Erso before heading toward the stairs. He began to follow her, but the butler held up a gloved hand, stopping them.

"Only you, Miss Elerair," he said.

She stopped, turning back to Erso. He tilted his head, urging her on. When she turned back, she found the butler already gone, leaving her to scramble up the steps behind him.

Once inside, the butler kept up his rapid pace, her little boots clicking at least twice as often on the marble floor. His pace gave her the distinct feeling he didn't normally walk like this with guests. She did feel embarrassed, of course, like she was dealing with Luthaine at the bank back home, but it was too late now.

As much as she focused on keeping up, though, it was hard not to stare, the inside of the palace even more stunning than the outside. To her right, tall windows revealed a giant courtyard enclosed by the outer wings, filled with carefully sculpted evergreens and littered with statues. Inside, any space left between the windows was covered with wall hangings, each one depicting a scene that must tell the history of the Anushai. Each table they passed held an intricate porcelain dish, and she gulped, suddenly terrified of knocking into them.

As they reached the end of the hallway, they turned left, emerging into an entry hall beside a sweeping marble staircase, apparently reaching the center of the palace. The front doors were easily thirty feet tall, looking as though they took a team of ten to open. At the top of the stairs, a balcony wrapped around the upper floors, its columns sculpted into giant beasts. There was a lion sitting proudly and a great black granite bear rearing on its hind legs. They even had a fire hawk, just like the bridges in Amoriai.

The butler cleared his throat, and she snapped back, only then realizing she'd fallen behind.

"While I can appreciate the spectacle of seeing the entry hall for the first time, Miss Elerair, the empress is very busy."

"I'm very sorry," she said, bowing in apology.

He simply nodded, walking on. He probably thought her just another peasant, floored by the beauty he found commonplace. Although, looking down at her dress, she realized she hadn't even thought to shape it.

As they rounded the side of the stairwell, a giant Essomuai fountain came into view in the center of the hall. It was just like the one in the temple, except its center glowed with brilliant gemstones. They were cut larger than any stone she'd ever seen, glinting in the light from the window as their colors swirled on the marble floor. But as they turned up the steps — angry butler or no — she couldn't help but gasp.

Above her, the landing held a final marble pillar, bigger than the rest, in the shape of what must be Essomuai herself, an incredibly beautiful woman with sweeping curves and a flowing dress. Instead of a single face, though, she seemed to have a dozen, the faces of the other animals folding out from the center like a fan. She met the statue's giant eyes, feeling like the goddess was staring through her.

"Miss Elerair," the butler said, waiting for her on the landing, "shall I presume you do not know the protocol for greeting the empress in the throne room?"

"Uh…no," she said, her neck hot with shame.

Hadn't she thought of anything before coming here? Rulers in the stories beheaded people for less! Suddenly, her gamble seemed foolish, just another daydream. But even here, in this beautiful place, she couldn't seem to shake Berill from her mind. She was too close to turn back now, wasn't she?

"Once they open the doors," the butler droned, "you will walk in silence with your eyes down until you reach a gold disc in the center of the hall. You must kneel and bow on it, touching your forehead to the ground. Do not look up until the empress mother invites you to. Speak only when spoken to, and you may call her Empress, Mother, or Your Majesty."

As he pulled out his watch again, she nodded to herself. It didn't sound like she'd missed anything important, though she'd find out the hard way if she had…

"One final thing," he said, pointing at her feet. "Please remove your shoes and stockings."

She cocked an eyebrow, thinking he must be joking, but he only glared at her in return. She hurriedly began to pull them off, stuck unlacing them while standing to avoid the indignity of sitting on the floor. A maid appeared out of thin air to take them from her, and the butler led her forward, the marble cold beneath her feet.

She started breathing quickly, though she tried desperately to summon her lessons with Beysal, searching for any stillness in herself. What happened next was out of her control, and she wouldn't be able to face it if she wasn't calm. She pictured the cave in her mind, putting her worries on a leaf and letting them float away. She just had to focus on the water, breathing in and out as it lapped against the basin.

"Miss Sumilnyeon Elerair for the empress mother," the butler said, his voice suddenly much higher than before. Another man in livery — a higher-ranking butler maybe? — nodded to the guards, and they pulled the doors open, revealing a dark room beyond. Sumi blinked, her eyes struggling to adjust. But the butler pushed her gently forward, and she stepped through, keeping her eyes firmly on the ground. She kept walking, though as she went into the darkness of the throne room, it was hard not to feel like being swallowed by a pit.

35

Under the leadership of Emperor Sulyeogang, elected on an emergency proviso with war powers, the four armies fought the Battle of Strussfaran in the second year of his reign (1607 N.E.) By far the bloodiest battle in memory, it finally brought a pause to the expansion of the Berillai menace. In order to hold their gains and ensure peace, the Lords and Ladies of the Houses elected Empress Kiyelpean of Shadow House for her expertise in treaty writing, ultimately writing and ratifying the Treaty of Trilathdrei. She was nominated by Lord Leonjen of Fire House with a vote of seven in favor, one in abstention, and two against.

-Voting Records of the Anushgiar Leyosil

—:—

Sumi crept forward in the darkness, staring hard at the floor as she walked across the marble. As the doors shut behind her, the gloom was complete, with almost no daylight slipping into the room. Thick incense clouded the air, and she heard the crackle of fires in braziers. She'd heard muffled voices from the other side of the door, but now that she'd passed through, it was deathly quiet. She could sense other people in the room but didn't dare raise her eyes to look.

After what seemed like an eternity, she finally reached the gold disc in the floor. It was as wide as she was tall and surprisingly cold. She stepped onto it as instructed, kneeling as she bowed her forehead to the ground. As she touched the metal, a buzzing filled her mind, like the phantom keyhole, making it hard to count her breaths. Was it the presence of the empress she was feeling? Or was it the disc itself? Still, she felt calmer somehow, the cool metal grounding her even as the wait seemed to stretch into forever.

"Please stand, child," a woman finally said. Her voice was low and smooth, speaking in perfect Berillai despite her accent.

She stood, unconsciously smoothing her dress. When she looked up, she found herself facing the empress mother of Anushai, the older woman watching calmly from her throne. Just like the painting on the ferry, she wore flowing purple robes, her head seeming to float above the silk as it spilled over the throne. She had a gold diadem on her head, and her hair was a brilliant white, falling in waves over her shoulders. Her hands — the only part of her visible beneath the cloth — were elegant, every finger with a different ring as they held to the edge of the throne.

"You've piqued my interest, child," Hiyelleom said, chuckling — a chorus of ladies-in-waiting echoing her from the shadows. "I had to see why a young woman from Berill had marched up to the palace with a Grass House pendant, of all things."

Sumi frowned. She'd seen the Essomuai shape in a thousand places in the kingdom, but what did that have to do with Grass House? She didn't know what to say, but it seemed she wasn't expected to speak yet, either.

"Tell me," the empress continued, "why did you introduce yourself with a first name in Anushai? Have you lived in our kingdom long?"

"No, Mother," she said, her mouth suddenly very dry. "I only just arrived, but I'm of mixed heritage."

"Interesting. Then how did you come across this pendant?"

"It was left to me by my grandmother, Your Majesty," Sumi said.

"And your grandmother's name, child?"

"Essolurei Elerair, Mother," she said.

At that, whispers broke out among the ladies that surrounded the empress. The stately woman held her composure, though; surely the butler would have told her as much already, no? Was it the name or the necklace that meant something to them? The empress lifted her hand in the air, the other ladies falling silent.

"Leave us," she said.

Hiyelleom still stared directly at her, so she began to bow again when the other ladies sprang up, disappearing in a whirl of silk. The guards stayed on, still as statues as they stared ahead.

"Just as I thought," Hiyelleom finally said quietly. "I knew your grandmother very well, Sumi."

Her mouth fell open, and she stared for a second before remembering herself. Still, a thousand questions blossomed in her mind. How in the world had Nela known the ruler of Anushai?

"Perhaps this conversation deserves a more private setting," the empress said, sighing. "Why don't you join me for tea?"

Hiyelleom made to stand, and suddenly, the room burst into action. One of the guards rang a gong, and doors began flying open all around the throne room. Maids appeared, lifting the train of her dress as other retainers moved in, picking up her things. The empress, however, didn't even seem to notice the swarm around her, moving into the hallway beyond with half a dozen guards beside her.

Sumi stood, frozen on the gold disc, unsure if protocol would let her follow. A maid suddenly appeared at her side with her boots and stockings — though it was a different one from before. As she yanked them on, the first butler returned, taking her by the elbow with a gloved hand.

"Come with me, miss," he said. "I'll escort you to the sitting room."

They followed the procession of servants into the hallway beyond, the light suddenly bright again as they were flanked by another courtyard. They kept about ten paces behind the empress — the butler with the same haughty posture from before, though she caught him watching her from the corner of his eye. He wasn't wrong about her, of course; she was still just a simple girl from Berill, but an invitation to tea had clearly left him guessing. Not that she wasn't guessing herself... Nela must have worked at the palace or something, but why wouldn't she mention something so amazing?

They moved further down the hallway, passing a series of large rooms, their double doors propped open, though they didn't turn inside. Each one looked like a sitting room, albeit with completely different styles. The first one they passed was done in red, with a giant fireplace in the center, its chimney running straight up to the roof. The next was done in blues, but instead of a fireplace, it had a fountain in the middle, the water filled with lily pads.

Finally, near the end of the hallway, the procession turned, filing into one of the last rooms on the right. She followed the butler to the doorway, where they waited outside the most beautiful room by far. More like a garden than a palace, it was filled with decorative stones, placed between the furniture along with huge planters of moss and ferns. Hiyelleom was already sitting on a wide, brocade couch, watching as the butler bowed, introducing her again.

"Miss Sumilnyeon Elerair," he said. Stepping up to a settee opposite the empress, he gestured for her to sit. He hadn't mentioned any protocol this time, though, so she curtsied, sitting as smoothly as she could with her dress beneath her.

"Thank you, everyone," the empress said. "Now, please leave us."

The room, having only just reached some sense of calm, burst into a frenzy again. The maids — who'd just returned with tea — placed it hastily between them as they backed out from the room. The guards snapped to attention, disappearing from their places on the wall until there were only two left, though they were different from the others. They wore no helmets, and actually looked remarkably alike, like father and son, one of them older with a long mane of white hair pulled into a bun. As the door finally shut, the room quiet again, she turned back to the empress.

"I hope you don't mind Ruseolem and Sulpeyon," Hiyelleom said. "They're like family; they never leave my side."

"No, Mother," Sumi said, shaking her head. Still, she was surprised Hiyelleom was willing to have just two to guard her — not that she meant her any harm, of course.

"Please help yourself to some tea. I would have you served, but a bit of labor is a small price to pay for privacy."

Sumi nodded, smiling gratefully as she carefully poured the tea, doing her best to add a lump of sugar without making a splash. The younger of the two guards, however, came and knelt beside the table, pouring for Hiyelleom.

"You know," the older woman said, sipping her tea, "your grandmother taught me that. She always hated when I was too reliant on my servants."

Sumi met the woman's eyes, her brow furrowed in confusion, though she took a quick sip of her tea to avoid looking rude. Still, it just didn't make sense. How had Nela been close enough to Hiyelleom to give her advice? And about tea, of all things!

"First," Hiyelleom said, "let me just say, I'm so sorry for your loss. A mutual friend wrote to me when your grandmother passed. She was a good woman, and she'll be missed. But please, speak freely, child, there's no need for ceremony here."

"Thank you," Sumi said slowly, still unsure of what to say even as a thousand questions raged through her mind. "How…did you know my grandmother?"

"She was my best and closest friend," the empress said.

Sumi, unfortunately, was halfway through another sip. She choked on her tea, coughing uncontrollably.

"Excuse me, Your Majesty," she said, finally catching her breath. "I'm sorry, I'm just…surprised."

"You mean you didn't know?"

Sumi shook her head.

"Nela…uh, I mean my *grandmother,* didn't talk about home very often. So I, uh…"

"That's so like her," Hiyelleom said, sighing. "To this day, I can't decide if she liked being frustrating or if she was just naturally secretive."

Still, she laughed, looking up at the ceiling.

"And to think of her being a Nela! She mentioned you in her letters, of course, but it never really struck me like it has today. I guess we all grow old eventually."

The empress's face grew serious, her smile fading.

"I suppose you don't know any of it. She probably didn't want you to, but you're here now, so I guess it's my story to tell. Your grandmother was Essolurei Saldalgiar, princess and heiress to Grass House."

Sumi shook her head, blinking. *She…what? That didn't make any sense. She was married to a sailor!* Nela was just like her, an ordinary person.

"I'm sorry, Your Majesty," she finally said, the words coming slowly. "Are you…sure we're talking about the same Essolurei?"

"Of course we are, child."

Hiyelleom set down her teacup, glowing as she turned into Nela — or what seemed like Nela, only far younger. Still, she would know that face anywhere, no matter how many wrinkles came off of it. She froze, completely absorbed by that face, the one she'd been missing nonstop since the funeral. Of course, she'd seen Nela's face in the mirror the first time she transformed, but that had been a shock, a dream. This time, she knew what she was seeing, and it was…*everything.*

The empress let her stare, seeming to understand her aching need. They actually looked somewhat similar, Hiyelleom wearing a version of Nela not too much older than herself, bearing a likeness in her youth that had disappeared with age. It was transfixing, every curl of hair, every dimple. Even her clothes, the empress's dress transformed into a soft green gown. Was that something that Nela used to wear? When she was…a princess? Hiyelleom finally spoke, her heart skipping a beat as she recognized Nela's voice.

"Do you think," the empress-Nela asked, "that I could see her as she was to you? After she left, I never saw her again."

Sumi nodded, closing her eyes. It took her no time at all to find Nela's door in Mu'lalat. The wood was soft and worn, and she suddenly realized it was the front door of their cottage. She reached out and touched it, and it seemed to pulse under her hand, bursting with decades of love. She opened the door, finding a cool, still pool. Nela sat beside it, smiling. What a gift to see her here. She had no grave to visit, but she could always find her in the halls. It took every ounce of strength she had not to simply stare forever. But the empress had done her a kindness, and she deserved one in return.

Glowing, she returned in Nela's form, and it was Hiyelleom's turn to look surprised. She maintained Nela's younger form, but her eyes widened, her hand slowly going to her mouth.

"It's good to see you again, old friend," she said in Anushai.

She shook her head, remembering herself.

"My apologies," she said, returning to Berillai, "it's just so different from only seeing her in a mirror."

Sumi nodded; they'd been thinking the exact same thing. The empress took a deep breath, collecting herself.

"Thank you for humoring me, dear. Why don't we get back to the purpose of your visit? I understand you have a request?"

The empress glowed, returning to her diadem and purple dress. Sumi followed suit, though she returned with her dress a bit more polished than before.

"Well..." Sumi said, touching her lips as if she could pull out the words, "I need your help. I know I've no right to it, but seeing as my people were from Anushai, I thought... Well, I didn't know where else to turn."

The empress clapped her hands together, smiling like a schoolgirl.

"So, one of you finally decided to take me up on my offer! I didn't think she would even bother to tell her family, stubborn as she was."

"Uh...I'm sorry, Your Majesty," she said, shaking her head, "I wasn't aware of any offer."

"Ah," Hiyelleom said, the smile falling from her lips. "I suppose not, if you didn't know the rest. Grass House ended abruptly when your great-grandfather died. There were bad debts, and with all of their land leveraged, Essolurei abdicated her title. I offered her a place in Stone House, as a duchess, but she ran off to Berill to be with— Well, you know all that. Anyway, I'd hoped you might be here to take her place — not with the title, of course, given your mixed heritage, but returning home, at least."

Sumi looked around the room, the larger-than-life sculptures, the exquisite furnishings. She could be a part of all this, a simple girl from a flower shop? She didn't belong here, of course, but if she could find a safe place... She thought of being in a country house, hidden from Parimu and surrounded by Erso and his family, finally able to offer them the safety they'd provided her. She could almost see herself there, surrounded by plants in a garden, green fields stretching out around them.

She'd have more time with Erso, maybe forever, offering him a home after everything he'd lost. And she could—

She thought of Nela again. As thrilling as it was to see her face after so long, she'd been different too, a younger woman locked in a different world. Beautiful dresses and palaces weren't what Nela had chosen for herself. She'd been offered a free ticket to live as royalty forever and rejected it, pouring her blood, sweat, and tears into Berill. She could never be a beautiful trinket locked inside a palace, and neither could Sumi. Maybe she couldn't have put it into words before now, but she knew it was true.

And yet, wasn't she being offered the very thing everyone seemed to yearn for? A place to hide, a life of joy, a chance at peace. But how could that peace ever be real if she knew what was beyond her garden walls? She would never be able to forget the pain and loss she'd seen in Amoriai or the home she left back in Berill. She hadn't come here to hide; she'd come to find a way back to her cottage, to her own beautiful life.

"Your Majesty," she said, her hands tight on her skirt, "thank you. It's an incredible honor, what you've offered me, but…I must refuse. I came here seeking your help with Berill. It was my Nela's chosen home, and it's mine too. My powers were discovered, and I had to run, but I came here thinking you could help. If you could intervene for me, if you could get me home… I don't know, somehow, I just hoped we could find peace between our people and the Berillai."

The empress chuckled, though her smile never touched her eyes. She was completely still, like she had hardened into stone.

"Well, it seems you did inherit something from your Nela," Hiyelleom said. "She tried to convince me of the same foolish notions all our lives. But of course, child, you must know that such a thing is impossible."

Sumi dropped her gaze, sinking into her chair. Of course, she was a fool. How could one audience with a ruler she'd never met change a hundred years of hatred? Even setting aside this…surreal story about Nela, she couldn't just magically change everything. She must seem like such a little girl, naive enough to think the empress could wave her hand, and everything would change.

"Bah!" the empress shouted, pinching the bridge of her nose. "Don't look so miserable. That's the trouble with you Grass House women, so soft, making me feel cruel when I hurt your feelings."

Sumi tried to keep her face completely still. She had almost felt a tear coming to her eye, but she didn't want to embarrass herself more than she already had — let alone worsen the already fragile reputation of

Grass House women. Though how Hiyelleom could ever think of Nela as soft was beyond her. The empress took a deep breath, meeting her eyes again.

"It's not as though I don't care, child — that's what I could never make your Nela see. It's just…there are realities I can't ignore." She took a deep breath. "Why don't you come with me? I have something to show you that may help."

Hiyelleom stood, and the younger guard fell in behind her, sweeping back into the hall before Sumi knew what was happening. The older guard waited for Sumi by the door, and as she scrambled to her feet, he gave her a small bow.

"If I might escort you, madam?" he asked.

"Of course," Sumi said, nodding quickly. He straightened and smiled at her, leading the way back into the hall.

As they left the sitting room, the empress was already down the hall, turning at the corner ahead. Sumi's guard fell in beside her, though he didn't look hurried, apparently knowing where they were going. She tried to match his easy pace, even as a tidal wave of thoughts crashed around her head. She knew what she wanted now, but how could she possibly achieve it, returning home with no help and no one to protect her?

"If you don't mind my saying so," the guard whispered, smiling, "I knew your Nela very well. She was a wonderful person, and I missed her dearly when she left."

"Thank you for saying that," she said, smiling sadly. "She…didn't tell me much. What's your name?"

"Ruseolem, madam," he said, inclining his head, "but Essolurei always called me Russ. I hope I haven't overstepped; it's not very often a guard speaks to a guest, but…your grandmother never was one to let decorum get in her way. I've served Stone House my whole life, but I knew your Nela from when she was only fifteen."

"She certainly wasn't one for rules," she said, chuckling. "Doesn't seem very grass-like, though, does it?"

Russ laughed, and somehow, she felt…*hopeful*. She still had no plan, but thinking of Nela at least made her want to keep trying. Nela had never been anything but herself, and even some forty years later, a guard from the palace still remembered her fondly. Even if she had to stay on the run for the rest of her life, she couldn't ever stop trying to live the way Nela had.

As they turned the corner, they found the empress in the courtyard, having descended a flight of stairs into a lush garden. It was filled with evergreens, carved into fanciful shapes: animals, seashells, and one that looked like Seongbelm. There were more guards on the other end — their tea thankfully never truly compromising Hiyelleom's safety. The empress was waiting for her by a fountain, and Russ urged her on, joining his son by the stairs.

Sumi stopped a few feet away — unsure of the proper distance to stand from royalty, though the empress didn't seem bothered. She looked calmly into the water, her hands folded in front of her. As a breeze came through the garden, she smelled something familiar over the flowers, something— *Nela's perfume.* She smiled; had Nela really worn the same perfume as the empress? No wonder she'd imported it all those years…

She waited quietly for the empress to speak, looking at the statues in the center of the fountain. It was…enormous. Nearly as tall as the second floor of the palace, it held dozens of bronze figures, all frozen in the panic of some kind of gruesome battle. There were men in the throes of death, swords rammed through them, though, otherwise, it was unlike any battle she'd ever heard of. Above the men were dozens of birds: hawks, eagles, owls, their beaks open in a battle cry. And there were animals among the soldiers on the ground as well: lions, bears, elephants, all doing battle with men on all sides, many of them howling in pain from arrows littering their bodies.

"The Battle of Strussfaran," the empress finally said in a quiet voice. The name seemed vaguely familiar from school, though now that she tried to summon it, she couldn't remember the details. But if it had been this horrible, how could she have possibly forgotten?

"When did this happen?" Sumi asked.

The empress gave her a disappointed look, though she still let out a dry chuckle, shaking her head.

"I suppose I shouldn't be surprised you don't know. It isn't something your people take as seriously as mine do. It was the end of our glory and the start of yours, after all. It was more than two hundred years ago, but it feels like I was there myself, studying it since I was a child. This one day has defined every step I've taken in my life. In fact, it probably set a path for all of us."

"This battle was with Anushai?" Sumi asked.

Hiyelleom nodded absently, staring into the bronze as if she were at the battlefield and Sumi was some dream she'd been having.

"Between both our kingdoms. In 1607 — 596 Posdeven in your calendar — the Berillai were expanding, and your king, Kolloven, wanted more farms, more sheep, more *everything*. They'd already taken Mesop land as far south as Ekaram, so they headed east into the Three Sisters."

She and Erso hadn't stopped in the Three Sisters, but she knew plenty of people with 'Sisters' blood,' as they called it, like Mr. Furttenhur. Still, what she'd seen from the boat was beautiful — rolling green pastures, farms by the sea — not a place where she could imagine this kind of carnage.

"They started with farmers, not soldiers," Hiyelleom continued, "living on unoccupied land. The Luterrin army finally drove them off, but when the Berillai returned seeking 'justice,' they routed Luterrin, starting the Four Kingdoms War."

That name *did* sound familiar, now that she heard it, but it felt like something they'd glossed over. Their history classes had always started with the founding, flying over the rest until the year the trains went in.

"In those days, almost every nation in the basin was our vassal, so of course, they came running to us for help."

Sumi looked closer at the birds above her. One of them looked remarkably like a fire hawk. The statue had been done in incredible detail, all of the plumage standing out in stark relief. She followed its wingtips to its chest and winced, finding an arrow through its heart.

"We brought a massive force across the sea," the empress continued, "finally meeting the Berillai just west of Strussfaran. They say the battle raged for five days, with enough blood spilt to fill the ocean twice."

She gestured toward the birds. "Our army had entire legions of Shapewalkers in those days. Some even shaped as squads, as you can see from the elephants. They fought valiantly, desperate to break the Berillai lines, but your people were prepared, churning out silver-tipped arrows for months, knowing we would come. The diary entries I've read talk of men falling from the sky, their transformations halted by the silver, screaming all the way to the ground."

Sumi felt her jaw clench, imagining falling like that. She could feel that all too personally — that very thing could have happened to them when they ran from the detective. Hiyelleom's face was blank, her own feelings long dulled by her study of these horrors, but her hands had gripped the lip of the fountain, her knuckles tight.

"We had fought well enough to hurt the Berillai badly, of course — it wasn't just our blood on the ground. The battle finally came to a standstill, and the treaty we signed, the Treaty of Trilathdrei, still endures, if only just. The Berillai realized the cost of taking on the Continent and agreed to stop their borders east of Strussfaran. Our losses were deep, though, and we lost magical blood we still have yet to replace. Though the Berillai decided to use commerce instead of force after that, and it's proven more effective than the sword by far."

Sumi nodded; that much had become painfully clear. Especially in Amoriai. The Berillai hadn't needed to do any conquering there; the Amoriai were happily destroying themselves at their instruction.

"But they won't be satisfied forever. It's been my life's work to protect this place — the last truly safe place to be a Shapewalker. I don't take your request lightly, child. Your own grandmother asked me for the same thing hundreds of times, but I cannot sacrifice my people. I am the stone upon which this empire rests. Still…"

She took a deep breath, meeting Sumi's eyes. Suddenly, she didn't look like a ruler anymore. She was just another woman, like Nela, concern creasing her eyes.

"Your Nela was the dearest friend I ever had. So, if I can keep you safe, I will. Stay here, and I can place you in any country manor under Stone House. Your Nela may have chosen Berill, but they never discovered what she was. Just choose to live, child."

Sumi felt a tear slip down her cheek, unable to hold it back this time. She thought of everything she'd lost, what her *people* had lost. The suffering never seemed to end. Of course, Hiyelleom wouldn't risk Anushai for her, but she was still willing to help. She could still live a life, stay with Erso, make another home. And yet… Nela had known this history, known all of Berill's faults, and she'd chosen it anyway. She'd made a life there, a family, a bridge between their peoples. Even if she failed, even if her own people killed her, how could she abandon them?

"I'm sorry," she said, bowing low, staring into the grass. "I don't deserve your kindness, but I have to go home. I have to find a way."

"I suppose it's too late to change the past," the empress said, looking up as if to stop from crying. When she met Sumi's eyes again, though, she was composed, the smooth facade of royalty returned.

"I wish you luck, girl. If you're half as stubborn as your Nela, perhaps you'll find a way."

Russ's son appeared at the empress's side, bowing as he handed Hiyelleom a stack of letters tied together with a bow.

"Thank you, Sulpeyon," she said, turning back to Sumi. "Whether you stayed or went, I thought you should have these; they're my letters with Essolurei."

She gestured for Sumi to take the stack, the paper yellowing with age.

"And this," Hiyelleom said, handing her a folded piece of parchment with a golden seal, "is a royal writ for the library at Sky House. You should go and read your family's records. Even if you go back to Berill, at least go back knowing who you are."

Holding the letters, it took everything in her not to cry again. The one on top even had Nela's handwriting.

"Are you sure?" she asked. "Maybe I can read the letters and send them back to you?"

"Think nothing of it," the empress said, waving one of her jewel-covered hands. "I have copies, and I won't be around forever, either. Maybe you'll learn something — you have sacred blood in your veins, and you shouldn't spill it over nothing."

At another wave from Hiyelleom, Russ came forward from the stairs, bowing like his son had.

"Ruseolem will escort you to the entrance. I'm glad you came, child. Be well."

"Thank you, Mother," she said, dropping into a deep curtsy. "It was an honor."

She followed Russ out, climbing the steps back into the palace. She caught one last glimpse of the empress, standing in the garden, staring at the statue. She looked down at the letters, feeling their weight. There were so many memories in them, so many years. In some ways, she'd never felt so lost, and yet, she'd never had such a brilliant light to guide her.

36

"Duyel zulhelm deomes huyol, buyel silgang shayosh minnelmes?"
"If all becomes dust in the end, should you not desire to burn the brightest?"

-Huwalgiar yal Chelmun
The Anushai Fire House Motto

—:—

Erso stood by the entrance, trying to look normal. But what was normal about this? Taking another drag from his pipe, he looked at his watch for the hundredth time, trying to determine the appropriate time to storm the palace and rescue Sumi. They hadn't told him to leave, but that didn't mean they liked him being there, either. He'd tried making conversation with the guards — which they were having none of — and even the stablehands in the carriage yard had given him the cold shoulder.

He eyed the building again, looking for openings. *Could* he even sneak in if he had to? A place like this must have channel watchers, like those old monks back home, trained to see even suppressed ripples in the depths of Mu'lalat. Still, he'd risk it — risk *anything* — if Sumi was in danger. His usual rat form wouldn't get him far in a fancy place like this, of course, but what else? Snails? Too slow. Spiders? Too creepy. He caught a shimmer of gold fluttering over a flower. Butterflies! Everybody liked butterflies. Maybe he could go over the roof to the interior gardens and look for windows that were open and then—

The door opened behind him, and he spun, finding Sumi, completely unharmed, thank the divine halls. Or maybe not completely unharmed… Her eyes were wide, and her mouth was a tight flat line, leaving him wondering if he should console her or run away. She flew down the steps, starting down the gravel walkway without stopping — and leaving him to scurry behind her.

"Sumi," he called after her, "you look like you saw a ghost or spit in the empress's tea. What happened?"

She stopped, looking at him as if seeing him for the first time. She reached out and grabbed his arm, bracing herself.

"My grandmother was a princess in Grass House," she said. She shook her head, suddenly talking a mile a minute. "Well, when there was still a Grass House anyway, so it doesn't change anything about me. But what a thing to find out, it's just—"

"Whoa, whoa," Erso said, taking a firm hold of her shoulder as he looked into her eyes. She didn't look concussed or anything, but was that good news or bad news?

"What do you mean?" he asked. "Your grandmother was…a princess?" He looked at the palace and back at Sumi. He certainly knew how to pick 'em, didn't he? She could be a, what, duchess? And she'd been running around with a back-alley scamp like him.

She put the letters she was carrying under her arm and lifted her emerald pendant, pushing it toward him on its chain.

"This!" she said. "This is a Grass House pendant. I just can't wrap my head around it. It all sounded normal in the palace, but now I don't know what to think!"

"Well, that's a good thing, right?" Erso asked. "Did that mean she could help you? Maybe they were cousins or something?"

Sumi shook her head, one hand going to her temple as she clamped her eyes shut.

"No," she said finally, opening her eyes. "The empress can't help me with Berill. All she offered was a place to hide."

"Well, that's great!" Erso said. "That's all we need, right? Somewhere safe to lay low, at least until Parimu leaves off. You can't go home, Sumi; there isn't anything back there. But a little peace and quiet in the countryside could do us some good."

"Peace and quiet," she said, repeating his phrase. She let out a single, hollow laugh. "The empress kept talking about peace, too…but what kind of peace is this?"

She took a deep breath, squaring her shoulders. "Listen, Erso, I've decided to go back to Berill on my own. I don't know how, but I have to try and change my people. I'm so sorry. Hiyelleom's offer… I thought of you, of your family, and I want to repay you all so badly, for *everything,* but I just can't. It's time for me to go."

She turned, starting back toward the inn as she tallied something on her fingers, her mind already on packing.

"Wait," he said, padding behind her. She glanced at him but didn't slow her stride. "We have to talk about this. You can't just go back. If you don't want to take the empress up on her offer, at least stay with me. I can keep you safe. Once we get Parimu off our trail, we'll be fine."

"Let's talk more at the inn," she said. "I want to be on my way as soon as I can." She lifted up her bundle of letters. "And I still have to read these and maybe get to Sky House, but I have to leave soon. Parimu could already be here, for all we know."

Sumi moved quickly down the hill and through the palace gardens, leaving him dazed in her wake, his thoughts a jumble. There was a pit in his stomach and his jaw felt tight. It was like watching a carriage go over a cliff. But he had to think of something. He had a feeling if he let her pack her bags, it would be too late. After a few minutes, they came out of the gardens and onto the wide boulevard north of the temple.

"Sumi, stop," he finally said, more loudly than he intended. She paused, and he pulled her off the crowded street beside a bench, though she didn't sit.

"Listen, let's just talk this out. I can't let you go back there. You've learned so much, and I know you can handle your transformations now, but going back to Berill... Parimu knows your face — the whole police department could, for all we know. Are you going to live your life as a completely different person? At some point, you'll slip — everyone does. Just...*don't.*"

"I'm sorry," she said, blinking hard like she was holding back a tear, "but I can't. I won't ask you to come; you've risked enough for me. But I can't keep running. This trip..."

She smiled, even as she still looked like she might cry. "It's been amazing, you've been amazing. But there's so much *awfulness* in the world, so much suffering. I don't blame you for running; you've had it worse than I could ever imagine. You deserve a *good* life, Erso, but I can't run anymore. Don't you see? I have to go home."

He opened his mouth, but his tongue felt dry, her words burying themselves in his mind. He felt...pain. His parents' faces flashed before his eyes, the memories of the theater burning, so many things he hadn't thought about in years. He shook his head — there was a reason he didn't think about those things.

"Sumi," he finally croaked out, "you can't."

She reached out, touching his face. It felt like lightning, even as she shook her head, draining every ounce of hope he had.

"Living with you has been a dream," she said. "I've loved every second of it, but you have a life to live, and I can't keep sticking myself in it."

She looked down the street in the direction of the inn. "We should keep moving. After I sort things out at the library, I mean to leave on the first ship I can get on. If I keep running now, I'll never stop."

He followed behind her, his shoulders slumped. She was right about one thing: you couldn't ever stop running in this life. The second you slowed down, the wolves were on you, tearing you apart. Still, this was better than no life at all, wasn't it? He ground his teeth. There was one thing she was dead wrong about, though. She wasn't something he'd been stuck with, some burden he was forced to carry. He had *chosen* her, would have done anything for her because she was unlike anyone he'd ever known.

Maybe that was the problem. She wanted a home, but she couldn't see she already had one. He wasn't foolish enough to think she'd ever be with him in *that* way, but she could still be part of his family. Beysal, Elo, Kel — they all adored her, and any of them would fight to keep her safe. He just had to convince her of that before it was too late.

They followed the stream until it took them around the temple. He tried harder to keep up with her, desperately searching for the right words. As they reached the inn, she finally slowed, looking up at Sky House where it rose up by the water.

"I hope they have what I need there," she said, looking down at the bundle of letters in her arms. "The empress thought I should know about my people, but...I just want to understand how Nela did it. If she had the courage to leave this place, I need to find it too."

"Sumi," he said, grabbing her arm, "your Nela wasn't on the run."

He could feel his voice rising but couldn't stop himself. "It isn't courage to get yourself killed," he said, nearly shouting.

She sucked in a breath, looking away. He felt like he was being torn in two. He needed to stop her, but he also didn't want to hurt her — *couldn't* hurt her. What was the right thing to say? How else could this story end? A thousand pictures surged up in his mind, a hazy picture of another life. Absurd as it seemed, he could see Sumi, in a house, children surrounding them. A *real* life, like Beysal had. But then he pictured Berill, a noose on the docks, and instead of Aelibis, it held Sumi, her beautiful leather boots dangling in the air before a jeering crowd. He pictured his mother, her body still and unmoving on the floor, or was it Sumi's? His dream didn't have to come true, but he couldn't allow this nightmare to, either.

"I didn't mean that you were a coward for running," Sumi said, finally meeting his eyes. She stepped closer to him, lifting a hand to touch his shoulder before pulling it back.

So, it was guilt she felt, thinking his anger was for his own pride. That was so like her, he almost wanted to laugh. Couldn't she see that all of this was for her sake?

"You don't owe me anything, Erso," she went on. "You've done so much for me. You've shown me so many other ways to live, and they're all beautiful. E'loseir and Beysal, making a life together, keeping the guild going. You, traveling from place to place, saving people. It's incredible. I've seen more things with you in a few months than I've seen in a lifetime. But I can't let my people go. Until we all have peace, then no peace is real. But you aren't a coward; you're the bravest person I've ever met. You gave me this chance to live; I just have to use it to try and change things. But you deserve to be free. I *want* you to be free."

"You're the tree, and I'm the wolf," he muttered under his breath.

"What?" she asked, her eyes searching.

He reached out, grabbing her hand and speaking before he could stop himself. "I love you, Sumi," he said. "It isn't freedom I want; it's you. I've lost too much, and I can't just watch you throw your life away. Not you, anyone but you. You aren't a burden, you're…everything. You don't have to go home to have a family; we can be your family. *I* can be your family."

She did cry then. Her face looked like a storm, joy and sadness sweeping across it. But which one was real? She looked at him for a heartbreaking moment before she squeezed her eyes shut, another tear rolling down her face.

"I never dreamed in a thousand years I'd hear you say that," she said, meeting his eyes, "and you have to know I feel the same. I think…I've loved you from that first pretzel. And I've thought about a life with you too; that's why I wanted to say yes to the empress. But…when it was right in front of me, I couldn't seem to take it. The Shapewalkers and the Berillai… I can't choose, and I can't live knowing I abandoned either of them. But I could never make you come with me. You're right, you've lost too much."

She reached out, cupping his face like it was a tiny, fragile bird.

"Just knowing you're out there, safe, will help me do what comes next. I have to go, and I won't make you choose. I love you, Erso Milak'erat."

She closed her eyes and took a deep breath, one final tear rolling down her perfect cheek. "Goodbye."

She turned and walked away, turning from the inn and toward Sky House, to the answers she thought she needed so badly. He watched her disappear down the street. His legs almost started to follow her again, but something held him back. It was that voice in his head that had been calling to him all this time: *Run, run, run.* It beat in his mind like a drum, as if it were his true heartbeat, the one he'd had since he reached into the ashes for his mother's bone. Sumi had just been a beautiful, foolish dream.

He really did love her — he hadn't even been able to admit that to himself until the words left his lips. But she was right; he couldn't follow her back to Berill just to watch her die. He had run from his mother that night, and he would run from Sumi now. He turned toward the inn. He would pay the bill, pack his things, and be on the next train to anywhere but here. Off to what remained of his world — his tiny, meaningless kingdom of ash and bone.

37

In the 45th year of Emperor Shaolmesun's reign (1789 N.E.), he left the world unto Essomuai. Despite the trials facing the empire, he brought many days of joy to the people with his festivals. However, the threats to the kingdom remained numerous, and for the safety of the empire, the Lords and Ladies of the Houses elected Empress Hiyelleom of Stone House. She was nominated by Lord Pulesai of Sky House with a vote of six in favor, none in abstention, and three against.

-Voting Records of the Anushgiar Leyosil

—:—

Turiem Yeilorn, ambassador to Anushai, wrote quickly in his study, trying to get his report done and off to Pont'dulairn as swiftly as possible. Some toady from the Royal Police was in Anushai, and the Foreign Office had instructed Yeilorn to escort him to see the empress. Leave it to Berill to send some overzealous navy man to gum up years of planning…

In fact, it was more than a few years — it was his entire life. He'd been working with Pont'dulairn since his first posting. It was a delicate balance, skimming just above the waves of tension, the military men always looking over their shoulders for some monster. Fools, all of them. Couldn't they see that Anushai cattle kept them in those nice boots they loved? Or that the mountain ranges north of Seongbelm held more gold than the entire Golden Coast combined? Not that they had a choice when ignorance came from the top, but he'd lived in Anushai for nearly two decades, and it was nothing like they feared.

But as hard as he'd worked, he'd also spent every day as ambassador watching Hiyelleom prepare for war. Surely Berill would win if it ever came to blows, but the military leaders back home seemed to think erasing them from the map was as simple as smudging the ink.

Hiyelleom had no inclination to be easy pickings, that was certain. He signed the letter, sealing it in a hurry as he called to his secretary. "Marteens!"

A moment later, the man popped his head in. "Yes, sir?" he asked. He was a very prim man, a bit too eager in his mind, but effective enough.

"Send this to the vice peer's office immediately," he said, standing from his desk and shrugging on his coat. "Is our guest here yet?"

"Yes," the man said, picking up the letter from the desk. "Detective Parimu is waiting in the anteroom, as you requested."

"Thank you, Marteens. I'll be back as soon as I can."

At least this would be an easy enough sacrifice to maintain their fragile peace. A single Shapewalker? That was no concern of his. The vice peer could be funny about things like that, but they couldn't very well disobey direct orders from the queen, especially on foreign soil. He just hoped Hiyelleom would go for it. She had always been reasonable, but you never knew you'd pushed too far until you went over the edge.

He walked through Marteens's office and into the hallway. It was a beautiful house they'd kept him in, with ocean views and just a short walk to the palace — even if the neighborhood surrounded him with Shadow House spies. Heading for the anteroom, he debated how to deal with Parimu. The man certainly had a reputation, but could he still be managed? The military types did tend to like their directions with a firm hand — not like the diplomats with their sensitive egos.

He opened the wide doors to the front hall, finding the detective standing at attention. Yes, he was a straight-laced one... As Parimu met his eyes, he made his decision, holding back the smile he usually used for greeting guests. It'd have to be the firm hand with this one. Still, the detective was a zealot, and he'd have to manage the political reality without offending the man's virtue.

"Detective Parimu," he said, taking his hand. The detective loomed above him, though he didn't use it to his advantage. He'd received one of the man's passphrases from the home office; that would be a nice touch. "The weather has been most unseasonable this winter," he said, signaling the man's fifth-tier passphrase.

"Alomidiar brings rain to Emillon," the detective returned, nodding in satisfaction as he visibly relaxed.

"Well," Yeilorn said, "as you've heard from the home office, things can be a bit sensitive up north. We'd like to see the queen's justice done, of course, but let me do the talking, and we should be able to get you what you need. When we arrive at the palace, stay just behind me. We're going to have to bow, and then we'll approach for the audience. Just do as I do, and everything should be fine."

"Thank you," the detective said, nodding gratefully, "I'll follow your lead, Ambassador."

"That's a good chap," Yeilorn said, clapping him on the shoulder. "Now, let's go; the empress could only fit us in for a fifteen-minute window after lunch."

Without waiting for an answer, the ambassador headed for the front doors, flinging them open and guiding Parimu into the street. It was just one Shapewalker, a single useless girl so peace could be preserved another day.

––––

Hiyelleom finished her lunch, ringing the bell as she returned to her letters, desperate to squeeze in some actual business while she still could. The day had been *unusual,* to say the least, leaving her feeling more off balance than she'd felt in years. First, there'd been the girl, dredging up all those old bloody arguments with Essolurei — and she hadn't even taken her up on her offer! Stubborn like her Nela. And now, as if that weren't enough, she had the Berillai ambassador coming for Wellonai knew what reason.

Prince Yelmeon of Shadow House, her acting foreign minister, had burst in shortly after the girl left, saying the Berillai were demanding an audience. *Demand* was a strong word, though she wasn't surprised. As hard as she worked, the barbarians were never satisfied. And Welaya, child that she was, seemed hell bent on careening into conflict. Still, if she did her job right, she could push war back another day, another day for her people to prepare.

There was a knock at the door, and Dannelei opened it, revealing Yelmeon. He was a reedy man, almost stereotypically of Shadow House stock, and his eyes darted to the sides. He bowed to her, though not a low one, as his station allowed. He was in many ways her equal, of course; he might even take the throne from her one day soon.

"Mother," he said in his soft voice, "Ambassador Yeilorn of Berill and Director of Reality Relsenair Parimu."

She narrowed her eyes at that — the director of reality? Quite presumptuous to bring a hunter of Shapewalkers into her own palace. She'd thought this would be about the Golden Coast and the mines she'd quietly taken over. In some ways, that was good, giving her more time for her plans in the north, but if the hunter was here…

The two men stepped in behind the minister — bowing properly, thank heavens, their foreheads to the ground.

"You may rise," she said, gesturing toward the couch across from her as they stood. The Parimu man was tall and clean shaven, and he stared at her, no doubt thinking her Queen of the Monsters. They both sat primly, the ambassador talking right away. He was an obsequious, tiresome man, but at least he lacked the bloodthirst so common in his countrymen. Thankfully, he also spoke half-decent Anushai.

"Empress Mother," he said, "please excuse the urgency of this meeting. We appreciate you fitting us into your busy schedule."

She waved a hand, urging him on. Parimu sat there with a tight look on his face, the look of someone trying to absorb a language he didn't know — while recognizing none of its words.

"I'll get right to it, then. There is a known criminal believed to have escaped from Berill to Anushai. Her Royal Highness Queen Welaya personally wants to see justice done in this matter, and she sent me to request your…assistance. I assured her that as a good friend to Berill, you would be most eager to help us in this rather *delicate* situation."

"I, as always," she said coolly, reaching for her tea, "am amenable to helping in any way that I can."

So, it was a criminal they wanted, and a Shapewalker, if this Parimu's presence meant anything. It wouldn't be good to have them snatching up people in her own territory, but depending on the circumstances, she would certainly be open to it. It wasn't like the ambassador had never done her a favor. Besides, he had put her in touch with Vice Peer Pont'dulairn, and *he,* for one, was a most useful friend to have.

"What is the name of this criminal, and what are they doing in my kingdom?"

"Her name is Sumilnyeon Elerair," the ambassador said. "But I assured the detective that Anushai is a law-abiding place, and she would find no haven here."

She was lucky she'd taken another sip of her tea — though she nearly choked on it. Still, it gave her the moment she needed to bring her face back under control. She put her tea down smoothly, the picture of composure. *On the run indeed…fool girl.* If she'd accepted her offer, she could have had Sumi halfway to the countryside by then. But now… Suppose the detective found Sumi anyway and caught her in a lie? She had no choice, even as a knot formed in her stomach. The girl had Essolurei's face in many ways, which only made it harder, but she was a hard woman, and she wouldn't sacrifice her hard-won peace for some girl from Berill, Saldalgiar or not.

"And what are the crimes of which this Elerair girl is accused?" she asked.

The detective looked her in the eyes, his gaze sharp and hawklike. He had perked up at the mention of Sumi's name. So, this hunt wasn't about politics for him — he was out for blood. Still, he said nothing.

"She has plotted treason against the crown," Yeilorn said.

He paused, not adding any more detail. Likely her only crime had been being a Shapewalker, though they wouldn't see it that way, surely. She looked at the dark eyes of the policeman, ignoring the ambassador. She saw in those eyes the hunger of the wolf, the maw that threatened to devour the world. The knot in her stomach squeezed her like a vise, but behind it, the siren call of peace still sang to her. She had sacrificed everything for it, and she would sacrifice again.

She looked to the side, where Ruseolem stood. He met her eyes, a hardness in them she hadn't seen before. This would be difficult for him. Still, after a moment, he looked down, bowing his head. His loyalty remained. She finally turned back to the ambassador.

"You will have my support, of course. I cannot spare any capitol police, but you are welcome to use your embassy guards. I will not interfere in any way."

At least she wouldn't use her own men to capture the girl. She didn't need any more blood on her hands, though she would stomach even that if she had to. She turned to Prince Yelmeon.

"Make sure the chief of police keeps his men out of their way."

All three men stood, making a proper exit bow, not all the way to the floor, but with waists fully bent.

"I thank you for your help," the ambassador said. Hiyelleom nodded her assent, and the men turned to go. Her face was still calm, but she was at war with herself. She had already given them permission to capture the girl, but she hadn't told them where she was. Perhaps such an offer would cement her with the ambassador — and save him back home. Her informants told her Yeilorn was seen as too soft on Anushai, and she would hate to have him replaced with a more loyal dog. She set her jaw. In for a mile, in for the whole climb.

"Ambassador," she said, just as the man reached the door, "I've heard the girl was seen heading to Sky House. I trust you won't disturb one of the Royal Houses with your men, but should you find the girl on her way out, that is entirely your affair."

He stood, looking at her for a moment, the briefest second to gauge her. *Yes,* she would need him, alright. Finally, the ambassador nodded.

"Thank you, Empress Mother," he said.

The door closed behind him, a door well and truly shut on her past and every foolish thing Essolurei had stood for.

"Goodbye, girl," she muttered to herself, "in another life, perhaps."

She turned back to her other business, eager to put this from her mind. Peace was everything, and she would have it, even if it was only for one more day.

38

"Weyol siom silmon yeljeom, et neyal duyek guyelmes nyeong."
**"The future is the eye of hope, and the bird sees farther than the
tallest bear."**

-Teongiar yal Chelmun
The Anushai Sky House Motto

—:—

Sumi made it to the waterfront, almost turning back a dozen times. Erso
loved her, something she could have only dreamed of just a day ago. But
she'd found her purpose too, and she couldn't let it go, even as her heart
seemed to crack in two. Even as she longed to run after him, she knew
she couldn't. Without her, he'd be safe. So, she kept moving, pushing
herself forward, even as her cheeks turned raw from wiping away her
tears. At least the tower of Sky House rose above her, like a star to guide
her through the storm.

The strange thing was how sure she felt about her purpose. Even as
the sadness threatened to crush her, she felt like — for the first time in
her life — she knew what the right path was. Somehow, that calm she
discovered in the throne room was still there, and she forced herself to
focus on it, kindling its tiny flame to keep her going. And hopefully, if
she looked hard enough, she'd find an ounce of Nela's strength inside
herself. She would likely think of Erso every second that she lived —
however long that was — but she would carry on, and she would laugh,
just like he'd always taught her.

Before she realized it, she'd crossed the city and was staring up at Sky
House, its white stone stark against the blue sky. Its masonry was so
smooth, it looked as if it'd been carved as a single piece, the bricks
unbroken as they rose to a lighthouse at the top. It was directly next to
the water, and its base extended over the wharf, reaching into the

constant splash of the surf. She walked up to the front of the building, where giant circular doors were built directly into the wall.

There were two guards flanking the entrance, wearing light-blue coats with sigils on the arm — presumably for Sky House. She walked up to the guard on the right, trying to act confident as she pulled out the letter from the empress.

"Excuse me," she said in Anushai, "I've been given a letter to access the library."

"Yes, madam," he said formally. He eyed her necklace as the others had, though she felt proud now that she knew what it stood for. He read over the letter, nodding.

"We appreciate you honoring Sky House with your visit," he said, bowing as his partner opened the door. "Please take the elevator to the second floor."

She thanked him, stepping through the door. It was much darker in the tower's base, lit by an opening by the water where the waves came crashing in, pushing against a set of giant wheels. She stared, watching as the contraption spun, its rotors disappearing into the wall. What on Wellonai could it be for?

"Do you need the elevator, miss?" a voice said. She spun, her eyes finally adjusted enough to see the man waiting on a metal disc in the middle of the room.

"Oh, yes," she said, "sorry. I was just surprised by…whatever this is."

"Beautiful, isn't it?" he said, smiling. He wore a blue coat like the guards outside, but his had a large jay stitched one arm, and he didn't wear a weapon. "It's a hydraulic pump. The Berillai beat us to the trains, but Sky House has had this elevator for over a hundred years. We missed electricity by a hair, but our engineers were the first to discover the water-powered piston."

"Incredible," she said, struggling to look away.

The man gestured for her to join him, so she stepped on the disc, her boot clicking against the metal. There was an opening above them where more light filtered down, but she didn't see any ropes or pulleys or anything. He pulled a lever in the floor, and the disc rose beneath them. She nearly jumped as it let out a great hiss, lifting them toward the ceiling.

"Nothing like the first time, eh?" the man asked, smiling.

She nodded, her eyes still wide as saucers. As they reached the top, the platform *became* the next floor, fitting seamlessly into the opening. She blinked in the light, suddenly surrounded by windows. The man pointed her toward a set of doors behind her, where another blue-clad man sat behind a massive desk. He was bent over a large ledger as she stepped up, quietly clearing her throat.

"Excuse me?" she said in Anushai.

"Yes?" the man asked, looking up.

"Um…I'm here for research. From the empress?"

He cocked an eyebrow at that but reached out and took the letter, his eyes widening as he skimmed the note. He jumped out of his seat, bowing as he gestured for her to follow.

"You should have said you were a Grass House acolyte!" he said, smiling. "I absolutely adored the house; their hospitals saved three in my family alone. Absolutely selfless what the princess did with the old house too, Essomuai bless her."

She smiled back, though she had no time to ask what he meant as he bowled her over with another wave of quick Anushai.

"Now, the note said you need house histories. I noticed your accent, and we should have Berillai copies of those. They'll be on the third floor in the western circle."

He pulled open one of the gilded doors, ushering her through. But as she crossed the threshold, she stopped, her breath catching as she saw the library. Built directly into the tower, the lighthouse soared above her, the white stone glowing in the light from hundreds of stained-glass windows. The ceiling was a mosaic like the sky itself, a glittering blue swept with whorls of white clouds and a gold sun where the beacon must have been. A giant spiral staircase wound upward through the center, the other floors in half-circle discs that narrowed as they climbed. And — as if that weren't enough — at the foot of the stairs was a giant gold statue, easily the size of her cottage back home.

The clerk didn't notice her stop at first, and he walked past her a few feet before he turned. "Oh, my apologies," he said, chuckling, "I forget sometimes." He pointed to the stairs. "Guests of the empress mother are free to escort themselves, so I'll let you take your time to look around. Just go up to the third floor when you're ready; there are servants there to help. I hope you'll order tea and make yourself comfortable."

He bowed again, smiling. "Enjoy your stay, Mistress Sumilnyeon."

"Thank you," she said, looking around her in a daze. She certainly hadn't expected to have the run of the place. Still, this might be the last time she saw anything like this before going home, and it would be nice to take her time.

She moved toward the center of the room, stopping beside the statue. Built on a giant golden disc, the metal was buffed to the point of gleaming and led to a sort of raised dais, where a glass enclosure held an altar. Around it were ten gold mirrors, each one carved into an ornamental shape. One looked like a tall tree had grown around it, while another was built into the mouth of a giant snake. The one directly behind the altar was shaped like a woman, tall and elegant like the statue of Essomuai in the palace. She leaned toward the closest mirror, a distorted golden blur staring back at her.

"What…is this?" she whispered to herself. Spotting a plaque at the statue's base, she squatted down, squinting at the Anushai script. *Essomkuyeon*, it read.

"Essomuai…fountain?" she mumbled, looking at the dais again. The altar did sort of have a dip in it, like the drinking fountains on some corners back home. But what was it for? As she stared at it, she started to feel a faint buzzing again, though it was much weaker than what she'd felt in the palace. She shook her head, blinking. She stood, staring up at the higher floors. A place this large must be filled with Shapewalkers, though no one seemed close by. Perhaps she was just overwhelmed — she'd had enough discoveries for a lifetime in a single day — but it felt like she was starting to hear the buzzing all the time.

She headed for the stairs, feeling a sudden twinge of sadness. If only she could have shared all this with Erso. But she could send him letters, couldn't she? Assuming he ever forgave her… But as long as she could stay alive, she hoped she'd at least have him as a friend. She couldn't bear to think of the alternative.

She climbed toward the first floor, where she saw dozens of servants scurrying about, Sky House sigils emblazoned on their jackets. Some carried books, while others loaded them onto small lifts, sending them to other floors. As she reached the second floor, she suddenly heard the trill of birds, looking up just in time to see a bluebird racing overhead. She stared, finding dozens of giant birdcages on the second floor, the doors open as the birds flitted about, landing on small trees set up in pots. She'd never thought the houses would take their sigils so literally, though the birds must be well trained if they were allowed to fly around a library.

Had Grass House been the same when Nela lived there? Maybe there had been dozens of grass cats roaming the halls back then. In fact, maybe that was why Nela hadn't put up a fight about adopting Amis… There had been a few times growing up when she'd caught Nela in the kitchen, talking to the cat in Anushai. Especially once Sumi started working, the two of them had been inseparable.

She finally made it to the third floor, and thankfully, it was an oasis of calm after the first two. There were stacks arranged in rings and plush blue sofas along the walls for reading. One or two of the little nooks were occupied, but it was much quieter. Still, there was a servant by the stairs who pointed her in the direction of the house histories. She went into the stacks, the shelves built into a curved shape to match the curving of the lighthouse.

She moved through the rows, stopping at the third ring as the man had told her. It was so organized! It would certainly be easier to find books here, though she still missed the chaotic darkness of her library back home. This one had live birds, but it still didn't feel like wandering in a forest the way Berill's did. There was something wonderful about how haphazard it was, sometimes feeling more like a museum of shelves than a library.

After a moment of looking, she found the book she needed. In the middle of the row, there was a book bound in gold with the title embossed in platinum on the side. It read *Anushgiar Leyosil* on the side and bore all ten house sigils. Next to it, there was a smaller version in Berillai, *The House Histories of Anushai* written on the side. That one wasn't bound in gold, but it still had the sigils on the cover.

She picked it up, running her finger fondly around the symbol of Grass House near the bottom. She found a chair against the wall and sank into the cushions with a sigh. She tried to stay seated properly — she was a Grass House guest here, after all — but after a day that felt more like a year, she was exhausted. She thought of ordering tea as the desk clerk had suggested, but the letters felt like they were burning a hole in her bag. Even the histories would have to wait until she got a handle on Nela.

She pulled them out, fanning them across the table beside her. There were ten in all. She took a deep breath and picked up the first one, unfolding it eagerly.

Hiyelleom, the letter began — no 'empress' in the address.

I was thrilled to receive your last letter, thank you for writing when things are so busy. It's not managing a kingdom, but little Sumi is quite a handful herself. She just did the most adorable thing—

She laughed, even as a tear slipped from her eye at hearing Nela's voice in her head again, especially in Anushai. She took a deep breath before reading on, losing herself in the letters as the past sucked her in.

39

In the First Year N.E., the people still celebrated Elomikarus's defeat. The Elders of Essomuai's children, however, knew peace could never last forever. They had divided the work of building the kingdom, yet they desired for one to lead them all, to be a Father or Mother to the people, Essomuai's hand to guide her ever-growing brood. They decided to vote amongst themselves and serve only so long as the needs of their people demanded. With refugees abounding and hungry mouths to feed, Saldal, Mother of the Grass, nominated her sister, Tudal, who knew how to work the earth. They all voted in agreement, eager to please Essomuai and build a home for their people.

**-Voting Records of the
Anushgiar Leyosil**

—:—

Forty Years Ago

Essolurei sat in her rooms in Stone House, looking out at the royal gardens. Soldiers moved back and forth on the gravel walkway below, on errands between the house and garrison. But she didn't look down, keeping her eyes glued to the waves of plants, trying to absorb something of their stillness. She ignored the palace, too — didn't want to think about the houses ever again if she could help it. The only indication the gardens were royal were the rows of red flowers, grown in honor of Emperor Shaolmesun.

She studiously avoided Seongbelm as well, eager to shut out thoughts of her father's crypt, where it had been cut deep into the stone. There were plenty of things to ignore, but it was worth looking at the scenery all the same. If she looked at the fine furnishings of her rooms any longer, she'd almost certainly go mad. Still, no matter where she looked, it seemed she'd find reminders of everything they'd lost. She sighed. It had all fallen apart so quickly.

Not that things had been going perfectly in Grass House. According to family lore, ever since Culyugang took the throne during a great sickness, family finances had been shoddy at best. The other houses liked to laugh at them, but who else was going to tend to the sick and poor? It was honorable what they did, even if it was only a fraction of what the poor were already forced to do for themselves. While the other houses bought up mines and forests across the empire, Grass House had built hospital after hospital. And, living frugally, generations of Grass House elders had been able to make do — for a while, anyway, until her great-grandfather.

Just after the Battle of Strussfaran, while the Treaty of Trilathdrei had secured a military stalemate, the Berillai had lit the Continent on fire with commerce. Suddenly, the elders of the other houses were tripping over themselves to catch up, buying up all the property they could, opening factories, building roads. Taxes had gone up on the houses to fund requisitions, and before long, Grass House was living hand to mouth. By the time her father took over, they were living on a shoestring.

Neither she nor Father had minded, of course. After Mother died, they mostly kept to themselves, reading in the great room and tending their own garden. Father had been the world's most likable man, of course, and somehow, every time the taxes were due, he made some kind of hardscrabble deal with a country cousin to make it all turn right in the end.

That was until he'd gotten sick himself… It wasn't like the cost of treatment had been out of reach. There were a hundred doctors within a mile who would have given their lives for Father. Every major hospital had been funded by Grass House, and most surgeons and apothecaries had received their training in their school on the first floor of the manor. It was just that, as he grew sicker, the careful juggling act suddenly came to an end. He wasn't able to perform his trick anymore, and the money dried up. One ball fell after another until the debtors were at their door.

And despite his diagnosis — some kind of wasting disease — she thought it was the worry that killed Father. He had been a joyful man outwardly, but whenever he thought she wasn't looking, the most incredible sadness would pass over his face. Still, even at the end, he'd managed to save the hospitals, writing to every doctor he knew — and having her write them when he could no longer hold a pen. By sacrificing all their lands, he'd cleared the debts on the hospitals, finding a consortium of doctors to take the deeds. And somehow, he even saved

Grass House Manor, raising funds from essom knew where to turn it into a hospital as well.

Of course, that meant she was homeless now, though moving into Stone House with Hiyel was a far cry from the squalor all too many of their subjects faced. Besides, she wouldn't have it any other way. Father — bless his soul — had raised her like himself, and he knew she'd be mortified if a single hospital was lost for her comfort. When Dr. Meolsemai came to take the keys, she'd handed them over gladly. Her father had done the impossible in her mind: holding on to his principles while beating the others at their game. There was honor in that. What was more Anushai than to shift your own form, escaping the cynics and scavengers alike?

"I'm proud of you, Peba," she whispered to her father, looking out at the gardens, tears wetting her face anew. She pulled her necklace up by its chain, kissing the emerald at its center. "Grass House lives on in your people."

Just then, a knock came at the door.

"Come in," she said in a firm voice, quickly wiping away her tears. One of the Stone House guards, Ruseolem — who also served as a sort of valet to Hiyelleom — came in. He put his hand over the sigil on his gray uniform, bowing deeply.

"Princess," he said, "tea is served, and Princess Hiyelleom requests your presence in the drawing room."

"Oh, thank you, Russ," she said.

Standing, she touched her own Stone House sigil as she curtseyed. She still usually wore her mother's old green dresses, but she had stitched the sigils onto all their shoulders. Russ held the door for her, trailing her down the hallway.

"You don't have to call me Princess now, you know," she said. She slowed her step, winking as she let him catch up. He'd bristled at her trying to walk beside him at first, but after three weeks, she was finally training him. "There isn't really a Grass House to be princess of any longer."

The rules were opaque at best, but in his deal relinquishing the manor, her father had lost their voting rights. Rather than letting her father's seat go to some opportunist, though, the other houses had closed ranks, simply removing the tenth seat from the voting hall. That was some small consolation, she supposed. It'd be much worse to have some businessman abusing their legacy.

"The people will remember," Russ said, "whether you bear the title or not. Not many have served the kingdom the way Grass House has."

His fake leg thumped hard on the marble flooring. He hid it well, but she knew what to listen for.

"That's rich coming from you," she said, chuckling. "You've earned enough medals to build your own ship."

"Duyel meyal reyong Essomuai," he said, quoting one of the old songs. *There is more than one way to show the face of Essomuai.* "If it weren't for Grass House surgeons, I'd be missing more than just a leg."

She turned, surprised, but he only smiled. He avoided mentioning his leg, but she'd forced him to let her look at it to make sure it was set right. Now, he brought it up on his own. It seemed she'd really cracked his shell after all.

"Well, I'm glad they saved you," she said. "There wouldn't be anyone to joke with otherwise. It's much too serious here, not what I'm used to at all."

They continued down the hallway in a warm, comfortable silence. The sitting room was on the east side of the house, so they had quite a bit of ground to cover. Stone House also served as the command office for the army, so there were dozens of meeting rooms crisscrossing the keep. It was a stoic place, far less cozy than Grass House had been, though it still held its own charms — if you knew where to look. Take the stone moldings, for example. In many places, the artisans had sneaked in little sculptures as they finished, her favorite being a squirrel by her bedroom, surrounded by nuts of every kind. They were small and just out of the lamplight, but she was the type to look.

As they passed the center of the house, a loud whistle erupted from below. She ran to the window, putting her face against the glass. There was a gigantic black monster taking up half of the parade ground as it belched a trail of smoke, Stone House's train prototype finally finished. Her breath fogged up the glass, matching the steam below, and she rubbed it clear with her sleeve.

It was *fascinating*. Who would have ever thought a hunk of metal could move itself? So many people talked about the Berillai in hushed, angry tones, but you had to hand it to them for ingenuity. Besides, the Continent needed something to push it forward. Like Father, always devouring medical journals and spending thousands on advanced equipment. It might have helped bankrupt them, but while the rest of the houses sat in their estates counting money, the world had leapt forward.

"Do you really think it'll work?" she asked, glancing at Russ where he'd stopped a few feet behind her.

"If anyone can do it, it's Stone House. But it better work sooner than later. One of the sergeants told me the Berillai are already laying tracks in the east. Soon they'll be able to move troops a hundred leagues a day."

"They can't be that bad, can they?" she asked.

"I suppose they must be," he said, shrugging. "We study Strussfaran at the academy; they call it *Heyalshulm.*"

Heyalshulm, the river of blood.

She tried to picture a battle that awful, but now, it was competing with a completely different set of feelings about Berill — and one sailor she'd met in particular… She'd been on the way to visit their hospital by the docks when he stopped her for directions. He was rugged and handsome, and best of all, he flirted with her like she was any other person. He hadn't recognized her necklace, speaking in extremely broken Anushai with no 'princess' this or 'your eminence' that.

She'd responded in Berillai — her brief tutoring at least more serviceable than his Anushai — and his eyes had widened.

"Well," he'd said, "gorgeous and brilliant."

She'd rolled her eyes, always ready to bat away any sign of flattery, but there had been a *glimmer* in his eye. For the first time in her life, it seemed she'd found someone she could take at face value. He'd asked her to tea, and they would be going this very afternoon before he left port.

She and Russ moved on, finally reaching Hiyel's sitting room. He shot her a look, begging to resume decorum in the presence of an actual member of Stone House. She tilted her head in assent, and he knocked on the door, announcing her arrival.

"The Lady Princess Essolurei Saldalgiar," he said in a baritone that didn't sound quite like himself.

"Oh, do come in," Hiyel called from behind the thick oak door as Russ pushed it open with a flourish.

She blinked at the brightness of the room, Hiyel's skylights filling it with sunlight even in the middle of the house. Sitting on a low gray settee, Hiyel had a granite-colored dress cascading around her, her usual tiara in her hair. She smiled radiantly when she saw Essolurei, gesturing at a tower of pastries in front of her.

"Come, come. Knowing you, you haven't eaten anything today."

Her stomach rumbled on cue, making Hiyel laugh, but she ignored the pastries for the moment, sitting as she looked around the room. Hiyelleom's sitting room always made her feel calmer. The first time she saw it, in fact — some fifteen years ago — she'd known immediately they would be friends. The strange rock sculptures, the moss growing on the walls, it was nothing like the gilded throne rooms other princesses made for themselves. Even as most thought their houses opposites —

hard-nosed Stone House and goody-goody Grass House — there was something strangely similar in how they approached being royal.

Finally, Essolurei leaned forward, taking a rose cake. She delicately bit the end, trying to avoid one of Hiyelleom's lectures about propriety. Still, she relished antagonizing Hiyel, so she started talking to her while her mouth was full.

"Whaf's the latest?" she mumbled through her food.

Hiyel gave her a stern look, the exact same one her father had always used when they were girls. Still, she kept her peace about the chewing and smiled instead, reaching to the table next to her and holding up a letter.

"I've just received a reply from my cousin in Taelosel," she said. "He wants to meet you. You remember the one, Prince Faelosem; very handsome, passionate about horses."

"Is this why you summoned me to tea?" she asked, cocking an eyebrow. Hiyel had been digging cousins out of the woodwork lately to try to marry her off, determined to make her a Stone House duchess. She'd love to be family with Hiyelleom, of course, it just…didn't feel right anymore — none of it did. Royalty had done nothing but take from her family, and she'd spent enough sleepless nights dreaming of a different life. The problem now was telling Hiyel.

"Well," Hiyelleom said, clicking her tongue, "I *brought* you here so you could eat something. You're much too skinny. But yes, the letter is another reason. Don't blame me for wanting to share the best news either of us has had in months."

"Hiyel," she said quietly, her voice drifting off into a sigh. "I…don't think I *want* to be a princess anymore."

She looked away at the floor, taking another bite of her cake to avoid speaking further. She heard the shuffle of Hiyel's dress as she got up from the couch, taking the chair next to her. She grabbed her hand, patting it between hers.

"Look, we've both been sick with grief," Hiyelleom said. "Your father was like my own Peba. No one ever treated me so kindly, and I'll miss him every day for the rest of my life. But we can't just throw everything away. Things are changing so fast these days. Everyone's saying Stone House will take the throne next, and I'll be Elder if my uncle abdicates. I don't just want you by my side, Rei; I *need* you with me."

"I'll always be there for you," she said, finally meeting Hiyel's eyes. "I just don't think I can be there in that way. I…don't believe in it anymore."

Hiyelleom's eyes narrowed in concern, looking like she was watching a child playing with matches — genuinely worried, but still full of classic Stone House condescension.

"*Dyeol sheng et myeol, bulgyeong shaldeom elshim,*" Essolurei said, quoting the second half of the Grass House motto. *The soil is a secret, but the grass always shows.* They'd had this argument a million times already. The Anushai weren't falling behind the Berillai because of some magic, missing technology; they were falling behind because they were stuck in one way of being. Essomuai hadn't set up the houses so they could fight each other, constantly vying for power. They needed to counteract the Berillai with better *beliefs,* not a better army. They needed to be as one.

"*Guyane siom feolem, chelan siom delyes,*" Hiyel answered with the first part of the Stone House motto, her mouth a thin line. *The light has many forms, but strength only one.*

They sat there for another moment, their hands still clasped, staring daggers at each other. Still, she couldn't stay mad at Hiyel. Essolurei lifted a hand, caressing her face.

"I love you better than a sister," she said, "and I don't want to fight. I have to leave for tea in the city, but I'll be back tonight, and we can talk more then."

She got up before Hiyelleom could stop her, smiling at Russ as he held the door for her. There would be time enough to fix things with Hiyelleom, but she couldn't spend the rest of her life behind gilded walls. Once she found her path, Hiyel would understand. In fact, maybe the path she was meant to take was right under her nose; you never did know when Essomuai would open a door for you. She quickened her step. She'd need time to get across town to meet her sailor, and if she was going to lure him in, she'd need more than just her signature perfume.

40

"Relonae suyyel kalyon ziyem, jolaeyeen siom komae."
**"Men can say a thousand words, but how they trade is their true
voice."**

-Heyalgiar yal Chelmun
The Anushai River House Motto

—:—

Sumi wiped more tears from her eyes, putting down the final letter. There had been a smattering from throughout the decades, each one full of pain and love. The two friends had never managed to escape their old pattern: Hiyelleom urging Nela to come back, Nela trying to bridge the gap between their worlds. And it had felt *surreal* to read those letters, passing through moments from her own life through Nela's eyes — and all the nights Nela had spent writing at the kitchen table.

Some of them had been almost too hard to read, like when Nela had written Hiyelleom to tell her Sumi's mother died. She had been so small then — and Nela such a rock — she never really realized what it must have felt like to lose her only daughter. Nela had written about not being able to eat for days, losing sleep, desperate with worry for her granddaughter. And yet, Nela had also written so lovingly about Sumi herself, bursting at the seams with things Nela could never bring herself to say out loud for some reason. If only she could have seen that letter when she was younger.

There were older letters too, giving her a window into the life her family had led before she was born. They told of Nela's struggles to adapt to a new country, Sumi's mother refusing to speak Anushai; so many tiny pains accumulating over time. Yet Nela had still always written passionately about Berill, her chosen home. She kept trying to convince Hiyelleom to bring their people together somehow — to make the world a better place for everyone, Shapewalker and human alike.

Sumi looked around the library with new eyes. She had needed to see the beauty of this place — the path Grass House didn't take, abandoning gilded beauty for a higher truth. But through the letters, she could see Hiyelleom's side too. It wasn't just about royalty. Anushai was incredible, and one of the only places on the Continent where it was truly safe to be a Shapewalker. Sumi couldn't just choose Berill and leave this behind; she had to fight to make the world safe for her people no matter which kingdom they lived in.

She took a deep breath, putting the letters away. She felt stronger, having communed with Nela in some way, but she wasn't finished yet. She needed to know her people's history. How had they built this place? Why was this magic in their blood? Hopefully, there would be answers about Essomuai, too. Was she a goddess or just an idea? The first time she'd learned about Essomuai and read her prayer, something had changed for her. And if she was going to change her kingdom, she'd have to find a way to change herself again, to be more than she ever thought possible.

She took the house histories, propping the massive book on her knees as she read about her people. It began in myth, telling the story of the goddesses and how they made the world. But it felt...*truer* somehow, so different from Umilai and Alomus fighting over the world, with humans nothing more than playthings to the gods. After all, she already held this story in her heart every time she changed her shape. And even if there was no one there to hear her, she'd prayed to Essomuai. Whatever her powers were, they were connected to her spirit in a very real way.

But more importantly, it felt like she finally had an origin story worthy of her people, casting her as something more than some demon sent to kill the king. In this story, they'd been created with purpose, to make peace and change the brutal course of history. Wellonai's three children — Vilodai, Essomuai, and Itorunai — had all played a role in creating the world and filling it with creatures. But Essomuai loved all things and had created the Shapewalkers to connect with them, to improve their lives.

Not that the story held no pain... Even in ancient times, it seemed the world had been eager to kill Shapewalkers, Essomuai's own sister, Vilodai, even sending the emperor, Elomikarus, to destroy them. But even then, the Shapewalkers had fought back with magic, turning away the enemy armies with nothing more than visions in the sky.

Even more interesting, though, were the things she already knew. In Anushai, Itorunai was the goddess of the wind, and her people called the storm-filled western sea Itorunai's Gap. Where would they have gotten that name without some kind of shared history? Even stranger, the story referred often to the power of metals, something she knew all too well from the detective's silver arrows. Apparently, there was power in anything from the earth — from Wellonai's body — and this extended to the gold of Essomuai and the fountain below. Could that be why the Berillai had so many mines, why they'd named the mother of their gods Velloni?

She devoured the pages, turning one after another until she reached the end of the first section. Turning the page, the title of the next chapter read 'The Font of Essomuai.' Could that be the *Essomkuyeon*? Even with the incredible legend fresh in her mind, she read on, desperate for something tangible.

Vilodai's rage still rumbled beneath the earth, and the Elders knew they would only face another Elomikarus if they failed to pacify her. Essomuai, too, could feel her sister's pain. Yet, as much as Essomuai had explored the world, she had never traveled to her sister's heart, where Vilodai had built up mountains and filled them with silver to keep her away. Essomuai called to her children, begging them to go and find her sister.

The Great Houses picked the strongest among them according to their gifts. Sky House sent a son who knew the birds, so he could chart their path. Grass House sent a daughter who could heal, and Flame House sent a teller of stories, so he could remember what occurred on their journey. When they were gathered together, Essomuai gave them a piece of her heart, an immense block of gold, to carry with them to Vilodai. Earth House provided many of their sigil, turned into oxen to carry the load.

They trekked for many months, dining with the fishermen of Ekosinar and trading with tribes of Relimorans until they reached their destination. The earth began to rise, and the weather became harsher as Itorunai's power ran up against Vilodai's. The way was rough and the mountains steep. The sun began to fail, and their only reminder of the light was their gleaming fragment of Essomuai.

Finally, they reached the Heart of Vilodai, where the mountains opened up into a cavernous maw diving deep into the earth. While the mountain peaks were frigid, the heat in the cave leapt up like a furnace, fueled by

Vilodai's rage. The children changed their forms to better dance with the fire of the cave, shrouding themselves in gold. Vilodai could have burned them all to dust on the spot, but she found herself curious. Even more than her revenge, she wanted to know of the world, to finally taste the life she'd been denied.

Sumi paused, her finger in the book, trying to picture the map of Wellonai. Vilodai's Heart was a real place, in the far eastern reaches of Mesop, where the Eltimeir River supposedly began. Was there really something hidden there?

In the center of Vilodai's Heart, they built the Font of Essomuai. They worked day and night, oblivious to the passage of days, lit only by the glowing gemstones of the mountain. They started with a dais, raising a fountain at its center and surrounding it with mirrors to hold the world's many forms. When it was done, one from each house stepped inside, joining their hands to sing the Song of Essomuai. From the beginning of time, they sang, shaping for Vilodai the many beauties of the world.

Vilodai watched silently at first, but soon, she began to smile, and as the Shapewalkers leapt as kittens, she began to laugh. They made themselves into thousands of flowers, and she began to weep, the beauty overtaking her. Vilodai had created many storms and rains, but now she saw where they had traveled, the grasses they had grown. Her weeping seemed to have no end, and as the Shapewalkers took their final form, her tears filled the cave, running down the mountain to form the mighty Seomkuyel, the river of a hundred names.

"See this great beauty, oh Vilodai!" the children called, "sent to you from our mother's heart to soothe yours. And greatest of all you have seen are the humans, your own children. We have taken many to our bosom, caring for them as our own. Let this font serve as our promise: a peace for all people and all creatures on Wellonai."

Vilodai listened in silence, and the elders nervously awaited as she deliberated. Finally, the heat of her cavern faded, and the gemstones glowed all the brighter, Vilodai finally speaking with the rumbling of the earth. "So it shall be," she said, and the pact was sealed. The Font of Essomuai still lays in that spot, and each year, the elders shall send a delegation to perform again the song.

Sumi pictured the statue below, the rounded altar at the center — that must have been where the Elders put their hands to shape the world's forms. What a fascinating story. Part of her really hoped it was true, of course. Still, true or not, there was something there for her. It showed her ancestors seeking peace, using their magic to calm a goddess filled with rage. It made her feel like she wasn't a fool for trying to change Berill. With nothing more than the beauty of their magic, her ancestors had changed the world.

She flipped through the rest of the book, finding a more formal history of the kingdom: voting records, timelines, even genealogies of the houses with sigils and mottos. She found the entry for Grass House, chuckling to herself as she finally recognized Nela's family motto for what it was. And at the end of the Grass House genealogy, she found the final entry: Essolurei Saldalgiar. This was her call — to fight as Nela had fought. She was the last Saldalgiar left now; the last Elerair too. And however poor a vessel she was, she'd have to carry that legacy — that hope — back to Berill, and trust it was enough.

She stood, quickly putting the book back as she headed for the exit. She wanted one last look at the fountain up close, and then it was time to go. She finally had what she needed, and she didn't want to delay another moment. Reaching the bottom of the stairs, she stopped at the giant golden statue, the fountain somehow even more mysterious now that she knew what it was meant to represent. She tried to picture her ancestors gathered around it, joining hands as they turned into all those beautiful shapes. She looked at the mirror of a woman, trying to picture the goddess. In the end, Pallinayum hadn't been able to decide if the Anushai really believed in Essomuai or not, but had her ancestors felt differently when they forged these mirrors?

She thought of the tower in Amoriai, to the night she escaped from jail in Berill, to reading Essomuai's poem in the library. She had prayed to Essomuai all those times, and she had felt something real in her heart. But was that enough to prove Essomuai's existence, or was she just tapping into the secrets of Shapewalking? She wished Nela was there to ask. But in that moment, even without Nela, she found that she believed. Even if Essomuai was only in her head, she would cling to her as tightly as she could.

She heard footsteps behind her, the clerk from the front desk reappearing with a book in his hands.

"It's a lovely statue, isn't it?" he asked.

"It's incredible. Is this…the fountain from the book?"

"From the house histories?" he asked, chuckling. "There probably never was a real *Essomkuyeon*, but it's a great reminder of our history. This was commissioned by the Sky House Elders when they built the library. At any rate, I'm glad you like it."

Sumi looked back at the fountain, nodding slowly. Perhaps it was only a metaphor. Still, it was awfully specific for something that wasn't supposed to be real… The clerk continued up the stairs, waving.

"Goodbye, Miss Sumilnyeon. I hope we'll see you again soon."

She smiled sadly. She would likely never come back to this wonderful kingdom. She might not even be alive in a month's time. Still, this had been a gift.

"Thank you," she said. "I hope so too."

She turned on her heel and walked out of the library, the glow of the statue firmly in her mind.

41

"Relonae silgang teon, kelshem weoljem tudal. Silgang muyal juyon, bilseom juyeom."
"Men want the sky but forget the soil. If you want trees, you must first plant seeds."

-Tudalgiar yal Chelmun
The Anushai Earth House Motto

—:—

Sumi stood outside the gate of Grass House, her eyes red from crying, staring up at the beautiful house. She'd gone back to the inn to pack her things, her tears flooding back when she found Erso's luggage missing. He was really gone. As much as she wanted to see him one last time, it was probably for the best. Her decision had been made, and she wasn't sure she'd have the strength to leave him again.

She had packed quickly, ducking out without the innkeeper seeing her. She was headed for the harbor next, but she just wanted to see Grass House again before she left. She put down her bag, leaning against the fence — and trying to feel something of Nela's presence in the cold metal. Hospital workers came and went, one or two of them eyeing her, though no one said anything. Maybe it was normal for old acolytes to come and mourn.

She noticed a plaque halfway down the fence and wandered toward it. Etched in bronze, it had the Grass House sigil at the top and a faded inscription underneath.

Liyal Saldalgiar zeolmsom, Junal Tuyashial jeol Saldalgiar em yeon seel Essomuai nel sheyol. Jeyong siom reyom jil penyeol. Yil jeolem jildel.

"Donated by Grass House," she whispered to herself as she translated it into Berillai. "Prince Tuyashial who rests with Essomuai. Always a

263

friend of the people, forever remembered."

She reached out, touching the plaque. Tuyashial, her great-grandfather. Had Nela written this before she left? She tried to picture how Nela had felt, losing so much, leaving everything behind. At the same time, her heart swelled with pride to think of all her family had done for this city. In that moment, part of her wished she could stay, to somehow be a part of this place. She'd even wash linens if she had to.

But that time was gone. The Saldalgiars had left this place in better hands, and she had her own people to see to in Berill. Like Nela had said in one of her letters to the empress: *A stone lives where it falls, but a field is made of years of sun and rain.* Change wouldn't come easily, but if she gave everything she had, she had to believe something new could grow. She—

"You've been a hard one to find, Miss Elerair," Detective Parimu said.

She turned, freezing as she saw the detective, like some kind of living nightmare. He was pointing a crossbow at her, a silver-tipped arrow in the groove. How could he be here like this? How had he found her so easily?

"Someone will see you," she stammered, her mind racing. "Th-this is Anushai."

She looked around her, for help, for somewhere to hide, but the street was suddenly empty. Where had all the people gone?

"Does justice have borders?" he asked, his eyes cold. "It was the Anushai capitol police who closed the street for me. It seems your time is up."

She kept her eyes glued to his crossbow. She had to get away. But could she find the stillness in her mind to shape? Could she really outrun an arrow? She had to try. She summoned Beysal's teachings, her mind searching for a form she could use. Something small. A *blue jay*, like in Sky House. She sucked in a breath, glowing, becoming smaller as the bolt left the arrow, slicing through her arm. She gasped, the transformation disappearing in a flash, a wave of energy blasting out from her and knocking them both to the ground.

She scrambled to her feet, fear pushing every other thought from her mind. She ran, throwing herself over the Grass House fence. Out of the corner of her eye, she saw Parimu stand. Another bolt shot at her but missed, clanging against the iron bars. Her shoulder seared with pain, but she ran as fast as she could, sprinting along the side of the house until she came across a cellar door.

"Please, please, please," she muttered, yanking at the door with her good arm. Luckily, it gave way, and she dropped down into the dim of the hospital's basement. She had to keep moving. Parimu would be right behind her, and she needed to find a way into the house and back out to the street. Her head was swimming, but she pressed on. She had…to keep…moving…

———

Erso stood at the train station, holding his ticket in a vise grip as he waited for the next train to Ekosinar. It would be slow going to Amoriai — the Anushai trains were a hodgepodge of random lines compared to the Berillai system — but he could use the time to thoroughly regret every decision he'd ever made. He chuckled, though there wasn't much humor in it. His face probably looked like a storm cloud too; the woman at the ticket window had nearly jumped when he reached the front of the line. Well, let them see his true face; it was likely the first time in his life it had shown what was really in his heart.

His heart — now, that really was a laughable concept. He tried to convince himself he was doing the right thing, that he had *responsibilities,* but what did that really mean? He cared about his family, and he didn't want Kel to grow up without an uncle, but how was this any different from every other time he left home? Every time could be his last, and he'd somehow manage to put aside his cowardice and save Sumi from that jail. But no…this *was* different. Getting out of Berill was risky, maybe even foolhardy, but going back? He thought of his mother again, the image of her dying slowly filling up his mind. How many times could he just watch things burn?

The train whistle blew, the last warning to board. He picked up his bag, starting for his car, though he stopped to look back at Anushai. He already knew he'd seen Sumi for the last time, but he looked anyway, hoping there was something left for him to see. The world seemed…*dimmer* than it had the past few months. These had been the best months of his life. It was like seeing the sun for the first time, feeling its heat on your face. How was he meant to go back to his cave, plodding along with his meaningless life?

He put his hand on the railing of the train car, about to haul himself up, when he stopped. His mother's face suddenly disappeared, replaced by Sumi's. So impossibly beautiful. He knew he couldn't just forget it, not this time, and he knew he couldn't let her leave knowing he had walked away, thinking it was easy for him. But it was more than that. Finally, everything *clicked.*

The problem wasn't that his mother died; it was that he hadn't died with her. He had jumped through the window that night, thinking he was doing what she wanted, getting to safety. But what was safety, anyway? There was nothing waiting for you on the other side. He knew that now, and he wouldn't let the same happen with Sumi. Even if they only lived one more month, he should live it with her, be *truly* alive. Maybe for the first time in a long time. And he would give everything he had to keep her safe. Even if he failed, he'd fail by her side.

"Train's leaving, sir," a conductor said, snapping him out of his trance. "On or off?"

Erso shook his head, blinking away his thoughts as he eased his foot back to the platform.

"Think it'll have to be off, mate," he said. "Seems I forgot something important."

He turned, dropping his bag as he took off at a run, his cane in hand. Forget the bag; it could all be replaced anyway. The only thing he couldn't replace was somewhere in this city, and he wouldn't waste any more time pretending he could live without her.

———

Sumi looked around the dark basement, finally spotting a door. Running over, she yanked on it, but it wouldn't budge.

"No!" she cried, but she already knew it was too late, the light dimming as a shadow blocked the cellar door. She turned to find Parimu looming in the doorway, his crossbow reloaded.

"Well," he said, his chest heaving just as hers was, "it seems you've nowhere else to go."

Her eyes darted to either side, looking for something, anything, but of course, he was right. She took a deep breath, searching for the calm, even as her heart pounded. She thought of Essomuai, thought of the cave, but she knew already in her bones she wouldn't be able to transform. The arrow had been silver — she was blocked. This would be the end. She faced Parimu. Somehow, though, she didn't feel afraid. She thought of Erso, glad he was free. That was all that mattered now.

Parimu stepped down into the cellar, his eyes on her, watching her for any sudden movement. She stared back defiantly. She was what she was, and even if he killed one more Shapewalker, this wouldn't end her people. She finally knew that, had finally learned the true lesson of Essomuai. Essomuai was Wellonai's blood, and she was in every single thing. And even if peace could be denied, it could never be forgotten. That's what all these people had been chasing, after all. Even when they were chasing phantoms of it, they yearned for the real thing, for what Essomuai offered: peace between all people, the promise of her song.

Suddenly, the cellar darkened again, a new shadow filling the doorway.

"Get away from her!" a voice shouted out. *Erso.* He launched down the cellar steps with a snarl, a sword in his hand, the same one he'd shaped back in Amoriai. Parimu just had time to turn, lifting his crossbow as Erso's sword smashed into it, knocking it to the ground. Parimu fell back, pulling his own sword as Erso attacked again.

The men fought, their swords meeting again and again, Parimu's flashing silver in the dim light. Erso wove like a dancer, moving quickly, though Parimu had still scored a few cuts, Erso's shirt already patched with red. That meant he wouldn't be able to transform, either. She had to do something. Sumi looked down at her left arm, finding it covered in blood. How much blood would it take to run the silver out? It didn't matter; there was no time, and she couldn't lose Erso, not without a fight.

She squeezed her eyes shut, reaching for Essomuai with everything she had. She pictured the pool in her mind, though there was a sort of haze over it, keeping her from stepping through. She was so close! It didn't matter if she died now, but she wouldn't let Erso fight alone. She shut out the image of the pool, shut out the sound of the swords clanging. She shut out the fear of Erso dying, the guilt, the pain, the doubt. She listened only to her heart, pounding in the void, and she called out to Essomuai.

"Save us," she said in Anushai. "Please, save us. Save Erso. We need you now."

She heard that phantom buzzing again, the one from all her dreams, only a thousand times more powerful. It was like she was surrounded by keyholes, the buzzing growing until it seemed to be inside her. Suddenly, a golden light flashed behind her eyes, the haze of the silver disappearing. She felt like she was floating, an enormous power rushing through her, her body suddenly *alive.* She could feel the hair on her head growing, reaching out with life, yearning to be. There was a humming in her ears now, more than a buzz, like singing from another room.

She pictured the pool, and the hall of Mu'lalat came to her immediately, no distance between her and the stillness of the water. The singing was louder, and she felt like she could almost make out the words — like it was a song she'd known her entire life but somehow forgotten. It was coming from down the hallway in the cave, where she could see a brilliant golden light.

She opened her eyes, and it was like a golden veil had come over the world. The men were still fighting, heaving for breath with their swords raised, but she could see Erso's keyhole, its faint glimmer transformed into a second sun, its massive golden glow over his heart. And she could *hear* it too, the humming in her ears changing to a deeper sound, like a tuba, like the laughter of a father or the tickle of a mustache. It sounded just like Erso. Suddenly, she knew his shape, and her own body vibrated to its rhythm, yearning to be him, to dance with his legs, to laugh with his laugh. She knew somehow that if she listened just a little longer, she'd hear his entire life, every day mapped into that beautiful sound.

She turned to Parimu, her fear suddenly gone as she saw a keyhole on him too. Erso had been right — Parimu was one of them. But his light was hidden, as if it were covered in gauze. His song was high-pitched, like a frightened bird, his soul standing on the edge of Mu'lalat but terrified to step through. His aura was a bright white, but it cast a strange shadow on the ground, like it was trying to escape its own light. Her heart ached as it vibrated to his rhythm. She didn't want to become him; she wanted to hold him, console him. She longed to scoop up that tiny bird, to release it and watch it fly.

She walked toward Parimu. He still didn't see her, his eyes only for Erso and the end of his sword. His muscles were tense, like a snake ready to strike again. She was only steps away when Erso finally saw her, his eyes widening in fear.

"Sumi, no!" he cried out.

Parimu turned, but before he could lift his sword, she touched his chest, and in a brilliant flash of light, they entered...*somewhere*. It was hard to tell if they even still existed. They may have been in Mu'lalat, but she couldn't see anything beyond a blinding light, white and gold, surging into the sky like a blazing fire, their songs beginning to mix and harmonize. She felt more than Parimu's body; she felt his soul. His life began to flash through her mind: a tiny village by the sea, a beautiful girl, and a grizzled man by a burning forge.

But she didn't just see these people, though; she *knew* them, and her light pushed toward them, trying to attune their songs as well. And finally, she saw Parimu, a thousand Parimus in every moment, at every age. She saw sadness and pain, and it felt like it was her pain. She felt like she wasn't enough, that she could never do enough. But were they her feelings or his? Suddenly, she became Parimu in that light-filled void, and before her appeared herself, her eyes wide.

"Where is this?" the other Sumi asked with Parimu's voice, trembling with fear. "What's happening?"

She spoke for the first time, the golden light trying to escape her in all directions. "We are being," she said, the words suddenly coming to her mind. "We are here."

The other Sumi shook her head frantically. "No, no, this can't be, I don't want this! I can't be…one of them…one of you!"

Sumi stepped forward in the void and put her hand to his heart again. "You are enough, Relsenair," she said, already knowing his given name somehow. "You have always been enough." Tears started to roll down the other Sumi's cheeks. "You are loyal, and you are brave. You care *deeply* for your people, but you don't have to be trapped in this cage. You can fly."

She wasn't sure how, but she turned them both into a bird, willing their forms into one shape. She felt like they were soaring, gliding through the air in that golden place. He pulled against her for a moment but then let go, swept up into the shape with her, the panic in his mind disappearing as they flew. She could feel his keyhole in her mind, and the shadow on it began to fade, melting away until only the light remained. She slowly let go of her wings, and Parimu stepped in, guiding the bird forward. He started to laugh, rolling the bird through the sky, swooping and banking as he flapped their wings.

Suddenly, they were standing again in the light-filled void, back in their own bodies.

"We aren't evil, Relsenair," she said, "and neither are you. Come home with me; let's set this right together. Berill needs you, but as you are, Shapewalker *and* policeman. If your color would not be, neither would be the field."

She felt something shift in him, his laughter still echoing in her mind. The vibration of his song crescendoed, growing all the brighter with no shadow to hold it back. Suddenly, the light disappeared, and they were standing together in the basement again. Parimu fell onto his knees, burying his face in his hands as he wept.

She felt dizzy, the light gone from her mind as it rushed out of her body and back to Mu'lalat. Her heart felt full enough to burst, but her limbs felt weak after holding that much power. She started to fall, but Erso was there, catching her as he lowered her to the ground.

She blinked her eyes open, finding Erso looking down at her, a frantic look in his eyes. But she smiled, and he visibly relaxed. She took one of his hands, patting it. "I'm okay," she said, "just a little tired."

"What was that?" he asked, shaking his head. "I've never seen anything like it. It was the brightest flash I've ever seen…like the sun was in the basement. I…thought I saw a bird moving in the light like you were shaping, but not even a second later, you were back, like nothing had ever happened. And as soon as you came out, Parimu stopped fighting."

Erso turned, look at Parimu, but she could hear the man still weeping.

"He stopped doing…*anything.* You saved us, Sumi."

"It was just a second?" she asked, pinching her forehead. "It felt like we were in there for days."

"In…where?" Erso asked.

"Mu'lalat?" she said, unsure. "I think we were with Essomuai, somewhere deep in the halls, deeper than I've ever gone. I…called on her, and…I don't know. It felt like I was channeling her."

She squeezed his hand tighter, smiling as she remembered Erso's song. "She knew you, Erso. She knew all of us. And you had the most beautiful song."

He grinned, looking shy. She reached up and grabbed his neck, pulling him in and kissing him. His mustache tickled her face, like lightning running across her lips. She could smell the spice of his cologne, and for just a moment, she thought she could hear his song again. It was quieter than before, but the soft buzz of his keyhole seemed to carry the same tune she'd heard in his heart, just behind his door in Mu'lalat. Something had changed, and she could hear the songs so clearly now. How had she never noticed before?

Erso pulled back, sucking in a breath as he stared at her. "Sumi, I'm so sorry, I never should have—"

"Shh," she said, putting a finger over his lips. "It's okay; thank you for coming back for me. I love you, Erso." She patted his face. "Now help me up; it's time we ended this."

She stood with Erso's help, somehow feeling both exhausted *and* refreshed, like new soil after a volcano erupts. And in the back of her mind, she could hear another song. She recognized it now, the song beneath the songs, the phantom buzz she'd heard so many times — *Essomuai's song.* It felt like it came from three different places at once: from the north, far off to the south, and in her own heart, filling the air around them. She stepped toward Parimu, but Erso grabbed her shoulder.

"Wait," he said, his eyes darting to the other man's sword. "Be careful."

"It's okay," she said, smiling, "he's one of us. He knows that now."

She stood next to Parimu, though he didn't seem to notice, his face in his hands as his body shook from sobbing.

"Relsenair," she said gently, touching his shoulder, "it's alright."

He looked up, wiping his eyes. "Miss Ele— Sumi," he said, blinking. "It's like I've known you my whole life — like I saw everything that ever happened to you. It…"

She nodded, offering her hand as she lifted him up. She opened her arms, and they embraced, like old friends, the hatred from just minutes earlier evaporated by Essomuai. She could still faintly hear his song too, just beneath his keyhole, and it felt *lighter*. It was still high-pitched like a bird, but a bird who was free, its song drifting on the wind.

She let go and turned, finding Erso there, standing warily in a sword stance still, his blade retrieved from the ground. Parimu noticed, tensing, but she put her hand back on his shoulder, stepping between them.

"We have to stop fighting now," she said. "It's time for peace. But a true peace — Essomuai's peace."

She chuckled, shaking her head.

"It's funny. I feel like ever since I left Berill, that's the only word I've heard. It's all anyone wants, even if they don't know how to get it. 'Peace will be when the Shapewalkers are dead; when the Berillai stop their wars; when our families are left alone.' But we need more, we *deserve* more. Until we all have peace — Shapewalkers *and* humans — then peace can never last. We have to go back, we have to show Berill what Shapewalkers can be, what all of us could be."

She looked between them, catching her breath after the words rushed out of her, like they had in the jail with Parimu all those months ago. She looked between them. "Will you two…come with me?"

Suddenly, she felt nervous. It wasn't like she had any more of a plan than when she'd run into the basement. Though that had been before she'd touched a goddess. But could she really risk their lives? Was it even up to her? She'd heard their songs, seen the pain in their hearts, and both these men deserved a chance to decide. After all, she'd thought sending Erso away would keep him safe, but he'd come back all the same. And Parimu, so loyal to his people, didn't he deserve a chance to change his people's fate?

"I go where you go," Erso said. "I'll never leave your side again."

She turned, facing Parimu, his eyes bloodshot from crying.

"I'll come if you'll have me," he said. He winced. "I just feel so ashamed, all the horrible things I've done…"

He shook his head, setting his jaw. "I'll risk anything to make it right. But what can we do? What can we change with only three?"

She thought of the golden light in her mind, the song in her heart. She thought of Nela, of Erso's parents, of Jalicyne. She thought of the library, the stories of her ancestors, the *Essomkuyeon.*

"I don't know yet," she said. "But I know I felt Essomuai, and I heard her song. I think we need to go to Vilodai's Heart, to find her fountain."

"Like the legend?" Erso asked. "Do you think it's real?"

Sumi looked at the ground, shaking her head, the golden light still fresh in her mind. "I might not have before today. But I can almost feel it now…"

She looked to the south again, where she could still faintly hear the song. What had the house histories called it? Essomuai's heart, a block of pure gold. She lifted up her necklace, holding the gold-backed pendant in her hand. Closing her eyes, she could hear the song there too, the tiny gold disc humming with Essomuai. If this tiny piece of the goddess was here, then she had to believe the fountain was out there too, somewhere in the mountains. She could hear Essomuai now, and whatever happened next, they had to find her. They had to sing her song.

42

They wandered out of the cellar, walking as if in a dream as they spilled onto the lawn and into a world that felt completely changed. Sumi stood between them, blinking in the light, knowing their destination but not the path to get there. Erso was still eyeing Parimu warily, and she put a hand on his shoulder. She couldn't blame him; it was only a moment ago they were crossing swords — even if it felt like years ago to her, buried under a lifetime of Parimu's memories.

The clouds broke overhead for just a moment, and a rare glimpse of sun shone on the grass. Sumi lifted her eyes to the sky, letting the light warm her face. These were the moments that they were fighting for, the tiny pieces of joy no one could take. She wanted that joy for all their people — Berillai, Amoriai, Anushai. The golden light of the sun, so similar to Essomuai's, felt like a promise that all of it was possible. It was just a glimmer on the horizon, but she felt hope. And somewhere to the south, she heard Essomuai's song. It sang in her heart, pulling her toward it and its promise of peace.

—:—

Come with us, and we will sing the song, the golden song of the thousand truths. This will be our song for all generations; may we never forget its rhythms and its arcs. By singing, we will honor our mother and her sacrifice, abiding by the final peace. Come with us, and we will sing. The song of all light, the song of our mother's children, the Song of Essomuai.

-Epilogue to the Anushgiar Leyosil

THE END OF BOOK TWO